WHAT THE GREEK
WANTS MOST

WHAT THE GREEK WANTS MOST

BY

MAYA BLAKE

First published in Great Britain 2014
by Mills & Boon, an imprint of Harlequin (UK) Limited,
Large Print edition 2015
Eton House, 18-24 Paradise Road, £ 13-5-15
Richmond, Surrey, TW9 1SR

© 2014 Maya Blake

ISBN: 978-0-263-25619-2

C46353610/

Printed and bound in Great Britain
by CPI Antony Rowe, Chippenham, Wiltshire

To my editor, Suzanne Clarke, for your unfailingly brilliant insight and support!

CHAPTER ONE

THEO PANTELIDES ACCELERATED his black Aston Martin up the slight incline and screeched to a halt underneath the portico of the Grand Rio Hotel.

He was fifteen minutes late for the black tie fund-raiser, thanks to another probing phone call from his brother, Ari.

He stepped out into the sultry Rio de Janeiro evening and tossed the keys to an eager valet who jumped behind the wheel of the sports car with all the enthusiasm Theo had once felt for driving. For life.

The smile that had teased his lips was slowly extinguished as he entered the plush interior of the five-star hotel. Highly polished marble gleamed beneath his feet. Artistically positioned lighting illuminated the well-heeled and threw the award-winning hotel's design into stunning relief.

The hotel was by far the best of the best, and Theo knew the venue had been chosen simply because his hosts had wanted to show off, to project a false image to fool him. He'd decided to play along for now.

The right time to end this game would present itself. Soon.

A sleek designer-clad blonde dripping in diamonds clocked him and glided forward on sky-high stilettos, her strawberry-tinted mouth widening in a smile that spelled out a very feminine welcome. And more.

'Good evening, Mr Pantelides. We are so very honoured you could make it.'

The well-practised smile he'd learnt to flash on and off since he was eighteen slid into place. It had got him out of trouble more times than he could count and also helped him hide what he did not want the world to see.

'Of course. As the guest of honour, it would've been crass not to show up, no?'

She gave a little laugh. 'No, er, I mean yes. Most of the guests are already here and taking pre-dinner drinks in the ballroom. If there's anything you need, anything at all, my name is Carolina.' She sent him a look from beneath heavily mascaraed eyelashes that hinted that she would be willing to go above and beyond her hostess duties to accommodate him.

He flashed another smile. '*Obrigado,*' he replied

in perfect Portuguese. He'd spent a lot of time studying the nuances of the language.

Just as he'd spent a lot of time setting up the events set to culminate in the very near future. For what he planned, there could be no room for misunderstanding. Or failure.

About to head towards the double doors that led to the ballroom, he paused. 'You said most of the guests are here. Benedicto da Costa and his family. Are they here?' he asked sharply.

The blonde's smile slipped a little. Theo didn't need to guess why. The da Costa family had a certain reputation. Benedicto especially had one that struck fear into the hearts of common men.

It was a good thing Theo wasn't a common man.

The blonde nodded. 'Yes, the whole family arrived half an hour ago.'

He smiled at her, effectively hiding the emotions bubbling beneath his skin. 'You've been very helpful.'

Her seductive smile slid back into place. Before she could grow bolder and attempt to ingratiate herself further, he turned and walked away.

Anticipation thrummed through his veins, as it had ever since he'd received concrete evidence that Benedicto da Costa was the man he sought. The road to discovery had been long and hard, fraught with pitfalls and the danger of letting his emotions override his clear thinking.

But Theo was nothing if not meticulous in his planning. It was the reason he was chief trouble-shooter and risk-assessor for his family's global conglomerate, Pantelides Inc.

He didn't believe in fate but even he couldn't dismiss the soul-deep certainty that his chosen profession had led him to Rio, and to the man who'd shattered what had remained of his tattered childhood twelve years ago.

Every instinct in his body yearned to take this to the ultimate level. To rip away the veneer of sophistication and urbanity he'd been forced to operate behind.

To claim his revenge. Here. Now.

Soon...

He grimaced as he thought of his phone call with his brother.

Ari was beginning to suspect Theo's motives for remaining in Rio.

But, despite the pressure from his family, neither Ari nor Sakis, his older brothers, would dare to stop him. He was very much his own man, in complete control of his destiny.

But that didn't mean Ari wouldn't try to dissuade him from his objective if he'd known what was going on. His oldest brother took his role as the family patriarch extremely seriously. After all, he'd had to step up after the secure family unit he'd known for his formative years had suddenly and viciously detonated from the inside out. After his father had betrayed them in the worst possible way.

Theo only thanked God that Ari's radar had been momentarily dulled by his newfound happiness with his fiancé, Perla, and the anticipated arrival of their first child.

No, he wouldn't be able to stop him. But Ari… was Ari.

Theo shrugged off thoughts of his family as he neared the ballroom doors. He deliberately relaxed his tense shoulders and breathed out.

She was the first thing he saw when he walked in. His lips started to curl at his clichéd thought but then he realised she'd done it deliberately.

The dress code for this event had been strictly black and white.

She wore red. And not just any red. Her gown was blood-red, provocatively cut, and it lovingly melded to her figure in a way that made red-blooded males stop and stare.

Inez da Costa.

Youngest child of Benedicto. Twenty-four, socialite...seductress.

Against his will, Theo's breath caught as his gaze followed the supple curve of a breast, a trim waist and the flare of her hips.

He knew each and every last detail of the da Costas. For his plan to succeed, he'd had to do what he did best. Dig deep and extract every last ounce of information until he could recite every line in the six-inch dossier in his sleep.

Inez da Costa was no better than her father and brother. But where they used brute force, blackmail and thuggery, she used her body.

He wasn't surprised lesser men fell for her Marilyn Monroe figure. A true hourglass shape was rare to find these days. But Inez da Costa owned her voluptuousness and confidently wielded it to her advantage. Theo's gaze lingered on her hips until she moved again, dropping into conversation with the consummate ease of a practised socialite. She had guests eating out of her hands, leaning in close to catch her words, following her avidly when she moved away.

As he advanced further into the room, she turned to speak to another male guest. The curve of her bottom swung into Theo's eye line, and he cursed under his breath as heat raced up through his groin.

Hell, no.

His fists curled, willing his body's unwanted reaction away. It had been a while since he'd indulged in a mindless, no-holds-barred liaison. But this was most definitely not the time for a physical reminder, and the instigator of that reminder was most definitely not the woman he would choose to end his short dry spell with.

He exhaled in a slow, even stream, letting the roiling in his gut abate and his equilibrium return.

As he made his way down the stairs to join the guests, the deep-seated certainty that he was meant to be here—in the right place at the right time—flared high.

If Pietro da Costa's love of excess hadn't led him down the path of biting off more than he could chew, this time in the form of commissioning a top-of-the-line Pantelides super-yacht he could ill afford, Theo wouldn't have flown down to Rio to look into the da Costas' finances three years ago.

He wouldn't have become privy to the carefully hidden financial paper trail that had led right back to Athens and to his own father's shady dealings almost a decade and a half ago.

He wouldn't have dug deeper and discovered

the consequences of those dealings for his family. And for him personally.

Memory stirred the unwanted threads of anxiety until it threatened to push its way under his control like Japanese knotweed. Gritting his jaw, he smashed down on the poisonous emotion that had taken too much from him already. He was no longer that frightened boy unable to stem his fears or chase away the screaming nightmares that plagued him.

He'd learned to accept them as part of his life, had woven them into the fabric of his existence and in doing so had triumphed over them. Which wasn't to say he wasn't determined to make those who'd temporarily taken power from him pay dearly for that error. No, that mission he was very much looking forward to.

Focusing his gaze across the room to where Benedicto and his son held court among Rio's movers and shakers, he strategised how best to approach his quarry.

Despite the suave exterior he tried to portray with his tailor-made suit and carefully cropped hair, Benedicto could never mask his lizard-like character for very long. His sharp, angular face and reptilian eyes held a cruelty that was instinctively felt by those around him. And Theo knew that he honed that characteristic to superb effect when needed. He bullied when charm failed, resulting in the fact that half of the people in this room had attended the fund-raiser tonight just to stay on Benedicto's good side.

Five years ago, Benedicto had made his political aspirations very clear, and since then he'd been paving the way for his rise to power through mostly unsavoury means.

The same unsavoury means Theo's own father had used to bring shame and devastation to his family.

Grabbing a glass of champagne, Theo sipped it as he slowly worked his way deeper into the room, exchanging pleasantries with ministers and dignitaries who were eager to find favour with the Pantelides name.

He noticed the moment Benedicto and Pietro zeroed in on his presence. Bow ties were surreptitiously straightened. Smiles grew wider and spines straighter.

He suppressed a smile, deliberately turned his back on the father and son and made a beeline for where the daughter was smiling up at Alfonso Delgado, the Brazilian millionaire philanthropist, who was her latest prey.

'If you want me to host a gala for you, Alfonso,

all you have to do is say the word. My mother used to be able to throw events like these together in her sleep and I've been told that I've inherited her talent. Or do you doubt my talents?' Her head tilted in a coquettish move that most definitely would've made Theo snort, had his eyes not been drawn to the sleek line of her smooth neck.

Alfonso smiled, his expression beginning to closely resemble adoration.

Forcing himself not to openly grimace, Theo took another sip of champagne and brushed off an acquaintance who tried to catch his eye.

'No one in their right mind would doubt your talent. Perhaps we can discuss it over dinner one night this week?'

The smile that started to curve her full, glossy lips forced another punch of heat through him. 'Of course, I would love to. We can also discuss that pledge you made to support my father's campaign…?'

Theo moved closer, deliberately encroaching on the space between the two people in the centre of the room.

Alfonso's attention jerked towards him and his smile changed from playboy-charming to friendly welcome.

'*Amigo*, I wasn't aware that you had returned

to my beloved country. It seems we cannot keep you away.'

'For what I need to achieve in Rio, wild horses couldn't keep me away,' he replied, deliberately keeping himself from glancing at the woman who stood next to Alfonso. He breathed in and caught her scent—expensive but subtle, a seductive whisper of flowers and warm sunshine.

His friend's eyes gleamed. 'Speaking of horses—'

Theo shook his head. 'No, Alfonso, your racehorses don't interest me. Speedboat racing, on the other hand… Just say the word and I'll kick your ass from one end of the Copacabana to the other.'

Alfonso laughed. 'No can do, my friend. Everyone knows underneath that tuxedo you're part shark. I prefer to take my chances on land.'

A delicate clearing of a throat made Alfonso turn, a smile of apology appearing on his face as he slipped back into playboy mode. For the ten years that Theo had known him, Alfonso had had a weakness for curvy brunettes.

Inez da Costa had curves that required their own danger signs. His friend risked being easy prey for whatever the da Costas had in mind for him.

'Apologies, *querida*. Please allow me to introduce you to—'

Theo stopped him with a firm hand on his shoulder. 'I'm perfectly capable of making my own introductions. Right now, I think you're needed elsewhere.'

Alfonso's eyes widened in confusion. 'Elsewhere?'

Theo leaned and whispered in his friend's ear. Shock and anger registered on Alfonso's face before his jaw clenched and he reined his emotions back in. His gaze slid to the woman next to him and returned to Theo's.

Taking in a deep breath, he held out his hand. 'I guess I owe you one, my friend.'

Theo took the proffered hand. 'You owe me several, but who's counting?'

'And I shall repay you. *Até a próxima.*'

'Until next time,' Theo repeated. He heard the disbelieving gasp from Inez da Costa as Alfonso walked away without another glance in her direction.

A thread of satisfaction oozed through him as he tracked his friend to the ballroom doors. Scanning the room, he saw Pietro da Costa's thunderous look in his sister's direction.

Theo lifted his glass to his lips and took a lazy sip then turned his attention to Inez da Costa.

Her large brown eyes were filled with anger as she glared at him.

'Who the devil are you and what did you say to Alfonso?'

CHAPTER TWO

THEO DIDN'T LIKE the idea that he'd been less than one hundred per cent thorough in covering every angle in his investigations.

His surveillance of Inez da Costa had been from afar simply because until recently he'd deemed her involvement in his investigation peripheral at best.

The extent of her role in her father's organisation had only come to light a few days ago. But even then he should've recognised her power.

Now, at the first proper sight of what was turning out to be the jewel in Benedicto da Costa's crown, the essential cog in the sinister wheel that his enemy was intent on using to his full advantage, he experienced a pulse of heat so strong, so powerful, he sucked in a quick breath.

Up close, Inez da Costa's heart-shaped face was flawless…breathtaking, her skin a silky, vibrant complexion even the best cosmetics couldn't hope to produce.

Not that she hadn't attempted to enhance her

beauty even further. Her make-up was impeccable, her lids smoky in a way that drew attention to her wide, doe-like stare.

Long-lashed eyes that bored into him with unwavering demand and a healthy dose of suspicion. Her nose flared with pure Latin ire and her full lips parted as she released another agitated breath.

The pictures in his dossier did her no justice at all. Flesh and blood wrapped in red silk from cleavage to toe, she made his senses ignite in a way he hadn't felt in a long time. The earlier pull deep in his groin returned. Harder.

'I asked you a question.' Her voice held a hint of dark sultriness that reminded him of a warm Santorini evening spent drinking ouzo on a deserted beach. And the mouth that framed her words, painted a deep matt red, reminded him of what happened on the beach after the ouzo had been consumed and inhibitions were at their loosest.

She glanced over his shoulder and Theo's jaw clenched at the thought that she was more concerned with the departing Alfonso than she was with him.

'Why is one of my guests walking out the door right this moment?'

'I told him that if he didn't want a noose slipped

around his neck before he was ready to be hog-tied, he needed to stay away from you.'

Her parted mouth gaped wider, showing a row of perfect white teeth. *'Excuse me—?'*

'You're excused.'

Eyes the colour of dark caramel flashed. 'How dare you refer to me as such—?'

'Careful, *anjo*, you're causing a scene. *Pai* would not be happy to see his event ruined by a tantrum now, would he?'

Her eyes didn't stray from his, her stare direct and cutting in a way that made it difficult for him to look away. Or maybe it was because, despite the boldly challenging stare, he spied a quickly hidden vulnerability that tweaked his radar?

'I don't know who you think you are but per-haps you need to be educated in the etiquette of social gatherings. You don't deliberately set out to insult your host or—'

'My intention was quite simple. I wanted to get rid of the competition.'

'The *competition?*'

The doors to the larger ballroom where the din-ner fund-raiser was to be held were thrown open. Theo turned to her. 'Yes. And now Alfonso's gone, I have you all to myself. And, as to who I am, I'm Theo Pantelides, your VIP guest of honour. Maybe you should add another bullet point to your rules of etiquette. That the hostess should know who her most important guests are?'

Her mouth started to drop open but she caught her reaction and pursed her lips.

'You're Theo Pantelides?' she muttered.

'Yes, so I suggest you make nice with me to stop me from leaving. One high net worth guest departing before dinner may be excusable. Barely. Two will certainly not go down well with your crowd. Now, smile and take my arm.'

Inez reeled under the steely punch packed behind the suave, sophisticated exterior and charming smile.

Theo Pantelides.

This was the man her father and Pietro had talked about. The one who would be taking over majority shares in Da Costa Holdings until after the elections. The one her brother Pietro had referred to as an arrogant bastard.

Well, he certainly was arrogant all right. The swiftness with which he'd dispatched Alfonso and assumed he could control her confirmed that assertion. As to whether he was a true bastard... well, that was something to be determined. But so far all signs pointed in that direction.

What she hadn't been aware of was that the man spoken of with such scorn would be so...visually breathtaking.

'I thought you would be older.' The words tripped from her tongue before she could stop herself.

'As opposed to young, virile and unbelievably handsome?' he drawled.

Shock jolted though her at his unapologetic, irritatingly justified confidence. Because he undeniably was. A full head of vibrant jet-black hair was common enough among her countrymen. Even his hazel eyes, sculpted cheekbones and square jaw were conventional in the polo-loving jet set crowd her father and brother encouraged her to associate with.

On this man, though, the whole combination had been elevated several hundred notches to an entirely different level of magnetism that demanded attention and got it. There was a quality about the way he carried himself, his broad shoulders unyielding, that spelled a tough inner core anyone would be foolish to mess with.

And yet that danger Inez could feel rising off him was...compelling. Alluring.

She found her gaze drifting over his face, past the tiny dimple in his chin to the dark bronze throat as he lazily swallowed a mouthful of champagne.

She inhaled a sharp dart of air as she watched his Adam's apple move. Then jerked back when her fingers flexed suddenly with the urge to touch him there.

Santa Maria!

She fought to remember her anger at this stranger. As much as she detested her role in tonight's events—the blatant begging for campaign funds disguised as a charity event—she couldn't let opportunities slip through her fingers.

It was the deal she'd made with her father.

An education in return for serving her time. In six short weeks she would be free to pursue her dreams. Free of her father's influence, of the sleazy, horrifying rumours that had been part of her childhood and what had driven her mother to quiet despair when she thought she wasn't being observed.

She needed to focus, not moon over how coarse this arrogant stranger's faintly stubbled jaw would feel against her skin.

'*Make nice?* After you rudely interrupted my conversation and sent my guest for the evening running without so much as a goodbye?'

'Think about that for a minute. Do you really

want a man who would abandon you so easily on the strength of a few whispered words?'

Genuine anger replaced the momentary sensory aberration. 'That you needed to whisper those words instead of state them in my hearing makes me wonder just how confident you are of your manhood.'

Inez was used to being the butt of male jokes. Pietro and her father had mocked and dismissed her career ambitions until the day she'd picked up her suitcase and threatened to leave home for good.

But she was still shocked when the man in front of her threw back his head and laughed. Even more so when the sight of his strong white teeth and the genuine twinkling merriment in his eyes sent her pulse racing. An alien tingling started in her belly and spread outward like fractured lightning.

'Did I say something funny?'

Light hazel eyes speared hers. 'I've been challenged on a lot of things, *querida*, but never over my manhood.'

The political career her father so desperately craved produced men who could fake confidence with the best of them. She'd seen political candidates on a clear losing streak fake bravado until they were on the verge of looking totally ridiculous.

This man oozed confidence and power so very effortlessly it was like a second skin. Couple those two elements with the dangerous magnetism she could feel and Theo Pantelides was positively lethal.

Over her thundering heartbeat, she heard the master of ceremonies announce that the fundraiser she'd so carefully orchestrated—the platform that would see her achieve her freedom—was about to begin.

Beyond one broad shoulder of the man who seemed to have sucked the air from the large ballroom, she saw her father and Pietro heading towards her.

Her father would want to know what had happened to Alfonso. The Brazilian businessman had promised to host a polo match on his large ranch where he bred the finest thoroughbreds. Securing a time and a date and a campaign donation had been her job tonight.

A much needed win this man had cost her.

Frustrated anger flared anew.

'This can be resolved very easily, Inez,' Theo Pantelides murmured in her ear. His voice was deep. Alluring. To hear him use her given name, the version her half-American mother had so lovingly bestowed on her, made her momentarily lose her bearings. A state that worsened when his hot breath washed over her neck.

Barely managing to suppress a shiver, she snapped herself back into focus. 'Don't say my name. In fact, don't speak to me. Just…just go away!'

Inez knew she was on the verge of displaying childish behaviour but she needed to regroup quickly, find a solution to a situation that had been so cut and dried fifteen minutes ago.

She watched her father and brother approach and the dart of pain that resided beneath her breastbone twisted. For a long time she'd yearned for a connection with them, especially after *Mãe* had been so cruelly ripped from their lives following a fall from a racehorse a week before Inez's eighteenth birthday. But she'd soon realised that she was alone in the pain and loneliness brought on by the loss of the mother who'd been her everything. Pietro had been given no time to grieve before their father had stepped up his grooming campaign. As for Benedicto himself, he'd barely finished burying his wife before resuming his relentless pursuit of political power.

The only other male she'd foolishly thought was honourable had turned out to be just as ruthlessly power-hungry as the men in her family.

Constantine Blanco—one lesson well and truly learned.

'I see the rumours were false after all,' the man who loomed, large and imposing, in front of her drawled in that deep voice of his, capturing her attention so effortlessly.

She pushed down the bitterness that swirled through her at the thought of what she'd allowed to happen with Constantine. How low she'd sunk in her need for love and a desire for a connection.

'What rumours?' She infused a carelessness in her voice she was far from feeling.

'The ones that said you exhibit grace and charm with each bat of your eyelids. At the moment all I can see is a hellcat intent on scoring grooves into my skin.'

'Then I suggest you stay away from me. I wouldn't want to ruin your *unbelievably handsome* face now, would I?'

She hurried away from his magnetic presence towards where the tables had been set out with highly polished sterling silver cutlery and exquisitely cut crystal. At twenty thousand dollars a plate, the event was ostensibly to raise money for the children trapped within Rio's *favelas*, a cause dear to her heart.

Shame it had to be tainted with power-hungry sharks, mild threats to secure votes and...devastatingly handsome rogues with piercing hazel eyes who made her breath catch in a frighteningly exciting way...

The direction of her thoughts made her stumble lightly. Catching herself, she smiled at a guest who slid her a concerned glance.

Each table was set for eight. Her father had insisted their table was placed in the centre, where all eyes would be on them.

With Alfonso's unexpected departure, the empty seat would stick out like the proverbial sore thumb once the Secretary of State and his wife and the other power couple had taken their places.

She had no choice but to bump someone to the high table. All she needed to figure out was who—

'Staring at the empty seat will not make your departed guest suddenly reappear, *senhorita*,' the deep voice uttered from behind her.

That hot shiver swept up her spine again.

Before she could summon an appropriately scathing retort, her chair and the one bearing Alfonso's name were pulled back.

'What are you doing?' she demanded heatedly under her breath. She continued to stare down at the place setting, unwilling to look up into those hazel eyes. Something in their light depths made her hyperaware of her body, of her increased heartbeat. As if she was prey and he was the merciless predator.

It was preposterous. She didn't like it. But it was undeniable.

'Saving your skin. Now, smile and play along.'

'I'm not a puppet. I don't smile on command.'

'Try. Unless you want to spend the rest of the evening sitting next to the equivalent of an elephant in the ballroom?'

Something in his voice made her forget her vow not to look into his eyes. Something...peculiar. Her head snapped up before she could stop herself.

Their eyes clashed. And she found herself in that hyperaware state again. She forced herself to breathe through it. 'You created the very situation you now seem intent on fixing. Why don't you save us both time and state what your agenda is?'

A look passed over his face. Too quickly for her to decipher but whatever it was made her breath catch in a totally different way from before. Warning spiked the hairs on her nape.

'I merely want to redress the situation a little. And, as talented as you seem to think you are at hiding it, I can see my actions caused you distress. Let me help make it better.'

'So you cause me grief then swoop in to save me like a knight in shining armour?'

'I'm no one's knight, *senhorita*. And I prefer Armani to armour.'

He pointedly held out her seat.

Casting a swift glance around, Inez saw that they were attracting attention. Short of causing a scene, there was nothing she could do. Willing her facial muscles to relax into a cordial smile, she slowly sat down and watched as Theo Pantelides folded himself into the seat next to her.

He reached for his champagne at the same time as she reached for her water glass. The brush of his knuckle against her wrist made her jump.

'Relax, *anjo*. I've got this,' came the smooth, deep reassurance.

A hysterical laugh bubbled up her throat, curbed at the last minute by a cough. 'Pardon me if that assurance brings me very little comfort.'

He lifted the glass she'd abandoned and held it out to her. 'Tell me, what's the worst that could happen?'

She took the glass and stared into the sparkling

water. The need to moisten her dry throat had receded. 'Believe me, the worst already has happened.'

For a long time she'd hidden from the truth—that her father had his heir, and she was a useless spare part.

Pain writhed through her and her breath grew shaky as her throat clogged with anger and bitterness.

'Get yourself together. Now isn't the time to fall apart. Trust me, Delgado may be a good friend but he has a wandering eye.' The hard bite to his tone cut a path through her emotions.

Setting the glass down, she faced him. 'I have been toyed with enough to last me a century, and I know your business here tonight has nothing to do with me, so do me a favour, *senhor*, and tell me straight—what do you want?' she whispered fiercely. She noted vaguely that her heartbeat was once again on rapid acceleration to sky-high. Her fingers shook and her belly churned with emotions she couldn't have named to save her life.

'First of all, cut out the *senhor* bit. If you want to address me in any way, call me Theo.'

'I will address you how I see fit, Mr Pantelides. And I see that once again you have failed to give me a straight answer.'

'No, I've failed to jump when you say. You need to be taught a little patience, *anjo*.'

She lifted a deliberately mocking brow. 'And you propose to be the one to teach me?'

That wide, breathtaking smile appeared again. Just like that, her pulse leapt then galloped with a speed even the finest racehorse would've strained to match.

What was going on here?

'Only if you ask nicely.'

She was searching for an appropriately cutting response when her father reached the table with the rest of the guests.

He cast her a narrow-eyed glance before his gaze slid to Theo Pantelides.

'Mr Pantelides, I had hoped for a few minutes of your time before the evening started properly,' her father said as he took his seat across the table.

Inez wasn't sure whether she imagined the slight stiffening in the posture of the man beside her. Her senses were too highly strung for her to trust their accuracy. Searching his profile as he stared at her father, nothing in his face gave any indication as to his true feelings.

'I'm all for mixing business with pleasure. However, I draw the line at mixing business with the plight of the poor. Let the *favela* kids have their cause heard. *Then* we will attend to business.'

The firm put-down sent an arctic chill around the table. The Secretary's wife gave a visible gasp and her skin blanched beneath her overdone make-up. Pietro, who'd just approached the table as Theo replied, gripped the back of his chair, anger embedded in his face.

Silence reigned for several fraught seconds. Her father flicked a glance at Pietro, who yanked back his seat and sat down. The hands her brother placed on the table were curled into fists and for a moment Inez wondered if his famous temper was about to be let loose on their guests.

Benedicto smiled at Theo. 'Of course. This cause is extremely dear to my heart. My own mother was brought up in the *favelas*.'

'As indeed you were, no?' Theo queried silkily.

Again, the Secretary's wife gasped. She reached for her wine glass and took a quick gulp. When she went to take another, her husband surreptitiously stayed her hand and sent her a stern disapproving look.

Her father nodded to the waiter, who stood poised with a bottle of the finest red wine. He took his time to savour his first sip before he answered.

'You are quite mistaken, Mr Pantelides. My mother managed to escape the fate most of her lot failed to and bettered her life long before she bore me. But I inherited her fighting spirit and her determination to do what I can for the bleak place she once called home.'

Theo's eyebrow quirked. 'Right. I may have been misinformed, then,' he said, although his dry tone suggested otherwise.

'I assure you misinformation is rife when it comes to the ploys of political opponents. And I have been told more than once that only a foolish man believes everything he reads in the papers.'

Theo slashed a smile that had a definite edge to it across the table. 'Trust me, I know a thing or two about what lengths newspapers will go to achieve a headline.'

'We seem to have lost Alfonso. Would you care to explain his absence, Inez?' Pietro's voice slid through the conversation.

Anger still rippled off him and Inez was acutely aware that he hadn't directly addressed Theo Pantelides.

Before she could speak, the man in question turned to her brother. 'He was called away suddenly. Emergency business elsewhere. Couldn't be helped. Since I was there when he took his leave, your sister offered me his seat and I graciously accepted, didn't you, *anjo*?'

She saw Pietro's eyes visibly widen at the blatant endearment. Just as swiftly, they narrowed and she could almost see the wheels spinning in a different direction as his gaze swung between her and Theo Pantelides.

No! Never! Her fingers curled into fists and she glared at him until he looked away.

'Well, perhaps Delgado's loss is our gain, *sim*?' her father prompted.

Again Theo smiled. Again her heart thudded hard at the sheer magnetism of his smile, even though it sorely lacked any humour.

The man was an enigma. He'd inveigled his way onto the top table, then proceeded to insult his host, just as he'd insulted her.

Inez had little doubt her father would unleash his anger at the slight later.

But right now she was more puzzled by the man next to her. What was his game plan? If he was in a position to acquire a controlling share of their company then clearly he was a man of considerable means. But he wasn't Brazilian. That much she knew. So why was he interested in her father's political ambitions?

She realised she was staring when that proud

head turned and gold-flecked hazel eyes captured hers, one eyebrow quirked in amusement.

Hastily averting her gaze, she picked up her glass and took another sip.

Thankfully, the master of ceremonies chose that moment to climb onto the podium to announce the first course and the first speaker.

Inez barely tasted the salmon mousse and the wine that accompanied it. Nor did she absorb the speech given by the health minister about what was being done to help the poor.

Her hyperawareness of the man beside her interfered with her ability to think straight. The last time she'd felt anything remotely like this, she'd wandered down a path she'd hated herself for ever since. She'd almost given herself to a man who had no use for her besides using her as a pawn.

Never again!

Six more weeks. She needed to focus on that. Once her father was on his campaign trail, she could start her new life.

She'd heard the rumours about her father's ruthless beginnings when she was growing up; a couple of her school friends had whispered about unsavoury dealings her father had been involved in. Inez had never found concrete proof. The one time she'd asked her mother, she'd been quickly admonished not to believe lies about her family.

At the time, she'd assured herself that they weren't true. But the passage of time had whittled away that assurance. Now, with each day that passed, she suspected differently.

'You look as if the world is coming to an end, *anjo*,' the man she was desperately trying to ignore murmured. Again the endearment rolled off his tongue in a deep, seductive murmur that sent shivery awareness cascading over her skin.

'I hope you're not going to ask me to smile again, because—' She gasped as he took her hand and lifted it to his mouth.

Firm, warm lips brushed her skin and Inez's stomach dipped in sensual free fall that took her breath away. Desperately, she tried to snatch her hand back.

'What the hell do you think you're doing?' she snapped.

'Helping you. Relax. If you continue to look at me like you want to claw my eyes out, this won't work.'

'What exactly *is* this? And why on earth should I play along?'

'Your brother and father are still wondering why Delgado left so abruptly. Do you want to suffer the third degree later or will you let me help you make it all go away?'

She eyed him suspiciously. The notion that there was something going on behind that smooth, charismatic façade didn't dissipate. In fact, it escalated as he stared down at her, his features enigmatic save for that smile that lingered on his wide, sexy mouth.

'Why do you want to help me?' Again she tried to take back her hand but he held on, one thumb smoothing over her inner wrist. Blood surged through her veins at his touch, her pulse racing at the spot that he so expertly explored.

'Because I'm hoping it would persuade you to have lunch with me tomorrow,' he replied.

His gaze flicked across the table. Although his expression didn't change, she again sensed the tension that hovered on the edge of his civility. This man didn't like her family. Which begged the question: what was he doing here investing in their company?

He swung that intense stare back to her and she lost her train of thought. Grabbing it back, she shook her head.

'I'll have to refuse the lunch offer, I'm afraid. I have other plans.'

'Dinner, then?'

'I have plans then, too. Besides, don't you have business with my father tomorrow?'

'Our business won't take longer than me signing on a dotted line.'

'A dotted line that gives you a permanent controlling share in my family's company?'

His eyes gleamed. 'Not permanent. Only until I have what I want.'

CHAPTER THREE

'AND WHAT IS it you want?'

'For now? Lunch. Tomorrow. With you.' Another pass of his thumb over her pulse.

Another roll of sensation deep in her belly. The temptation to say yes suddenly overcame her, despite the warning bells shrieking at the back of her mind.

She forced herself to heed those warning bells. Her painfully short foray into a relationship had taught her that good looks and charm often hid an agenda that would most likely not benefit her or her heart. And Theo Pantelides had metaphorical skull and crossbones stamped all over him.

'The answer is still no,' she replied, a lot sharper than she'd intended.

His lips compressed but he shrugged. As if her answer hadn't fazed him.

And it probably hadn't. He was one of those men who drew women like bees to pollen. He could probably secure a lunch date with half of the women in this room and tempt the other married half into sin should he choose to.

With his dark, exquisite looks and deep sexy voice, he could have any woman he chose to display even the mildest interest in.

The thought that he would do just such a thing punched so fierce a reaction in her belly that she suppressed a shocked gasp.

What on earth is wrong with me? She needed to get herself back under control before she did something foolish—like discard her plans for tomorrow in favour of spending more time with this infuriatingly self-assured, visually stunning man.

Giving herself a fierce pep talk, she pulled her hand from his grasp.

She folded her hand in her lap and wrapped her other hand over her wrist. But suddenly her own touch felt…inadequate.

She was saved from exploring the peculiar feeling when the lights dimmed and the projector started reeling pictures of miles and miles of rusted shingle roofs that formed the world famous Rio *favelas.*

Her father climbed onto the podium to begin his speech.

The tale of despair-driven prostitution, violence, gang warfare and kidnapping of innocents, and the need to do whatever was needed to help was one she'd heard at many fund-raisers and charity dinners.

She clenched her fist. Knowing that half the people in here, dripping in diamonds and tuxedos worth several thousand dollars, would've forgotten the plight of the *favela* residents by the time dessert was served made her silently scream in frustration.

The need to get up, to walk out almost overwhelmed her but she stayed put.

There would be no running. No walking away from the work she'd committed herself to, nor walking away from the formative minds that were depending on her.

Fierce pride tightened her chest at the part she was playing in the young lives under her charge. And the fact that she'd managed to change that part of her own life without her father or brother's interference.

She refocused as her father finished his speech to rousing applause. The projector was shut off and the lights grew brighter.

She reached forward for her glass of wine and noticed that she was once again the focus of Theo's gaze.

'Should I be offended that I'm being so comprehensively ignored?' he asked.

'It's not a state you're used to, I expect?' With her surroundings once more in focus, she noticed the looks he was getting from women on other tables. She didn't delude herself that any of them were interested in his views on politics or world peace. No, each and every one of them would vie for much more personal, much more physical contact with the lean, broad-shouldered man next to her, whose hands casually caressed his wine glass stem in a way that made her think indecent thoughts.

She noticed the young famous actress on the next table where Theo should have been sitting gazing over at him, and again felt the sharp edge of an unknown emotion pierce her insides.

His smile grew hard. 'You'd be surprised.'

Curiosity brought her gaze back to his. 'Would I? How?'

'That question makes me think you've formed an opinion of me.'

'And that answer convinces me that you're very good at deflecting. You may fool others, but you do not fool me.'

He stared at her for a moment before one corner of his mouth lifted. Abruptly, he stood and held out his hand. 'Dance with me, *anjo*, and enlighten me further as to what you think you know about me.'

The demand was silky and yet implacable. In full view of the other guests, her refusal would be extremely discourteous.

Her heart hammered as she slowly slid her hand into his and let him draw her to her feet.

Emotions she was trying and failing to suppress flared up at the warmth and firmness of his grip. Fervently, she prayed for time to speed up, for the evening to end so she could be free of this man. Her reaction to him was puzzling in the extreme and the notion that she was being toyed with unsettled her more with each passing second.

As they skirted the table to head for the dance floor, her gaze met her father's. Expecting approval for accommodating the man whose business he was so obviously keen to garner, she was taken aback when she saw his icy disapproval.

Through the elite Rio grapevine she knew Alfonso Delgado's net worth and knew he couldn't afford to acquire a controlling share of Da Costa Holdings. So why did her father disapprove of a man who was clearly superior in monetary worth to Alfonso?

'You really have to do better with your social

skills than this. Or I'll have to do something drastic to retain your attention.' The hard bite to Theo's voice slashed through her thoughts. 'Or were you really that into Delgado?'

'No, I wasn't.'

Her immediate denial seemed to pacify him. 'Then tell me what's on your mind.'

Inez found herself speaking before she could snap at him not to issue orders. 'Have you ever found yourself in a position where everything you do turns out wrong, no matter how hard you try?'

'There have been a few instances.' He pulled her close and slid an arm around her back. Heat transmitted to her skin via the soft material of her dress and flooded through her body. This close, his scent washed over her. Strong but not overpowering, masculine and heady in a way that made her want to draw even closer, touch her mouth to the bronze skin just above his collar.

Deus!

'You think this is one of those occasions for you?'

'I don't think; I know.'

'Why?'

Her laugh grated its way up her throat. 'Because I have a perfectly functioning brain.'

'You're worried because your father and brother are displeased with you?'

'Everything else this evening has gone according to plan except...'

'Delgado. You're worried that your father offered you up on a silver platter because he seems to think you're a prize worth winning and now he'll demand to know what you did wrong.'

Her eyes snapped to his, the insult surprisingly painful. 'What do you mean by *seems to think*? What do you know about my father? Or about me, for that matter?'

Theo forced himself not to tense at the question. Or let the fact that her body seemed to fit so perfectly in his arms impact on his thinking abilities. 'Enough.'

'Do you always go around making unfounded remarks about someone you've just met?'

He let a small smile play over his mouth. 'Enlighten me, then. Are you a prize worth winning?'

'There's no point enlightening you because it will serve no useful purpose. After tonight you and I will never meet again.'

She took a firm step back. Attempted to prise herself out of his arms. He held her easily, willing back the thrum of anger and bitterness that rose like bile in his throat.

'Never say never, *anjo*.'

Her fiery brown eyes glared at him. 'Don't.'

He feigned innocence. 'Don't what?'

'Don't keep calling me that.'

'You don't like it?'

'You have no right to slap a pet name on some-one you just met.'

The hand holding hers tightened. 'Calm down—'

'No, I won't calm down. I'm not an angel. I'm certainly not *your* angel.'

'Inez.' A warning, subtle but effective.

Inez's pulse stalled, then thundered wildly through her veins.

'Don't,' she whispered again. Only this time she wasn't sure what she pleaded for.

He leaned closer until his mouth was an inch from her ear. When he breathed out, warmth teased her earlobe. 'Don't use your given name? It's either that or *anjo*. All the other words are only appropriate for the bedroom.'

Heat flamed through her belly as indecent thoughts of rumpled sheets, sweaty bodies and incandescent pleasure reeled through her mind.

She shook her head to dispel the images and heard his low laugh.

When she stared up at him, his eyes blazed down at her with a hunger that smashed through her body. Her nipples slowly hardened and the fire raged higher as his lips parted on another heart-stopping smile. Unable to help herself, her eyes dropped to the sensual curve of his mouth.

'I think it's my turn to say *don't*. Not if you don't want to be thrown over my shoulder and raced to the nearest cave.'

She forced a laugh despite the sensations rushing through her. 'This is the twenty-first century, *senhor*.'

'But what I'm feeling right now isn't. It's very basic. Primeval, in fact.'

He swerved her out of the path of another couple and used the move to draw her even closer. At the fierce evidence of his arousal against her stomach, Inez swallowed hard.

Her confusion escalated.

Constantine had been charismatic and breath-taking in his own right. But he'd never made her feel like *this*, not even in the beginning…before everything had gone disastrously wrong.

Thinking of the man who'd broken her heart and betrayed her so cruelly threw much needed ice over her heated senses. She'd made a fool of herself over one man. Foolishly believed he was the answer to her prayers. She was wise enough now to know Theo Pantelides wasn't the answer to any prayer, unless it was the crash and burn type.

'I believe I've fulfilled my obligatory dance duty to you. Perhaps you'd like to find a more unwitting female to club over the head and drag to your cave?' She injected as much indifference into her voice as possible.

'That won't be necessary. I've already found what I'm looking for.'

Theo watched several emotions chase over her features before Inez da Costa regained her impeccable hostess persona.

Although he silently cursed himself for his physical reaction, he was thankful she realised her effect on him.

Let her think she held the power. Allow her to believe that he could be manipulated to her advantage. Or, rather, her father's advantage.

Her reaction to Delgado's departure had shown him that fulfilling her role as her father's Venus flytrap was most important to Inez da Costa. Or was it something else? Did she hope to bag *herself* a millionaire while serving her father's purpose? She came from a family ruthless in its pursuit of wealth and power. Was that her underlying agenda?

That knowledge demanded that he rethink his strategy. The conclusion he'd arrived at was surprising but easily adaptable.

He had an opportunity to kill a few more birds with one stone. With any luck, he would conclude his business in Rio in a far shorter time than he'd already anticipated if he played his cards right.

Inez tried to wrench herself from his grasp once more. The primitive feelings he'd mentioned so casually a moment ago resurfaced. When she tugged harder, he forced himself to release her. Her soft hand slid from his, leaving a trail of sensation that made his groin pound and his blood heat.

The plan he'd hatched solidified as he gazed down into her heart-shaped face, saw her fighting to stop her clear agitation from messing with her breathing.

Theo hid a smile.

Either she was offended at his primitive declaration or she was turned on by it. Since she wasn't slapping his face, he concluded that it was the latter.

His gaze dropped lower, and the sight of her tightly beaded nipples against her gown made his own breathing stall in his chest. Lower still, her tiny waist gave way to those tempting hips that his palms ached to explore.

Even as he talked himself into believing his re-action would ultimately serve his purpose, a part of Theo was forced to acknowledge that he hadn't reacted this strongly to a woman in a very long time. Everything about her brought his senses to roaring life in a way only the thought of revenge had for the past decade.

Revenge...retribution over the person who had created such chaos in his life.

He gritted his teeth as the sound of tinkling laughter and animated conversation refocused his mind to his task and purpose.

'Good evening, Mr Pantelides. I hope you enjoy the rest of your evening,' Inez said stiltedly.

She turned and walked off the dance floor be-fore he could reply. Not that he felt like replying. Although he'd mostly kept on track throughout the evening, a large part of him had become far too consumed by her seductive presence.

Inez da Costa was only one part of the game. To keep on track he needed to keep his head in the *whole* game.

He headed for the bar and sensed the moment Benedicto and his son halted their conversation and moved pincer-like towards him.

Dreaded anxiety washed over his senses but he forced himself to breathe through it.

I am no longer in that dark, cold place. I am in light. I am free...

He tersely repeated the short statement under his breath as he tossed back the shot of vodka and set it down with cold, precise care.

He was no longer weak. No longer helpless.

And he most certainly would never be put in a position to beg for his life. Ever again.

By the time they reached him, he'd regained control of his body.

'Senhor Pantelides—'

'We're about to become business partners—' his gaze slid over Pietro's head to where Inez was holding court in a group of guests; the sleek line of her neck and the curve of her body sent another punch of heat straight to his groin '—and hopefully a little bit more than that. Call me Theo.'

The younger man looked a little taken aback, but he rallied quickly, nodded and held out his hand. 'Theo...we wanted to hammer down a time to discuss finalising our agreement.'

He took Pietro's hand in a firm grip. Benedicto started to offer his hand. Theo deliberately turned away. Catching the bartender's eye, he held up his fingers for three more drinks. By the time he faced them again, Benedicto had lowered his hand.

Theo breathed through the deep anger that churned through his belly and smiled.

'Tomorrow. Ten o'clock. My office. I'll have the documents ready for us to sign.'

This time it was Benedicto who looked taken aback. 'I was under the impression that you wanted to iron out a few more details.'

Theo's gaze flicked back to Inez. 'I had a few concerns but they no longer matter. Your campaign funds will be ready in the next twenty-four hours.'

Father and son exchanged triumphant looks. 'We are pleased to hear it,' Benedicto said.

'Good, then I hope the three of you will join me for dinner tomorrow evening to celebrate our new deal.'

Benedicto frowned. 'The three of us?'

'Of course. I expect that, since this is a family company, your daughter would wish to be included in the celebrations? After all, the company was her mother's family's business before it became yours, Senhor da Costa, was it not?' he queried silkily.

The older man's eyes narrowed and something unpleasant slid across his face. 'I bought my father-in-law out over a decade ago but yes, it's a family business.'

Bought out using money he'd obtained by inflicting pain and merciless torment.

The bartender slid their shots across the polished counter.

Theo picked up the nearest shot glass and raised it. 'In that case, I look forward to welcoming you all as my guests tomorrow evening. *Saúde.*'

'*Saúde,*' Benedicto and his son responded.

Theo threw back the drink and this time didn't hold back from slamming it down.

Again he saw father and son exchange looks. He didn't care.

All he cared about was making it out of the ballroom in one piece before he buried his fist in Benedicto da Costa's bony face. The urge to tear apart the man who'd caused his family, caused *him,* so much anguish reared through him.

The sound of his phone vibrating in his jacket pocket brought a welcome distraction from his murderous thoughts.

'Excuse me, gentlemen.' He walked away without a backward glance, gaining the double doors leading out to the wide terrace before activating his phone.

'Heads up, you're about to get into serious trouble with Ari if you don't fess up as to why you're really in Rio,' Sakis, his brother, said in greeting.

'Too late. I've already had the hairdryer treatment earlier this evening.'

'Yeah, but do you know he's thinking of flying down there for a face-to-face?'

Theo cursed. 'Doesn't he have enough on his hands being all loved up and taking care of his pregnant fiancé?' He wasn't concerned about a confrontation with Ari. But he was concerned that Ari's presence might alert Benedicto to Theo's true intentions.

So far, Benedicto da Costa was oblivious as to the connections Theo had made to what had happened twelve years ago. The older man had been very careful to erase every connection with the incident and sever ties with anyone who could bear witness to the crime he'd committed. He hadn't been careful enough. But he didn't know that.

Having another Pantelides in Rio could set off alarm bells.

'You need to stall him.'

'He's concerned,' Sakis murmured. Theo heard the same concern reflected in his brother's voice. 'So am I.'

'It needs to be done,' he replied simply.

'I get that. But you don't need to do it alone.

He's dangerous. The moment he guesses what your true intentions are—'

'He won't; I've made sure of it.'

'How can you be absolutely certain? Theo, don't be stubborn. I can help—'

'No. I need to see this through myself.'

Sakis sighed. 'Are you sure?'

Theo turned slowly and surveyed the ballroom. Rio's finest drank and laughed without a care in the world. In the centre of that crowd stood Benedicto da Costa, the reason why Theo couldn't sleep through a single night without waking to hellish nightmares; the reason anxiety hovered just underneath his skin, ready to infest his control should he loosen his grip for one careless second.

Inexorably, his eyes were drawn to the female member of the diabolical family. Inez was dancing with a man whose blatant interest and barely disguised lust made Theo's fist curl over the cold stone bannister.

His stomach churned and adrenaline poured through his system the same way a boxer experienced a heady rush in the seconds before a fight. This fight had been long coming. He would see it through. He had to. Otherwise he feared his demons would never be exorcised.

He'd lived with them for far too long, and they needed to be silenced. He needed to regain complete, unshakeable hold of his life once more.

His other hand tightened around his mobile phone, his heart thundering enough to drown out the music. He spoke succinctly so his brother would be in no doubt that he meant every word.

'Am I sure that I need to bring down the man who kidnapped and tortured me for over two weeks until Ari negotiated a two million ransom for my release? *Hell, yes.* I'm going to make him feel ten million times worse than what he did to me and to our family and I don't intend to rest until I bring all of them down.'

CHAPTER FOUR

'A DOUBLE-SHOT AMERICANO, *por favor*.' Inez smiled absently at the barista while she tried to juggle her sketchpad and fish out enough change from her purse to pay for the coffee.

It was barely nine o'clock and yet the heat was already oppressive, even more than usual for a Thursday morning in February. Normally, she would've opted for a cool caffeine drink but her energy levels needed an extra boost this morning.

She'd slept badly after the fund-raiser last night. And what little sleep she'd managed had been interspersed with images of a man she had no business thinking, never mind dreaming, about.

And yet Theo Pantelides's face had haunted her slumber...still haunted her, if truth be told.

The last time she'd seen him he'd been leaning against the terrace bannister outside the ballroom, his eyes fixed firmly on her. Inez wasn't sure why her attention had been drawn outside.

All she knew was that something had compelled her to look that way as she danced with a guest.

Even from that distance the tension whipping through his frame had been unmistakable, as had the blatant dark promise in his eyes as his gaze raked her from head to toe.

More than anything she'd wished she could lip-read when she'd watched his lips move to answer whoever was at the other end of his phone conversation.

That last look plagued her. It'd held hunger, anger and another emotion that she couldn't quite decipher. Brushing it off, she smiled, accepted her coffee and headed outside. She was a little early for her class with the inner city kids but she hadn't wanted to spend another moment at the tension-fraught breakfast table with her father and brother this morning.

In contrast to Pietro's third degree as to what exactly had happened with Alfonso Delgado, her father had been cold and strangely preoccupied. The moment he'd stood abruptly and left the table, she'd made her excuses and walked away.

Even Pietro's reminder that they had a dinner engagement she couldn't recall making hadn't been worth stopping to query. All she'd wanted was to get out of the mansion that felt more and more as if it was closing in on her.

'*Bom dia, anjo.*' The deep murmured greeting brought her thoughts and footsteps to a crashing halt.

Theo leaned casually against a gleaming black sports car, a pair of dark sunglasses hiding his eyes from her. But her full body tingle announced that she was the full, unwavering focus of his gaze. Her breath stalled, her heart accelerating wildly as her pulse went into overdrive.

'What the hell are you doing here?' she blurted before she could stop her strong reaction.

Aside from the devastation his tall, lean suited frame caused to her insides, the thought that he could discover where she was headed or what she did with her Tuesday and Thursday mornings made her palms grow clammy. By lunchtime today, if Pietro were to be believed, Theo would be firmly entrenched as a business partner in her family's company. Which meant constant contact with her family. Which meant he could disclose parts of her life she wasn't yet ready to disclose to her family.

'Are you following me?' she accused hotly as she approached him, her senses jumping with the possibilities and consequences of her discovery.

'Not today. My trench coat and fedora are at the laundry.'

'Keep them there. In this heat, you'd boil to death.'

A smile broke across his face. 'Do I detect a little unladylike relish in your voice, *anjo*?'

'What you detect is high scepticism that you're here by accident and not following me,' she snapped.

'You give me too much credit, *agape mou*. I asked for the best coffee shop in the city and I was directed here. That you're here too merely confirms that assertion. Unless you go out of your way to sample bad coffee?'

Before she could respond, he straightened and reached for the hand wrapped around her coffee. Curling his hand over hers, he brought his lips to the small opening on her coffee lid and tilted the cup towards him.

He savoured the drink in his mouth for a few seconds before he swallowed.

Inez fought to breathe as she watched his strong throat move. The slow swirl of his tongue over his lower lip caused darts of sharp need to arrow straight between her legs.

'Delicious. And surprising. I would've pegged you for a latte girl.'

'Which goes to show you know next to nothing about me,' she retorted.

He slowly raised his sunglasses and speared her with his mesmerising eyes. Although a smile hovered over his sensual lips, some unnameable tension hovered in the air between them. A charged friction that warned her all was not as it seemed.

Hell, she knew that. Theo Pantelides spelled danger. Whether smiling or serious, dallying with him was akin to playing with electricity. Depending on his mood, you could either receive a mild static frizzle or a full-blown electrocution. And she had no intention of testing him for either.

'*Sim*, I don't know enough about you. But I intend to remedy that situation in the near future.'

She shrugged. 'It is your time to waste.'

He merely smiled and turned towards his car.

'I thought you came to get coffee?' she probed, then bit her lip for prolonging a meeting she wanted over and done with. Last night she'd told herself to be thankful that she would never see this man again. And yet, here she was, feeling mildly bereft at the notion that he was leaving.

He paused and his gaze slid over her. Immediately, she became supremely conscious of the white shorts and blue tank top she'd hurriedly thrown on this morning. Her hair was caught up in a ponytail because it helped keep it out of the way during her class. Her face was devoid of make-up except for the light sunscreen and the gloss she'd passed over her lips. All in all, she projected a much different image this morning than the sophisticated hostess she'd been last night.

Catching herself wondering whether he found her wanting now, she mentally slammed the thought down. She didn't care what Theo thought of her.

'I have the kick I need to keep me going. See you tonight.'

'Tonight? Why would you be seeing me tonight?' she demanded.

His smile slowly disappeared as his gaze slid over her again. This time, his hot gaze held an element of possessiveness that made her fight to keep from fidgeting under his keen scrutiny.

Stepping back, he activated a button on his car key and the door slid smoothly upward. She watched, completely captivated, as he lowered his tall masculine frame inside the small space. A touch of a slim finger on a button and the engine roared to life.

'Because I want to see you. And I always get what I want, Inez,' he said cryptically, his tone suddenly hard and biting. 'Remember that.'

* * *

I always get what I want.

Another shiver of apprehension coursed down her spine.

All through the two art and graphic design classes she taught from ten till midday, the infernal words throbbed through her head as if someone had set them on repeat.

She managed to keep her focus, barely, as she demonstrated the differences between charcoal and pencil strokes to a group of ten-year-olds. Once or twice she had to repeat herself because she lost her train of thought, much to the amusement of her pupils, but the satisfying feeling of imparting knowledge to children who would otherwise have been left wandering the streets momentarily swamped the roiling emotions that Theo had stirred with his unexpected appearance this morning.

The suspicion that he had been following her didn't go away all through her hurriedly taken lunch and the meeting she'd scheduled with the volunteer coordinator at the centre.

Her decision to forge her own path by seeking a permanent position at the centre had solidified as she'd tossed and turned through the night.

Seeking her independence meant finding a paying job. To do that she needed more experience, which she hoped her longer hours spent volunteering would give her.

Thanks to her father's interference, all she had was one semester at university. It wasn't great but, until such time as she could further her education, it was better than nothing. That plus her volunteering was a starting point.

A starting point that was greatly enhanced when the coordinator agreed to increase her hours to three full days.

She was smiling as she activated her phone on the way to her car after leaving the centre.

The first text was from Pietro, reminding her that they were dining out that evening. With Theo Pantelides.

The unladylike curse she uttered won her a severe look of disapproval from an elderly lady walking past. The urge to text back a refusal was immediate and visceral.

After last night and this morning, exposing herself to the raw emotions Theo provoked was the last thing she needed.

And even more than her suspicions this morning, she had a feeling he'd engineered this dinner. Hell, he'd as much as taunted her with it with his last words to her this morning.

As much as she tried to think positive and hope that the dinner would be quick and painless, a premonition gripped her insides as she slid behind the wheel and headed home.

'*Filho da puta.*' Her brother's habitual crude cursing wasn't a surprise to her. That it had seemingly come out of nowhere was.

'What's wrong?' She eyed him as they stepped out of the car at the marina of the exclusive Rio Yacht Club just before seven p.m.

She pulled down her box-pleated hem and wished she'd worn something a little longer than the form-fitting mid-thigh-length royal-blue sleeveless dress. The traffic had been horrendous and she'd arrived home much later than planned. The dress had been the nearest thing to hand. Now she stared down at the four-inch black platform heels she'd teamed with it and grimaced at the amount of thigh and legs on show.

The light breeze lifted a few strands of her loose hair as she turned to her brother and saw him jerk his chin towards the largest yacht moored at the far end of the pier. 'Trust Pantelides to rub my nose in it,' he said acerbically.

She looked from the sleek black, gold-trimmed

vessel back to her brother. 'Rub your nose…what are you talking about?'

With a sullen look, he strode off down the jetty. 'That's my boat.'

'*Yours*? When did you buy a boat?'

'I didn't. I couldn't. Not after the mess up with *Pai*'s last campaign. That boat was supposed to be mine!' Dark anger clouded his face.

Her heart jumped into her throat. 'Pietro, a boat like that costs millions of dollars. Besides that very unsubtle hint that I in any way stood in the way of your acquiring it—which is preposterous, by the way—there's no way you could ever have afforded a boat like that, so—'

'Forget it. Let's go and get this over with. It's bad enough *Pai* pulled out of coming tonight. Now I have to schmooze for both of us. You have to play your part, too. It's clear Pantelides's got a thing for you.'

Disgust and anger rose in her and she snatched her hand away from Pietro when he tried to lead her down the gangplank.

'I won't participate in another of your soulless schemes. So you may as well forget it right now.'

'Inez—'

'No!' Feelings she'd bottled up for much longer than she cared to think about rose to the surface.

'You keep asking me to throw myself at prospective investors so you can fund *Pai*'s campaign. You're his campaign manager and yet you can't seem to function without my help. Why is that?'

Pietro's eyes darkened. 'Watch your mouth, sister.'

'Show me some respect and I'll consider it,' she challenged.

'What the hell has got into you?'

'Nothing that hasn't always been there, Pietro. But you need me to point it out to you so I will. I'm done. If you want me to accompany you as your *sister* to Theo Pantelides's dinner, then I will. If you have another scheme up your sleeve, then you might as well forget it because I am not interested.'

Her brother's lips pursed but she saw a hint of shame in his eyes before his gaze slid away. 'I don't have time to argue with you right now. All I ask, if it's not too much, of course, is that you help me secure this deal with Pantelides, because if we lose his backing then we might as well pack up and head back up to the ranch in the mountains.' He set off down the jetty.

She hurried to keep up, picking her way carefully over wooden slats. 'But I thought everything was done and dusted this morning?' she asked when she caught up with him.

Anxiety slid over Pietro's face. 'Pantelides cancelled the meeting. Something came up, he said. Except I know it was a lie. I have it on good authority he was parked outside a coffee shop chatting up some girl when he was supposed to be meeting us to finalise the agreement.'

Inez stumbled, barely catching herself from toppling headlong into the water a few feet away.

'You're having him watched?' How she managed to keep her voice even, she didn't know.

Petulance joined anxiety. 'Of course I am. And I'd bet my Rolex that he's doing the same to us.'

The thought of being the subject of anyone's surveillance made her skin crawl, even though a part of her had reluctantly accepted the truth: that her father's business dealings weren't always legitimate. But hearing her brother admit it made her stomach turn.

And if that was the way Theo Pantelides conducted his business as well…

She pressed her lips together and looked up as Pietro strode past the potted palm lined entrance to the Yacht Club.

'Aren't we dining in there?'

He shook his head. 'No. We're dining on my... on *his* boat,' he tossed out bitterly.

Inez glanced at the yacht they were approaching.

This close, the vessel was even more magnificent. Its sleek lines and exquisite craftsmanship made her fingers itch for her sketching pad. She was so busy admiring the boat and yearning to capture its beauty on paper that she didn't see its owner until she was right in front of him.

Then everything else ceased to register.

He wore a black shirt with black trousers, his dark hair raked back from his face. Under the soft golden lights spilling from the second deck his sculpted cheekbones and strong jaw jutted out in heart-stopping relief.

At the back of her mind, Inez experienced a bout of irritation at the fact that he captured attention so exclusively. So effortlessly.

Even as he shook hands with Pietro and welcomed him on board the *Pantelides 9*, his eyes remained on her. And God help her, but she couldn't look away.

On unsteady feet, which she firmly blamed on the swaying vessel, she climbed the steps to where he waited. When his eyes released hers to travel over her body, she grappled with controlling her breath. She reached him and reluctantly held out her hand in greeting.

'Thank you for the dinner invitation, Mr Pantelides.'

With a mocking smile, he took her hand and used the grip to pull her close. Despite her heels, he was almost a foot taller than her, easily six foot four. Which meant he had to lean down quite a bit to whisper in her ear, 'So formal, *anjo*. I look forward to loosening your inhibitions enough to dissolve that starchy demeanour.'

Her pulse, which had begun racing when his palm slid against hers, thundered even harder at his words. 'I can see how not having a woman fall at your feet the moment you crook your finger can present a challenge, *senhor*. But you really should learn the difference between playing hard to get and being plainly uninterested.'

His eyebrow quirked. 'You fall into the latter category, of course?' he mocked.

'*Sim*, that is exactly so.'

He looked towards where Pietro had accepted a glass of champagne from a waiter and was admiring the luxuriously decorated deck, at the end of which a multi-coloured lit jet pool swirled and shimmered.

When his gaze re-fixed on hers, there was a

steely determination in his eyes that sent a shiver down her spine. All the earlier alarm bells where Theo was concerned clanged loudly in her brain.

'Then I will have to get a little more inventive,' he murmured silkily before dropping her hand.

Inez clenched her fist and fought the urge to rub the tingling in her palm. She didn't want him getting inventive where she was concerned because she had a nasty feeling she wouldn't emerge unscathed from the encounter.

But she kept her mouth shut and followed him onto the deck. The cream and gold décor was the last word in luxury and opulence. Plump gold seats offered comfort and a superior view onto the well-lit marina and the open sea to their right. To their left, the lights of Rio gleamed, with the backdrop of the huge mountain, on top of which resided the world-famous Cristo Redentor.

A sultry breeze wafted through the deck as a waiter served more flutes of champagne. She took a glass as Pietro rejoined them. His glass was already half empty and she watched him take another greedy gulp before he pointed a finger at Theo.

'I wish you'd given me the chance to make you another offer for this boat before you pulled the plug on our sale agreement, Pantelides.'

Theo's jaw tightened before he answered. 'You had several opportunities to make good but you failed to close the deal. So I cut my losses.' He shrugged. 'Business is business.'

Pietro bristled. 'And cancelling our meeting today? Was that for business too, or pleasure?'

Theo's eyes caught and held hers. Inez held her breath, wondering if he was about to give her up. His eyes gleamed with a mixture of danger and amusement. Somehow he'd sensed that he held her in his power. And he relished that power. Her hand trembled slightly as she waited for the axe to fall.

'I'm not in the habit of discussing my other business interests, or my pleasurable ones, for that matter. But, suffice it to say, what kept me away from our meeting was very much worth my time.' His gaze swept down, lingering over her breasts and hips in a blatant appraisal that made her breathing grow shallow. When his eyes returned to hers, Inez was sure all the oxygen had been sucked out of the atmosphere.

'Our business together should be equally worth your time,' Pietro countered.

Theo finally set her free from his captivating gaze. Narrow-eyed, he glanced at Pietro.

'Which is why I rescheduled for this evening.

Of course, your father chose not to grace us with his presence. So the song and dance continues, I guess.' The hard edge was definitely in his tone again, prompting those alarm bells to ring louder.

Pietro muttered something under his breath that she was sure wasn't complimentary. He snapped his fingers at the waiter and swapped his empty glass for a full one.

'Well, we'll be there at the appointed time tomorrow. We can only hope that you will not be delayed…elsewhere.'

The upward movement of Theo's mouth could in no way be termed a smile. His eyes flicked back to her. 'Don't worry, da Costa, I intend to hammer out the final points of our agreement tonight. When I turn up to sign tomorrow, it will be with the knowledge that all my stipulations have been satisfied.'

The firm belief that his statement was connected to her wouldn't dissipate all through dinner. As a host, Theo was effortlessly entertaining. He even managed to draw a chuckle from Pietro once or twice.

But Inez couldn't shake the feeling that they were being toyed with. And once or twice she caught the faintest hint of fury and repulsion on his face, especially when her father's name came up.

She shook herself out of her unsettling thoughts when the most mouth-watering dessert was set down before her.

Whatever Theo was up to, it was nothing to do with her. Her father had managed their family business with enough savvy not to be drawn into a scam.

With that comforting thought in mind, she picked up her spoon and scooped up a mouthful of chocolate truffle-topped cheesecake.

Her tiny groan of delight drew intense eyes back to hers. Suddenly, the thought of dishing out a little of the mockery he'd doled out to her tingled through her. Keeping her gaze on his, she slowly drew the spoon out from between her lips, then licked the remnants of chocolate with a slow flick of her tongue.

His nostrils flared immediately, hunger darkening his eyes to a leaf-green that was mesmerising to witness. With another swirl of her tongue, she lowered the spoon and scooped up another mouthful.

His large fist tightened around the after-dinner espresso he'd opted for and she momentarily expected the bone china to shatter beneath his grip. But slowly he released it and sat back in his chair, his eyes never leaving her face.

'Enjoying your dessert, *anjo*?' he asked in that low, rough tone of his.

She hated to admit that the endearment was beginning to have an effect on her. The way he mouthed it made heat bloom in her belly, made her aware of her every heartbeat…made her wonder how it would sound whispered to her at the height of passion. *No!*

'Yes. Very much.' She fake smiled to project an air of nonchalance.

He smiled at her mocking formality. 'Good. I'll make a note of it for the next time we dine together.'

Before she could tell him she intended to move heaven and earth to make sure there wouldn't be a next time, Pietro lurched to his feet. 'I never got the chance to inspect my…this boat before the opportunity to buy it was regrettably taken away. You won't mind if I take a look around, would you?' he slurred.

Theo motioned the hovering waiter over. He murmured to him and the waiter went to the deck bar and picked up a handset. 'Not at all. My skipper will give you the tour.'

A middle-aged man with greying hair climbed onto the deck a few minutes later and escorted a swaying Pietro towards the stairs.

Inez watched him go with a mixture of anxiety and sympathy.

'He's drunk.' Her appetite gone for good, she set her spoon down and pushed the plate away.

'You say that as if it's my fault,' he replied lazily.

'Did you really have to do that?' She glared at him.

He raised a brow. 'Do what, exactly?'

'This was supposed to be Pietro's boat.' No matter how unrealistic that notion had been, her brother didn't deserve to be humiliated like this.

'*Supposed* being the operative word. We had a *gentleman's* agreement.' That hard bite was back again, sending trepidation dancing along her nerve ends. 'He didn't hold out his end of the deal.'

'Regardless of that, do you have to rub his nose in it like this?' she countered.

'As I said before, I'm a businessman, *anjo*. And I currently have a yacht worth tens of millions of dollars that needs an owner. The Boat Show starts next week. I relocated aboard in order to get it in shape for prospective buyers, otherwise our dinner would have taken place at my residence in Leblon and your brother's delicate feelings would've been spared.'

She frowned. 'You're selling the boat?' The thought of the beautiful vessel going to some unknown, probably pompous new owner made her nose wrinkle in distaste. The design was exquisite, unique…sort of like its owner. As hard as she tried to imagine it, she couldn't see anyone else owning the boat besides Theo. Not even Pietro. Its black and gold contrasts depicted darkness and light in a complementary synergy—two fascinating characteristics she'd glimpsed more than once in Theo.

'Needs must.'

She looked around the beautiful deck, imagined its graceful lines awash with sunlight, and sighed.

Theo's eyes narrowed as he stared across at her. 'You like the boat.'

'Yes, it's…beautiful.'

He watched her for a few minutes then he nodded. 'Let's make a date for Sunday afternoon. We'll take her out for a quick spin.'

She laughed. 'Unless I'm mistaken, this is a four hundred foot vessel. You don't just take her out for a *quick* spin.'

'A long spin, then. I need to make sure it runs perfectly. If you still like it when we return to shore, I'll keep it.'

Her heart lurched then sped up like a runaway freight train. 'You would do that…for me?'

'*Sim*,' he replied simply.

Genuine puzzlement, along with a heavy dose of excitement she didn't want to admit to, made her blurt, 'Why?'

He strolled lazily to where she stood. This close, she had to tilt her head to catch his gaze. *Darkness and light.* He might have been smiling but Inez could almost reach out and touch the undercurrent of emotions swirling beneath his civility. She jumped slightly when he brushed a forefinger down her cheek.

'Because I intend to keep you, *anjo.* And while you will not have a lot of choice in the matter, I'm willing to make a few adjustments to ensure your contentment.'

CHAPTER FIVE

THEO WATCHED HER grapple with what he'd just said. Unlike her brother, she wasn't inebriated—she'd barely touched her glass of the rich Barolo 2009 he'd specially chosen for their dinner.

She shook her head in confusion. 'You intend to *keep* me?'

Her skin, satin-smooth beneath his touch, begged to be caressed. He gave in to the urge and traced her from cheek to jaw. When she withdrew from him, he followed. He stroked the pulse beating in her neck and pushed back the need to step closer, touch his mouth to the spot.

He'd learnt two things last night.

The first was that Benedicto da Costa, for all his cunning and veneer of sophistication, was still a greedy, vicious snake who thought he could con millions of dollars out of an unsuspecting fool like him.

The second was that Inez da Costa could be a key player in the slow and painful revenge he intended to exact for the wrong done to him. It didn't hurt that the chemistry between them burned the very air they breathed.

In the past Theo had made several opportune decisions by switching tactics at the last minute and making the most of whatever situation he found himself him.

With the newfound information at his fingertips, he'd found a way not only to end the da Costas once and for all, but also to make a tidy profit to boot.

He barely stopped himself from smiling as he looked down into Inez's face. She really was stunningly beautiful. With a mouth that begged to be explored.

'Mr Pantelides?'

'Theo,' he murmured, anticipating her refusal to use his first name.

She blew out an exasperated breath. 'Theo. Explain yourself.'

The unexpected sound of his name on her lips sent a pulse of heat through his body. Followed swiftly by a feeling he recognised as pleasure.

With a silent curse he dropped his hand. Pleasure featured nowhere on his mission to Rio. Nor was standing around, gazing into the face that reminded him of the painting of an angel that used to hang in his father's house.

Pain. Reparation. Merciless humiliation. Those were his objectives.

'There's no hidden message in there, *anjo*. For the duration of my stay in Rio I expect you to make yourself available to me, day and night.'

Her genuine laughter echoed around the open deck. When he didn't join in, she quickly sobered. 'Oh, I'm sorry. But I believe you have me confused with a certain type of woman you must encounter on your travels.'

Theo let the insult slide. He'd told his skipper to take his time with the tour, but even his trusted employee couldn't keep Pietro away for ever. And it looked as if he needed to step up this part of his strategy in order to forward his overall objective.

'I was supposed to sign documents that guaranteed your father's campaign funds this morning but I didn't turn up. Aren't you even a little bit curious as to why?'

A touch of confusion clouded her brown eyes but she shrugged one silky-smooth shoulder that shimmered softly under the deck lights. 'Your business with my father is not my concern.'

A little of that control he kept under a tight leash threatened to slip free. 'You don't care where the money comes from as long as you're kept in the style to which you've grown accustomed, is that it?'

Her eyes widened at the acid leaching from his tone. 'You may think you know me but, I assure you, you've got things wrong—'

'Have I? From where I'm standing it's very evident you're the bait he uses to trap weak, pathetic fools into opening their wallets.'

Her ragged gasp accompanied a look of outrage so near authentic Theo would've believed her reaction had he not seen her in action with Delgado last night.

'If it is your intention to be offensive to show your *machismo*, then *bravo*, you've succeeded,' she threw at him and whirled away.

He caught her wrist before she could take a step.

'Let me go.'

'I've yet to outline my plans, *anjo*.'

'I think you've *outlined* enough. I won't stand here listening to your unfounded insults. I'm going to find Pietro. And then we're leaving.' She tried to free herself. He tightened his grip until he could feel her pulse under his fingers. Furious. Passionate.

His groin stirred and he forced himself to ignore the throb of arousal determined to make itself known. 'You're not leaving here until we have this discussion.'

'What we're having is not a discussion, *senhor*. What you're doing is holding me captive, torturing me with—'

She broke off, no doubt in reaction to his hiss of fury and the flash of icy memory that made his whole body go rigid for one long second.

Theo released her, turned away sharply and shoved his hand through his hair. He noted his fingers' faint trembling and willed himself to stop shaking.

'Th…Theo?' Her voice came from far away, filled with confusion and a touch of concern.

He willed away the effect of the trigger words and forced himself to breathe. But they pounded through his brain nonetheless—*captive, prisoner, torture, darkness…*

Fingers closed over his shoulder and he jerked around. *'Don't!'*

She jumped back, snatching back her hand. It took several more seconds for him to recall where he was. He wasn't in some deep, dark hole in a remote farm in Spain. He was in Rio. With the daughter of the man who continued to cause his recurring nightmares.

'What's…what's wrong with you?' she asked with a wary frown.

He drew in a steady breath and gritted his teeth. 'Nothing. I'll get to the point. The agreement was that I'd take control of Da Costa Holdings and keep a fifty per cent share of the profits in exchange for liquidated funds to finance your father's political campaign. However, the papers your father had drawn up contain a major loophole that I can easily exploit.'

Slowly, his panic receded and he noticed she was absently rubbing her wrist. He quickly replayed his reaction to her touch and breathed a sigh of relief when he confirmed to himself that he hadn't grabbed her in his panic.

She continued to rub her skin and slowly another earthy emotion replaced his roiling feelings. He welcomed the pulse of arousal despite the fact that he had no intention of falling prey to the easy wiles of Inez da Costa. No matter how mouth-watering her body or how angelic her face.

'Shouldn't you be telling my father this, give him a chance to fix the loophole before you sign?'

He smiled at her naiveté. 'Why should I? I stand to gain by signing the agreement as it's drawn up.'

Her brow creased. 'Then why tell me about it?

What's to keep me from telling my father about it the moment I leave here?'

'You won't.'

One expertly plucked eyebrow lifted. 'Again, I think you underestimate me.'

He strode to the extensively stocked bar and poured himself a shot of vodka. 'You won't because if you do I won't sign the agreement in any form. And the offer of financial backing vanishes.'

All trace of colour left her face. 'So this is a blackmail attempt. To what purpose?'

'The purpose needn't concern you. All I want you to know is that there is a loophole which I can choose to exploit or leave alone, depending on your cooperation.'

'But what is to stop you from going ahead with whatever you have planned after I've cooperated with…what exactly is it you want from me?'

'That's the simple part, *anjo*. I want to keep you. Until such time as I tire of you. Then you will be set free.'

When the full meaning of his words finally became clear, ice cascaded down Inez's spine. Despite the warm temperature, she shivered.

Oh, how easily he said the words. As if her answer meant nothing to him. But of course it did. He'd been planning this for a while. The meeting this morning outside the coffee shop—which she was now certain hadn't been coincidental—the dinner invitation that he'd probably known her father wouldn't be able to attend due to his long-standing monthly dinner with the oil minister, the invitation to the yacht, which was sure to cause a reaction in her brother, letting Pietro drink far more than he should've so he'd get her alone...

'You planned this,' she accused in a hushed tone because her throat was working to swallow down her rising anger.

'I plan everything, Inez,' he replied simply.

She looked into his face. The indomitable determination stamped on his harsh features sent a wave of anxiety through her.

She started to speak, to say the words that seemed unreal to her and her mouth trembled. His gaze dropped to the telling reaction and she immediately clamped her lips together. Showing weakness would only get her eaten alive.

Not that she wouldn't be anyway. A bubble of hysteria threatened. She swallowed and held his gaze.

'You want me to be your *mistress*?'

He laughed long and deeply. 'Is that what you would call yourself?'

She flushed. 'How else would you describe what you've just demanded of me? This *keeping* me? What you're suggesting is archaic enough to be described as such. Or does *plaything* more suit your pseudo-modernistic outlook?'

'No, Inez. I don't like the term plaything either. I have no intention of playing with you. No, what I foresee for us is much more grown up than that.' The sexual intent behind the statement was unmistakable.

Rather than being offended or shocked, Inez found herself growing breathless. Excited.

No!

'Yes,' he murmured as if he'd read her mind.

'Whatever term you slap on your intentions, I refuse to be a part of it. I'm going to find my brother—'

He slowly sank onto the plush seat, curved his hand along the back of the chair and levelled one ankle over his knee. 'And tell him that you've dashed his hopes of a possible high profile position in your father's administration because you couldn't take one for the team? I don't think you're in a position to refuse any demands I make, *anjo*.'

'Stop calling me that! And I won't be a pawn

in whatever game you're playing with my father and brother. Pietro is well aware of that.'

'Really? Since when? Wasn't serving on your father's campaign the reason you dropped out of university? Clearly, you play a part in your father's political ambitions or you wouldn't have been trying to fleece poor Alfonso. Why stop now when you're so close to achieving your goals? And why claim innocence when it's something you've done before?'

The hurt that scythed through her was deep and jagged. She wasn't aware she'd moved until she stood over him, glaring down at the arrogant face that wore that oh, so self-assured smile.

'I've never wanted to be this...this person you think I am. I was merely trying to help my family. I misjudged the situation and—'

'You mean you fell in love with your mark.'

She swallowed. 'I don't know what you're getting at.' But deep down she suspected.

'I mean you were set a target and you fell in love with your target. Isn't that what happened with Blanco?'

Light-headedness assailed her as he confirmed her suspicion. 'You know about Constantine?'

'I know everything I need to know about your

family, *anjo*. But by all means enlighten me as to why you've been so misjudged.'

His cynicism raked her nerves raw. 'I made a mistake, one that I freely admit to.'

'What mistake do you mean, *querida*? I want to hear it.'

'I misjudged a man I thought I could trust.'

'You mean you meant to use him but found out he intended to use you too?' he mocked. 'Some would call that poetic justice.'

Recalling Constantine's public humiliation of her, the names he'd called her in the press, her stomach turned over. 'You're despicable.' She raised her chin. 'And assuming you're even close to being right, won't I be a fool to repeat that mistake again?'

'No.'

'No?'

His eyes fixed on hers. Serious and intense. 'Because this time you know exactly what you're getting. There will be no delusions of love on either of our parts. No pretence. Just a task, executed with smooth efficiency.'

'But you intend to parade me about as your… lover? What will everyone think?'

He shrugged. 'I don't care what everyone thinks. And I don't much think that bothers you either.'

She shivered. 'Of course it bothers me. What makes you think it won't?'

'You're the ultimate young Rio socialite. You have a dedicated following and young impressionable girls can't wait to grow up and be you.' His mockery was unmistakable.

Heat crept up her cheeks. 'That's just the media spinning itself out of control.'

'Carefully fuelled by you to help your father's status. You're always seen with the right offspring of the right ministers and CEOs. You're the attraction to draw the young voters, are you not?'

She couldn't deny the allegation because it was true. Nor did she want to waste time straying away from the more serious subject of the demand he was making of her.

The demand she wouldn't—*couldn't*—consent to.

But there was something about him…a reassurance…and expectation of acquiescence that made the hairs on her nape stand on end.

'What happens if I refuse this…this sleazy proposal?'

'I sign the agreement then use the company as I wish. I could dismantle it piece by piece and sell it off for a neat profit. Or I could just drive down the share price and watch the company implode from the inside out. But that's all boring business. What do you care?'

Her fists clenched. 'I care because my grandfather built that company from nothing.'

'And now your father's willing to hand it over to a complete stranger just so he can further his political career.'

She pursed her lips and fought not to react. She'd been deeply concerned when she'd first heard how her father planned to raise funds for his campaign. Concerns that had been airily brushed away with reassurances of airtight clauses.

Clauses which Theo had apparently easily loopholed.

Maybe it wasn't too late. She could tell him to go to hell and warn her father and brother about the danger their proposed business partner presented and advise them to walk away. Surely that would be better than admitting the lion into their midst and letting him wreak havoc at whim?

Light hazel eyes watched her with a predatory gleam. 'If you're thinking of warning your family, I'd think twice. Remember how easily I dispatched Delgado?'

She stiffened, recalling how a few whispered words had caused one investor in her father's campaign to walk away. 'You don't mean that,' she tried.

He slowly rose from the chair and towered over her. Every protective instinct screamed at her to step back but she stood her ground. Any show of weakness would be mercilessly pounced on.

'Do you want to test me, *anjo*?' The blade of steel that hovered over the endearment sent a shiver down her spine.

She slowly uncurled her fists and forced herself to breathe. 'What do you expect me to do?'

His smile was equally as predatory as the look in his eyes. 'You will inform your father and brother tomorrow that you and I are an item— our meeting last night sparked a chemistry so hot we couldn't *not* be together.'

A tiny sliver of relief eased her constricted chest. 'If that's all you want, I'm sure I can convince them—'

His mocking smile stopped her words.

'After you tell them that, you'll pack your bags and move in with me.'

Shock slammed her sideways. 'Are you serious?'

He gripped her chin and held her pinned under his gaze. 'I've never been more serious in my life.'

'But…why?'

'My reasons are my own. You just need to do as you're told.'

Do as you're told. Constantine had tried to blackmail her with those very words. When she'd refused he'd spread rumours about her in the newspapers.

Anger grew in her belly. But it was a helpless anger born of the knowledge that there was nothing she could do. Once again she was trapped in a hell that came from trying to do what was right for her family.

Only this time she was to truly pay with her body. In a stranger's bed. Her heart tripped before going into fierce overdrive.

She gazed at Theo's face, then his body. A body she would in the very near future become scorchingly intimate with. The horror she'd expected to feel oddly did not materialise.

'How long exactly will I be expected to *do as I'm told*?' she snapped.

'Until after the elections.'

A horrified gasp escaped her throat and she forcibly wrenched herself from his grip. 'But… that's…the elections are *three months* away!'

'*Sim*,' he replied simply.

'*Sim*? You expect me to put my life on hold for

the next three months, just like that?' She clicked her fingers.

He raised an eyebrow. 'Do you want me to repeat the part about you not having a choice?'

She searched his face, trying to find meaning behind his intentions. 'What did my father do? Did he best you at a deal? Bad-mouth you to investors? Because I can't see what would make you want to go down this path of trying to get your own back.'

She watched his eyes darken, and his nostrils flare. All traces of mockery were wiped from his face as he stared down at her. Only she was sure he wasn't really seeing her.

His usual intense focus dulled for several seconds and his jaw clenched so tight she feared it could crack. Whatever memory he was reliving caused volcanic fury to bubble beneath the harsh, ragged breath he expelled and this time she did take that step back, purely for self-preservation.

Voices sounded on the deck below. In a few minutes Pietro and the skipper would return from their tour. Inez wasn't sure whether to be grateful for the disruption or frustrated that her opportunity to find out Theo's reasons for demanding her presence in his bed had been thwarted.

His gaze sharpened, flicked towards the steps and back to her.

'It's time for your answer. Do you agree to my terms?'

She shook her head. 'Not until you tell me— *what are you doing*?' she blurted as he snapped out an arm and tugged her close.

One large bold hand gripped her waist and the other speared through her hair. Completely captured, she couldn't move as he angled her face to his. The unsettling fury was still evident in his darkened eyes and taut mouth. Despite the heat transmitted from his grip, she shivered.

'You seem to think you can talk or question your way out of this, *anjo*. You can't. But perhaps it was a mistake to expect a verbal agreement. Perhaps a physical demonstration is what's best?'

Despite his rhetorical question, she tried to answer. 'No...'

'Yes!' he muttered fiercely. Then his mouth smashed down on hers.

She'd been kissed before. By casual boyfriends in her late teens who she'd felt safe enough with.

By Constantine, in the beginning, before he'd revealed his true ruthless colours.

Nothing of what had gone before prepared her

for the power and expertise behind Theo's kiss. Her world tilted beneath her feet as his tongue ruthlessly breached the seam of her lips. Hot, erotically charged and savagely determined, he invaded her mouth with searing passion. Bold and brazen, he flicked his tongue against hers, tasting her once and coming back for more.

The shocked little noise she made was a cross between surprise and her body's stunned reaction to the invasion.

The hand at her waist pressed her closer to his body. Whipcord strength, sleek muscles and his own unique scent brought different sensations that attacked her flailing senses.

Fire lashed through her belly as liquid heat pooled between her thighs. Her breasts, crushed against his chest, swelled and ached, her nipples peaking into demanding points with a swiftness that made her dizzy.

Deus!

Feeling her world career even faster out of control, she threw up her hands. Hard muscle rippled beneath her fingers. The need to explore slammed into her. Before she could question her actions, she slid her hands over his warm cotton-covered shoulders to his nape, her fingers tingling as they encountered his bare skin.

He jerked beneath her touch, pulled back with a tug on her hair. Breathing harshly, he stared into her eyes for several seconds. Hunger blazed in his, turning them a dark, mesmerising molten gold that stole what little breath she had from her lungs. Then his eyes dropped lower to her parted mouth.

A rough sound rumbled from his throat. Then he was kissing her again. Harder, more demanding, more possessively than before.

Inez pushed her fingers through his hair as arousal like she'd never experienced before bit deep. This time, when his tongue slid into her mouth, she met it with hers. Boldly, she tried to give as much as she got, although she knew she was hopelessly inadequate when it came to experience.

The hand around her waist tightened and she was lifted off her feet. Seconds later, she found herself on the bar stool, her legs splayed and Theo firmly between thighs exposed by her stance. He came at her again, the force of his sensual attack tilting the stool backwards.

She threw out her hands onto the counter to keep from toppling over. Theo growled beneath his breath, his hands moving upward from her waist to cup her breasts. He moulded her willing, aching flesh so expertly she whimpered and arched into his hold. Beneath her clothes, her tight nipples unfurled in eager anticipation when his thumbs grazed over them. The deep pleasurable shudder made him repeat the action, eliciting a soft cry of pleasure from deep inside her.

'Inez!'

The rapier-sharp call of her name doused her with ice-cold water. She wrenched herself from Theo's hold...or at least she tried to.

The hands that had dropped from her breasts to her waist at the sound of Pietro's return stayed her desperate flight.

'What the *hell* do you think you're doing?' Pietro growled, no longer looking as drunk as he'd been half an hour ago.

'If you need it explained to you, da Costa, then I'm wondering who the hell I'm getting into business with.'

Her brother flushed in anger. 'I wasn't talking to you, Pantelides. But maybe I should ask you what you're doing, pawing my sister like some mad animal.'

Inez desperately tried to pull her dress down. But Theo stood firmly between her thighs, making the task impossible. Her sound of distress drew his attention from Pietro. He stared down at her for a second before he adjusted his stance. But although he allowed her to close her legs and pull her dress down, his hands didn't drop from her waist. If anything, they tightened, their hold so possessive she fought to breathe.

'Inez was going to tell you tomorrow. But I guess tonight's as good a time as any.'

Pietro's gaze shifted from Theo's face to hers. 'Tell me what?'

'Do you want to do the honours, *anjo*? Or shall I?' he queried softly.

Her heartbeat accelerated but not with the arousal pounding through her bloodstream. She heard the clear warning in Theo's tone. Anything short of what he'd demanded of her would see her family ruined completely.

She opened her mouth. Closed it again and swallowed hard.

A trace of fear washed over Pietro's face. Despite their strained relationship, there'd been times in the past when they'd been close. She knew how much a political career of his own some day meant to him. How much he was pinning his hopes on what her father's campaign would mean to him personally.

She tried again to speak the words Theo demanded she speak. But her vocal cords wouldn't work.

'Would someone hurry up and tell me what's going on?'

Fierce hazel eyes drifted over her face in a look that spelled possession so potent her breath caught.

Theo curled his arm over her shoulders and pulled her into the heat of his body. He drifted his mouth over her temple in an adoring move so utterly convincing she reeled at his skilful deception.

She was grappling with that, and with just how much of the kiss they'd shared had been an exercise in pure ruthless seduction on his part, when he spoke.

'Your sister and I have become...enamoured with each other. We only met last night but already I cannot bear to be without her.' His voice held none of the mockery from before, sparking another stunned realisation of his skill. He stared down at her and she caught the implacable determination in his eyes.

When his gaze reconnected with Pietro's she

stared, mesmerised, at his profile then shivered at the iron-hard set to his jaw.

'Tomorrow she will be moving out of your home. And into mine.'

CHAPTER SIX

'*LIKE HELL YOU are*,' Pietro repeated for the hundredth time as their chauffeur-driven car stopped outside the opulent Ipanema mansion she'd grown up in.

She quickly threw open the door and hurried up the steps leading to the double oak front doors although she knew escape wouldn't be easy. Pietro was hard on her heels.

'Did you hear what I said?' he demanded.

'I heard you loud and clear. But you fail to realise I'm no longer a child. I'm twenty-four years old—well over the age when I can do whatever the heck I want.'

He slid a hand through his hair. 'Look, I know I may have pushed you into playing a greater part in *Pai*'s fund-raising campaign. But…I don't think getting involved with Pantelides is a good idea,' he said abruptly.

Inez's heart lurched at his concern but she couldn't reassure him because she herself didn't know what the future held. 'Thank you for your concern but like I said, I'm a grown up.'

He swivelled on his heel in the vast entrance hall of the villa. 'Are you really that into him? I know what I saw on his deck tells its own story but you only met him last night!'

'I hadn't met Alfonso Delgado before last night either and yet you expected me to charm him.'

'*Charm* him, not move in with him!'

'There's no point arguing with me. My mind is made up.'

Pietro's face darkened. 'Is this some sort of rebellion?'

Inez sighed. 'Of course not. But I'd planned to move out anyway, once you and *Pai* started on the campaign trail.'

'Move out and go where? This is your home, Inez,' he replied.

She shook her head. 'My world doesn't begin and end in this house, Pietro. I intend to rent an apartment, get a job.'

'Then don't start by ruining yourself with Pantelides.'

Her throat clogged. 'My reputation is already in shreds after Constantine. I really have nothing left to lose.'

She turned to head up the grand staircase that

led to the twin wings of their villa. Behind her, she could still hear Pietro pacing the hallway.

'This doesn't make any sense, Inez. Perhaps a good night's sleep will bring you to your senses.'

She didn't answer. Because she didn't want to waste her time telling him the decision had already been made for her.

For Theo to have gone to the effort of staging that kiss and paving the way for the lies she had to perpetuate, she knew without a shadow of a doubt that his demands were real.

He'd gone to a lot of trouble to set up tonight's meeting. She would be a fool to bait him to see if he would carry out his threat.

Her heart hammered as she undressed and stepped beneath the shower. Slowly soaping her body, she found her mind drifting back to their kiss. The incandescent delirium of it was unlike anything she'd felt before.

Her fingers touched her lips, and they tingled in remembrance.

Tomorrow she was inviting herself into the lion's den to be devoured whole for the sake of her family.

A hysterical laugh became lost in the sound of the running water.

Pietro was finally showing signs of being the

brother she remembered before their mother died. Shame that she'd had to sacrifice herself on the altar of their family's prosperity before he'd come round. As for her father...sadness engulfed her at the thought that even if he knew of her sacrifice, he probably wouldn't lift a finger to shield her from it.

Theo's gaze strayed to his phone for the umpteenth time in under twenty minutes and he cursed under his breath.

He'd called Inez this morning and they'd agreed a time of eleven o'clock, two hours before he was due to sign the documents at her father's office.

It was now eleven twenty-five and there was no sign of her. No big deal. She was probably stuck in traffic. Or she hadn't left her home on time, especially if she was packing for a three-month stay.

Besides, women are always late.

Even as a child he'd known this. His mother had never been on time for a single event in her life.

His mother...

Memory rained down vicious blows that had him catching his breath. His mother, the woman who'd been nowhere in sight, either before or after he was kidnapped and held for ransom by Benedicto da Costa's vicious thugs.

For weeks after he'd been rescued and returned home, broken and devastated by his ordeal, he'd asked for his mother. Ari had made several excuses for her absence. But Theo had been unable to reconcile the fact that the mother who'd once treated him as if he'd been the centre of her world suddenly couldn't even be bothered to pick up the phone and enquire about her mentally and physically traumatised child.

No. She'd been too preoccupied with wallowing in her misery following her husband's betrayal to bother with her own children.

Ari had been the one to hold them together after their family was shattered by the press uncovering their father's many shady dealings and philandering ways.

For a very long time he'd laboured under the misconception that out of the three brothers he was the most special in their father's eyes. That just because he was the miracle baby his parents had never thought they'd have, he was their favourite. His kidnapping and what he'd uncovered since had mercilessly ripped that indulgent blindfold away.

Finding out that his father had known about Benedicto da Costa's escalating threats and that he'd done nothing to warn or protect him had forced the cruellest reality on him.

And his mother's response to all that had been to abandon him, together with her other two children, and go into hiding.

Hearing of his father's eventual death had made him even angrier at being robbed of the chance to look his father in the eye and see the monster for himself.

Because, even now, a pathetic part of him clung to the hope that maybe his father hadn't known the full extent of the kidnapping threat; hadn't known that Benedicto da Costa's reaction to being thwarted out of a business deal would be to kidnap a seventeen-year-old boy, and have his torture photographed and sent to his family to pressure them into finding the millions of dollars owed to him.

His phone rang, wrenching him out of the bitter recollections. Glancing down at the number, a bolt of white-hot anger lanced through him. He forced himself to wait for a couple more rings before he answered it. 'Pantelides.'

'*Bom dia*. I've just had a very interesting conversation with my daughter.' Theo detected the throb of anger in Benedicto da Costa's voice and a grim smile curved his own lips. 'She seems determined to pursue this rather *sudden* course of action where you're concerned.'

'Your daughter strikes me as a very determined woman who knows exactly what she wants,' he replied smoothly.

'She is. All the same, I can't help think that this decision is rather precipitate.' There was clear suspicion in Benedicto's voice now.

'Trust me, it's been very well thought through on my part. Tell me, Benedicto, has she left yet?'

'*Sim*, against my wishes, she has left home,' he replied, his voice taut with displeasure.

A wave of satisfaction swept through Theo. 'Good. I'll await her arrival.'

'I hope this will not delay our meeting,' the older man enquired.

'Don't worry. The moment I welcome your daughter into my home, I'll head to your offices.'

An edgy silence greeted his answer and Theo could sense him weighing his words to perceive a possible threat. Finally, Benedicto answered, 'We should celebrate our partnership once the documents are signed.'

Theo's mouth twisted. Benedicto had already moved on from the subject of his daughter. And he noticed there had been no admonition to treat her well, *or else*…

But the knowledge that Benedicto had intensely disapproved of Inez's intentions and had called him to air that disapproval was good enough for him.

'Great idea. Unfortunately, I'll be busy for the next few nights. Perhaps some time next week Inez and I will have you and Pietro over for dinner.'

The fiery exhalation that greeted his indelicate words made Theo's grin widen.

'Of course. I'll look forward to it. *Até a próxima,*' Benedicto said tightly.

Theo ended the call without responding. He absorbed the pulse of triumph rushing through his bloodstream for a pleasurable second before he exhaled.

His plan was far from being executed. But this was a brilliant start.

He looked out of the floor to ceiling window at the sparkling pool and the beach beyond and tried to push away the images that had visited him again last night and the single hoarse scream that had woken him.

A full body shudder raked his frame and he shoved a hand through his hair. Although he'd long ago accepted the nightmares as part of his existence, he loathed their presence and the helplessness he felt in those endless moments when he was caught in their grip.

The single therapy session he'd let Ari talk him into attending had mentioned triggers and the importance of anxiety-detectors.

He laughed under his breath. Putting himself within touching distance of the man responsible for those nightmares would be termed as fool-hardy by most definitions.

Theo chose to believe that exacting excruciating revenge would heal him. *An eye for an eye.*

And if he had to suffer a few side-effects during the process, then so be it.

He tensed as his security intercom buzzed. Crossing the vast sun-dappled room, he picked up the handset.

'*Senhor*, there's a Senhorita da Costa here to see you.'

A throb of a different nature invaded his blood-stream. 'Let her in,' he instructed.

Replacing the handset, he found himself striding to the front door and out onto his driveway before he realised what he was doing.

Hands on his hips, he watched her tiny green sports car appear on his long driveway. The top was down and the wind was blowing through her loose thick hair. Stylish sunglasses shielded her eyes from him but he knew she was watching him just as he was studying her.

She brought the car to a smooth stop a few feet from him and turned off the ignition. For several seconds the only sound that impinged on the late morning air was the water cascading from the stone nymph's urn into the fountain bowl. Then the sound of her seat belt retracting joined the tinkling.

'You're late,' he breathed.

She pulled out her keys and opened her door. 'It took a while to uproot myself from the only home I've ever known,' she said waspishly.

A touch from a well-manicured finger and the boot popped open. He strolled forward, viewed its contents and his eyes narrowed.

'And yet you only packed two suitcases for a three-month stay?' he remarked darkly. 'I hope you don't think you can run back to *Pai*'s house each time you need a new toothbrush?'

She got out of the car.

From across the width of the open top, she glared at him. 'I can afford to buy my own toothbrush, thanks,' she retorted.

Theo nodded. 'Good to hear it.' Unable to stop himself, his gaze travelled down her body.

Faded jeans moulded her hips and her cream

scooped-neck silk top left her arms bare. Its short-in-the-front, longer-at-the-back design exposed a delicious inch of golden, smooth midriff when she turned to shut her door and the air lifted the light material.

Heat invaded his groin, once again reminding him of their kiss last night.

The kiss that had blown him clean away and rendered him almost incoherent by the time her brother had rudely interrupted them.

Hell, she'd been so responsive, so intoxicatingly passionate, she'd gone to his head within seconds. What had set out as a hammering-a-point-home exercise to convince her he meant business had swiftly morphed into something else. Something he'd still been struggling to decipher when she'd been hustled off his boat by her suddenly protective brother.

One thing he'd been certain of was that had Pietro been a few more minutes returning to the top deck, Theo was sure he would've had his hands on her bare skin, exploring her in a more earthy way, propriety be damned.

Luckily, he'd come to his senses. And, from here on in, he intended to focus on his plan and his plan alone.

She went to the boot and bent over to lift the

first case. The sight of her rounded bottom made a vein throb in his temple.

He stepped forward, grabbed the cases from her and handed them to his hovering butler. 'I'm running late for my meeting. We should have done this last night like I suggested.'

He'd tried. But she'd stood her ground and he had quickly decided that there was nothing to be gained from getting into a slanging match with Pietro da Costa. That he'd also realised that his change of timing was to do with that kiss and nothing to do with his carefully laid plans had had him sharply reassessing his priorities.

'I'm here now. Don't let me stop you from leaving if you wish to.'

He smiled at the undisguised hope in her voice. 'Now what kind of host would I be if I desert you the moment you turn up?'

'The same as the one who blackmailed me into this situation in the first place?' she replied caustically.

There was a thread of unhappiness in her voice that grated at him.

'This will go a lot easier if you accept the status quo.'

'You mean just shut up and *do as I'm told*?' she

snapped bitterly as she slammed the boot shut and walked towards him.

Unease weaved through him. With restless shoulders, he shrugged it away. 'No. You can protest all you want. I just want you to be aware of the futility of it.'

She snorted under her breath, a sound that made his smile widen. She had spirit, and wasn't afraid to bare her claws when cornered. Which made him wonder why she withstood the unreasonable control from her father. Were material benefits so important to her?

The heavy glass front door slid shut behind them and he watched her reaction to his house. It was an architectural masterpiece, and had featured in several top magazines before he'd bought it a year ago and ceased all publicity of the award-winning design.

'Wow,' she breathed. 'This place must have cost you a bomb.'

Theo had his answer. Disappointment scythed through him as he watched her move to the bronze sculpture he'd acquired several weeks back.

'I saw the exhibition on this two months ago. This piece is worth a cool half million,' she gasped in wonder. 'And that one—' she pointed to another smaller sculpture he'd commissioned by his favourite New York artist '—is an exclusive piece, worth over two million dollars.'

His lips twisted. 'Should I be worried that you know the monetary value of every piece of art in my house?'

She whirled to face him. 'Excuse me?'

'I hope we can engage in more meaningful dialogue than how much everything is worth. I find the subject of avarice...distasteful.'

Her gasp sounded genuinely hurt-filled. 'I wasn't...I'm just...that's a horrible thing to say, Mr Pantelides.'

His eyebrow lifted. 'I thought I kissed all the formality out of you last night?'

She flushed a delicate pink that made her skin glow. Her expressive brown eyes slid from his and she turned back to examine the room.

It was then that he noticed the faint bruises on her left arm. He was striding to her and lifting her arm to examine the marks before his brain had connected with his body.

'Who did this to you?' he demanded.

Her surprised gaze snapped from his to her arm. Her flush deepened as she swiftly shook her head. 'I...it doesn't matter; it's nothing—'

He swallowed hard. 'Like hell it is.' The idea that his demands on her might have caused this to happen to her made a thread of revulsion rise in his belly. He forced it down and concentrated on her face. 'Tell me who it was.'

She swallowed. 'My father.'

Pure fury blurred his vision for several seconds. 'Your *father* did this to you?'

She gave a jerky nod.

Why the hell was he surprised? 'Has he done anything like this before?' he bit out.

She pressed her lips together in a vain attempt not to answer. A firm grip of her chin, tilting it to his gaze, convinced her otherwise. 'Once. Maybe twice.'

His vicious curse made her shiver. Theo examined the marks, which would grow yellowish by nightfall, and pushed down the mounting fury. 'That son of a bitch will never touch you again.'

Shock made her gasp. 'That *son of a bitch* is my *father*. And I've given you what you wanted, so I expect you to hold up your end of the bargain.'

He frowned with genuine puzzlement. 'Why do you tolerate this, Inez?' He glanced from the bruises to her face. 'You're more than old enough to live on your own. Hell, if money and a rich lifestyle are what you crave, you're sufficiently resourceful to find some wealthy guy who would—'

She snatched her arm from his grasp. It was

then that he realised he'd been caressing her soft skin with his thumb. He missed the connection almost immediately.

'I certainly hope you're not about to suggest what I think you are?'

Keen frustration rocked him into movement. 'I'm curious, that's all.'

'I'm not here to satisfy your curiosity. And perhaps you've been lucky enough to be granted a perfect family but not everyone has been afforded the same luxury. We made do with what we... Did I say something funny?' she snapped.

He cut off the mirthless laughter that had bubbled up at her words. 'Yes. *You're damned hilarious.* You obviously don't know what you're talking about.'

She stared at him with confusion and a little trepidation. 'No. But how can I? We only met two nights ago. And now I'm here, your possession for the foreseeable future.'

The simple statement twisted like live electricity between them. The look in her eyes said she was daring him to react to it. But the off-kilter emotions swirling through his chest made him back away from it. He shouldn't have dealt with her so soon after speaking to Benedicto. He should've left Teresa, his housekeeper, to see to her needs.

He turned and headed for the door. 'I'll show you upstairs. And then I need to go.'

Striding into the hallway, he started up the grand central stairs that led to the upper two floors of his house. After a few steps, he noticed she wasn't behind him.

Turning, he found her paused on the second step, her gaze once again wide and wondrous as she stared around her.

'What?'

'There are no concrete walls.' She looked up at the all-encompassing glass around her. 'Or ceilings.'

He resumed climbing the stairs. 'I don't like walls. And I don't like ceilings,' he threw over his shoulder.

She hurried after him and caught up with him as they neared the first suite of rooms. She regarded him for a few seconds then bit her lip.

He paused with a hand on the doorknob. 'What?' he asked again, trying and not succeeding in prising his gaze from her plump lips.

'I'm not sure whether to take that as a metaphor or not.'

'*Anjo*, there's no hidden meaning behind my words. I literally do not like concrete walls or ceilings.'

She frowned in puzzlement. 'I don't understand.'

'It's very simple. I don't like being closed in.'

'You're...*claustrophobic*?' She whispered the word as if she wasn't sure how to apply it to him.

He shrugged and hurriedly threw open the door, a part of him reeling at what he'd just admitted. 'We all have our flaws,' he retorted.

'Were you born with it?'

His jaw clenched once. 'No. It was a condition thrust upon me quite against my will.'

'But...you seem...'

'Invincible?' he mocked.

Her lips pursed. 'I was going to say self-assured.'

'Appearances can be deceptive, *querida*. After you.' He indicated the door he'd just opened.

She stopped dead in the middle of the room. From where he stood, Theo could see what she was seeing. With the glass walls and white carpet and furnishings and nothing but the view of the blue sky and sea beyond, the vista was breathtaking.

'*Deus*, I feel as if I'm floating on a cloud,' she murmured with an awe-filled voice.

'That is the primary aim of the property. Light, air, no constrictions.'

He'd learned to his cost that constrictions triggered his anxiety and fuelled his nightmares. Which was why every single property he owned was filled with light.

'It's beautiful.'

The strong pulse of pleasure that washed through him had him stepping back. Things were getting out of hand. He needed to walk away, go to his meeting with Benedicto and remind himself why he was in Rio. This need to bask in Inez's presence, touch her skin, indulge in the urge to taste her sensual lips once more needed to killed. He had to stick to his game plan.

'Make yourself at home. I'll be back later. We're going out this evening. Dinner at Cabana de Ouro, then probably clubbing. Wear something short and sexy.'

Her eyes widened at his curt tone but he was already turning away. He didn't stop until he reached the landing. On a completely unstoppable urge, he looked over his shoulder. Through the glass walls, he saw her frozen in the middle of her suite, her eyes fixed on him.

She looked lost. And confused. And a little relieved.

With grim determination he turned and headed down the stairs. And he hated himself for needing the reminder that Benedicto da Costa had damaged not just him, but his whole family.

The payback should be equal to the crime committed.

The black satin boy shorts she chose to wear were plenty stylish and sexy. They also moulded her behind much more than she was strictly comfortable with but everything else she'd hastily packed was too formal for dinner at Cabana de Ouro, the trendy restaurant and bar in Ipanema. Coupled with the dark gold silk top, with her hair piled on top of her head and gold hoops in her ears and bangles on her wrist, she looked good enough for whatever club Theo intended to take her to after dinner.

Clubbing wasn't strictly her entertainment of choice. But since, for the next twelve weeks, Theo expected her to obey his every command, the least she could do was learn to pick her battles. And she'd already endured one battle this morning in the form of confrontation with Theo. And found out he was claustrophobic.

He'd been right; she'd secretly imagined him to be invincible. The way he carried himself, the innate authority and self-assurance that seemed part of his genetic make up, she'd had no trouble seeing him best each situation he found himself him.

Hearing him admit to a deep flaw that most grown men would be ashamed of had floored her. Coupled with his concern when he'd seen the marks her father had inflicted when she'd announced she was moving in with Theo, she'd been seriously floundering in a sea of uncertainty by the time he'd left her bedroom.

She examined the marks on her arm now and released a shaky breath to see that they were fading. She was shrugging on the shoulder-padded waist-length leather jacket that went with the outfit when she heard Theo's Aston Martin roar into the driveway.

Her fingers trembled as she fastened the long-chained gold medallion necklace at her nape.

He'd left her so abruptly this morning she hadn't had the time to question him about sleeping arrangements. A closer examination of her suite after he'd left had revealed no presence of another occupant, and after talking to Teresa, his housekeeper, she'd found out that the *senhor's* suite was directly above hers, taking up the whole glass-roofed top floor of the house.

The fact that she wouldn't be expected to share his bed immediately should've pleased her. Instead she was more on edge than ever. Or maybe that was what he wanted? That she should be kept guessing, kept on a knife-edge of uncertainty like some sort of game?

Deus!

She'd barely spent one day under his glass roof and already she was being driven mad. His response to her admiring his sculptures had been too infuriating for her to explain how she'd come to acquire such knowledge of sculptures—her late mother's talent. If he wanted to believe Inez appreciated beautiful art purely with dollar signs in her eyes, that was his problem.

Her breath caught as she heard distinct footsteps in the hallway. Teresa had shown her how to shroud the bedroom glass for privacy and she'd activated it before she'd gone in to take a shower. It was still shrouded now although she could make out a faint outline of the towering man who knocked a few seconds later.

'Come in.' She cringed at the husky breathlessness of her voice.

The heavy glass swung back and Theo stood framed in the doorway.

Light hazel eyes locked on her with the force of a laser beam for several seconds before they travelled slowly down her body.

Before meeting him, Inez would've found it hard to believe she could physically react so strongly to a look from a man. Constantine, with all his misleading smiles and false charm, had never affected her like this, not even when she'd believed herself in love with him.

With Theo the evidence was irrefutable—in the accelerated beat of her heart, the tightening and heaviness of her breasts and the stinging heat that spread outward from her belly like a flash fire.

She watched his mouth drop open as his gaze reached her shorts and her own mouth dried at the look that settled on his face.

'What the hell are you wearing?'

'What? I'm wearing clothes, Mr Pantelides,' she snapped, once she was able to get her brain working again.

He stepped into the room and the door slid shut behind him. All at once, she became aware of the sheer size of him, of the restriction in her breathing and the fact that her eyes were devouring his magnificent form.

'Let's get one thing straight. From now on you'll address me as Theo. No more *senhor* and no more Mr Pantelides, understand?'

'Is that an order?' She tilted her chin to see his face as he stopped before her.

'It's a friendly warning that there will be con-sequences if you don't comply.'

'What consequences?' she huffed.

'How about every time you call me *senhor* I kiss that sassy mouth of yours?'

CHAPTER SEVEN

'EXCUSE ME?' HER voice was a little more breathless. With excitement. *Deus*, what was wrong with her? This man was threatening her family, was effectively turning her life upside down for the sake of some unknown grudge. And all she could think of was him kissing her again.

'No, you're not excused. Use my first name or I'll kiss it into you. Your choice. Now tell me what the hell you're wearing.' His gaze dropped back to her shorts, his eyes glazing with hunger so acute, her heart hammered.

'These are shorts. You said "short and sexy".'

His mouth worked for a few seconds before he nodded. 'I said short, but I don't think I meant that short, *anjo.*'

Heat raced up her neck and she barely managed to stop her hand from connecting with his face. 'They are not that bad.'

His rasping laugh made her face flame. 'Trust me, from where I'm standing, they're lethal.'

'I have nothing else to change into. Everything else is too formal for a club.'

Dark eyes rose, almost reluctantly, to clash with hers. 'I find that very hard to believe.'

'It's true. I didn't have enough time to pack properly. Besides, I didn't take you for…'

His eyes narrowed. 'Didn't take me for what?'

She shrugged. 'You don't strike me as the club-bing type.'

One corner of his mouth lifted. 'Have you been forming impressions about me, *anjo*?'

She kicked herself for that revelatory remark. 'Not really.'

He looked down at her shorts one more time and he turned abruptly for the door. 'I'll be ready to go in fifteen minutes. You can tell me what other impressions you've formed about me at dinner.'

Inez exhaled and realised she hadn't taken a full breath since he'd walked into her presence. Her whole body quivered as she shoved her feet into three-inch platforms and made sure her cell phone and lipstick were in the black and gold clutch.

She caught sight of herself in the hallway mir-ror as she made her way down and cringed at the feverish look in her eyes.

Reassuring herself firmly that it was anger at

Theo for his overbearing treatment of her, she made her way to the living room.

Floodlights illuminated the pool and gardens in a stunning display of shimmering light and shrubbery. Like every single aspect of the building, the sight was so breathtaking her fingers itched with the need to draw.

Setting her clutch down, she went to the large duffel bag she'd brought down this afternoon and took out her sketchpad and pencil.

She was so lost in capturing the vista before her, she didn't sense Theo enter the room until his unique scent wrapped itself around her.

She jerked around to see him standing close behind her, his eyes on her picture.

'You draw?' he asked in surprise.

Unable to answer for the loud hammering of her heart, she nodded.

He reached forward and plucked the pad from her nerveless fingers. Slowly, he thumbed through the pages. 'You're very talented,' he finally said.

Expecting a derogatory remark to follow, like his comment on his art this morning, her eyes widened when she realised he meant it. 'You really think so?' she asked.

He closed the pad and handed it back to her,

his eyes speculative as they rested on her face. 'I wouldn't say it otherwise, *anjo*.'

Pleasure fizzed through her. 'Thank you.' She smiled as she stood. Crossing over to her duffel bag, she bent to place the pad back into it.

'*Thee mou!*'

She dropped the pad and hastily straightened. 'What?'

'You bend over like that while we're out and I will not be responsible for my actions, understood?' he growled.

Her mouth dropped open at the dark promise in his voice. A shudder ran through her body as hunger further darkened his eyes. She licked her lip nervously as the atmosphere thickened with sensual charges that crackled and snapped along her nerves.

'We…we don't have to go out if what I'm wearing offends you…Theo,' she ventured hesitantly, sensing that he held himself on the very edge of control.

He inhaled deeply, his chest expanding underneath the dark green shirt and black leather jacket he wore with black trousers. 'That's where you're wrong. What you're offering doesn't offend me in the least. But I'm a red-blooded, possessive male who is finding it difficult not to roar out his primitive reaction to the idea of other men looking at you.' He said it so matter-of-factly she couldn't form a decent response. 'But I'll try to be a *gentleman*. Come.' He held out his arm.

With seriously indecent thoughts of Theo fighting to the death for her flitting through her mind, she crossed the room to his side.

He led them out and held the passenger door of his car open. The first few minutes of the ride to Ipanema was conducted in silence. Every now and then, he raked a hand through his hair and slid a glance at her naked thighs. Each time, he exhaled noisily.

A wild part of her wanted to flaunt herself for him, revel in his very physical reaction to her attire. Another part of her wanted to run and hide from the volatile emotions swirling through the enclosed space of the luxurious sports car.

By the time they drew up in the car park of the exclusive restaurant her pulse was jumping with anxiety. She forced the feeling down and followed him into the restaurant. Finding out they were dining in the even more exclusive upper floor led to all sorts of renewed anxiety as she preceded him up the steps.

The moment they were seated, he leaned forward. 'The moment we return home, I'm burning those shorts.'

She glared at him. 'No, you are not, *senhor!* They're my favourite pair.'

'Then frame them and mount them on a wall. But you most definitely will not be wearing them out again.'

That wild streak widened. 'I thought you would be man enough to handle a little…challenge. Are you saying you're not?'

His eyes narrowed. 'Don't bait a hungry lion, *querida*, unless you're prepared to be devoured,' he grated out.

'Did you tell your last girlfriend how she should dress too?' she challenged.

His mouth compressed. 'My last girlfriend was under the misconception that the more frequently she walked around naked the more interested I would be in her. She lasted ten days.'

Inez's curiosity spiked, along with an emotion she was very loath to name. 'How long did your longest relationship last?'

'Three weeks.'

Her breath caught. 'So why three *months* with me?' she asked.

He looked startled for a moment then he shrugged.

'Because you're not my girlfriend. You're so very much more.'

Inez was struck dumb by his reply. A small foolish part of her even felt giddy, until she reminded herself that she was intended to be nothing but his *mistress*. Again unfathomable emotions wrapped themselves around her heart. She cleared her throat and fought to keep her voice even. 'Why *misconception*?'

'Very few women manage to catch and keep my interest for very long, *anjo*.'

'Because you get bored easily?' she dared.

His lashes swept down for a few seconds before they rose again to capture hers. 'Because my demons always win when pitted against the rigours of normal relationships.'

'*Demons?*'

'*Sim, anjo*. Demons. I have a lot of them. And they're very possessive.' A wave of anguish rolled over his face, then it was gone the next instant. He nodded to the hovering *sommelier* and ordered their wine. Another pulse of surprise went through her when she noticed it was the same wine she'd served at the fund-raiser and her favourite.

'The burning is now off the table. Hell, you can even keep the damn shorts. But, for the sake of my sanity, can we agree that you don't wear them outside?' he asked with one quirked eyebrow.

She pretended to consider it. 'What is your sanity worth to me?'

'You think you're in a position to bargain with me, Inez?' he asked, his voice deceptively soft.

'I never pass up an opportunity to bargain.'

He regarded her silently for several minutes. Then he shrugged. 'As long as I achieve my goals in the end, I see no reason why the road to success shouldn't be littered with minor obstacles. Tell me what you desire.'

'Is that what I am, a minor obstacle?'

'Don't miss your opportunity with meaningless questions.'

The need for clarity finally forced her to speak. 'I wish to know exactly what you want of me.'

'Sorry, I cannot answer that.'

She frowned. 'Why not?'

'Because my needs are…fluid.' The peculiar smile accompanying his answer sent a tingle of alarm down her spine.

'So I am to live in uncertainty for the next three months?'

'The unknown can be challenging. It can also be exciting.'

'Is that why you came to Rio? To seek challenge and excitement?'

For several seconds he stared at her. Then he slowly shook his head. 'No, my reason for being in Rio is specific and a well-planned event.'

Inez shivered at the succinct response. 'I can't help but be frightened by your answer.'

Her candid admission seemed to surprise him. 'Why is that?'

'Because I have a feeling it has something to do with my family. Pietro has his flaws but he's never done anything without my father's express approval. Besides, you're much older than him, which makes it unlikely that he's the one you came here for. You're here because of my father, aren't you?'

It took an astonishing amount of control not to react to her simple but accurate summation of the single subject that had consumed him for over a decade.

Thinking back, he realised he'd given her several clues to enable her to reach this conclusion. Somehow, in the mere forty-eight hours that he'd known her, Inez had managed to slip under his guard and was threatening to uncover his true purpose for being in Rio.

He also realised that he'd given her much more leeway than he'd ever intended to when he'd formulated his plan. Inviting her to compromise? Inviting her to state her desires with the knowledge that he was seriously considering granting them?

After his hasty departure this morning he'd realised that he'd let those marks on her arms sway him into going easy on her. *Because he hadn't wanted her to think he was a monster like her father?*

The man who hadn't so much as asked after his daughter when Theo had attended his office to sign the agreement papers?

The man whose eyes had shone with greed and triumph even before the ink had dried on the documents?

No, he was nothing like Benedicto da Costa. He wasn't about to lose any already precious sleep wondering about that little statement.

What he had to be careful of was that his enemy's daughter didn't guess his intentions. He was so very close to having Benedicto right where he wanted him. He couldn't afford to be swayed by a heart-shaped face or the most sinfully sexy pair of shorts he'd ever seen in his life, no matter how acute the ache in his groin.

'Will you please tell me why you're after my

father?' she implored softly. The concern on her face appeared genuine and he suddenly realised that, despite Benedicto's treatment of her, Inez cared for her father.

His nostrils flared as bitterness rocked through him. He'd once been in that same position, foolishly believing that the father he'd idolised and loved beyond reason cared just as deeply for him. That he wasn't the fraudster and philanderer the press were making him out to be.

Now, he wanted to rip the blindfold from her eyes, make her see the true monster in the man she called *Pai*. Make her see that her love was nothing but a manipulative tool that would be used against her eventually.

Except he had a strong feeling she already knew, and chose to overlook it. Which made his blood boil even more.

'Why, do you plan to sacrifice yourself to save him?' he taunted.

She gasped, dropping the sterling silver fork she'd been nervously toying with. 'So, it *is* my father!'

He cursed under his breath. 'If you so much as breathe a word in his direction about your suspicions, I'll make sure you regret it for the rest of your life.'

She paled. 'You really expect me to sit back and watch you destroy him?'

'I expect you to hold up your end of the bargain we struck. Live under my roof in exchange for me leaving the loophole in the contract alone. Are you prepared to do that or do I need to plot another plan of action?' he asked, not bothering to hide the threat in his voice.

She stared back at him apprehensively. Her chin rose and her brown eyes burned holes in him but she nodded. 'I'll stick to our agreement.'

When their wine was served, he watched her take a big gulp and curbed the desire to follow suit. He was driving and needed to restrict his drinking. Nevertheless, a sip of the Chilean red went a way to restoring a little order to his floundering thoughts.

Thee mou, he hadn't even fired the first salvo and things were getting out of hand. Why on earth had he shared the presence of his demons with her? And that comment about her being so much more than a girlfriend? He silently shook his head and sucked in a control-affirming breath.

Their dinner progressed in near silence. Theo reminded himself that his main reason for bringing her out hadn't been for conversation. When she refused dessert, he settled the bill quickly and rose to help her out of her seat.

Fire shot through his groin, hard and fierce, as he was once again confronted with the risqué shorts. While they'd been seated, he'd managed to tamp down the effect of those shorts on his raging libido.

Now, as she walked in front of him, he was treated to a mouth-watering sight of her deliciously rounded bottom and stunning legs. With each sway of her hips, he grew harder until he wondered if he had any blood left in his upper extremities that hadn't migrated south.

He was reconsidering his decision not to burn the shorts at the earliest opportunity when he caught a male diner staring in blatant appreciation at her legs.

His growl was low but unmistakable. The man hastily averted his gaze but Theo was still simmering in primitive emotions when they reached the car park.

He followed her to the passenger side but, instead of opening the door for her, he braced his hand on either side of her and leaned in close. With her front pressed against the door, her bottom was moulded into his groin in such a way that she couldn't fail to notice his state of arousal.

Her breathing quickened, but she stayed put. 'What are you doing?'

'Delivering the punishment I promised.'

'Sorry?'

'You called me *senhor* when we were in the restaurant.'

She tried to turn around but he pressed her more firmly against the car. 'I…don't remember.'

'Of course you do. You also thought I wouldn't act on my promise in full view of other diners, didn't you?'

'No, I wasn't—'

'Maybe you were right. Or maybe we both knew I'd want to do more than just kiss you.'

'You're wrong…'

'Am I?'

'Yes…'

'So you'd prefer I let this one slide?' He rocked his hips against her bottom and her breath hitched. 'You won't think me weak?'

Her shocked laugh heated the air around them. 'Only someone foolish would think you weak.'

'I'm not sure whether there's a compliment in there. Is there?'

Her head fell forward, exposing the seductive line of her neck. 'Am I to pander to your ego too, Theo?'

He laughed. 'How can you appear submissive and yet taunt me at the same time?'

She lifted her head and turned to stare at him. Whatever she saw in his face made her squirm harder. Provocatively. Her gaze dropped to his mouth and Theo could no more resist the temptation than he could breathe.

Fingers sliding beneath her knotted hair to hold her still, he caught her mouth in a fierce kiss. Every emotion he'd experienced since waking that morning was delivered in that kiss—passion, arousal, confusion, anxiety and anger. He pinned her against the car so she couldn't move, couldn't put those seductive hands on his body.

Although he missed her touch, a part of him was thankful because, had she had access, he would've lost even more of his mind than he suspected he was losing.

He registered the brief flashes behind his closed eyelids but didn't break the kiss. He suspected Inez had no idea what had just happened. And even if she had, she wouldn't have suspected the true reason behind the paparazzi shots because she was used to being the darling of the press.

Well, she was in for a rude awakening...

She started to open her mouth wider, to return his demanding kiss.

He slowly lifted his head. When she made a tiny sound of protest and tried to recapture his mouth, he forced himself to step away. He'd achieved one part of what he'd set out to do. The second part was a short drive away.

Curving his arm around her waist, he peeled her away from the door, opened it and deposited her inside, all the time trying not to stare down at her legs and imagine how they would feel wrapped around his waist.

He swallowed hard as he rounded the hood and slid behind the wheel.

'Time to head to the club before I give in to the urge to deliver more punishment.'

Her eyes dropped to his mouth and he barely suppressed a groan as she licked her lips.

'For your mercy, I will teach you how to samba like a true Brazilian,' she replied huskily.

Inez lay among the white sheets the next morning, trying hard not to relive the events of the night before but it was as futile as trying to stop a tidal wave.

They'd eventually emerged from the nightclub at two in the morning. She'd been flushed and sweaty from being plastered to Theo's superb body for three straight hours. But the wild racing of her heart had nothing to do with her exertions on the dance floor and everything to do with the man who'd focused on her as if she was the only woman in the whole club.

And *Deus*, had he danced like a dream? Far from tutoring him on the correct steps of her native dance, she'd found herself following his lead as he'd moved expertly on the dance floor.

When he'd caught her to him, her back to his front and replayed the scene in the car park, but this time to music, she'd seriously feared her heart would beat itself to expiration.

In that moment, she'd forgotten that there was a sinister purpose to Theo's plan; that he'd all but admitted she was being used as a pawn in some deadly game he was playing with her father. When he'd laid his stubbled jaw against her cheek and hummed the sultry samba music in her ear, she'd closed her eyes and imagined what it would be like to belong—truly belong—to a man like Theo.

Turning over in bed, she groaned in disbelief at how susceptible she'd been to his hard body and magnetic charisma. *Santa Maria*, she'd been all but putty in his hands.

Luckily, the fresh air and the long drive back had hammered some sense into her. The moment they'd returned, she'd bidden him a curt *boa noite*, left him standing in the hallway and retreated as fast as her sore feet would carry her.

And she intended to carry on like that. She might not know what his end game was, but she refused to be a willing participant in his campaign.

The last thing she wanted to do was to fall for another manipulator like Constantine.

She was here only because she had no choice but she didn't intend to idle away her time in this house. Theo expected her to stay here for three months, which meant whatever he had planned was not to be executed immediately. Perhaps she could convince him to change his mind in that time.

Yeah, and fairy tales really did come true...

Or she could find out exactly what his intentions were.

She'd seen the look in his eyes when he spoke about her father. Whatever vendetta he'd planned, he intended to see it through.

Helplessly, she rolled over in bed and her eyes lit on the bedside clock. She jerked upright and threw the sheet aside. She might not have anywhere to be on this Saturday morning but lazing about in bed past ten o'clock wasn't her style.

She jumped into the shower, shampooed her hair and washed her body with quick, regimented movement ingrained in her from her time at the Swiss boarding school her father had sent her to just to impress his friends.

Leaving her damp hair to dry naturally, she pulled on an aqua-coloured sundress and slipped her feet into low-heeled thongs. Smoothing her favourite sunscreen moisturiser over her face and arms, she left her room and headed downstairs.

Teresa was crossing the hallway carrying a *cafetière* of freshly made coffee and indicated for Inez to follow her.

She led her out to the terrace that overlooked the immense square infinity pool. Light danced off the water but her attention was caught and held by the man seated at the cast iron oval breakfast table.

His white short-sleeved polo shirt did amazing things to his eyes and olive-toned skin. And loose green shorts exposed solid thighs and lightly hair-sprinkled legs that made her mouth dry before flooding with moisture that threatened to choke her.

'*Bom dia, anjo*. Are you going to stand there all morning?' he mocked.

She forced her legs to move and took the chair he indicated to his right.

'Coffee?' he asked, his voice deep and low.

'Yes, please.' Her voice had grown husky and emerged barely above a whisper.

He nodded to Teresa who smiled, filled her cup then made herself scarce.

Inez sipped the hot brew just as a delaying tactic so she didn't have to look at him.

So far she'd seen Theo in formal evening wear and smart casual and each look had threatened to knock her sideways. But seeing him now, with so much of his vibrant olive skin on show, threatened to topple her completely. She took another hasty sip and choked as the liquid scalded her mouth.

Grabbing the napkin to stop herself from dribbling like an idiot, she looked up and caught his mocking smile. 'You'd rather blister yourself than converse with me?'

She swallowed and fought to present a passable smile. 'Of course not. I was just enjoying the…view.' She indicated beyond his shoulder, where the garden extended beyond the pool and sloped down to the sandy white beach and sparkling ocean.

With a disbelieving smile, he picked up the

paper next to his plate and shook it out. 'If you say so—'

Her horrified gasp made him lower the newspaper. 'Something wrong?'

'Is that a picture of *us*?' she demanded through a severely constricted throat. The question was redundant because the picture taking up the whole of the front page was printed in vivid Technicolor.

He'd already seen it, of course, so he didn't bother to glance where her appalled gaze was riveted. 'Yes. Fresh off the morning press.'

'*Meu deus!*' She reached out and snatched the broadsheet out of his grasp. It was even worse up close. 'It looks as if…as if—' Disbelief caught in her throat, eating the rest of her words.

'As if I'm taking you from behind?' he supplied helpfully.

Humiliating heat stained her cheeks. '*Sim,*' she muttered fiercely. 'With your jacket covering me that way it looks as if I'm wearing nothing from the waist down! It's…it's disgusting!'

He plucked the paper from her hand and studied the picture. 'Hmm, it certainly is…*something.*'

'How can you sit there and be so unconcerned about it?' The picture had been taken with a high-resolution camera but, with the low lighting in the car park, the suggestiveness in the picture could be misinterpreted a thousand ways. None of them complimentary.

'Relax. We weren't exactly having sex, were we?'

'That's not the point.' She grabbed the paper back and quickly perused the article accompanying the gratuitous picture, fearing the worst. Sure enough, her father's political campaign had been called into question, along with an even more unsavoury speculation on her private life.

If this is what they do in public we can only imagine what they do in private…

Her hands shook as she threw the offending paper down. 'I thought this was a reputable paper.'

'It is.'

'Then why would they print something so…offensive?'

'Perhaps because it's true. We were kissing in the car park. And you were pushing your delectable backside into my groin as if you couldn't wait till we got home to do me.'

She surged to her feet, knocking her chair aside. Her whole body was shaking with fury and she could barely grasp the chair to straighten it.

'We both know I was not!'

'Do we? I told you those shorts were a bad idea. Do you blame me for getting carried away?'

'Oh, you're *despicable!*'

'And you're delicious when you're angry,' he replied lazily, picked up the paper and carried on reading.

The urge to drive her fist through the paper into his face made her take another hasty step back.

She abhorred violence. Or at least she had before she'd met Theo Pantelides. Now she wasn't so sure what she was capable of…

'Aren't you going to eat, *anjo*?' he asked without taking his eyes off the page.

'No. I've lost my appetite,' she snapped.

She fled the terrace to the sound of his mocking laughter and raced up to her room, her face flaming and angry humiliation smashing through her chest.

He found her on the beach an hour later. She heard the crunch of his feet in the warm sand and studiously avoided looking up. She carried on sketching the stationary boat anchored about a mile away and ignored him when he settled himself on the flat rock next to her.

He didn't speak for a few minutes before he let out an irritated breath. 'The silent treatment doesn't work for me, Inez.'

She snapped her pad shut and turned to face him. His lips were pinched with displeasure but his eyes were focused, gauging her reaction...almost as if her reaction mattered.

'Having my sex life sleazily speculated about in the weekend newspaper doesn't work for me either.' She blinked to dilute the intense focus and continued. 'I agree that perhaps those shorts were not the best idea. But I saw the other diners in that restaurant. There were people far more famous than I am. But still the paparazzo followed us into the car park and took our picture.'

Inez thought he tensed but perhaps it was the movement of his body as he reached behind him and produced a plate laden with food. 'It's done. Let's move on.'

She yearned to remain on her high horse, but with her exertions last night, coupled with having eaten less than a whole meal in the last twenty-four hours, it wasn't surprising when her stomach growled loudly in anticipation.

He shook out a napkin and settled the plate in her lap. 'Eat up,' he instructed and picked up her sketchpad. 'You have an hour before the stylist arrives to address the issue of your wardrobe.'

She froze in the act of reaching for the food. 'I

don't need a stylist. I can easily go back home and pack up some more clothes.'

'You'll not be returning to your father's house for the next three months. Besides, if your clothes are all in the style of heavy evening gowns or tiny shorts, then you'll agree the time has come to go a different route?'

She mentally scanned her wardrobe and swiftly concluded that he was probably right. 'There really is no need,' she tried anyway.

'It's too late to change the plan, Inez.'

And, just like that, the subject was closed. He tapped the plate and, as if on cue, her stomach growled again.

Giving up the argument, she devoured the thick sliced beef sandwich and polished off the apple in greedy bites. She was gulping down the bottled water when she saw him pause at her sketch of a boat.

'This is very good.'

'Thank you.'

He tilted the page. 'You like boats?'

'Very much. My mother used to take me sailing. It was my favourite thing to do with her.'

He closed the pad. 'Were you two close?'

'She was my best friend,' she responded in a

voice that cracked with pain. 'Not a day goes by that I don't miss her.'

His fingers seemed to tighten on the rock before they relaxed again. 'Mothers have a way of affecting you that way. It makes their absence all the harder to bear.'

'Is yours…when did you lose yours?' she asked.

He turned and stared at her. A bleak look entered his eyes but dissolved in the next blink. 'My mother is very much alive.'

She gasped. 'But I thought you said…'

'Absence doesn't mean death. There are several ways for a parent to be absent from a child's life without the ultimate separation.'

'Are you talking about abandonment?'

Again he glanced at her, and this time she caught a clearer glimpse of his emotions. Pain. Devastating pain.

'Abandonment. Indifference. Selfishness. Self-absorption. There are many forms of delivering the same blow,' he elaborated in a rough voice.

'I know. But I was lucky. My mother was the best mother in the world.'

'Is that why you're trying to be the best daughter in the world for your father, despite what you know of him?'

His accusation was like sandpaper against her skin. 'I beg your pardon?'

He shook his head. 'Don't bother denying it. You know exactly what sort of person he is. And yet you've stood by him all these years. Why— because you want a pat on the head and to be told you're a good daughter?'

The truth of his words hit her square in the chest. Up until yesterday, everything she'd done, every plan of her father's she'd gone along with had been to win his approval, and in some way make up for the fact that she hadn't been born the right gender. She didn't want to curl up and hide from the truth. But the callous way he condemned her made her want to justify her actions.

'I'm not blind to my father's shortcomings.' She ignored his caustic snort. 'But neither am I going to make excuses for my actions. My loyalty to my family isn't something I'm ashamed of.'

'Even when that loyalty meant turning a blind eye to other people's suffering?' he demanded icily.

She frowned. 'Whose suffering?'

'The people he left behind in the *favelas* for a start. Do you know that less than two per cent of the funds raised at those so-called charity events you so painstakingly put together actually make it to the people who need it most?'

She felt her face redden. His condemning gaze raked over her features. 'Of course you do,' he murmured acidly.

'It happened in the past, I admit it, but I only agreed to organise the last event if everything over and above the cost of doing it went to the *favelas*.' At his disbelieving look, she added, 'I do a lot of work with charities. I know what I'm talking about.'

'And did you ensure that it was done?'

'Yes. The charity confirmed they'd received the funds yesterday.'

One eyebrow quirked in surprise before he jerked to his feet. Thrusting his hands into his pockets, he turned to face her. 'That's progress at least.'

'Thank you. I don't live in a fairy tale. Trust me, I'm trying to do my part to help the *favelas*.'

'How?'

She debated a few seconds before she answered. 'I work at an inner city charity a few times a week.'

His gaze probed hers. 'That morning outside the coffee shop, that was where you were going?'

'Yes.'

'What does your father think?'

She bit her lip. 'He doesn't know.'

His mouth twisted. 'Because it will draw attention to his lies about his upbringing? Everyone knows he was born and raised in the *favelas*.'

'It's part of the reason why I didn't tell him, yes. But he denies his *favela* upbringing because he's…ashamed.'

'And yet he doesn't mind anyone knowing about his mother?'

'He thinks it gives him a little leverage with the common man to be indirectly associated with the *favelas*.'

'So he likes to rewrite his history as he goes along?'

'Perhaps. I don't delude myself for one second that my father doesn't bend the rules and the truth at times.'

His harsh laugh made her start. 'Right. Are you talking about, oh, let's see…doing ninety on a sixty miles per hour road, or are we talking about something with a little more…teeth?'

That note she'd heard before. The one that sent a foreboding chill along her spine, that warned her that something else was going on here. Something she should be running far and fast from. 'I…I'm not sure what you're implying.'

'Then let me spell it out for you. Are we talking about harmless anecdotes or are we talking about actual deeds? You know—broken kneecaps? Ruptured spleens. *Kidnap for ransom*?'

Her hand flew to her mouth. 'What the hell are you talking about?'

'Come on, you know what your father is capable of. Do I need to remind you of what he did to you when you displeased him?'

She followed his gaze to the marks on her arm and slowly shook her head. 'I don't excuse this but I refuse to believe he's the monster you describe.'

His mouth twisted. 'I'll let you enjoy your rosy outlook for now, *querida*. I, too, felt like that once about my own father.'

'Is that what you're going to do to my father? Make him accountable for the things he's done?'

For several heartbeats she was sure he wouldn't answer her, or would change the subject the way he'd done in the past. But finally he nodded.

'Yes. I intend to make him pay for what he took from me twelve years ago.'

Her breath froze in her lungs. 'What did he take from you?'

He turned abruptly and faced the water, his stance rigid and forbidding. But Inez found herself moving towards him anyway, a visceral need driving her. She reached out and touched his shoulder. He tensed harder and she was reminded of his re-action to her touch on his boat. 'Theo?'

'I don't like being touched when my back's turned, *anjo.*'

She frowned. 'Why not?'

'Part of my demons.'

Her gut clenched hard at the rough note in his voice. 'Did…did my father do that to you?'

'Not personally. After all, he's an upright citi-zen now, isn't he? A man the people should trust.' He whipped about to face her.

'But he had something to do with your claus-trophobia. And this?'

'Yes.'

'Theo—'

'Enough with the questions! You're forgetting why you're here. Do you need a reminder?'

She swallowed at the arctic look in his eyes. All signs of the raw, vulnerable pain she'd glimpsed minutes ago were wiped clean. Theo Pantelides was once again a man in control, bent on revenge. Slowly, she shook her head. 'No. No, I don't.'

CHAPTER EIGHT

THEIR CONVERSATION AT the beach set a frigid benchmark for the beginning of her stay at Theo's glass mansion.

The next two weeks passed in an icy blur of hectic days and even more hectic evenings. They'd quickly fallen into a routine where Theo left after a quick cup of coffee and a brief outline of when and where they would be dining that evening.

On the second morning when she'd told him she was heading for the charity, he'd raised an eyebrow. 'What sort of work do you do there?'

'Whatever I'm needed to do.' She'd been reluctant to tell him any specifics in case he disparaged her efforts as a rich girl's means of passing the time till the next party.

He'd returned to his coffee. 'Your time is your own when I'm not around. As long you're back here when I return, I see no problem.'

That had been the end of the subject.

After repeating his warning not to mention anything to her father he'd walked away. The man who'd shown her his pain and devastation had completely retreated.

His demeanour during their time indoors was icily courteous. However, when they went out, which they did most evenings, he was the attentive host, touching her, threading his fingers through her hair and gazing adoringly at her.

It was after the fifth night out that she realised he was pandering to the paparazzi. Without fail, a picture of them in a compromising position appeared in the newspapers the very next morning.

But while she cringed with every exposing photo, he shrugged it off. It wasn't until her third weekend with him, when the newspapers posted the first poll results of the mayoral race, that she finally had her suspicions confirmed.

He was swimming in the pool, his lean and stunning body cutting through the water like the sleekest shark. The byline explaining the reasons behind the voters' reaction had her surging to her feet and storming to the edge of the pool.

'Is this why you've been taking me out every night since I moved in? So I'd be labelled the slut daughter of a man not fit to be mayor?' She raised her voice loud enough to be heard above his powerful strokes.

He stopped mid-stroke, straightened and slicked back his wet hair. With smooth breaststrokes he swam to where she stood barefoot. Looking down at his wet, sun-kissed face, she momentarily lost her train of thought.

He soon set her straight. 'Your father isn't worthy to lead a chain gang, never mind a city,' he replied in succinct, condemning tones. 'And before I'm done with him, the whole world will know it.'

Despite seeing the evidence for herself two weeks ago at the beach, despite knowing that whatever her father had done to him had been devastating, she staggered back a step at that solid, implacable oath.

He planted his hands on the tiles and heaved himself out of the water. It took every ounce of her self-control not to devour him with hungry eyes. But not looking didn't mean not feeling. Her insides clenched with the ever-growing hunger she'd been unable to stem since the first night he'd walked into her life. And, with each passing day, she was finding it harder and harder to remain unaffected.

It seemed not even knowing why she was here, or the full extent of how Theo intended to use her to hurt her father, could cause her intense emotional reaction to his proximity to abate.

Which made her ten kinds of a fool, who needed to pull her thoughts together or risk getting hurt all over again.

'So you don't deny that you used me as bait to derail my father's campaign?'

Hazel eyes, devoid of emotion, narrowed on her face. 'That was one course of action. But you haven't been labelled a slut. I'll sue any newspaper that dares to call you that,' he rasped.

Her laughter scraped her throat. 'There are several ways to describe someone without using the actual derogatory word, Theo.'

He paused in drying his hair and looked at her. Slowly, he held out his hand. 'Show me.'

She handed the paper over. He read it tight-jawed. 'I'll have them print a retraction.'

Dismay roiled through her stomach, along with a heavy dose of rebellious anger.

'That's not the point, though, is it? The harm's already done. You know this means I'll have to stop volunteering, don't you? I can't bring this sort of attention to the charity.'

He frowned and she caught a look of unease on his face. 'I'll take care of this.'

'Forget it; it's too late. And congratulations; you've achieved your aim. But I won't be paraded about and pawed in public any more, so if you're planning on another night on the town you'll have to do it without me.'

His gaze slowly rose to hers and he resumed rubbing the towel through his hair. 'Fine. We'll do something else.' He threw the paper on the table.

She regarded him suspiciously. 'Something like what?'

'I promised you a trip on the yacht. We'll sail this evening and spend tomorrow aboard. Would you like that?'

At times like these, when he was being a courteous host, she found it hard to believe he was the same man who was hell-bent on seeking revenge on her father for past wrongs.

She'd given in to her gnawing curiosity after his revelations on the beach and searched the Internet for a clue as to what had happened to him. All she'd come up with were scant snippets of his late father's dirty dealings before Alexandrou Pantelides had died in prison. As far as she knew, there was no connection between Theo's family and hers. The Pantelides brothers, one of whom was married and recently a parent, and the other engaged to be married, were a huge success in the oil, shipping and luxury hotel world. Theo's job as a troubleshooter extraordinaire for the billion-dollar conglomerate meant he never settled in one place for very long. An ideal job for a man whose personal relationships were fleeting at best.

And a man tormented by a horde of demons.

She looked closer at him, tried to see the man behind the wall, the man who'd bared his soul for a brief moment when he'd spoken of his mother's abandonment.

But that man was closed off.

'What does it matter what I want? Frankly, I'm surprised my father hasn't been in touch about this.'

'He has. I refused to take his calls.'

'I didn't mean you. Since I was also the subject in these photos, I'm surprised he hasn't called me to vent his anger.'

His eyelids swept down and shielded his gaze from her. Apprehension struck a jagged path through her. 'He has, hasn't he?'

'He tried. I suggested that perhaps he refrain from contacting you and concentrate on kissing babies and convincing little old ladies to cast their ballot in his favour.'

Shock rooted her to the ground. 'How dare you take control of my life like this?'

'Would you rather I gave him access so he airs his disappointment?'

'What do you care? It's a little late to protect me, don't you think?'

His jaw tightened. 'For as long as you remain under my roof, you're under my protection.'

'*Meu deus*, please don't pretend you care!'

She realised how close she was to tears and swallowed hard. Fearing she would break down in front of him, she whirled round, intent on heading for her room. She made it two steps before he stopped her.

Flinging away the towel, he cupped her cheeks with both hands. 'Stop getting yourself distressed about this.'

'Is that another command?'

His eyes narrowed. 'You're angry.'

'Damn right I am. I wish I'd never set eyes on you. In fact I wish—'

His mouth slanted over hers, hot, hungry and all consuming. Her groan of protest was less than heartfelt and devoured within a millisecond.

A part of her was furious that he'd resorted to kissing her to shut her up. But it was only a minuscule part. The rest of her body was too busy revelling in the feel of his warm bare back and the fine definition of muscles that rippled beneath her caress.

His hands speared into her hair, imprisoning

her for the invasion of his tongue as he took the kiss to another level.

His first kiss over two weeks ago had been a pure threat and the two that followed a show of mastery. This kiss was different. There was hunger and passion behind it, but also a gentleness that calmed her roiling emotions and slowly replaced them with a different sensation. Need clamoured inside her; a need to be closer still to his magnificent body; a need to dig her hands into his back and feel him shudder in reaction.

His groan was smothered between their melded lips as she dug her fingers even deeper. Power surged through her when he jerked again.

One hand dropped to her bottom and yanked her lower body into his groin. His erection was unmistakable. Bold, thick and hot, it pressed against her belly with insistent power that made her heartbeat skitter out of control.

She wanted him. Above and beyond all sense, she wanted this man. Her willpower, when it came to the chemistry between them, was laughably negligible.

But she couldn't give in. *Couldn't…*

The gentleness she'd sensed in him was false, she reminded herself fiercely. The bottom line was that in a few short weeks he would walk away. Leave her and her family devastated.

'I'm losing you. Come back, *anjo*,' he murmured seductively against her mouth. He ran his tongue over her lower lip and her knees weakened.

When he cupped her bottom and squeezed, she desperately summoned all her resolve and pushed against his chest. 'No.'

He raised his head and she saw behind the wall. He was as caught in this insane chemistry as she was. A little part of her felt better.

'I can change your mind, Inez. Regardless of what I intend for your father, what is between us is undeniable.'

'Do you hear yourself? You think I should forget everything else and sleep with you just because you made me feel a certain way?'

'That's generally the reason why men and women have sex.'

'But we're not just any man and any woman, Theo, are we?'

He stiffened, and a hard look entered his eyes. 'Are you saying that you've been in love with every man you've slept with?' he queried.

She froze and prayed her humiliation wouldn't show on her face as she tried to stem the memory of Constantine's treatment of her.

His cruel rejection was still an ache beneath her breastbone.

'Inez?' Theo interjected harshly.

'My past relationships are none of your business.'

His slightly reddened mouth twisted. 'Far be it for me to request to be lumped in with your other lovers, but isn't it a touch hypocritical to apply one criteria to me that you haven't done with one of your lovers, in particular?'

'If you're referring to Constantine, let me assure you that you have no idea what you're talking about.'

His hand tightened around her waist. 'Then enlighten me. Why did he dump you?'

Inez broke free. 'We weren't compatible.'

'Or he found out the true reason you were with him and wanted nothing to do with you?'

'No. That wasn't why…' She screeched to a stop as the words stuck in her throat.

'So what was it? Did you really love him or did you convince yourself you did in order to achieve your aims?'

She bit her lip as he shone a light on the stark question. Had she blown her feelings out of proportion? Constantine had been charismatic, yes, but he'd never created the decadent chaos that Theo created in her.

When she'd imagined love, she'd always imagined passion, hunger and a keen pleasure even the slightest thought of that special someone brought. She'd believed herself in love with Constantine and yet she'd never experienced those emotions.

Well, she most definitely wasn't feeling them now.

'I believed my emotions were genuine at the time. But he didn't. He believed I was using him to further my father's campaign.'

'What did he do?' he asked. She looked into his eyes and fooled herself into thinking she saw a thawing of the hardness there.

'He made painful digs at me whenever he gave interviews. He made the tabloids call my character into question…much the same way you're doing now.'

He dropped his hand. 'It's not the same—'

'Yes, it is. Look Theo, I just want to be left alone to do my time.'

He paled. 'You're not in prison, Inez.'

She put much needed distance between them. 'Am I not? How else would you describe my presence here?'

* * *

Theo watched her walk away and curled his fists at his sides. The urge to call her back was so strong he forced himself to exhale slowly to expel the need. Her reference to her presence under his roof as a prison sentence had stung badly.

But hell, the truth was irrefutable. He'd forced her to make a choice, and no amount of dinner dates or designer shopping sprees would gloss over the fact that he'd set the tabloids on her as a way to dismantle her father's campaign.

Witnessing her clear distress just now had made his chest ache in a way that confused and irritated him.

Perhaps he needed to step up his agenda, end this dangerous game once and for all and move on with his life.

His brothers would certainly agree. He'd been avoiding their calls for the best part of a fortnight, replying only by email and with curt one-liners that he knew would only go so far before something gave.

He gritted his teeth against the prompt to deliver a swift killing blow to Benedicto da Costa.

His own ordeal hadn't been swift. It'd been long and tortuous. The punishment should fit the crime. Any hesitation on his part now merely stemmed from the afterglow of the chemistry between him and Inez. He freely admitted that theirs was a strong and potent brand, more intense than anything he'd ever experienced before.

It was messing with his mind, the same way the thought of her ex-lover had made him see red for several long seconds. But there was no way he was letting it impede his goal.

Which meant he had to come at this problem from another angle.

He swallowed the acrid taste in his mouth at the thought that Inez had put him into the same class as Constantine Blanco.

Slowly walking back indoors, he turned over the dilemma in his mind. By the time he reached his suite and changed out of his swimming trunks, a smile was curving his lips.

An hour later, he watched her descend the stairs, her duffel bag slung over her shoulder and an overnight case in her hand.

'Did Teresa tell you to pack your swimming gear?'

She regarded him warily. 'Yes. But I thought we were just taking the boat out?'

He shrugged. 'I thought you would welcome the opportunity to sunbathe away from the prying lenses of the paparazzi? There are several decks on the yacht that you can sunbathe on. Or we can swim in the sea, dine alone under the stars. Would you like that?' he asked, then felt a jolt at how much he wanted her to answer in the affirmative. In the past, he'd never taken the time to seek out what pleased his girlfriends beyond the usual gifts and fine dining. It was why he operated his relationships on a strict short-term basis with as little maintenance as possible.

Inez was far from low maintenance. And yet he found himself even more drawn to her.

She glanced pointedly over his shoulder. 'I'll think about it and let you know.'

His unsettled feelings escalated. He reminded himself that they were heading for his boat. She liked his boat. Perhaps she would relent enough to forget that she was angry with him. Forget about Blanco and forget that she was being blackmailed.

Theo was still debating why her feelings meant so much to him when he pulled up at the marina.

'You've been smiling ever since we set sail.'

Her voice was full of heavy suspicion. Theo's smile widened as he tilted his face up into the sunshine. 'Have I? It must be the weather.'

'The weather has been the same for the last month,' she replied sourly.

He slowly lowered his head and captured her gaze with his. 'Then it must be the company.'

A delicate wave of heat surged up her neck into her cheeks, making him wonder, as he had more than once these past two weeks, how she could have been involved with someone like Blanco and still blush like a schoolgirl.

Theo had looked into Constantine Blanco and had not been surprised to find that he was cut from the same cloth as Benedicto. It was perhaps why Da Costa had chosen to ally himself with the younger man politically. He'd sent his daughter to spy on Blanco and had been double-crossed in the bargain.

Theo's smile slipped as he recalled her hurt when he'd thrown her relationship with Blanco at her. He reached for the glass of wine that had accompanied their late afternoon meal and took a large gulp.

The guilt tightening in his chest since her accusation at the pool squeezed harder.

What the hell was going on with him?

'Have you decided whether you're selling the boat or not?' she asked.

In the sunlight, her black hair gleamed like polished jet, making him burn to feel its silkiness beneath his fingers.

He stared into his drink. 'Maybe. I'll have to weigh up practical usage versus the desire to hang on to something beautiful.'

'But you're a billionaire. Isn't collecting toys part and parcel of your status?'

'I wasn't always a man of means. In fact my brothers and I worked our backsides off to achieve the level of success we enjoy now.' His smile felt tight and strained.

'Your brothers…Sakis and Arion…'

He looked up in surprise. 'You've been playing around on the Internet, I see.'

She raised her chin. 'I thought it wise to learn a little bit more about my enemy.'

The label grated. Badly. 'What else did you try to discover while you were rooting around my family tree?'

'Your brother Sakis had some trouble with a saboteur on one of his oil tankers.'

He nodded. 'We dealt with that quite satisfactorily.'

'And now your brother Ari is engaged to the widow of the man who tried to throw your company into chaos?' She frowned.

A reluctant grin tugged at his mouth. 'What can I say; we thrive on interesting challenges.'

'You also seem to make enemies with the people

you do business with. So far you've led me to believe it was my father who wronged you. How do I know it's not the other way round? That you're not here because you deserved everything you got?'

The stem of the wine glass snapped with a sickening crack. Even then it took the cold wine seeping into his shirt to realise what he'd done.

The top part of the glass landed on the table, rolled off and smashed onto the deck.

Inez gasped. 'Theo, you're bleeding!' She surged to her feet and sprang towards him.

'Stop!'

'But your finger…'

'Is nothing compared to what will happen to your foot if you take another step.'

She glanced down at the broken glass an inch from her bare foot and glanced back at his bleeding forefinger. Anguish creased her pale features.

'Sit down, Inez,' he instructed tersely.

'Please, let me help,' she implored.

Gritting his teeth, he grabbed a napkin and formed a small tourniquet around the gaping wound. 'It's not deep but will need to be cleaned properly. There's a first aid kit behind the bar.'

She nodded, slipped on her sandals and dashed for the bar. Theo stood and moved from the dining table to the wraparound sofa to give the crew member who'd arrived on deck room to sweep up the broken glass. He glanced up as Inez rushed back and set the kit on the coffee table.

Her eyes were turbulent with worry as she glanced from his face to the blood-soaked napkin.

'Are you going to stand there staring at me all evening? I'm bleeding to death here.'

With a hoarse croak, she jerked into action. She carefully cleaned the wound with antiseptic and applied gauze before securing it with a plaster. All through the procedure, she darted quick, apologetic glances at him.

As he stared at her, he felt a different sort of jolt run through him. One he hadn't been aware he was missing until he felt it.

Care. Concern. Fear for him.

When was the last time anyone besides Ari and Sakis had felt like that about him? When was the last time his own mother lavished such attention on him? Inez slid him another worried glance and his breath shuddered out.

'Calm yourself, *anjo*. I'll live. I'm sure of it.'

She exhaled noisily and her agitated pulse pounded at her throat. '*Sinto muito*,' she said in a rush.

'Don't apologise. It wasn't your fault.'

'But…if I hadn't accused you of…'

'You're operating in the dark and want to find out the truth. I respect that. But I can't tell you what my business with your father is until I'm ready. You have to respect that.'

'But…this…' She glanced down at his finger and shook her head. 'Your reaction…the claustrophobia and the touching thing…I can't help but fear the worst, Theo,' she whispered.

Against his will, his chest constricted at the anguish in her voice. He wanted to comfort her. Wanted to take that look of anticipated pain from her face. He wanted to kiss her until they both forgot why she was his prisoner and why he was beginning to dread the day he had to set her free.

He swallowed hard.

'Let's make a deal. For the next twenty-four hours, no talk of your father or the reason why I'm in Rio. Agreed?'

Her mouth wobbled and her teeth worried her bottom lip as she glanced back at his finger. Her eyes were no less turbulent when they rose to his but he saw determination flare in their depths. 'Agreed.'

Theo stood at the railing on the third floor deck and watched her swim in the pool on the second deck the next morning. She moved like a water nymph, her long black hair streaming down her back as she scissored her arms and legs underwater.

He gripped the rail until his knuckles turned white but still he couldn't take his eyes off her.

'I'm waiting for an answer, Theo,' came the weary voice at the end of the line.

Theo sighed. 'Sorry, remind me again what the question was.'

Ari grunted with annoyance. 'I asked you why I couldn't have one peaceful breakfast without opening the papers to find you wrapped around some poor girl. Seriously, my digestive system has sent me a stern memo. Either I treat it better and not subject it to such images or it goes on permanent vacation.'

Theo heard Perla, his soon-to-be sister-in-law, laughing in the background.

'The answer is simple. Don't read the papers.'

Ari sighed. 'How long is this going to go on for?'

'Everything should be signed, sealed and delivered in a week or two,' he responded, rolling his shoulders to ease the tension tightening his muscles. Another sleepless night, plagued with nightmares. He'd given up on sleep somewhere around three a.m.

'You sound very sure.'

His grip tightened around the phone. As he'd lain awake he'd briefly toyed with the idea of ending this vendetta sooner. And he'd been stunned when the idea had taken firm hold. 'I am.'

'And nothing you're doing down there will affect the wedding? Don't forget it's in two weeks. If you can prise yourself away from that piece of skirt for long enough—'

'She's not a piece of skirt,' he snarled before he could catch his response. Ari's silence made him hurry to speak. 'I'll be at your wedding.'

'Good, since you've missed most of the rehearsals, I'll send you the video of what you need to do. Make sure you get it right; we'll do a quick rehearsal when you get here. I'm not having you mess things up for Perla.'

'Sure. Fine,' he murmured.

He followed the curvy, sexy shape underneath the water and held his breath as Inez broke the surface and rose out of the pool. Dripping curves and sun-kissed skin made his body clench unbearably. He wanted to trace every single inch of her with his hands, his mouth, his tongue. 'Oh, and tell Perla I'm bringing a guest.'

His brother muttered a curse and relayed the message. Theo heard Perla's whoop of delight. 'The love of my life grudgingly agrees but suggests that perhaps, next time, you could be courteous enough to give us a heads-up sooner?'

'Next time? You mean you'll be getting married for a third time?'

He hung up to more pithy curses ringing in his ears and found himself smiling. Without taking his eyes off the figure below, he descended the spiral staircase and walked towards the bikini-clad goddess reaching for the towel on the shelf next to the pool.

Her back was turned and he slowed to a stop as the sight of her tiny waist and curvy hips made blood rush through his veins. Lust twisted through his gut, hard and demanding.

Hell, this was getting unbearable.

He threw his cell phone on the breakfast table and watched her jerk around to face him. The towel she was holding to her hair stilled.

'Hi.'

'Good morning. Enjoy your swim?'

'It was very refreshing,' she replied huskily, her eyes following him warily as he strode towards her. 'So, what's the plan for today?' she asked.

I want to haul you off to my bed and keep you

underneath me until we both pass out from the pleasure overload.

He wrenched his gaze from her full breasts, lovingly cupped by damp white triangles, and concentrated on breathing. 'We're headed for Copacabana. We'll stop for something to eat then head back tonight. Or if you want we can stay on the boat and leave in the morning?'

She thought about it for a second and nodded. 'I'd love to draw the boat in the moonlight.'

'Then that's what you shall do.'

Her gaze turned puzzling, weighing.

'What's on your mind?' he asked.

She shook her head slightly and slowly folded the towel. 'Sometimes I feel as if I'm dealing with two people.'

Something hard tugged in his chest. 'Which one do you prefer?'

'Are you joking? The person you are now, of course.'

He froze as the tug tightened its hold on him. His breath came in short pants as he closed the distance between them. 'I thought we weren't going to delve into our issues today.'

'You asked me what was on my mind.'

He nodded. 'I guess I did.' He stared into the

pure, make-up-free perfection of her face and something very close to regret rose in his gut.

'Now it's my turn to ask you what's on your mind, Theo,' she murmured thoughtfully.

'It's completely pointless, of course, but I'm wishing we'd met under different circumstances.'

Her mouth dropped open. 'You are?'

The urge to touch grew, and he finally gave in. He traced his thumb over her lips and felt them pucker slightly under his touch. 'As I said, it's pointless.'

'Because you would've been done with me within a week?' she ventured.

'No. I would've kept you for much longer, *anjo*. Perhaps even for ever.'

He forced himself to step away. Once again she'd slid so effortlessly under his skin, opened him up to wishes and possibilities he'd forced himself never to entertain after what their respective fathers and his mother had done to him. She was making him believe in impossible dreams, feelings he had no business experiencing.

He strode quickly towards the pool. A cold dip would wash away the fiery need and alien emotions tearing his insides to shreds. He hoped.

He emerged twenty minutes later to find her polishing off the last of her scrambled eggs and coffee. Over the past fortnight he'd noticed that she ate with a gusto that triggered his own appetite. Or *appetites*.

As he poured his coffee and helped himself to fruit, she reached for the ever-present duffel bag and pulled out her sketchpad.

'Have you thought of doing something with your talent?' he asked.

A shadow passed over her face before she tried to smile through it, but he guessed the reason behind it. Her father. 'I will once I resume my education. I put pursuing my degree on hiatus for a while.'

He didn't need to ask why. 'Until when?'

She shrugged and searched for a fresh page in her pad. 'I haven't decided yet.'

Theo tried not to let his anger show. They'd called a truce for twenty-four hours.

'What will you study when you return?'

'I love buildings and boats. I may go into architecture or boat design.'

He glanced from her face to the pad. 'Boat design, huh?'

She nodded.

He picked up his coffee and regarded her over the rim. 'Why don't you design me one?'

'You want me to design a boat for you?'

'Yes. I'm sure your research showed you what sort of designs we specialise in. It has to be up to the Pantelides standard. But use your own template. Make it state-of-the-art, of course.'

'Of course,' she murmured but he could see the gleam of interest in her eyes as she stared down at her pad.

Her pencil flew across the paper as he devoured his breakfast. She didn't look up as he rose and rounded the table to where she sat. He didn't glance down at her drawing; he was too absorbed with the sheer joy on her face as she became immersed in her task.

Even when his finger drifted down her cheek to the corner of her mouth she barely glanced up at him. But her breath hitched and she jerked a tiny bit towards his touch before he withdrew his hand.

As he walked away, Theo marvelled at how light-hearted he felt.

CHAPTER NINE

THEY DROPPED ANCHOR about a mile away from Copacabana Beach and took a launch ashore.

Inez looked to where Theo stood, legs braced, at the wheel of the launch. The wind rushed through his dark hair, whipping it across his forehead. Stupid that she should be jealous of the wind but she clenched her fingers in her lap as they tingled with the need to touch him.

I would've kept you for much longer, anjo. *Perhaps even for ever.*

Try as she had for the last few hours, she couldn't get his words out of her head. They struck her straight to the heart in unguarded moments, made her breath catch in ways that made her dizzy. Every time she pushed the feeling away. But, inevitably, it returned.

She was in serious trouble here…

A shout from nearby sunbathers drew her attention to the fact that they were not alone any more.

She watched the surge of people and the noise of

tourists enjoying a Sunday stroll along the beach roads and suddenly felt as if she was losing the tenuous connection she'd made with Theo last night and this morning. Which was silly. There was no connection. Just a precarious truce.

And an exciting task designing a Pantelides boat, which had made joy bubble beneath her skin all day.

He brought the launch to a smooth stop at the pier and turned off the engine. Jumping out with lithe grace, he held out his hand to her, the smile on his face making her breath stutter in her chest as she slipped her hand into his.

'I'm in the mood for some traditional food and I know just the place for it. You happy to trust me?'

Safely on solid ground, she glanced up and found herself nodding. 'Yes.'

His eyes darkened. 'It's a bit of a walk.' He glanced at her high-heeled wedges with a cocked eyebrow.

'Don't worry about me. I was born in heels.'

'Then I pity your poor *mãe*.'

She laughed and saw his answering smile.

Gradually they fell silent and his gaze drifted over her face, resting on her mouth for a few seconds before he tugged on her hand. 'Come on, *anjo*.'

He led her along the pier and towards the streets. Ten minutes later, she stared in surprise when they stopped outside a door with a faded sign and a single light bulb above it.

'I hear they serve the best *feijoadas* in Rio,' he said, his gaze probing her every expression.

Inez forced the lump in her throat down as she stared at the sign that had been very much part of a long ago, happier childhood. 'It's true. I…how do you know about this place?'

The hand he'd captured since they alighted from the boat meshed with hers, causing her heart to flutter wildly as he brought it to his lips and kissed the back of it. 'I made it my business to find out.'

Again tears choked her and she couldn't speak for several moments. 'Thank you.'

He nodded. 'My pleasure.'

They stopped in the doorway to allow their eyes to adjust to the candlelit interior.

'*Pequena estrela!*' A matronly woman in her late forties approached, her face lit up with a smile.

After exchanging hugs, Inez turned to introduce Theo.

'Camila and my mother were best friends. I

used to have supper here many times after school when I was a kid.'

Theo responded to the introduction in smooth, charming Portuguese that had the older woman blushing before she led them to a table in the middle of the room.

'You want the usual?' Camila asked after she'd brought over a basket of bread and taken their wine order.

Inez glanced at Theo. 'Will you let me choose?'

He sat back in his chair, his gaze brushing her face. 'It's your show, *anjo*.'

She rattled off the order and added a few more dishes that had Camila nodding in approval before she bustled off.

Alone with Theo, she tried to calm her giddy senses. Not read too much into why he'd brought her here of all places. But her emotions refused to be calmed.

He was making her feel things she had no business feeling, considering their circumstances. Her heart was very much in danger of being devastated. And this time the danger signs were not disguised as they'd been with Constantine. She was walking into this with her heart and eyes wide open...

'You're frowning too hard, *querida*.'

Plucking a piece of bread from the basket, she fought to focus on not ruining their truce. 'I think I may have ordered too much food.'

'You have a healthy appetite. Nothing wrong with that.'

'It's that healthy appetite that keeps me on the wrong side of chubby.'

'You're not chubby. You're perfect.'

Her hand stilled on the way to her mouth. In the ambient light, she witnessed the potent, knee-weakening look of appreciation on his face. The look slowly grew until hunger became deeply etched into his every feature.

Desire pounded through her, sending radial pulses of heat through her body to concentrate on that needy place between her legs. '*Obrigado*,' she murmured hoarsely.

He nodded slowly, leant forward and took the piece of bread from her hand. Tearing off a piece, he held it against her mouth. When she opened it, he placed it on her tongue and watched her chew.

Then he sat back and ate the remaining piece.

She eventually managed to swallow and cast around for a safe topic of conversation that didn't involve her father or the dangerous emotions arcing between them.

Whether he noticed her floundering or not,

she smiled gratefully when he asked, 'Did your mother grow up around here?'

'No, both she and Camila grew up near the Serra Geral, although she spent part of her childhood in Arizona where my grandmother was from. Their fathers were ranch-owning *gauchos* and neighbours but after they both married they moved to Rio and stayed in touch. Camila is like a second mother to me…'

'Da Costa Holdings isn't a cattle business, though,' he replied, then stiffened slightly.

She smiled quickly, wanting to hold onto the animosity-free atmosphere they'd found. 'No, after my grandfather died, my mother sold the ranch and let my father expand the company instead.' She breathed in relief when Camila returned with their wine and first course.

The older woman's warm smile and effusive manner further lightened the mood. By the time she took her first sip of the bold red wine the slightly chilly interlude had passed.

Theo complimented her on the food choice and tucked into the grilled fish starter. The conversation returned to safer topics and eventually turned to his previous career as a championship-winning rower.

'Why did you stop competing?'

He shrugged. 'I tried a few partners after Ari and Sakis retired. The chemistry was lacking. In a sport like that chemistry is key.' He topped up her wine and took a sip of his own.

'You've been lucky to have had the opportunity to do something you loved,' she replied wistfully.

His smile looked a little taut around the edges. 'Luck is a luxury that normally comes along as a result of hard work.'

She glanced down into her wine. 'But sometimes, no matter how hard you try, fate has other ideas for you.'

His eyes narrowed into sharp laser-like beams. 'Yes. But the answer is to turn it to your advantage.'

'Or you can walk away. Find a different option?'

One corner of his mouth lifted. 'Walking away has never been my style.'

She slowly nodded. 'You wouldn't have won championships if you were a man who walked away.'

His expression morphed into something that resembled gratitude. She couldn't claim she understood all his motives but she was beginning to grasp what made Theo tick. As long as he could see a problem in any area of his life, he would not walk away until it was resolved. It was why he was the troubleshooter for Pantelides Inc.

She'd watched footage of him rowing. His grit and determination had held her enthralled throughout the feature and she would be lying now if she didn't admit it was a huge turn-on.

'But there's also strength in walking away. You walked away from rowing rather than risk partnering up with the wrong person.'

He stiffened. 'Inez...'

She fought the urge to back down. 'I don't want to mess up our truce but I want you to just think about it. There's no shame in forgiving. No shame in letting the past *stay* in the past.'

His eyes grew dark and haunted. 'What about my demons?'

'Do you have a cast-iron guarantee that they will be vanquished by the path you've chosen?'

He frowned for several seconds before his eyes narrowed. 'You're right. Let's not mess up the truce, shall we?'

'Theo...'

'*Anjo*. Enough. Have some more wine.' He smiled.

And, just like that, her pulse surged faster. Hell, everything he did made her pulse race. She took a sip and licked her lips as the languorous effect of the wine and the captivating man sitting opposite her took hold.

She really needed to stop drinking so much. She pulled her gaze from the rugged perfection of his face as Camila returned to offer them coffee.

Inez declined and looked over to see his eyes riveted on her.

'I think we need to get you back to the boat.'

Laughter that seemed to be coming easier around him escaped her throat. 'You make me sound as if I've been naughty,' she said after Camila collected their empty plates and left.

'Trust me, I would tell you if you'd been.'

'Well, the night is still young and I'm not ruling anything out.' She laughed again.

His mouth curved in one of those devastating smiles as he reached for his wallet and extracted several crisp notes.

'I say it's definitely time to get you back and into bed.'

Her breath caught. He didn't mean what she thought he meant. Of course he didn't. But images suddenly bombarded her brain that had her blushing.

As she said goodbye to Camila and headed outside, she prayed he wouldn't see her reaction to his words.

'Hey, slow down, you'll break your ankle rushing in those heels.' He caught up with her outside and slid a hand around her waist.

The warmth of his body was suddenly too much to bear. 'It's okay, I'm fine.' Her voice emerged a touch too forceful and he glanced sharply at her.

'What's wrong?'

She raked an exasperated hand through her hair and tried to stem the words forming at the back of her mind. They came out anyway. 'You're supposed to be my enemy. And yet you brought me to one of my favourite places in the world. You're being so kind and attentive and I can't help...I... I want you.'

The transformation that occurred sent her senses reeling. From the charming, desirous dinner companion, Theo turned into a hungry predatory beast in the space of a heartbeat.

He pulled her into a dark alley between two high-rises. Her heart hammered as he held her against the wall and leaned in close.

'You don't want to say things like that to me right now, Inez,' he grated harshly.

His mouth was so tantalising close, she shut her eyes to avoid closing the gap between them and experiencing another potent kiss. 'I don't want to be saying them either. I can't seem to stop myself because it's the truth.'

'That's just the wine talking,' he replied.

She nodded then groaned when he leaned in closer. Heat from his body burned hers and his breath washed over her face. When his stubbled jaw brushed her cheek, she bit hard on her lower lip to stop another groan from escaping.

'Open your eyes, Inez.'

She shook her head. '*Nao...por favor...*'

'What are you begging me for?' he whispered in her ear.

A deep shudder coursed down her spine. 'I don't know...' She stopped and sucked in a desperate breath. 'Kiss me,' she pleaded.

With a dark moan, he touched his mouth to the corner of hers. Fleeting. Feather-light. Barely enough.

Her hands gripped his waist and held on tight. '*Please*,' she whispered.

'*Anjo*, if I start I won't be able to stop. And neither of us wants to spend the night in jail for lewd behaviour.'

She finally opened her eyes. He stood, tall, dark, devastatingly good-looking and tense, with a hunger she'd never seen in a man's eyes. That it was directed at her made her pulse race that much harder.

'Theo.' Her fingers crept up to his face, dying to touch his warm olive skin. 'Let it go. Whatever my father did, revenge would only bring you fleeting satisfaction.'

His jaw tightened but he didn't look as forbidding as he'd looked before. 'It's the only thing I've dreamed about for the last twelve years.'

Her hand crept up to settle over his heart. 'Have you stopped to think that obsessing about it may just be feeding the demons?'

One large hand settled over hers and he stared fiercely down at her. 'Are you offering me another way to quiet them, *anjo*?'

'Maybe.'

He captured her hand and planted a kiss in her palm. When he glanced down at her, a feverish light burned in his molten eyes. 'He doesn't deserve to have you as a daughter.'

'I can say the same about your parents but we play the hand that is dealt us the best way we can. And when it gets really bad I try to remember a happier time. Surely you must have some happy memories with your mother? And was your father really all bad?'

His mouth tightened. Then, slowly, he shook his head. 'No. It wasn't always bad.'

'Tell me.'

He frowned slightly. 'They thought Sakis would be their last child. I came as a surprise, or so my mother tells me. She used to call me her special boy. My father...he took me everywhere with him. He had a sports car—an Aston Martin—that I loved riding in. We'd take long drives along the coast...' He stopped and his eyes glazed over.

She kept silent, letting him relive the memories, hoping that he would find a way to soften the hard ache inside him. But when his eyes refocused, she saw the raw pain reflected in them.

'I'm not a father, and I probably never will be. But even I know those things are easy to do when life's a smooth sail. The true test comes when things get rough. I find it hard to believe that my brothers and I were ever in any way special to our parents when they turned their backs on us when we needed them most. He could've saved me, Inez—' He stopped abruptly and her heart clenched with pain for him.

'How?'

'One simple phone call to warn me and I wouldn't be here...I wouldn't be afraid of going to

sleep each night because of hellish nightmares…'
A deep shudder raked his tall frame.

'Oh, Theo,' she murmured. He leaned into the
hand she placed on his cheek for several seconds
then he pulled away and tilted her chin up.

The vulnerable man was gone. 'This changes
nothing. I am what I am. Do you still want me?'

She swallowed. 'Yes.'

Something resembling relief swept through his
eyes. 'You have half an hour and a lot of head-
clearing air before we're back on the boat. I suggest
you use that time to think carefully about whether
you want this to go any further. Because, once we
cross the line, there won't be any going back.'

CHAPTER TEN

THEO THREW THE reins of the launch to the waiting crew member and turned to help her out. Her bare feet hit the landing pad and she swayed a little when the boat rocked.

Contrary to her thinking he would rush her back to the boat after his pronouncement, Theo had taken his time walking her back down the streets to the promenade and onto the beach that led to the pier.

Hell, he'd even taken the time to help her out of her shoes so they could walk along the shore.

But the plaguing doubt that perhaps he didn't want her as much as her screaming senses craved him evaporated the moment she looked into his eyes.

Burnt a dark gold by volcanic desire, he stared down at her for several seconds before he demanded in a hoarse voice, 'Well?'

She licked her lips and watched his agitated exhalation. 'I still want you.'

'Are you sure? There will be no room for regret in the morning, Inez. I won't allow it.'

'I'm not drunk, Theo. Besides, I wanted you this morning and I wasn't drunk then. Or last week, or the first night we met.'

His nostrils flared as he dragged her close on the deserted lower deck. 'That first night, you felt what I felt?'

An impossible attraction that had no rhyme or reason? 'Yes,' she answered simply.

He swung her up in his arms and strode into the galley and down the steps into his large, opulent suite. Somewhere along the line, her shoes fell from her useless hands. She knew they had because her fingers were buried in his hair, and her mouth was on his by the time he kicked the door shut behind them.

Their tongues slid erotically against each other as they explored one another, his forceful, hers growing bolder by the second. Because she knew he liked it, she nipped his bottom lip with her teeth.

His deep growl echoed inside her before he pulled away. Eyes on hers, he slowly lowered her body down his sleek length. Hard muscles and firm thighs registered against her heated skin and even after her feet hit the plush carpet she held onto him, fearful she'd dissolve into a pool of need the moment she let go.

'I need to undress you,' he said raggedly.

Unable to look away from him, she nodded. The dark purple knee-length dress was form-fitting and secured by a side zip. After a couple of minutes of frustrated searching, she laughed and pointed to the hidden zip beneath her arm.

With a dark curse, he lowered it and tugged the dress over her head.

He dropped the dress. He swallowed. Then he stared so hard she stopped breathing.

'*Thee mou*, you're so beautiful,' he groaned.

The feeling suffusing her was different from her reaction to the incandescent hunger in his eyes. It was pleasure that he liked what he saw, that he might well pardon her for her inexperience.

Eager to experience more of the feeling, she reached for her bra clasp.

'No,' he commanded. He grabbed her hands and placed them on his chest. 'That's my job. *You* don't move.'

He drifted his fingers up her sides, eliciting a deep shiver that brought a satisfied smile to his lips. Her bra came undone a second later and he glanced down at her heavy breasts.

'Do you know how long I've waited to taste

these?' He cupped one globe in his hand, lowered his head and flicked his wet tongue repeatedly over her nipple.

Fire scorched through her veins and her head fell back as pleasure surged high.

'Theo,' she gasped as he delivered the same treatment to her other nipple. Caught in the maelstrom of sensation, she wasn't aware her nails were digging into his pecs until he hissed against her skin.

'Take my shirt off, *querida*. I want to feel those nails on my bare skin.'

Fingers trembling, she complied with his demand, pulling the shirt off his broad shoulders and down his arms before giving in to the need to caress his bronzed skin. Heated and satin-smooth, his muscles bunched beneath her touch as she explored him.

But, much too soon, he was pulling her hands away, catching her around the waist and striding to the bed.

Depositing her in the middle of the king-sized bed, he stood staring down at her, one hand on his belt. The power and girth of him knocked the breath out of her lungs and a momentary unease sliced across her pleasure.

So far, Theo hadn't commented on her inexperience but the evidence would become glaringly apparent in a few minutes. She opened her mouth to tell him but he was crawling over the bed towards her, his intense focus paralysing her to everything but the pleasure his eyes promised.

He kissed her again, deeper, more forceful than all the times before. She gave in to her need and buried her hands in his hair, scraped her nails along his scalp and won herself a deep groan of pleasure from him. His lips moved along her jaw to nip her earlobe before going lower to explore her neck and lower.

Once again, he suckled her breasts and once again she lost the ability to think straight.

'You love that, don't you?' he observed huskily when he raised his head.

'*Sim*,' she groaned.

'There are many more pleasures, *anjo*. So many more.'

His lips trailed down her midriff…he kissed his way to the top of her panties before he gripped the flimsy material in his hands. Expecting them to be ripped off—a notion that made her wildly breathless—she was surprised when he slowly and gently lowered them down her legs and drew them off.

Equally slowly, taking his time to savour her,

he kissed her from ankle to inner thigh. When his mouth skated over her secret place, her hips arched off the bed in delirious anticipation.

She'd never imagined she'd want a man to go down on her but now she couldn't imagine *not* feeling Theo's mouth on her heated core.

At the touch of his mouth, she cried out, her body twisting as pleasure scythed through her. He tasted her so very thoroughly, his tongue, teeth and lips working in perfect harmony to drive her straight out her mind.

She slid ever closer to breaking point, both fearing and yearning for what lay ahead.

Theo slipped his hands beneath her bottom and pulled her even closer to his seeking mouth. With quick expert flicks of his tongue, he sent her careening over the edge.

Her scream was an alien sound, hoarse and pleasure-ravaged, her grip on the sheets tight as she was buffeted by blissful sensation.

He continued to kiss her until she calmed, then kissed his way up her body to seal her mouth with his.

The earthy taste of her surrender seemed to trigger an even more primitive reaction in him. By the time he lifted his head, his eyes were almost black with hunger.

'Did Blanco make you feel like this?' he grated.

She shook her head. 'No.'

Satisfaction gleamed in his eyes. 'By the time I finish making you mine, you will not remember anyone else who came before me.'

Knowing he would discover her inexperience in a matter of minutes, she took a sustaining breath and blurted, 'I never slept with Constantine. Theo, I'm a virgin.'

He froze in the act of reaching for a condom. Several expressions raced over his face before he spoke. 'So I'm to be your first lover?'

She gave a jerky nod. 'Yes.'

Theo absorbed the news and tried to weigh which was the greater emotion swirling through him—shock or elation. The shock was understandable. But the elation, the fact that he was *pleased* he was to be her first? It'd never crossed his mind that she would be a virgin. But suddenly a few things fell into place. Her blushes, her furtive innocent looks, her surprise at his demanding kisses.

Another feeling rose to curl itself around his chest. Possessiveness.

The fact that he was to be her first made him want to beat his chest like a wild jungle animal.

He ripped the condom packet open and stared down at her.

The look of apprehension forced him to slow down. He was moving too fast, possibly scaring her. Time to turn it down a notch.

'I'll go as slow as you want, *querida*, but I won't stop,' he warned. He couldn't. He'd come too far. He wanted her too much.

I would've kept you... Perhaps even for ever.

His own words echoed in his head and yet another emotion swept over him. If they'd met in another time, would she be the one? The idea of Inez as his wife, the mother of his children if he'd been normal, washed over him. His heart raced as he stared down at her, so beautiful, so giving.

Thee mou, what the hell was he doing wishing for the impossible? He wasn't normal...

'I don't want you to stop,' she replied. Then she performed one of those actions that illuminated her inexperience. Her gaze flicked down to his groin and she bit her lip. She had no idea how hot that little gesture made him.

A groan ripped from his chest and effectively wiped away the useless yearning.

Planting his hands on either side of her, he parted her thighs with his and settled himself at her entrance.

'Hold onto me, and feel free to dig your nails into my back if it all gets too much.' He attempted a smile and felt a touch of relief when she returned it.

The seductive bow of her mouth called to him and, leaning down, he drove his tongue between her lips. Gratifyingly, she opened up to him immediately. He deepened the kiss and swallowed her groan.

Carefully, he nudged her entrance, fed himself slowly into her wet heat.

He froze as she tensed. 'Easy, *anjo*. Relax,' he murmured soothingly against her mouth.

With a rough little sound she complied. Except now the tension was channelled into him. The feel of her closing around him threatened to tear him apart. Lying in the cradle of her hips, a sense of wonderment stole over him he'd never felt before. And he wasn't afraid to admit it scared the hell out of him.

'Theo.' She said his name with a touch of imploration and frustration that ramped up his tension. Never had he wanted to make it more right for a sexual partner.

He pushed deeper and felt the resistance of her innocence. Those nails dug in. Pleasure roared through him as he pulled back and looked into her beguiling face.

A face that held a touch of apprehension and breathless anticipation.

'Please, Theo. I want you.'

Her husky entreaty was the final straw. With a hoarsely muttered apology, he breached the flimsy barrier and buried himself deep inside her.

She made a sound of pain that pierced his heart then her head was rolling back on a long moan that echoed around the room. He waited until she had adjusted to him. Then he pulled out and rocked back in.

'*Meu deus*,' she voiced her wonder.

'Inez...' he waited until her glazed eyes focused on him, then he repeated the move '...tell me how you feel.'

'*Fantastico*,' she groaned, and Theo was sure she didn't realise she spoke her native tongue.

Her fingers spiked into his hair and when he thrust into her, she met him with a bold thrust of her own. His breath hissed out.

'You're a fast learner, *querida*.' He increased the tempo and gritted his teeth for control when she immediately matched his pace.

All too soon her back arched off the bed, her chest rising and falling in agitation as she neared her climax. Hot internal muscles rippled along his length and he shut his eyes for one split second to rein in his failing grip on reality. Leaning lower, he took one tight nipple and rolled it in his mouth. Her cry of pleasure was music to his ears. He treated its twin to the same attention then lowered himself on her. Sliding his arms under her shoulders he brought her flush against him and thrust in fast, deep movements.

She screamed once before her teeth closed over the skin on his shoulder. Deep shudders rocked through her as her bliss pulled her completely under.

She bit him harder, her nails scouring his back as she rode the unending wave.

When her head fell back towards the pillow, he raised his head and looked at her face. The expression of wonder and ecstasy sheening her eyes finally sent him over the edge.

With a roar torn from deep inside him, he gave into the shattering release.

He clamped his mouth shut as new, confusing words threatened to burst free. Praise? Gratitude? Hell, *adoration*? When had he ever felt those emotions in connection to a woman he'd just bedded?

He buried his face in her neck and let the ripples of pleasure wash him away in silence. Until he could fathom just what the hell was going on beyond the chemical level with Inez, he intended to keep his mouth shut.

Inez slowly caressed her hands down his back, not minding at all that she was pinned to the bed by his heavy, muscled weight. Right at that moment, she couldn't think of a better way to suffocate to death. The thought made her giggle.

Theo turned his head and nuzzled her cheek. 'Not the reaction I expect after a mind-blowing orgasm but at least it's a happy sound.'

Immediately her mind turned to the dozens of women he'd pleasured before her. Hot green jealousy burned through her euphoric haze and her hands stilled.

'Hey, what did I say?' His voice rumbled through her. When she didn't immediately answer, he raised his head and stared down at her. 'Inez?'

'It's nothing important,' she replied. And it wasn't.

Earlier this evening, she'd tried to make him see a different way. But he'd refused. This thing between them would last until his vendetta with her father was satisfied. She had no business thinking about what women had come before her or who would replace her once he was done with her family and with Rio.

She endured his intent gaze until he nodded and rose. The feeling of him pulling out of her created a further emptiness inside that made her heart lurch wildly.

Deus, she needed to get a grip. Her hormones were a little askew because she had experienced her first sexual act.

No need to descend into full melt-down mode.

She watched him leave the bed, his body in part shadow in the lamp-lit room. He entered the bathroom and returned a minute later with a damp towel. When she realised his intention, she surged up and tried to reach for the towel.

'No,' he murmured softly. 'Lie back.'

Her face heating up, she slowly subsided against the pillows and allowed him to wash her.

Incredibly, the hunger returned as he gently saw to her needs and when he finally glanced back at her his nostrils were flared, a sign she'd come to recognise as a control-gathering technique.

Her nipples puckered and her body began to react to the look on his face.

'You need time to recover.'

Her body refuted that but her head knew she needed to take time to regroup. When she nodded, he looked almost disappointed. He returned the towel to the bathroom but left the light on as he came back to bed. Getting into bed, he pulled the covers over their bodies and pulled her into his arms.

She settled her hand over his chest and felt his steady heartbeat beneath her fingers. They lay there in silence until another giggle broke free from her jumbled thoughts.

'I'm beginning to get a complex, *anjo*.' He brushed his lips over her forehead.

'I believe this is the part where we make small talk after sex but I can't come up with a single subject.'

She felt his smile against her temple. 'Wrong. Normally this would be the part when I either leave or do what I just did to you all over again.'

Her heart caught. 'And?'

'I'm trying to rein in my primal instincts and not flatten you on your back again.'

Feeling bolder than was wise, Inez opened her mouth to tell him that he needn't hold it back for much longer. Instead a wide yawn took her unawares.

It was his turn to laugh. 'I think the decision on small talk has been shelved in favour of sleep.' He turned her face up to his and pressed his mouth to hers. Within seconds the kiss threatened to combust into something else. He pulled back with a groan and tucked her against him. 'Sleep, Inez. Now,' he commanded gruffly.

With a secretly pleased smile, she slid her arm around his waist, already feeling the drowsy lure of sleep encroaching.

She woke to moonlight streaming through the windows. The bedside lamp glowed and she judged that she'd been asleep for a few hours.

Beside her, Theo lay on his side, tufts of sleep-ruffled hair thrown over his forehead. In the soft lighting he looked younger and peaceful but still so damn sexy her breath caught just looking at him.

She suddenly needed to commit his likeness to paper. Her pad was next door in her suite. Slowly extracting herself from the arm he'd thrown over her, she pulled on his shirt and went to retrieve it.

Returning just as quietly, she settled herself cross-legged at the foot of the bed and began to draw. Every now and then she paused and took a breath, unable to fathom the circumstances she found herself in.

She was in bed with a man who was bent on

destroying her family. And yet the overwhelming guilt she expected to feel was missing. Instead she yearned to save him from the demons that she'd glimpsed in his eyes when he spoke of his nightmares.

She swallowed as a well of sadness built inside her. Despite his outward show of invincibility she'd seen his battle. A battle he believed only revenge would win for him…

She froze as Theo made a sound. It was somewhere between a moan of pain and the bark of anger. His hand jerked out and then closed into a tight fist.

His whole body tensed for a breathless second before his chest started to rise and fall in agitated pants.

She dropped the sketchpad. 'Theo?'

'*No. No! No! Thee mou, no!*' The words were hoarse pleas, soaked with naked fear.

Both hands shot out in a bracing position and his head twisted from side to side.

'Theo!' She rose to her knees, unsure of what to do.

'No. Stop! *Arghh!*' With a forceful lunge, he jolted upright with a blood-curdling cry. Sweat poured down his face and he sucked in huge gulping breaths.

'*Deus*, are you okay?' The question was hopelessly inadequate but it was all she could manage at that moment. Because her heart was turning over with pain for what she'd just witnessed him go through.

She reached out and he jerked back away from her. 'Don't touch me!'

'Theo, it's me. Inez.' Tentatively, she reached out and touched his arm.

He shuddered violently and lurched away from her, staring blankly at her for several seconds before his face grew taut and haunted.

'Inez,' he said with a dark snarl. 'I fell asleep?'' There was self-loathing in the question, as if he hated himself for having lowered his guard enough to let the demons in.

Her stomach flipped and her fingers curled into her palm. 'Yes. You…you had a nightmare.'

His mouth twisted with a cruel grimace. 'No kidding. What the hell are you doing here?' he snapped, looking around the room with unfocused eyes.

She frowned. 'We…um, we fell asleep together after…' She stopped as heat rushed up her face.

He turned back to her and his gaze slowly travelled over her. He brushed the hair out of his eyes and gradually the dull green lightened into golden hazel. 'We had sex. I remember now.'

She flinched and watched him with wary eyes.

With sure, predatory moves, he lifted the tangled sheet off his body and prowled to where she was poised on her knees. He stopped a hairsbreadth from her.

'Can I…can I touch you?' she asked, unwilling to have him pull away from her, but a part of her longed to soothe the turbulent blackness in his eyes.

His mouth pinched and he took several steadying breaths before he spoke. 'You want to comfort me?'

'If you'll let me.'

Another deep shudder and he closed his eyes. His head lowered until his forehead rested between her breasts. His arms closed around her and tightened so hard she couldn't move. They stayed like that until his breathing steadied.

'Theo?'

'Hmm?'

'Tell me about your dream.'

He tensed immediately and she bit her lip. He raised his head and stared at her.

'Take my shirt off,' he commanded, his voice hardly above a tortured whisper.

Concern spiked through, despite the heat his words generated. 'Theo, you just had a nightmare—'

'One I want to forget.' His hands were on the back of her thighs, hard and demanding as they caressed up to her bottom. He cupped the globes with more roughness than before but there was no pain in the caress. 'Inez, if you want to help me, do it.'

She drew the shirt over her head and dropped it. His eyes devoured her breasts and his tongue darted out to rest against his bottom lip.

Between her legs, liquid heat dampened her folds and he groaned in dark appreciation as his seeking fingers found her core.

'So ready. So tight,' he rasped. With almost effortless ease, he picked her up, pivoted off the bed and sat on the side. Grabbing a condom, he slipped it on and positioned her legs on either side of him.

'You will *make* me forget.' The words were almost a plea but with a promise of things to come. 'Yes?'

Before she could do so much as nod, he pressed her down on top of him. She cried out as he filled her with his hot, heavy length. His hard grip on her hips controlled the rhythm, which grew more frantic with each thrust.

'Theo,' she gasped as pleasure scalded her insides and rushed her towards ecstasy.

'Shh, no talking,' he instructed.

Biting her lip, she stared into his face.

Torment, anger, pleasure and more than a dose of anxiety mingled into an oddly fascinating tableau. He was still caught up in the hell of his nightmare and her heart broke over his anguish.

She tried to catch his gaze, to transmit a different sort of comfort from the carnal that he clearly sought but he avoided her eyes. Instead he buried his face between her breasts and mercilessly teased her nipples until she whimpered at the torture.

He increased his thrusts, bouncing her on top of him with almost superhuman strength that had her reeling.

Her orgasm crashed into her, flattening her under its fierce onslaught before proceeding to completely drown her.

Through the thunderous rush in her ears, she heard his guttural roar as he achieved his own ruthless release.

Sweat slicked their skin and their breaths rushed in and out in frantic pants. This time, though, there were no pleasurable caresses and giggling was the last thing she felt like doing.

With lithe grace, he twisted around and deposited her on the bed. Without speaking, he strode into the bathroom.

Inez lay on the bed, grappling with what had just happened. In the last twenty-four hours she'd glimpsed the man tortured by his nightmares, had seen a side to Theo she was certain very few people saw. Instead of guarding her own heart, she wanted to open herself up even more to him, find a way of taking away his pain and torment.

Had she not learnt her lesson with Constantine?

No, Theo was nothing like that man who'd taken delight in humiliating her. The retraction Theo had promised had appeared in the online evening edition of the newspaper and she was sure she'd seen a look of contrition in his eyes when he'd watched her read it.

Darkness and light.

She was deeply, almost irreversibly attracted to both. Again her heart twisted and she looked towards the bathroom.

A crash came a second later, followed by a pithy curse. She was off the bed and running into the bathroom before she could think twice.

'I'm fine!' he ground out.

She hesitated in the doorway and watched him. His fingers were curled around the marble sink and his head was bent forward. 'What's wrong, Theo?'

'Dammit, woman, I'm not made of glass. And I've been grappling with my nightmares long before you came along, so leave me alone!'

Hurt shredded her inside. 'Don't push me away.'

He locked eyes with her in the mirror and sighed. 'You're too stubborn for your own good, you know that?'

'Maybe, but before you throw me out I need the bathroom,' she lied.

'Fine; it's all yours.'

He started to turn. That was when she saw his scars. '*Meu deus*, what happened to you?' she whispered raggedly.

His glance ripped from her face to where she pointed to his left hip. The marks were puckered and too evenly spaced and shaped to be an accident. But still her mind couldn't grasp the idea that someone had deliberately inflicted pain on him.

'You mean you haven't guessed already, *querida*? *Your father* happened.'

CHAPTER ELEVEN

INEZ STAGGERED BACKWARDS until her legs hit the vanity unit and she collapsed onto it. 'I don't… you're saying my *father* did this to you?' She shook her head in fierce disbelief.

Theo's mouth twisted. 'Not personally, no. He hired thugs to do it.'

She felt the blood drain from her head. Had she not been seated, she would've swayed under the unbelievable accusation.

'But…why?'

He grabbed a towel and secured it around his waist. 'You did your research on my family. You know what happened to my father.'

She nodded. 'He was indicted for fraud, bribery and embezzlement.'

'Among other things. He was also involved with some extremely shady people.'

He turned and strode from the bathroom.

She followed him, the fear she'd harboured for

a long time blooming in her chest. 'And my father was one of these shady people?'

Theo turned and watched her. Shocked knowledge flared in her eyes. For a brief moment, he sympathised with what she was going through. Having the truth blown up in front of you wasn't easy.

In his deepest, darkest moments he still couldn't believe how painfully raw he felt at his father's abandonment.

'My father owed him a lot of money on some crooked scheme they were working on when he was arrested and all our assets were frozen. Your father took exception to being out of pocket. When he realised he wouldn't be paid, he decided to pursue a different route.'

Her haunted eyes dropped to the scars covered by the towel and quickly looked away.

'So I'm here to pay for my father's sins,' she whispered raggedly.

That had initially been his plan. Somewhere along the line that particular plan had become questionable. But he'd be damned before he'd admit that.

'Your father made me pay for my father's. Money and power were his bottom line, and he wanted payback. Nothing else mattered to him, not even the tortured screams of a frightened boy...'

He compressed his lips as her mouth dropped open and anguish creased her face. 'How old were you?'

He raked a hand through his hair. Even as a voice shrieked in his head to stop baring his raw wounds, he was opening his mouth.

'I was seventeen. I was returning from a night out with friends when his goons grabbed me. He had me smuggled from Athens to Spain and threw me into a hole on some abandoned farm in Madrid. Ari found me there two weeks after I was taken. After he damned near bled every single cent he could find from every relative and casual acquaintance in order to stump up the two million dollars ransom that your father demanded.'

Her hands flew to her head, her fingers spiking through the long tresses to grip them in a convulsive stranglehold. 'Please tell me when you say a *hole*...you don't mean that *literally*?' The words were a desperate plea, as if she didn't want to believe how real the monster that was her father.

His smile cracked his lips. 'Oh, yes, *anjo*. A twelve-foot-deep *literal* hole in the ground with vertical sides and no hand or footholds. No light.

No heat. One meal a day with a bucket for my necessaries.'

'No…'

'*Yes!* And you know what his men did for *fun* when they were bored?'

She shook her head wildly, her eyes wide and horror-struck as he loosened the towel from around his waist and exposed his puckered skin. 'Cigar tattoos, they called them.'

Tears welled in her eyes and fell down her cheeks. Still shaking her head, she walked to the bed and sank down on it. She buried her face in her hands and a gut-wrenching sob ripped from her throat. After the first one, they came thick and fast.

His chest tightened with emotions he was very loath to name. Each sob caught him on the raw, until he couldn't bear to hear another one.

'Inez! Stop crying,' he instructed hoarsely after five minutes.

She shook her head and sniffled some more.

'Stop it or I'll throw you overboard and you can swim to shore.'

That got her attention. She brushed her hands across her cheeks and speared him with wide, imploring eyes.

'If the only people you saw were his men, how did you know it was my father?'

He couldn't fault her for trying to find a different reality to the one he'd smashed her world with. Hell, he'd done that for a long time after his father had been indicted. 'I followed the money.'

She frowned. 'What?'

'I traced the ransom my brother paid through dummy corporations and offshore accounts. It took a few years but I finally found where it ended up.'

'In my father's account?'

'Yes. And since then I've made it my business to find out how every single cent was spent.'

Her shoulders slumped and tears welled again. He could tell the ground had well and truly shifted beneath her feet.

After several seconds, she raised her head.

'Okay. I'll do whatever you want. For however long you want.'

It was his turn to feel the ground shift under his feet. Shock slammed through him as he realised just how much he wanted to take her. To hang onto her.

But not for the sake of revenge. For an altogether different reason; because he wanted her. Not for her father but *for her*.

He shook his head. 'Inez...'

'I can never buy back those two weeks that were taken from you or the horror you've had to live with. But I can try and find a way to make up for what was done to you.'

'How? By giving me your body whenever and wherever I ask for it?'

She paled a little. But the brave, spirited woman he'd come to see underneath all that false gloss raised her chin. 'If that's what you want.'

His mouth twisted. 'I don't want a damned sacrificial lamb. And I sure as hell don't want you throwing yourself on your sword for that bastard's sake!'

'Then what do you want? You have his company. His campaign is falling apart. He will be left with nothing by the time you're done with him. How much more suffering do you need before you let go of this anger? When will you feel pacified?'

Theo started to answer, then realised he had no answer. The satisfaction he'd thought he'd feel was hollowly absent, as was the deep-seated sense of triumph he'd always thought he would feel when this moment came.

Looking into her face, he saw the pain and confusion reflected there and his puzzlement increased. The ground was still tilting beneath his feet but he'd been on this path for too long to let go.

Hadn't he?

He forced his gaze to meet hers.

'I will let you know when I'm adequately appeased.'

Over the next week, she watched as he slowly dismantled her father's campaign piece by piece. Allegations of impropriety surfaced, triggering an investigation. Although nothing was found to indict Benedicto, his credibility suffered a death blow and any meaningful points he'd managed to retain in the polls dropped to nothing.

On the Monday morning after returning from their sailing trip, the calls to her cell phone started. Both her father and Pietro bombarded her with messages and texts, demanding to know what was going on.

She hadn't needed Theo to warn her not to take their calls. After his revelation, each time she saw her father's name pop up on her screen, her stomach churned with pain and disgust.

Although she'd long suspected that her father's business dealings weren't as pure as the driven snow, she'd never in her wildest dreams entertained the idea that he would condone the brutality that Theo had described. Each time she saw his scars—and she'd seen them every night since their return, when he'd moved her into his suite— a merciless vice had squeezed her heart.

And that vice had tightened every time he'd cried out in the middle of the night after another nightmare.

She'd been surprised that first night after their return when he'd pulled her close after a fiery lovemaking and instructed her to go to sleep.

When he kept her with him the following night, she'd boldly asked him why.

'I don't want to be alone,' he'd stated baldly. And each time he'd come awake he'd reached for her, wrapping his trembling body around her and holding on tight until his nightmare receded and his breathing returned to normal.

More and more, her foolish heart had begun to believe that her presence was making the nightmares, if not any less horrific, then at least tolerable.

Or she could just be living in a fantasy land where her mind and heart had no idea what language the other was speaking. Because she was beginning to believe that her heart was more involved in Theo's welfare than was wise. And yet she couldn't control it enough to make it stop wrenching in pain when he suffered another nightmare, or soar with joy when he took her to the heights of ecstasy. Even the knowledge that some time in the very near future, after his goal to destroy her father was achieved, Theo would pack up his bags and leave Rio for good, made her heart ache in a way that was almost a physical pain.

Santa Maria, she was losing her mind—

'There you are. Teresa told me you're still here. I thought you'd be at the centre by now.' She'd shared more details of her volunteer work with him during the times when he'd been *Normal Theo*, not *Revenge Theo*. And she'd been ridiculously thrilled when he hadn't been judgemental or condescending.

She looked up as he entered the living room and crossed to where she sat, applying finishing touches to the sketch she'd been working on since breakfast an hour ago. She'd thought he'd left for the day but obviously she'd been mistaken.

Glancing up at his lean, solid frame and gorgeous face, her heart performed that painfully giddy flip again and she glanced away. 'I took a day off. I'm…I'm still thinking of resigning.'

He stilled then dropped to his haunches in front of her. 'Why?'

She struggled to breathe as his scent surrounded her, making her yearn to lean in closer. 'This whole thing with my father has brought unwanted attention to people who are already struggling with life's difficulties. I don't think it's fair on the children.'

A look resembling regret passed through his eyes before he blinked it away. After a full minute, he murmured, 'No, it's not. But you won't resign.'

Her heart caught. 'Why not?'

'Because I won't allow you to give up something you love doing. The publicity about your father will go away. I'll make sure of it.'

She met mesmerising hazel eyes. 'Why are you doing this?'

He shrugged. 'Perhaps I'm beginning to realise that I was mistaken about how much collateral damage I was prepared to accept.'

Collateral damage. She was grappling with that when he spoke again.

'I have something for you.'

She glanced warily at him. 'Beware of Greeks bearing gifts. I'm sure I've read that warning somewhere.'

His smile held a certain chill but was heart-stopping nonetheless. 'For the most part, I'd urge you to heed that warning. But this one is completely harmless.' He pulled something from his back pocket and presented it to her. The look in his eyes made her stomach flip as she glanced from his face to the box.

'What is it?' she asked.

'Open it and see.'

She opened the velvet case and gaped at the platinum-linked, three-tiered diamond choker nestling between the two catches.

'Are you trying to make some sort of *macho* statement?'

He shook his head in confusion. 'Sorry, *anjo,* you've lost me.'

'This is a *choker.* You want everyone to see that you own me?'

He frowned. 'What the hell are you talking about?'

'Why a choker? Why not a simple diamond pendant?'

'I asked my jeweller to send a few pieces. I liked the look of that one. So I chose it. No big deal, no mind games. I thought you'd like it,' he finished tersely.

She bit her lip and wondered if she was reading too much into it. Much like she was reading far too much into her feelings for Theo and what would happen when things ended.

'It's a beautiful piece of jewellery. But frankly it's a bit ostentatious for my taste.' She snapped the box shut and held it out to him. 'Besides, since my role as paparazzi bait is over, I don't see where I would wear something like that.'

His jaw tightened and he pushed the box back at her. 'I was just coming to that. Ari is getting married next weekend. You're coming with me as my plus one.'

She couldn't stop her mouth from gaping open any more than she could stop breathing. 'You want me to drop everything and fly to Greece with you?'

'I'm sure you can work something out with the charity. I'm happy to make a donation to cover your absence if you like.'

'I...'

'And we're not going to Greece. Ari and Perla are getting married at their resort in Bermuda.'

'Different continent, same response.'

His eyes narrowed. 'Do I need to remind you that we're only three weeks into our agreement?'

Her fingers trembled and she threw the box down on the sofa. 'No, you don't need to remind me. Call me foolish, but I thought we were getting beyond that.'

'I'm trying to, Inez.'

'Then ask me nicely. For all you know, I may be busy next weekend and would need to rearrange my plans for you.'

He raised an eyebrow. 'Busy doing what?'

'Splitting the atom. Shaving my legs. Rehearsing to join a circus troupe. What does it matter? You didn't bother to ask. You only brought me trinkets and ordered me to be ready to fly off to Bermuda.' Her mouth trembled and she firmed it.

'You're angry.'

'You're very observant.'

'Tell me why.'

She laughed. Even to her ears it sounded as if it could've easily cut glass. His eyes narrowed as she shook her head. 'What would be the point?'

'The point would be that I would listen.'

She placed her feet on the carpet and tried to stand. He caught her hips and kept her seated in front of him.

This close she could see the hypnotic gold flecks in his eyes. She wanted to drown in them. Wanted to drown in him. She tried to calm her racing pulse.

His gaze dropped to her mouth, then down to

her chest and a different sort of fever took hold of her.

'That necklace—'

'Is just a necklace. I thought I'd give it to you now so you could get an outfit to match for the wedding.'

'And the trip?'

'I need a plus one. I need *you*. And you can hate me if you want but I'm not prepared to leave you here so Benedicto can hound you.'

'I can take care of myself.'

His eyes narrowed. 'I don't doubt that. But can you tell me that he won't view your refusal to take his calls this last week as a betrayal?'

Her heart skittered. 'And you think he'll harm me in some way?'

He glanced meaningfully at her arm, then back to her face. 'Sorry, *anjo*, I'm not prepared to take that chance.'

Darkness and light. Tenderness and ruthlessness. It was what kept her emotions on a knife-edge where this man was concerned.

'Will you come to Bermuda with me? Please?'

She glanced at the velvet box. 'I will. But I'm not wearing that necklace.'

'Fine. We'll find you something else.'

'I don't need anything—' Her argument died

on her lips when he picked up her sketchpad. She grabbed at it but he held it out of her reach. 'Theo, hand it over.' She breathed a secret sigh of relief when her panic didn't bleed through her voice.

'You're supposed to be designing me a boat.'

'I'm still working on it. I'll show it to you when it's done.'

His gaze brushed her face and settled on her mouth. The intensity of it made her insides contract. After a minute he handed the pad over and rose. 'I look forward to it. We're dining in tonight. I'm in the mood for an early night.'

He left the room just as silently as he'd entered. She realised her fingers were clamped white around her sketchpad and slowly relaxed them.

She flipped through the pages until she came to the one she'd been drawing. It was one of many featuring Theo asleep. She stared at it, seeing the vulnerability and gentleness in his face that he covered up so efficiently when he was awake. When he was asleep he was all light, no darkness. There was a boyishness about him that she only caught rare glimpses of during the day.

Darkness and light. Unfortunately, her heart refused to be picky about which it preferred because, awake or asleep, Theo had captured her emotions so efficiently she was beginning to fear she was falling in love with him.

The nightmare started the way it always did. A glow of light signalled the men's arrival. Followed by the rope ladder and the heavy descent of thick boots, tree trunk thighs and towering thugs.

Each time he'd fought back. A few times he'd landed blows of his own. But each time they'd eventually overpowered him. The tallest, toughest one, the one who favoured those smelly cigars, always laughed. It was the laughter not the pain that triggered his screams. It was a never-ending grating sound that churned through his gut and tripped his heart rate into overdrive.

He felt the scream build in his throat and readied himself for the roar.

Gentle but firm hands shook him awake.

'Theo…*querido!*'

He kept his eyes shut and reached for her, holding on tight as the images receded. The irony of it wasn't lost on him, the thought of how much he now needed the daughter of the man who was responsible for reducing him to a helpless wreck night after night for the last twelve years.

As he held on to her the thought that had plagued him for several days now took hold. He no longer wanted to pursue this vendetta. Yesterday, he'd found himself requesting that the board vote a different way to what he'd originally planned. They'd been stunned. He'd been twice as stunned.

He'd mentally shrugged and told himself there was no reason to turn his back on a healthy profit but he'd known he'd changed his mind for a different reason.

Benedicto was all but finished.

But ending it now would mean Inez would be free to walk away from him. And the very thought of that made him break out in a cold sweat.

He'd managed to buy himself a little more time by persuading her to come with him to Ari's wedding.

After that…

His insides churned as he lay in the darkness and felt her soft hands soothe him.

He pushed away thoughts he wasn't brave enough yet to truly examine.

'*Querido*, are you awake?' she breathed softly.

His heart flipped and his arms tightened convulsively around her soft, warm body. 'I'm awake, *anjo.*'

'I'm not an angel, Theo.'

'You are.'

'If I were an angel, I'd have the power to banish

your nightmares,' she replied in a voice fraught with pain.

It took several seconds to realise she ached for him.

Pulling back, he stared into her face.

'You didn't do this to me, Inez.'

Her eyes clouded. 'I know. But that doesn't mean I don't wish you healed.'

His smile felt skewed. 'There's no cure for me, sweetheart,' he said, although he was beginning to doubt that. Just as he was beginning to think that the answer lay right there in his arms. If only there was a way...

'Are you sure? There's therapy—'

'Tried it. Didn't work,' he replied. When he heard the curtness in his voice he soothed an apologetic hand down her back.

She relaxed against him and he buried his face in her hair and breathed her in.

'What happened?'

'What, with the therapy?'

She nodded.

He slowly opened his eyes and stared into the middle distance. 'They spoke about triggers, breathing techniques and anxiety-detectors. There was mention of electro-shock therapy or good old-fashioned pills. I never went back for a second session.'

Her head snapped up. 'You mean all that was at your first session?'

He smiled and kissed her gaping mouth. 'I believed what was wrong with me couldn't be fixed by therapy.'

'*Believed*?'

He realised what he'd said and his breath caught. Was he grasping at straws where there were none?

'I'm beginning to think things aren't as hopeless for me, *anjo*.'

She paled a little but continued to hold his gaze. Slowly, she nodded. Her luxuriant hair spilled over her shoulder onto his chest as she stared into his eyes. 'I really hope you find closure one day, Theo.'

Simple, frank words, said from the heart. But they froze his insides as surely and as swiftly as an arctic wind froze water.

Because he was seriously doubting that he would ever find peace without this woman in his arms.

CHAPTER TWELVE

THEY BOARDED THEO'S private jet late the next Friday. The moment they stepped on board, Inez sensed something was wrong.

Theo paced up and down, his agitation growing the closer they got to take-off.

When the pilot came through, Theo sent a piercing glance at him and the man hurried into the cockpit.

'Theo, sit down. You're making your pilot nervous.'

He barked out a short laugh and threw himself into the long sofa opposite her chair. His fingers drummed repeatedly on the armrest. 'Don't worry; he's used to it.'

'Used to what?'

'My aversion to enclosed spaces,' he answered tersely.

'Your claustrophobia.' Her heart squeezed as she watched his fingers grip the armrest and the skin around his mouth pale.

Unbuckling her seat belt, she crossed to the sofa and sat down next to him. A sheen of sweat coated his forehead and when his eyes sought hers she read the anxiety in them. Reaching around him, she secured his seat belt then took care of her own as the plane taxied onto the runway.

Taking the arm closest to hers, she pulled it over her shoulder and settled herself against him. He tugged her close immediately, his breathing harsh and uneven.

She hugged him harder, and when he tilted her face up to his she went willingly.

He kissed her with a desperation that tore through her soul. For long, anxiety-filled minutes, he took what she offered, until the need for air drove them apart.

'You get that we cannot kiss all the way to Bermuda, don't you?' she said, laughing.

'Is that a challenge? Because I bet I can,' he threw back with a heart-stopping smile.

Inez noticed that his breathing was no longer agitated and breathed a sigh of relief.

'No, it's not a challenge.' She rested her head on his shoulder and caressed his hard jaw. 'How do you normally get through flying?'

His jaw tightened for a second before he relaxed.

'Mild sleeping pills before take-off normally does the trick.'

'Why not today?'

'You're here,' he said simply. After a minute, he asked, 'Why are you helping me?'

'I cannot forget that my father did this to you. And no, I'm not offering myself as a sacrificial lamb. But I don't want to see you suffer either. I want to help any way I can.'

The reminder that her father loomed large between them grated more than he wanted to admit. 'For how long?' Theo demanded more harshly than he'd intended.

She stiffened. 'Sorry?'

'Are you counting the days until I set you free?' he pressed.

Her eyelids swooped down, concealing her expression. 'I…we have an agreement—'

'Damn the agreement. If you had a choice now, today, would you stay or would you leave?'

'Theo—'

'Answer the question, Inez.'

'I'd choose to stay…'

The bubble of joy that started to grow inside him burst when he registered her flat tone. 'But?'

'But… this could never go anywhere.'

A sense of helplessness blanketed him. 'Why not? Because I blackmailed you?'

She shook her head. 'No. Because a relationship between us would be impossible.

Theo's vision blurred at her words. He'd pushed her too far. Hung onto his vendetta for too long. His mouth soured with ashen hopelessness. 'I guess we both know where we stand.'

When she moved away, he fought not to pull her back. She stayed close—out of pity? His mouth curled. He told himself he didn't care but the voice in his head mocked him.

He cared, much more than he'd bargained for when he'd forced her to make that stupid choice. The idea of her walking away from him made his insides knot with a pain far greater than he'd ever known.

The plane hit a pocket of turbulence, throwing her against him. When she stayed close, he let her. Forcefully, he reminded himself of one thing.

He'd never meant to keep her for ever.

The Pantelides Bermuda resort was a breathtaking jewel set amid swaying palm trees and sugar-white sand. The sun beat down on them as Theo drove the open-top Jeep towards their villa.

Stunning buildings connected by dark wooden bridges under which the most spectacular water features had been constructed made for a visual masterpiece. All round them bold colour burst free in a heady mix of blues, greens and yellows that begged to be touched.

Their sprawling whitewashed villa featured high ceilings, cool tiled floors and a four-poster bed that dominated the master bedroom.

A tense Theo who hadn't said more than a dozen words to her since they landed, instructed the porter to place their cases in the master bedroom and tipped the man before walking outside onto the large wooden deck.

'There's a barbecue later this afternoon. Perla thought we might want to rest before then. You can go ahead and rest if you want to. I'll go and catch up with Sakis and Ari.'

He walked away from her and headed out of the door.

The clear indication that she wasn't welcome stung, although why she was surprised was beyond her.

He'd held ajar the possibility of continuing this thing between them and she'd slammed the door shut.

A small part of her was proud she hadn't grasped

the suggestion with both hands, while the larger part, the part that had fallen head over heels in love with Theo in spite of all the chaos surrounding them, reeled with heart-wrenching pain at what the future held.

But, as she'd told herself over and over again on the plane as he'd shut his eyes and surprisingly dozed off, she was taking the right steps now to prevent even more heartache later.

Because there was no way Theo would ever reconcile himself to having her as a constant reminder. Certainly not enough to love her.

The reality was that they'd fallen into bed as a result of some crazy chemistry. Chemistry fizzled out. Eventually, the constant reminder that a part of her was responsible for his inner demons and outer scars would grate and rip at whatever remained after the chemistry was gone.

He was better off without her.

Her heart protested loudly at that decision. Ignoring it, she went into the bedroom and lifted her case onto the bed. The cream sheath she'd bought for the wedding needed to be hung out before it creased beyond repair.

Unzipping her case, she opened it and froze. A red velvet box, similar to the black one Theo had presented her with a few days ago lay on top of her clothes.

With shaky hands she picked it up and opened it. The stunning necklace sparkling in the sunlight made her gasp.

The platinum chain had a small loop at one end, with a large teardrop diamond at the other that slipped easily through the hoop. The design was simple and elegant. And so utterly gorgeous she couldn't stop herself from caressing the flawless stone.

Swallowing a lump in her throat at the thoughtfulness behind the necklace, she jumped when a knock came at the door. Thinking it was Theo who'd forgotten to take a key, she opened the door with a smile.

Only to stop when confronted by two stunningly beautiful women, one of whom was heavily pregnant, while the other carried a small baby in her arms.

'Sorry to descend on you like this, only Theo was a bit vague about whether you were actually resting or if you were up for a visit.' The women exchanged glances. 'I've never seen him so scatty, have you?' the pregnant redhead asked the blue-eyed blonde.

'Nope, normally he's quick off the mark with

those hopeless one-liners. Today, not so much. Anyway, we thought we'd come on the off-chance that you were *not* resting and say hello...oh, my God, that necklace is gorgeous!' The redhead reached out and traced a manicured forefinger over the diamond.

Then she looked up, noticed Inez's open-mouthed gaze and laughed. 'Sorry, I'm Perla soon-to-be Pantelides. This is Brianna Pantelides, Sakis's wife. And this little heartbreaker is Dimitri.'

'I'm Inez da Costa. I'm a...' she paused, for the first time holding up her relationship with Theo to the harsh light of day and coming up short on explanations '...business associate of Theo's.'

The two women exchanged another glance and she rushed to cover the awkward silence. 'Please, come in.'

Brianna paused. 'Are you sure?'

'*Sim*...yes, I'm sure. I was just unpacking...' she started and noticed Perla's frown.

'Why are you doing that yourself? We have two butlers and three villa staff attached to each residence.'

'I think Theo sent them away,' she said, then bit her lip as Perla's eyebrows shot upward.

'Did he? Ari did that once too, when we first

arrived here four months ago. Then we proceeded to have an almighty row.' She smiled at the memory and placed her hand lovingly over her swollen belly.

Brianna laughed and walked to the sofa. Settling herself down, she opened her shirt and adjusted her son for a feed.

Perla sat on the sofa too and they both stared back at her. Their open curiosity made her nape tingle.

'We won't keep you long. I just wanted to run the itinerary by you because, frankly, I don't trust the men with the information. We have a casual dinner tonight, followed by a quick rehearsal. Most of the guests arrive in the morning and the wedding is at three o'clock, okay?'

'Okay.' She ventured a smile and Brianna's eyes widened.

'Gosh, you're stunning! How did you meet Theo again?'

'Brianna!' Perla admonished with a laugh.

'What?'

Inez fiddled with the clasp of the velvet box and pushed down the well of sadness that surged from nowhere. These two women were not only almost family, they were friends too. Whereas her family was in utter chaos and she had no friends to speak of.

She forced another smile. 'He had some business in Rio. I was…am helping him out with it.'

'Right. Okay.' Perla struggled upright and nudged Brianna. 'We'll leave you alone. I think the guys are rowing in about an hour. It's an experience you don't want to miss if you've never seen it before.'

Brianna gently dislodged her drowsy baby from her breast and laid him on her shoulder, gently patting his back as she stood.

The door opened as they neared it and Theo's large frame filled the doorway.

His gaze zeroed in on her, then dropped to the box still clutched in her hand before coming back up. Her throat dried at the sight of him and the ever present tingle that struck her deep within flared heat outward.

'Um, Theo?' Perla ventured.

'What?' he snapped without taking his eyes from Inez.

'You need to move from the doorway so we can leave.'

He snorted under his breath and entered the villa. He turned with his hand on the door, causing Brianna to roll her eyes. 'We've given Inez the schedule so you have no excuse to be late.'

'I'm never late.'

'Yeah, right. You were almost two hours late for Perla's engagement party and an hour late for Dimitri's christening.'

'Which therefore means I'll only be half an hour late for this wedding. Now, please go and pester your other halves and leave me alone.'

The women grumbled as they left. He turned from the door with a smile on his face but it slowly dimmed as his gaze connected with hers.

'Did they harass you?' he asked, a touch of wary concern in his eyes.

She shook her head. 'No. They were lovely.'

'I don't know about lovely but I tolerate them.' Contrary to his words, his voice held a fondness that made her chest tighten.

Theo understood family. Enough that he'd been devastated when his had been broken. And yet he'd wanted to rip hers apart.

Despite understanding the reason behind his motives, the thought still hurt deeply.

'Inez?'

She turned sharply and headed back to the bedroom. He followed and grabbed her wrist as she reached out to set the box down.

'What's wrong?'

Her throat clogged. 'What *isn't* wrong?'

His eyes narrowed. 'If Brianna or Perla said something to upset you—'

'No, I told you they were wonderful! They were kind and funny and…and incredible.' Tears threatened and she swallowed hard.

'You only met them for twenty minutes.'

'It was enough.'

'Enough for what?'

'Enough to know that I want what they have. And that I'll probably never have it. So far my record has been beyond appalling.'

He frowned. 'You don't have a record.'

'Constantine used me to get dirt on my father and—'

'I don't want you to say his name in my presence,' he interrupted harshly.

'And what about you? You make me hope for things I have no right to hope for, Theo. What sort of fool does that make me?'

'No, you're not a fool. You're one of the bravest, most loyal people I know.' He said the words gravely. 'It is I who is the fool.'

Theo's words echoed through her mind as she watched the brothers row in perfect harmony across the almost still resort water a short while later.

He took the middle position with Sakis in front and Ari at the back. She watched, spellbound, as his shoulders rippled with smooth grace and utmost efficiency.

'Aren't they something to watch?' Perla sighed wistfully.

'*Sim*,' she agreed huskily.

'I think they do that just to get us girls all hot and bothered,' Brianna complained but Inez noticed that she didn't take her eyes off her husband for one second.

When the men eventually returned to shore, the two women joined them and were immediately enfolded into the group.

Theo glanced her way, a touch of irritation in his eyes. Seconds later, he broke away from the group and came towards her.

'I didn't expect you to be down here. You should be resting.'

'I was invited. I hope I'm not intruding.'

'If you were invited then you're not intruding. Come and join us.' He grabbed her hand and led her to where Ari and Sakis were turning over the boat to dry the underside.

The two brothers gave her cursory glances but

barely spoke to her. When Ari abruptly asked Theo to accompany him to the boat shed, her stomach fell.

Perla organised a Jeep to take her back to their villa and when Theo returned half an hour later, his jaw was tight and his movements jerky as he swept her off her feet and strode into the bedroom.

He made love to her with a fierce, silent passion that robbed her of speech and breath before he clamped her to his side and slid into sleep.

Her eyes filled with tears and she hurriedly brushed them away. It was no use daydreaming that things would ever magically turn rosy between her and Theo.

As much as she wanted to wish otherwise, they were on a countdown to being over for good.

The wedding was beautiful and quietly elegant in a way only an events organiser extraordinaire like Perla could achieve despite being seven months pregnant. Inez watched the bride and groom dance across the polished floor of the casino, transformed into a spectacular masterpiece that stood directly on the water, and fought the feelings rampaging through her.

Theo would never be hers. She would never

have a wedding like this or have him gazing at her the way Ari was gazing at his new wife.

She would never feel the weight of his baby in her belly or have it suckle at her breast.

Despair slowly built inside her, despite knowing deep down that Theo had done her a favour by bringing her here. He didn't need her to save him from whatever nightmares plagued him. He had a family that clearly adored him, who would be there for him when he chose to let them in.

She needed to stop moping and get on with her life.

Her time in Theo's house and his bed was over. In retrospect, she was thankful she'd let him talk her into keeping her volunteer position. It was a lifeline she was grateful for in a world skidding out of control. The things she couldn't control she would learn to live without.

A tall figure danced into her view and her eyes connected with the man who occupied an astonishingly large percentage of her mind. In his arms was an elegantly dressed woman with greying brown hair and a sad expression. She said something to him and he glanced down at her. His smile was gentle but wary and Inez saw her sadness deepen.

Inez heard the soft gurgle of a baby over the

music and turned to see Brianna next to her. 'That's their mother.' She nodded to Theo's dance partner. 'Their relationship has been fraught but I think they're all finding their way back to each other.' She glanced at Inez with a smile. 'I hope that you two find your way too.'

Inez shook her head. 'I'm afraid that's impossible.'

Brianna laughed. 'Believe me, I've seen the impossible happen in this family. I've learned not to rule anything out.' She smiled down at her child and danced away with him towards her husband.

Tears stung her eyes as she watched Sakis enfold his wife and son in his arms.

'What's wrong now?' Theo's deep voice sounded in her ear.

She blinked rapidly and pasted a smile on her face. 'Nothing. Weddings…they make me emotional. That's all.'

His eyes narrowed speculatively on her face before he took hold of her elbow. 'Dance with me.'

He led her to the dance floor and pulled her close.

'You have a big family,' she said, more for something to fill the silence.

'They can be a pain in the rear sometimes.'

'Regardless, you all seem to watch out for each other.'

He shrugged. 'Force of habit.'

'No, it's not. Does Ari know who I am?'

His mouth tightened. 'He suspects. I didn't enlighten or deny because it's none of his business. He's welcome to draw his own conclusions. Why do you ask?'

'Because he's been watching me like a hawk since we got here and he hasn't spoken more than two words to me. That's what I mean. What you have with your brothers isn't habit. It's love.'

His mouth twisted in a way that evidenced his dark pain.

'*Love* hasn't conquered the nightmares that have plagued me for all these years, Inez.' The raw pain in his voice made her throat clog. She forced a swallow.

'Because you haven't allowed it to. You resisted any attempt at help because you thought you had to face this demon alone, do things your way.'

The honest barb struck home. He was silent for the rest of the song. Then abruptly he spoke. 'I didn't want to appear weak. I hated myself every time I couldn't walk into a dark room or down an unlit street. I haven't been able to cope with the smell of cigars without breaking out in a cold sweat. Do you know what that feels like?' he asked in a harsh undertone.

She shook her head. 'No, but I know it will never go away if you keep it buried.'

Her warmth, her strength hit him hard and he wanted to reach for her with all he had. Suddenly, everything he'd ever craved, ever wished for seemed coalesced in the woman before him.

'It's no longer buried. A month ago I was still the messed-up boy Ari dug up from that hole twelve years ago. But you did something about that.'

'No, I'm not responsible for that.'

His hand cupped her nape and he whispered fiercely in her ear. 'You are. You've seen me, Inez. I can't sleep with the lights off. I used to panic whenever someone shut a door behind me. That's why I surrounded myself with glass. With you by my side I flew here with no need for sleeping pills.'

'Even though you refused to speak to me for hours.'

He exhaled. 'Things are upside down and inside out right now. Let's just…we'll get through this wedding and head back to Rio. And we will damn well fix this thing between us. Because I'm not prepared to let you go yet.'

CHAPTER THIRTEEN

'I TOLD YOU, you're so much better than a damn sleeping pill.'

Inez laughed as Theo tugged her dress down and lifted her out of it. Leaving it on the floor of the master cabin bedroom, he waited for her to kick her shoes off before he crossed over to the bed. The diamond pendant he'd looked incredibly pleased that she'd worn lay nestled between her breasts.

'Keep that on,' he instructed, just as the plane jerked through turbulence and they fell onto the bed together, a tangle of hard and soft limbs and hot, needy kisses.

'I'm glad I have my uses,' she said, laughing, when he let her up for air.

His face grew serious as he stared down at her. 'You've attained the ultimate purpose in my life, *querida*. Now more than ever you're my saviour: *my* angel.' He cradled her head as he kissed her.

Inez closed her eyes and imagined that she could

feel his soul through his reverent kiss. She studiously ignored the voice that mocked that she was deluding herself.

When he finished undressing her with gentle hands, she tried to stem her tears as he made love to her with a greedy passion that touched her very soul.

Afterwards she held him in her arms as he fell asleep. Unable to sleep, her mind drifted back to the wedding.

Theo had introduced her to his mother and again she'd witnessed the sadness in her eyes. When he'd hugged her at the end of the evening and murmured gently into her ear, his mother had burst into tears. Inez had watched as the brothers closed around her and soothed her tears.

She was still watching them when Ari had glanced her way. His measured smile and thoughtful nod in her direction had made her swallow. It hadn't been acceptance but it hadn't been the chilly reception he'd given her either.

As they'd packed to leave, Inez had asked Theo about what had happened with his mother.

'She fell apart completely after my father was arrested. She left Athens and locked herself away at our house in Santorini,' he'd replied in an offhand manner, but Inez had seen his anguish.

Recalling his words about abandonment, she'd gasped, 'She wasn't there when you were kidnapped, was she?'

Heart-shredding pain washed over his face, but a moment later it was replaced by a look even more soul-shaking. Forgiveness. 'No. She wasn't. But I had Ari and Sakis. They were strong for me. And they were that way because of her. I told her that tonight because I think we both needed to hear it.'

His words had resonated deep inside her. But most of all it had been his statement on the dance floor that continued to flash across her mind. *I'm not prepared to let you go yet.*

Her heart lurched. He meant to keep her in his bed for a while yet. Like a trophy he wasn't prepared to relinquish. And her foolish heart performed a giddy little samba at the thought of having a few more moments with him.

She woke to kisses on her forehead and her cheek and opened her eyes to bright sunshine.

'Good, you're awake. We just landed.'

She yawned widely. 'Already? I feel as if I just fell asleep.'

He laughed. 'It's three o'clock in the afternoon. And we have much to do before tonight.'

She stared at his wide grin and her heart lifted

with happiness. 'You seem in very good spirits, *querido*,' she commented.

He gathered her close in his arms and gazed down at her. 'There is a reason for that.'

'Tell me,' she murmured softly.

His face turned serious, his eyes fierce as he watched her. 'For the first time in twelve years, I slept through the night without a nightmare,' he muttered hoarsely.

Theo watched her face light up with shocked pleasure before she reached up to clasp his face. Her kiss was gentle and sweet. 'Oh, Theo. I'm so happy for you.'

'I'm happy for *us*,' he replied. With another kiss, he got up and started dressing. 'Get a move on, sweetheart, unless you wish to give the customs guy an eyeful when he boards.'

With a yelp she got up and pulled her clothes on.

Theo's phone started ringing the moment they stepped off the plane. And it wasn't until they were back home that she remembered what he'd said on the plane.

'What did you mean—"we have much to do before tonight"? We're not going out, are we?' She groaned.

He took the phone from his pocket and checked

it as another text message came through. She waited impatiently for him to finish.

'No, we're not going out. But we have a guest coming.'

'A guest? Who?'

'I've invited your father to dinner.'

Inez staggered as if a bucket of ice had been poured over her.

'My father is coming here?'

'Yes.'

'And you didn't think to inform me of this? What makes you think I want to see him?'

'We have to. It's time to get this thing over and done with, once and for all.'

'And you don't care how I feel about it?'

'I thought we agreed to fix things when we return to Rio?' he asked with a frown.

'Yes, but when you said *we*, I thought you meant us, you and me. More fool me. Because there is not me without my father, is there?'

'What are you talking about? Of course there is.'

'Then why would you go behind my back to arrange this?'

A tic started in his temple. 'Because it's my fault you're in the middle of all this.' He sighed and clawed a hand through his hair. 'I got a chance to fix things with my mother in Bermuda. We may never get back what we had but I'll take that over nothing. Whatever relationship you choose to have with your own father from here on in is up to you. But this is a hardship I caused in your life and one I have a duty to fix.'

The fight fizzed out of her but the fear that something had gone seriously wrong between the airport and home wouldn't go away.

At seven on the dot, the doorbell rang. She passed her hand over her black jumpsuit and tucked a lock of hair nervously behind her ear as she stood by Theo's side.

The butler entered the living room, followed by her father.

Benedicto da Costa drew to a halt. His narrowed gaze slid from Theo to her, his face a mask of dark anger and cold malice she'd forced herself to overlook in the past.

Now she saw him for who he really was. Images of Theo's scars flashed through her mind and her hands fisted at her side.

'I won't shake your hand because this isn't a social visit,' he rasped icily to Theo. 'And I won't be dining with you, either.'

'Perfectly fine by me. Frankly, the quicker we

get this over with the better. But let me remind you that you're here only because of Inez. She may be your daughter but she's under my protection now. I suggest you don't lose sight of that fact. What business you and I have will be finished by week's end.'

Her father's gaze swung back to her. 'Are you just going to stand there and let him speak to your father that way? You disappoint me.'

'That's no surprise. I've been a disappointment from the moment I was born a girl, *Pai*.'

'Your mother will be rolling in her grave at your behaviour.'

She raised her chin. 'No, actually. *Mãe* told me every day she was proud of me. She also encouraged me to follow my dreams. She wanted to be a sculptor. Did you know that?'

'What's your point?'

'She was talented, *Pai*. But she gave it up for you. It was her, not you, who taught me what loyalty and family meant. You were only focused on exploiting that loyalty for your own selfish needs.'

His face tightened and his eyes flickered to Theo, who'd been standing by her with his arms folded, a half smile on his face.

'Is this what I came here for? To be lectured by an ungrateful child?'

Theo shrugged. 'I'm finding it quite entertaining.'

Benedicto growled and shot to his feet. 'If there is a point, *son*, I suggest you get to it.'

Theo grew marble-still, his smile disappearing in the blink of an eye. Pure rage vibrated off his body and Inez watched his nostrils flare as he sucked in a control-sustaining breath.

'*I am not your son*. And you are not worthy to be a father. It's a shame you didn't learn how to be a better parent from the mother who gave birth to you in that *favela* you deny you grew up in. And don't bother denying it again. I know everything there is to know about you, da Costa.'

For the first time since he'd walked in, Benedicto grew wary. He strolled to the drinks cabinet and took his time examining all the expensive spirits and liqueurs displayed.

Without asking, he poured a measure of single malt whisky and took a bold sip. 'So I bent the truth a little. So what? You've already discredited my campaign. What do you want? My company? Is that your end game? You want to pick up the shares for Da Costa Holdings for peanuts? Well, over my dead body.'

Theo's laugh was menacing enough to cause her skin to tingle in alarm. 'Trust me, a few weeks ago it would've been my pleasure to grant you your wish. But you're wrong on that score. Your company is of no interest to me.'

His wariness increased. 'What's changed?'

Theo's eyes flicked to her and her heart thudded. 'Your daughter.'

'Really?'

Inez shook her head in astonishment. 'Do you really not know who he is, *Pai*?' she asked.

Theo's mouth curved in a mirthless smile. 'Oh, he knows who I am. He's just hoping that *I* don't know what he did twelve years ago.'

Benedicto swallowed, his gaunt face growing pale until he looked ashen. 'I have no idea what you're talking—'

She rushed towards him, anger, pain and disappointment coiling like poisonous snakes inside her. 'Don't you dare deny it. *Don't you dare!*' Her voice cracked and a sob broke through her chest. 'You had a boy kidnapped and tortured! For money. How could you?'

Eyes she'd once thought were like her own turned black with sinister rage. 'How could I? I did it for you. The fancy clothes you strut about in and that fancy car you drive? Where do you think the money came from? I needed it to save the company. Anyway, it was my money. Why did I have to go back to farming just because Pantelides couldn't keep it in his pants or stop his bit on the side from blowing the whistle on him?'

Inez's hand flew to her mouth, her insides icing over. '*Santa Maria*, you truly are a monster.'

Her father's jaw tightened and he addressed Theo. 'Is this the point where you hand whatever file you've gathered on me over to the authorities?'

Theo's mouth twisted. 'So you can bribe your way out of jail? No.'

Benedicto frowned. 'Then what the hell do you want?'

Theo glanced over at her and a look of almost relief washed over his face, as if a weight had been lifted off his shoulders. 'That's up to Inez. And only her. I'm done with you.'

Inez raised her suddenly heavy head and looked from one man to the other.

One stood tall, proud and breathtaking. A man she'd been so determined not to let in. But whose tortured vulnerability had drawn her to him, made her see beneath his skin to the frightened child who was desperately seeking answers.

Choking tears filling her eyes, she turned to the monster who was her father. 'I have nothing else to say to you. I don't want to see you ever again. Goodbye.'

Turning sharply from both men, she rushed out of the room and fled up the stairs.

Theo wasted no time in throwing Benedicto out once Inez left the room. He'd meant what he said—he was done with seeking retribution…had been done almost from the moment he'd met Inez.

Perhaps unwisely, he'd thought the meeting with Benedicto would be swift and cathartic. Instead, he'd brought Inez even more anguish.

He slashed his fingers through his hair as he vaulted up the stairs that led to his third floor suite. Perhaps she'd been right. He'd ambushed her in his rush to get this situation sorted between them.

But he would make it right for her. They would get through this. They had to. The feelings he'd tried hard to smother had blown up in his face when he'd woken on the plane this afternoon. With the absence of anxiety and fear, the purest reason why he wanted to wake up each morning with Inez had shone through.

The feelings had been so intense he'd almost

blurted it out. But he'd decided to wait until she'd confronted her father.

Now he wished he hadn't. He was wishing he'd provided her with that additional support of knowing how much she meant to him before he'd let her father loose on her.

Pursing his mouth in determination, he pushed the bedroom door open. 'Inez, I'm sorry for—'

The sight that confronted him silenced his words and turned his feet to clay. She stared at him, eyes red-rimmed with freshly shed tears.

Because of him. But even that pulse of deep regret couldn't erase the sight before him.

'What are you doing?' he asked, although the part of his brain that hadn't frozen along with his feet could work it out.

Two suitcases were open on the bed, one filled with her clothes. *She was packing...*

The silk top in her hand trembled before she turned and threw it in her case. Then her fingers curled around the edge of the lid.

When she looked at him again, more tears filled her eyes.

'Thank you for opening my eyes to what he truly is,' she murmured huskily.

'Shelve the thanks and tell me what you're doing,' he replied tersely.

One hand swiped at her cheek. 'I'm leaving, Theo.'

'You're what?' His voice rang with disbelief. 'You're going back to your father's house?'

She shuddered from head to toe. 'No. I could never live there again.'

He frowned. 'Then where are you going?'

She gave a tiny shrug. 'I'll stay with Camila.'

He finally got his feet to work and paced to where she stood. When she grabbed her shorts, he ripped them from her hand and threw them on the bed. 'I seem to be missing a link somewhere, sweetheart. Why don't you take a beat and fill me in?'

'I can't stay here.'

A merciless vice squeezed his chest. 'Why not?'

Her face creased in fresh anguish. 'Because he is right. The food he put on our table; the clothes on my back; our fancy education. They *all* came from your suffering.'

'For God's sake—'

She carried on raggedly. 'I never stopped to think about it but I remember the day he came home twelve years ago and told my mother our troubles were over. We weren't exactly poor before then, but after he pressured my mother into selling the ranch he made some bad investments and the company suffered for it. They argued a lot and I used to go to bed every night praying for a miracle just so they'd stop arguing. Can you imagine how I felt when my prayers were answered? And now, all these years later, I find out that what I'd prayed for came at the cost of your—' She choked to a stop, then frantically threw more clothes into the case.

Theo couldn't find an answer as desperately as he tried. He was watching her torture herself and he could do nothing to stop it. '*Anjo*—'

'No. I'm *not* an angel, Theo. I'm a child of the monster, a heartless devil who tortures children and doesn't feel an ounce of regret for it. How can you even bear to look at me?'

'Because you're *not* him!' he interjected fiercely. He took her hands and forced her to face him. 'You're not responsible for his actions. Stay, Inez. We said we would talk about us once we were done with him.'

'But there is no us, is there? We…we just fell into bed because of the circumstances that brought us together. If it hadn't been for my father you'd never have set foot in Brazil.'

'So you're walking away because you think we were never meant to be?' He watched her, forced himself to think how he would feel if she walked away from him. The realisation of what was happening washed over him and ashen despair filled his chest.

'I'm walking away because you need to put everything and everyone associated with your ordeal behind you. Otherwise you will never heal properly.'

He dropped her hand and stared down at her. The ice that had started to build inside him since he'd walked into the room hardened. It crept around his heart and Theo swore he heard it crack. His eyes scoured her beautiful tearstained face, looking for a tiny chink. A tiny ray of hope that would offer deliverance from the quicksand of devastation he could feel himself sinking into.

'So that's it? That's your final decision. You're doing this for my sake but I have no say in the matter?' He couldn't stop the bitterness from lacing his voice.

Her answer was to step back and gather up the last of her clothes. With trembling fingers, she zipped up the cases and lifted them off the bed.

'Inez, answer me!'

She stilled at the door. '*Adeus*, Theo.'

'Go to hell!' he snarled back.

* * *

'Table Four need a second helping of *feijoadas*. And a bottle of Rioja.' Camila bustled into the kitchen, checked on the bubbling pot Inez was stirring and nodded in approval. '*Fantastico*. I'll be back in a minute for that order.' She sailed back out on a giddy whirlwind.

Inez wiped her sweating brow and looked over her shoulder. 'Pietro, you grab the bottle; I'll serve up the *feijoadas*.'

Her brother rolled his eyes. 'Who made you queen of the kitchen?'

'I did, when I won the coin toss earlier.'

Her grin came easier today—much easier than it had for far longer than she wanted to dwell on. She still couldn't go for more than ten seconds without thinking of Theo but if she could joke with her brother, that was a good sign that this hollow, half-dead devastation she carried inside her would eventually ease. Right?

'I still think you cheated,' Pietro grumbled.

She lifted one shoulder. 'I'll let you explain to Camila, then, why the Rioja isn't here when she returns, *sim*?'

'Tomorrow, I'm tossing the coin.' He sauntered down the stairs into the basement that served as the restaurant's larder and wine cellar. The smell of the cheese Camila kept in the small space could be overpowering and she smiled again as Pietro made gagging noises.

If there was a bright side to be seen, it was that, amid all the chaos and heartache, somehow she and her brother had grown closer than she'd ever dreamed possible.

They both were yet to decide what they wanted to do with their lives after choosing to walk away from their father and the company, but Camila had encouraged them to take their time. To heal. To reconnect.

When her mother's childhood friend had offered them a job in her restaurant they'd both jumped at it. She'd worked it around her volunteer work and, between the two jobs, it kept her plenty busy.

Keeping herself occupied stopped the tight knot of pain inside her from mushrooming into unbearable agony. In the dark of the night when she lay wide awake and aching was time enough to suffer through the hell of wondering if she was doomed to heartache for ever.

Of wondering if Theo had left Rio in the three weeks since their final bitter encounter. Of wondering if his nightmares were gone for good or if her brief presence in his life had made them worse.

Her hand trembled and she immediately curled it into a fist. Theo was strong. He would survive…

Yes, but he called you his saviour. His angel. And you walked away from him.

'No,' she breathed through the pain ripping through her. She'd done the right thing—

'No what? If you tell me I've got the wrong wine, you'll have to go and get it yourself.'

She shook her head blindly and turned gratefully to the door as Camila walked in. Her quick but assessing glance at her made Inez frown.

'We have a new booking. Table One. And an order of *feijoadas* for one.'

'Wow, you're on fire tonight, sis.'

She ignored Pietro. 'Okay, I'll serve it up and—'

'No, I didn't take a drink order. And I think they want an appetiser first too. Can you go take care of it?'

Inez's eyebrow shot up. 'Me? But I'm not dressed to serve.'

'Pfft. This isn't the Four Seasons, *meu querida*. Besides, it's time you took a break from that hot stove. Tidy your hair a bit and go and take the order.'

Inez looked down at her black skirt and grey T-shirt. It wasn't standard waitress attire but, as Camila had said, this wasn't the Four Seasons. She tucked a strand of hair behind her ear and caught the worried look in the older woman's eyes. It was an expression she'd spied a few times and she reached out and shook her head before the concern could be voiced.

'I'm fine.'

Camila's mouth pursed. 'Good. Then go and attend to Table One.'

With a weary sigh, she washed and dried her hands on her apron. Unfastening it, she hung it on the hook and avoided her image in the small mirror by the door. Her red face from manning the stove for the last three hours would depress her even more.

Plucking a pencil, notebook and menu from the kitchen stand, she nudged the swinging doors with her hip and turned towards Table One.

'You...' she choked out.

Through the drumming in her ears she heard the items in her hand clatter to the floor. A couple of diners glanced her way. Someone picked up the scattered items and placed them in her numb hands. She opened her mouth to thank them but no words emerged.

Every atom in her body was paralysed at the sight of Theo Pantelides.

She heard movement behind her. 'You can't

stand here all night, *pequena*. Life will pass you by that way,' Camila said solemnly.

She exhaled shakily and forced herself to move.

Those light hazel eyes never left her as she approached his table. He looked as powerful and as magnificent as ever, even if his cheekbones seemed to stand out a little more than she remembered. His hair had grown a little longer and looked a little dishevelled.

'Sit,' he rasped.

Her heart lurched at the sound of his voice. Licking her dry lips, she shook her head. 'I can't. I'm working.'

'I've received special dispensation from Camila. Sit,' he commanded again.

She sat. He stared at her for a full minute, his eyes raking over her face as if he had been starved of her... Or he was committing her face to memory one last time?

White-hot pain ripped through her. 'Why are you here, Theo?' she blurted.

His eyes rose from her mouth to connect with hers. The breath he took was deep and long. 'I was clearing out the house and I found something you left behind.' He reached down near his feet and laid her sketchpad on the table.

She stared at it, drowning beneath the weight of

her despair. 'Oh, thank you.' She paused a second before the words were torn out of her. 'So you're leaving Rio?'

He shrugged. 'There's nothing left for me here.'

Tears burned her eyes as her heart shredded into a million useless pieces. 'I…I wish you well.'

He made a rough sound under his breath. 'Do you?' he asked sarcastically. She glanced up sharply but he wasn't done. 'Problem is, I'd believe those blithe words from the woman sitting across from me. But the woman who drew these…' he flicked over the pages of the sketchpad a few times before he stopped and pointed '…this woman has guts. She was brave enough to draw what was in her heart; what cried out from her soul. Look at her.'

She kept her eyes on his face, her whole body trembling wildly as she gave a jerky shake of her head.

'Look at her, dammit!'

She sucked in a breath. And looked down. The first sketch was the one she'd made of him after they'd made love that first time on the boat. The ones that followed were variations of that first sketch. She'd captured Theo in various poses, each one progressively more lovingly detailed until the final one of him with his brothers, laughing together at the wedding. She'd drawn that from memory on their final night in Bermuda. Staring at the finished picture had cemented her feelings for him.

He turned the page and the image of Brianna and Sakis's baby stared back at her. Dimitri already bore the strong, captivating mark of the Pantelides family. It was that template that she'd used in the following sketches, when capturing her own secret yearning of what her and Theo's baby would look like on paper had been too strong to resist.

'You must think I'm some sort of crazy stalker.'

'There is no stalking involved when the subject is just as crazy about the stalker,' he rasped in a raw undertone.

Her heart flipped into her belly and her whole body trembled. 'You can't be. Theo, I'll ruin your life.'

'I thought my life was ruined before I met you. I was consumed by rage and a thirst for revenge. I let the need for revenge swallow me whole, blinding me to what was important. Family. Love. I thought there was nothing else worth fighting for. But I was wrong. There was you. My life *will* be ruined. But only if you're not in it.'

The tears she'd tried to hold back brimmed and

fell down her cheeks. Theo cursed and looked around. 'What's through there?' he asked.

'It's a room, for private parties.'

'Is there a party tonight?'

Before she'd finished shaking her head he was standing and tugging her after him. He kicked the door shut and turned to her.

'Listen to me. You told me I would never see you as anything but the child of a monster. But you forget you're also the child of a loving mother who celebrated every day the special person you are. How do you think she would feel to see you buried here, punishing yourself for what your father did?'

She shut her eyes but the tears squeezed through anyway.

'Open your eyes, Inez.'

She sniffed and complied, staring up at him with blurred vision. 'Now, truly open your eyes and see the wonderful person you are. See the person I see. The brave, talented person who drew those pictures.'

'Oh, Theo,' she cried.

'You have a dream. A dream I want to be a part of.' His hands shook as they traced her face.

'I want that dream to become reality so badly.'

'Then please forgive me for blackmailing you and give us that chance.'

She pulled back. 'Forgive you? There is nothing to forgive. If anything, I should be thanking you for shaking me out of my bleak existence. Even before I truly knew you, you empowered me to fight for what I wanted.'

'So will you fight for us? Will you give me the chance to prove to you that I'm worthy of your love and let me show you how much you mean to me?'

She touched his face and inhaled shakily when he turned to kiss her palm. '*Meu querido,* I fell in love with you so ridiculously soon after meeting you, I swear I'll never confess to you when it happened.'

His stunned laugh brought a wide smile to her face. '*Anjo...*' When her smile dimmed, he shook his head. 'Don't bother to argue with me. I love you with every breath I take. You're my angel and I'll keep repeating it until you believe it.'

'We're not going to have a very smooth-sailing future, are we?'

'No,' he concurred with a laugh then kissed her until her head swam with delirious pleasure. 'But that will be part of our story. And, speaking of smooth sailing...'

'*Sim?*'

'I sent a couple of your sketches to our design guys in Greece. They're interested in talking to you about them. If you're up for it?'

Her mouth dropped open. She waited until he'd kissed it shut before she tried again. '*Really?*'

'Really. And I should bring you good news more often. That happy wriggle does incredible things to my—'

She clamped her hand over his mouth and glanced, alarmed, over his shoulder, just as two text messages beeped in quick succession. He groaned and was about to activate them when a knock sounded on the door.

'*Hell*, I knew I should've found a quieter place for this.'

The door opened and Pietro entered with a bottle of champagne and two glasses.

Theo's expression grew serious as he watched him approach.

Pietro set the bottle and glasses down and stared back at Theo. 'You took care of my sister when I was too much of a *burro* to do so. I'll be for ever in your debt.' He held out his hand.

After several seconds, Theo shook it. 'Don't mention it. Any man who's not afraid to call himself an ass is all right in my book.'

With a self-conscious laugh, Pietro turned to leave.

'Thanks for the drinks,' Theo said. 'But how did you know?'

Inez suppressed a giggle. Pietro rolled his eyes and nodded to the far wall. 'There's a partition to the kitchen. Camila's been spying on you since you came in.'

Theo glanced behind him as the partition widened and Camila beamed at them. Her gaze rested on Inez. 'Your *feijoadas* are good enough, but I always believed your destiny lies elsewhere.' She blew a kiss and shut the partition.

Pietro left and Theo stared down at her. 'Are you ready to start our adventure, *agape mou*?'

'What does that mean?'

'It means *my love*.' His smile dimmed. 'I learnt to speak Portuguese for the wrong reasons. I will teach you Greek for the right ones.'

Her grip tightened on his shirt. 'Were you really planning to leave Rio?'

'Yes. After I persuaded Benedicto to sign over the company into your and Pietro's names, I was done with that soulless vendetta. The thought that I'd lost you in the process nearly killed me.'

'I...what? You got him to sign over the company to us? Theo, we don't want it!'

'It was your grandfather's, then your mother's. It's right that it should be yours and Pietro's. If you don't really want it, I'm sure you'll find a beneficial way to dispose of it.'

She nodded. 'It would go a long way to help the inner city centre and the *favela* kids.'

'Great, we'll make it happen.'

Her heart contracted as she stared into his warm eyes. 'I love you, Theo. Thank you for coming back for me.'

'I couldn't not return, *anjo*, because without you I'm lost.'

She lifted her face to his and he slanted his mouth over hers in a deep, poignant kiss that brought fresh tears to her eyes.

'We need to talk about these tears,' he said drily, then huffed in irritation as his phone beeped again.

'Your brothers?' she guessed.

'And their wives. Ari wants to know if I'm still alive. Sakis wants to know if he can hire you to design his next oil tanker.'

She laughed. 'And their wives?'

He glanced down at the screen and back at her. 'They want to know if they can start planning our wedding.'

She took the phone, flicked the off switch and slipped it into his back pocket. Gripping his waist, she raised herself on tiptoe and leaned close to his ear.

'We will reply to each one of them in the morning. Right now, I want you to take me back to the boat and make love to me, make me yours again. Is that okay?'

'It's more than okay, my angel. It's what I plan to do for the rest of our lives.'

The look of love and adoration in his eyes as he took her hand and walked her out of the room was forever branded on her heart.

* * * * *

MILLS & BOON®
Large Print – April 2015

TAKEN OVER BY THE BILLIONAIRE
Miranda Lee

CHRISTMAS IN DA CONTI'S BED
Sharon Kendrick

HIS FOR REVENGE
Caitlin Crews

A RULE WORTH BREAKING
Maggie Cox

WHAT THE GREEK WANTS MOST
Maya Blake

THE MAGNATE'S MANIFESTO
Jennifer Hayward

TO CLAIM HIS HEIR BY CHRISTMAS
Victoria Parker

SNOWBOUND SURPRISE FOR THE BILLIONAIRE
Michelle Douglas

CHRISTMAS WHERE THEY BELONG
Marion Lennox

MEET ME UNDER THE MISTLETOE
Cara Colter

A DIAMOND IN HER STOCKING
Kandy Shepherd

MILLS & BOON®
Large Print – May 2015

THE SECRET HIS MISTRESS CARRIED
Lynne Graham

NINE MONTHS TO REDEEM HIM
Jennie Lucas

FONSECA'S FURY
Abby Green

THE RUSSIAN'S ULTIMATUM
Michelle Smart

TO SIN WITH THE TYCOON
Cathy Williams

THE LAST HEIR OF MONTERRATO
Andie Brock

INHERITED BY HER ENEMY
Sara Craven

TAMING THE FRENCH TYCOON
Rebecca Winters

HIS VERY CONVENIENT BRIDE
Sophie Pembroke

THE HEIR'S UNEXPECTED RETURN
Jackie Braun

THE PRINCE SHE NEVER FORGOT
Scarlet Wilson

He found he looked forw **with her every day. And now she was bringing hope into his life by agreeing to have his baby. *Their* baby.**

He put down his fork and reached for her small hand. 'You won't change your mind, will you, Chantal?' he said huskily.

She felt the warmth of his hand around hers and skin against skin seemed almost erotic. She could feel deep down that being with Michel was affecting her more than it should.

'No, of course I won't change my mind.' She stood up. 'Dessert?' she asked briskly.

He could feel something like an electric current running between them. Inside him was a powerful feeling of wanting to take Chantal in his arms and hold her until the feeling went away. He stood up and put his arms around her, drawing her close. This didn't make sense. She should be pushing him away, telling him to stick to the plan. He bent his head to kiss her.

She parted her lips as every sense in her body ignited with passion and longing. She was feeling overwhelmed by the sensual fluidity of her body as she moulded herself against Michel's hard, virile, muscular frame. She was melting away as he held her tightly. There was a powerful force gripping her. She didn't even want to stir in his arms in case the dream ended.

He lifted her into his arms, carrying her towards the door. There was no need for words as he carried her upstairs. They were both intent on giving in to the magic of the moment. There was no need to justify his actions or her compliance. Life was too precious to banish moments like this.

Dear Reader

I've returned once more to my favourite part of France for the setting of HER MIRACLE TWINS. I fell in love with the area when I strolled hand in hand one summer's day along a favourite beach with my boyfriend John, who was soon to be my husband. Later we took our children. Now some of our children and grandchildren live not far from this beach.

I still walk along the same beach if I'm searching for a new romantic story. Although my husband died a few years ago I still feel the inspiration he used to give me when I needed to conjure up a romantic hero.

The beach is set in a beautiful area of hills and valleys near fashionable Le Touquet and the picturesque old town of Montreuil-sur-Mer. It's a perfect background for the romance of Chantal and Michel. In HER MIRACLE TWINS we also meet up again with Chantal's cousin Julia and her husband Bernard, who were the hero and heroine in SUMMER WITH A FRENCH SURGEON. Chantal, like her cousin Julia, has many emotional obstacles to overcome before she finds true love and happiness.

I hope you enjoy reading this romantic story as much as I enjoyed writing it.

Margaret

HER MIRACLE
TWINS

BY
MARGARET BARKER

First published in Great Britain 2014
by Mills & Boon, an imprint of Harlequin (UK) Limited,
Large Print edition 2014
Eton House, 18-24 Paradise Road,
Richmond, Surrey, TW9 1SR

© 2014 Margaret Barker

ISBN: 978 0 263 23889 1

Harlequin (UK) Limited's policy is to use papers that are natural, renewable and recyclable products and made from wood grown in sustainable forests. The logging and manufacturing processes conform to the legal environmental regulations of the country of origin.

Printed and bound in Great Britain
by CPI Antony Rowe, Chippenham, Wiltshire

Margaret Barker has enjoyed a variety of interesting careers. A State Registered Nurse and qualified teacher, she holds a degree in French and Linguistics, and is a Licentiate of the Royal Academy of Music. As a full-time writer, Margaret says, 'Writing is my most interesting career, because it fits perfectly into family life. Sadly, my husband died of cancer in 2006, but I still live in our idyllic sixteenth-century house near the East Anglian coast. Our grown-up children have flown the nest, but they often fly back again, bringing their own young families with them for wonderful weekend and holiday reunions.'

Recent titles by the same author:

SUMMER WITH A FRENCH SURGEON
A FATHER FOR BABY ROSE
GREEK DOCTOR CLAIMS HIS BRIDE
THE FATHERHOOD MIRACLE

These books are also available in eBook format from www.millsandboon.co.uk

To John, my inspiration always.

CHAPTER ONE

'IT WAS THAT wretched stone just under the surface that tripped me up, Michel. Look at that dreadful, jagged monster. Somebody must have—'

'Chantal, keep still, will you? I'm trying to assess how much damage you've done.'

'Damage I've done? I'm trying to keep still but— Ow, that hurt!'

Sprawled on the sand, Chantal glared up at the tall, athletic man in white running shorts and black tee shirt who was now kneeling on the sand beside her. He appeared to have come from nowhere as she'd tripped and hurt her ankle. She deduced he must have been running behind her, but he was barely recognisable as the suave director of Accident and Emergency she was used to seeing as she worked alongside him at the Hôpital de la Plage.

'If you weren't my boss I'd...'

He looked down at her, smiling in the most patronisingly irritating yet surprisingly sexy way, his fingers firmly supporting her swelling ankle. She told herself to concentrate on the pain, which would help her to stop fantasising about something that was never going to happen to her again—especially with the usually serious, work-focussed Dr Michel Devine.

'I'm going to have to carry you up the beach to my car up there on the promenade so I can get you back to the hospital.'

'No! I don't want to be carried. Just help me to my feet so I can hop as far as—'

'Be quiet, Dr Winstone, and that's an order!'

She frowned as she decided to give in to him. He always got his own way in Urgences but she'd never seen him quite so domineering before. She couldn't help admiring the expression on his face. It made him appear even more desirable as a man. And she didn't do desirable any more. Not since last September.

She decided the pain was addling her brain, filling her head full of mad ideas. Weird feelings she would never have contemplated since she'd changed completely on that awful night.

Effortlessly, Michel picked her up and carried her in his arms across the sand. The pain in her ankle was now becoming more intense. She decided to give in completely. He was, after all, the most experienced expert in accidental injuries for miles around, probably in the whole of France. And it was a good feeling to simply relax in his arms.

Yes, she should be grateful he'd come along when he had. And the pleasant feeling of strong, muscular, masculine arms around her helped to counteract the pain. Since the two-timing Jacques had done the dirty on her she'd never expected to tolerate a man's arms around her again.

As he was loading her into the back seat of his car she put on a contrite tone of voice and told him she was sorry.

'Sorry for what? Being a difficult patient? Forget it. I get to see them every day. Once I've shown them how to co-operate, as I did with you, we get on fine. Your childish behaviour was because you were suffering from shock, probably still are.'

He was looking directly into her eyes now, an expression of concentration creasing his fore-head. She found herself admiring his warm, brown, expressive eyes.

'How's the pain now? Worse?'

She nodded as a particularly sharp spasm passed through her ankle. 'Mmm. Do you have any—?'

He was already pulling out a strip of painkillers from his glove compartment. 'Swallow those two with this water.' He opened a new pack. 'Now, try to keep the ankle as still as you can. I'll get it X-rayed as soon as we get back to hospital.'

She lay still as Michel drove off. The welcome sight of the Hôpital de la Plage came into view and she gave a sigh of relief.

'It was the warm spring sunshine that tempted me out this Sunday morning,' she muttered, almost to herself, as Michel drove up to the front entrance of the hospital. 'I should have stayed in bed.'

'So should I. I hadn't planned that I would have to work on my day off.'

He switched off the engine as a porter arrived to remonstrate with the owner of this car parking in an ambulance space.

'Oh, sorry, Dr Devine. I hadn't recognised you. I see you've got a patient on the back seat so— Oh, it's you, Dr Winstone. Are you all right?'

'No, she's not all right. Could you please bring a stretcher and then park my car in the staff car park?'

Chantal could tell that Michel was reverting to type after his initial attempt to be patient with her. She remained very still and quiet as a nurse came out to help the porter load her onto the trolley. Michel supervised while holding her right ankle to prevent any further damage as they trundled along to X-Ray.

'Good news No fractures.' Michel was pointing out the X-rays illuminated on the screen.

She raised her head from the pillow.

'Thank heavens for that. So it's simply a sprain.

I'll get the ankle strapped up and I'll be on duty again tomorrow morning.'

He frowned. 'Chantal, there's nothing simple about a sprain, as you well know. I think you've been lucky that you haven't torn the surrounding ligaments but there's been mild stretching of the ligaments which will have to be dealt with. The treatment is to minimise the pain. You've started on the paracetamol. Two five hundred mg every six hours will take the edge off it. For the first three days you need complete rest, ice-pack applications pressed on to the injury for fifteen minutes every two hours and—'

'Michel, I can't possibly do all that. I've got too much to do.'

'Exactly. That's why I'm going to put you in a side ward attached to Female Orthopaedic. I take no chances with my staff. Deal with a sprain properly at the beginning and future problems shouldn't arise.'

Chantal lay back on the trolley, looking up at the bright lights above her head. Michel was on the phone to the orthopaedic sister. He was smiling now. 'Yes, we're coming along now if that's

OK with you, Sidonie? Good. Yes, you know Chantal, Dr Winstone. She's been with us in Emergency since February. We'll go over the treatment she needs when I arrive. I've got hold of a porter at last. Be with you in a couple of minutes.'

Half an hour later Chantal was safely settled in an orthopaedic bed, wearing the most unglamorous hospital pyjamas. Her right leg was elevated on hard orthopaedic cushions, Sister Sidonie was applying an ice pack to the painful area. Michel was watching her every move as if ready to criticise.

'Ow!' Chantal found it impossible to check her cry as Sister pressed on the painful area.

Michel was nodding his approval. 'That's exactly right, Sister. More pressure on the injury just there. Keep it like that for fifteen minutes. Here, let me show you the exact pressure required to reduce this inflammation.'

Taking over from Sister Sidonie, he placed his fingers on Chantal's ankle.

'Michel!'

'Yes, I expect that did hurt a bit but you'll thank me for this later.'

Chantal lay back against the pillows and gave in. She didn't know what he had in mind for the thanks she would have to give him. Even through the pain he was inflicting she got a thrill at the touch of his fingers. Most bizarre. She'd worked with this man for over two months and hadn't ever thought of him in this way. As she'd suspected earlier, the pain must have addled her brain. She'd gone back to childhood days and was imagining he was a knight in shining armour who'd come to rescue her from danger, probably on a white horse instead of simply jogging along the beach.

'That's better.' He smiled and patted her hand.

His teeth were very white, she noticed now, very even. His dark hair, which was hanging down over his forehead as he leaned over her, gave him a rumpled, little-boy look, something she'd never seen before as he worked efficiently on his patients. But it was those sexy dark brown eyes that were impossibly attractive. How come they hadn't registered with her until this morning?

'Sister, I'll be back later in the day. Reapply the pack for fifteen minutes every two hours. In about four days we'll be able to put the ankle in a tubular compression bandage and get the physiotherapist to introduce massage, ultrasound therapy and gentle joint movement.'

Chantal raise her head. 'Michel, when can I go back to my room in the medics' quarters?'

'That will depend on your progress. Hopefully in a few days we should be able to get you up on crutches. Once you can move around with the use of a stick I might let you go back to your room so long as you don't take any weight on the right ankle. You may even spend an hour or so in Emergency doing paperwork or something non-strenuous. We'll have to see how you get on.'

She couldn't help noticing that he'd reverted to his totally professional manner with her. She was just another patient requiring attention on his day off. Fine. He was just another medical colleague. When these unusual flights of fancy left her she would revert to type as well.

He was glancing at his watch. 'Any questions before I have to go?'

She suddenly felt a moment of panic. 'When will you be coming back?' As soon as she'd asked the pathetic question she regretted it. What was the matter with her? The pain gave her an excuse perhaps but she hoped he didn't read anything into it.

Sidonie was smiling at her in a reassuring, almost maternal way. 'It's OK, Chantal, we'll take care of you.'

'I'll be back this evening. Don't worry. A month from now you'll wonder what all the fuss was about.'

She certainly would. As she watched the lithe, athletic figure disappear through the door she was experiencing mixed emotions. Somehow she felt she was getting to know the real person beneath the dour façade Michel presented to his professional colleagues. Her emotions this morning were dangerously out of order. She too had always elected to present a façade to her colleagues to cover up the agony she'd been through before she'd started working here.

Sidonie applied more pressure with the ice pack. 'Quite a charmer, isn't he?'

Chantal hesitated. 'Well, I wouldn't say that. He's good at his job.'

'Oh, he's devoted to his job. You know his wife died don't you? Over three years ago, I believe. Apparently, she died of cancer and he's never got over it. We all fancied him when he arrived to be Director of Emergency, over a year ago now.'

Sidonie gave an expressive sigh. 'Well, who wouldn't fancy him? Tall, dark and handsome and built like an athlete. But he made it quite clear to all of us that he wasn't interested in relationships. He's the sort of man who obviously adored his wife and will never take a long-term girlfriend. Definitely not remarry, that's for sure! She must have been a very special woman to deserve such loyalty from him.'

Sidonie paused in her observations and gave another sigh. 'That's unfortunate for all the unmarried staff who lavish attention on him. If I wasn't a forty-year-old married woman with two children I'd fancy him myself.'

She removed the ice pack and smiled down at her patient. 'You've been working in Emergency since February, haven't you? I heard you were on the medical staff of a hospital in Paris before you came here. How does the Hôpital de la Plage compare to your previous hospital?'

Chantal hesitated. 'Well, it's different. Actually, it's like coming home for me. You see, I was born just a few miles away in Montreuil. My English father died when I was seven. My French mother resumed her teaching career after that and she took me to live in Paris where she'd got a job. That's where she brought me up, although we always used to return to this area and stay here during the long summer vacation.

'This coastline feels like my second home because I know it so well. When I was old enough I did my medical training in Paris and took a staff position when I qualified.'

Sidonie put the ice pack down on a trolley and sat down beside her patient. 'Was it because you regard this area as your second home that you chose to leave Paris?'

Chantal looked at the figure of the kindly woman and found her experienced presence very comforting. She welcomed a girly chat to take her mind off the pain and the unexpected turn of events today.

She lay back against her pillows. 'It was a sudden decision. Very sudden.'

She drew in her breath as the awful memory of that fateful day flooded back to her.

'One minute I was on cloud nine, in love with the man of my dreams, three months pregnant with his much-wanted baby.'

She hesitated. Should she, indeed could she, go on? What did she have to lose?

'Then the phone rang and everything changed.'

Her voice was quavering as she gathered her thoughts. Was it really a good idea to unload the sordid details onto someone who was a colleague?

The orthopaedic sister was watching her with a deeply sympathetic expression on her face, as if anticipating what was to come. Oh, it would be good for her to get it off her chest. She'd bottled it up ever since she arrived at the Hôpital de la Plage. It was about time she relaxed and socialised a bit more. It wasn't her fault she'd been totally hoodwinked by a despicable, two-timing scoundrel.

She could hear the sound of a heavy trolley being pushed past her door through the swing doors into the ward and the murmur of the nurses and patients as the doors opened.

A nurse knocked, before opening her door. 'Dr Winstone, would you like some lunch?'

Chantal shook her head. 'No, thank you, Nurse.'

Sidonie turned her head. 'Is everything OK in the ward, Sylvie?'

The young nurse smiled. 'Fine, Sister. A nice quiet Sunday for once.'

'I'll be back to check the medicines after you've served the lunch. Pay attention to the patients on extra fluids, won't you?'

'Of course, Sister.' She turned back to her patient. 'So what happened after the phone rang?'

Chantal moved her good foot into a more comfortable position at the side of the cushions supporting her injured ankle as that fateful evening last September came flooding back.

'I was in the kitchen in my apartment, roasting a chicken for our supper, I remember. My boyfriend had phoned earlier to invite himself round that evening so I'd picked up a chicken at the supermarket on my way home from hospital.'

She swallowed hard. 'The phone rang. I answered it. It was a woman's voice. She asked if Jacques was there. I called him over and went on preparing the meal. I assumed it was probably one of his private patients. He seemed to have lots of those. He was such a charming person. Unpredictable, though. I never knew when he was going to turn up.'

Already she could feel the bitterness welling up inside her. 'He took the phone into the sitting room. I could hear his voice, very low, more like a whisper. Then suddenly he started shouting. 'No, you mustn't do that! No, you can't come here. You can't!'

Sidonie sat very still as she waited for Chantal to continue. She could see how upset she was.

'He slammed down the phone and came back into the kitchen. His face was drained of all colour and he was trembling. At the same time I could hear footsteps on the stairs coming up from the ground floor of my apartment block. Then hammering on the door.'

'Who was it?'

'His wife. I had no idea he was married. It transpired that she'd been caring for her sick mother in the south of France for a few months. A friend had tipped her off that her husband was being unfaithful and had given her my address and phone number.'

'So what happened when his wife arrived?'

Chantal cleared her throat. 'She started shrieking at him. Hitting him in the chest with her fists. He grabbed her wrists, fending off the blows as he tried to placate her. He said he could explain everything. How pathetic! The evidence was there before the poor woman's eyes, for heaven's sake. I found myself feeling sorry for her.'

'So, did she start shouting at you?'

'No, that was the strange thing. She barely glanced at me. It was her pig of a husband she was mad with. I'd heard enough about his womanising as she continued to hurl abuse at him. I just wanted it all to stop. So I opened my door and asked them both to leave.'

'And then?'

'They noticed me at last. His wife grabbed his arm and pulled him towards the door. I continued to hold the door wide open. She was still shouting. I told them both again to get out of my apartment. After they'd gone I went into my bedroom. My brain had gone numb. I lay down on the bed and closed my eyes, willing myself to sleep.'

No, she couldn't tell her any more of the agony that had come afterwards, not now anyway. She wanted to move forward with her life. She was a different person from the innocent, trusting woman she'd been. The heartbreaking experience later that night had changed her for ever. She couldn't even speak about her miscarriage.

'I'm sorry, Sidonie, to burden you with all this.'

Sidonie leaned across and patted her hand. 'Thank you for sharing a confidence with me. I feel privileged to have been told something of your background. You always seemed so quiet and withdrawn when you first started working in Emergency. I hadn't realised the suffering you'd been through. If ever you need a shoulder to cry on...'

'Thanks, but I've done all the crying I'm going to do. The past is over. It's the present and the future that are important to me now.'

She must have fallen asleep after Sister had gone back into the ward. The sun, which had been shining full into her window, had dipped below the rooftops of the hospital. She became aware of someone being in the room and turned to look at her bedside chair.

'I hope I didn't wake you?'

'Julia! What a lovely surprise.' She held out her arms at the sight of her cousin then winced as she unwittingly moved her damaged ankle.

Julia rose to her feet. 'Don't try to move, Chantal.' She bent down and kissed her cheek. You looked so peaceful when I came in. Sister said you would probably be waking up soon.'

'Oh, it's so good to see you again. How did you know I was here?'

'Well, Bernard phoned Sidonie this afternoon to say he was coming in to Orthopaedics to check on the patient he'd chosen for teaching purposes tomorrow morning. Bernard always asks their permission, checks these patients carefully and makes sure they know that he will be supervising his students all the time. I remember when I was one of his students I was always so impressed with the care he took to ensure the patients knew exactly what they were letting themselves in for.'

'I love to hear about when you were one of Bernard's students and you found him so difficult and demanding as a professor while you were studying with him for that prestigious exam in orthopaedic surgery.'

Julia laughed. 'He was only being difficult, he told me afterwards, to ensure I got the best results. After that I managed to thaw him out and… well, you know how it all ended. Marriage and a baby on the way. Anyway, Sister Sidonie told Bernard you were in the side ward here, having sprained your ankle and stretched the ligaments. That must be really painful. I just had to come and check how you are and if there was anything you need.'

'I can't fault the way they've treated me. Right from the time Michel picked me up off the beach'

'Michel? What on earth were the two of you doing on the beach together?'

Chantal, well aware of the insinuating grin on her cousin's face, quickly set her straight with the basic details, starting with the important fact that they hadn't gone to the beach together. Michel had arrived just as she'd tripped up on a killer of a stone absolutely lying in wait for her.

'Ah, I see. So Michel brought you back to hospital, set up your treatment and then disappeared.'

'He's coming back this evening to check on me. How's young Philippe?'

Julia's expression softened. It was always obvious that she adored her husband's son from his first marriage.

'He's fine. Marianne—you remember our brilliant housekeeper who's been with the family since she was sixteen? Well, she's at home with Philippe. We told him we were going to see you but that he couldn't come to see you this time because he had an early start tomorrow. School in the morning, so it was an early night tonight. Marianne was giving him supper when we left and we'll be back in time to read him a bedtime story.'

Chantal gave a nostalgic sigh. 'I always loved the bedtime stories you and I had when we were staying together at your house or mine in Montreuil before Mum and I went to live in Paris, didn't you?'

Julia smiled. 'We lived more like sisters in those days, just like our mothers had been, didn't we?'

Chantal giggled. 'And because our mothers are identical twins I used to wake up sometimes in the night at your house, calling out for my mother. When your mother came in I was convinced she was mine. Oh, hello, Bernard.'

Her cousin-in-law came over and kissed her cheek. 'How are you getting on, Chantal? Are they treating you OK?'

'I'm being spoiled rotten.'

'Even by the exacting Michel?'

Someone else was pushing open the door. Chantal watched as Michel advanced into the crowded side ward. He grinned as he overheard Bernard's comment about him.

Bernard shook his colleague's hand. 'Sorry, Michel, I didn't know you were coming back this evening. Such devotion to duty.'

Michel raised an eyebrow. 'And on my day off too!'

'Actually, we were just leaving. Promised to be back home before Philippe goes to sleep. He adores Marianne but there's nothing like a paternal voice reading the bedtime story, is there?'

Bernard held out his hand to help his wife as she got to her feet.

She smiled up at him. 'Oh, so you're volunteering to read the story tonight, are you?'

'Don't want to tire you out, my love.' He placed a hand gently over Julia's pregnant bump. 'Only a few weeks to go now.'

'Don't forget you promised to make me godmother,' Chantal said.

'You'll be the most perfect godmother,' Julia said as she bent over the bed to give her cousin a kiss.

After they'd gone Michel lost no time in checking out her injured ankle. He looked down at her as his experienced fingers gently palpated the damaged area. She winced but refrained from comment as she looked up at him. His expression was so sensitive, so caring, so totally wrapped up in what his patient had suffered and was going through. She told herself that was all she was, another patient. And that was how she wanted their relationship to remain.

'Good. The swelling's going down. Sister's done a good job this afternoon.'

He sat down in the chair beside the bed. 'Anything you'd like to ask before I go?'

She found herself wishing she dared ask him to stay longer but instead she shook her head and told him she was sure the nurses would continue to take care of her. Better to dampen down the ridiculous feelings she was experiencing. Who needed male company anyway? Certainly she didn't.

He stood up. 'I'm sure they will. I'll go and see Sister now and find out who's on duty this evening. You must have some supper, Chantal. Got to keep up your strength. I'll be back in the morning to see you.'

She watched as the door closed after him, willing the sad feeling to go away. She knew she mustn't allow these insane seductive feelings about Michel to enter her mind. In her post-Jacques life she'd convinced herself that she could never trust a man with her heart again. She would never open herself up to potential pain. She must remind herself every day and never weaken her resolution.

Michel drove out of the staff car park at a furious rate. He slowed as he started to ascend the narrow winding road to the top of the hill. This was always where he began to relax after he'd been on duty. But today he found it harder than usual to switch off, even though technically, it had been his day off.

Reluctantly he admitted to himself that the problem was Chantal. Ever since she'd joined the staff in Emergency in February he'd been aware of her. She was different from all the others. Someone whose company he enjoyed. But it was a totally platonic feeling. It had been more than three years since Maxine had died and his love for her had grown stronger. Every day he still grieved. But somehow when he was with Chantal he became interested in her as a woman.

Surely, that didn't mean he was being unfaithful to the memory of Maxine, did it? It just meant he was a full-blooded normal male and being with an attractive, intelligent woman like Chantal stirred him. But he wouldn't allow himself to go along with those feelings. Being with her today, touching her skin, smelling the scent of her body had brought it all to a head. He certainly didn't want to act on any of these feelings. Heavens above, she'd been his patient today! He would have to hand her on to a colleague for further treatment.

He got out of the car in his driveway and looked out over the stunning sea view. He turned to watch the sun setting over the hill. He was alone, as he was meant to be for the rest of his life. To love a woman was to risk the bitter pain he'd felt when Maxine had been taken from him. He couldn't risk that again. Not in one lifetime.

CHAPTER TWO

As MICHEL DROVE his car down the hill above St Martin sur Mer he was feeling apprehensive. Even the glorious sea view couldn't distract him from thinking about his work in Emergency today. It had been a month since he'd picked up Chantal from the beach and taken her back to the Hôpital de la Plage. He'd made sure he'd referred her to the orthopaedic ward the day after he'd treated her.

He swallowed hard as he changed into a lower gear. His reasons were obvious only to himself and his colleagues hadn't questioned his decision Basically, they'd followed his advice on the treatment plan he'd recommended and Chantal had been an exemplary patient. Today was the first day she was going to work with him in Emergency for a full day, without the aid of her stick.

He'd been impressed with her absolute determination to cope with the work he'd given her during the last two weeks she'd spent in Emergency on light duties, always aided by her stick and always within reaching distance of a chair in case she became tired.

As he drove through the hospital gates he told himself to stop worrying about her. She was a feisty girl, dependable in any situation. Always cool and unflustered with whatever problems a patient posed. An absolute natural in their department. She'd be able to cope today when he'd scheduled her to work the whole day.

Switching off the engine in the car park, he managed to convince himself that she wasn't his problem. He'd prescribed her treatment and the result was that she had a healthy, viable ankle that shouldn't cause problems in the future. So he should stop thinking about her. There was work to be done and Chantal was just another colleague in his department...wasn't she?

It was ironic that she was the first person he saw as he pushed open the swing doors into Emergency. He couldn't help smiling at her. She looked so young and fresh and raring to go this morning. He had to remember not to treat her any differently from his other colleagues.

'Ready to work all day?'

'Of course! I've dealt with a couple of patients already. No problem.'

She covered the few steps between them, consciously walking correctly, as she'd practised with the physiotherapists; heel toe, heel toe.

'Very good.'

She grinned, unable to stop feeling pleased with herself at his praise.

'Oh, I've had only the best treatment, you know. And I was determined to get back to normal working life as soon as I possibly could.'

'I know you were.' He averted his gaze, which was full of admiration. As his phone rang 'Well, then, let's see what we're landed with today,' he said, getting out his smartphone to scroll through his messages. 'Hold on a moment, Chantal. I may need your help immediately. I'm getting a message through about a car crash on the motorway.'

Even as he spoke the doors to Emergency swung open and a couple of porters with patients on trolleys followed each other inside. From outside the building came the sound of another ambulance arriving.

'Dr Devine,' the first porter called. 'This woman is in pain and she won't stop screaming. She's completely hysterical. I can't—'

'Let me help you,' Chantal said in a soothingly calm voice as she moved to meet the porter.

'I'll deal with the second patient,' Michel said. 'Contact me whenever you need me.'

Chantal had already directed the porter to take their patient into the nearest vacant cubicle and was leaning over her, trying to reassure her that she was safe. The screams had now turned to sobs as the patient clung to Chantal's hand.

She was aware that Michel had just arrived and was taking his place at the other side of the trolley.

'I've handed my patient to a colleague so I can get the general picture of where I'm needed most. I thought you might need some help here.'

He could see Chantal was having a soothing influence on the hysterical patient as she gently asked her name.

'Josephine,' the patient whispered now in between sobs. 'I will be OK, won't I?'

'Yes, you will. I'm Dr Chantal Winstone and I'm going to do everything I can to help you. Now, tell me where it hurts Josephine. Let me...'

As Chantal began to pull back the blanket covering her patient she was immediately aware of her condition. She was a large lady but it wasn't just due to obesity. She was definitely pregnant.

Chantal held back her own emotions, the feelings she'd had about pregnancy ever since she'd lost her own much-wanted baby sometimes overwhelming. It was only a fleeting memory of the horrors of her miscarriage that came to her. She was a doctor and should be totally dispassionate about any medical situation. When she was needed she had to deal with the case as expertly as possible.

She took a deep breath and for a split second her eyes met Michel's. She mustn't show her conflicting emotions in front of him. The patient always came first.

'Josephine, when is your baby due?' she asked quietly.

'I don't really know with this one, Doctor. This will be my fifth, you see, and I've been so busy I haven't really had time to get to the doctor's. I know I've missed a few periods but I've lost count and… Oh, help me…'

By the time the screaming started again Chantal had removed the blanket and was checking her patient's abdomen. The contraction she could now feel was very strong. A swift examination of the birth canal showed her that the cervix was well dilated.

She glanced up at Michel. 'Call Obstetrics to send a midwife. We can't move our patient up to them at this late stage. And if you could bring me that gas and air apparatus over there by the door?'

Her full attention was back on her patient. 'Breathe deeply, Josephine, deep breaths, breath through the pain. Thanks, Michel.'

She took the mask he'd prepared and fixed it over her patient's face. 'There we go, breathe through now, yes, that's good, very good, keep going like that, Josephine.'

Michel found himself marvelling at how calm

Chantal was through all this. No one else in the team who'd rescued their patient from her crashed car on the motorway had suspected she was pregnant. They were working fluidly together now. He'd moved to check on the dilation of the cervix.

'The cervix is fully dilated now, Chantal. I can see the head. Don't let Josephine push until the next contraction. I need to adjust the cord.'

'Pant for the moment, Josephine, breathe short breaths. Excellent. Well done. I'll tell you when you can push. Not yet. OK, now, push, bear down into your bottom, the baby's head has made an appearance. Yes, a little rest for you now...'

She was watching for another signal from Michel. As their eyes met she saw the relief in his, he saw the enigmatic emotions that the baby's delivery had set in motion. Yes, she was deeply involved, not just giving this delivery her all in terms of expertise and experience. She was deeply moved even though outwardly she remained calm and in control.

He wondered if she had an issue with childbirth. Had she had a bad experience somewhere in her own past? Whatever had happened to her, she was a joy to work with now. They dovetailed together as they worked well together.

Josephine was clinging to Chantal's hand.

'You're doing fine, Josephine.'

Michel signalled for a final push. As the baby moved down the birth canal he took it into his hands and it began to cry lustily.

'Here you are, Chantal.'

He was handing her the baby wrapped in a dressing sheet. As she took the baby from him he could see the tears in her eyes, the deep involvement she had with this birth, the tender way she held the precious bundle in her arms. For a moment their eyes met over the baby and Chantal let out a sigh of relief.

'Thank God,' she whispered huskily. 'A live birth is always a miracle.'

For a moment she didn't appear aware of her surroundings. Seconds later she cleared her throat and became totally professional again as very gently she handed the baby to her patient.

'Here's your daughter, Josephine.'

Now it was Josephine's turn to shed tears of joy. 'A daughter! After four boys she's very welcome. I shall call her Chantal, Doctor. You've been so kind to me. I couldn't have got through this without you.'

'Oh, I think you could,' Chantal said, dabbing her eyes with a tissue as she turned away from the joyful scene of mother and baby together.

Suddenly she was aware that Michel was beside her, his hand on her shoulder. 'Are you OK, Chantal?'

'I'm fine.' she said firmly, turning to look up into his eyes. 'It's always an emotional experience when a baby is born, isn't it?'

He was holding onto his own mixed emotions now. He had to get a grip on himself where Chantal was concerned. She disturbed him too much and at this moment he wasn't sure why.

A midwife came into the cubicle. 'I came as soon as I could but— Oh, I see I was too late. Sorry about that but we're very busy in Obstetrics at the moment.'

'Don't worry,' Chantal told her. 'I'll hand Josephine and her daughter over to you now. I haven't done the postnatal checks yet. This is a fifth baby and Josephine was involved in a car crash earlier.'

'I'll leave you to it, Chantal,' Michel said, as he heard her starting on the patient's history with the midwife. 'I'll check on what's happening to the other new patients. May I suggest you take a break before you work on your next patient?'

She glanced at him enquiringly. What was he implying?

'It's your first day back on full-time duties,' he said, quietly before turning away and leaving the cubicle.

After filling the midwife in with Josephine's details she left her patient and the new baby in her care. Josephine clung to her hand. 'Do you have to leave me, Dr Chantal?'

'I'm afraid so. But you'll be well looked after when you're taken to the postnatal ward.'

She bent down to say goodbye to the baby. The little rosebud mouth was moving as if acknowledging her. She could feel tears prickling behind her eyes as she swiftly became professional again and left the cubicle.

She'd taken Michel's advice and had a short break in the staff coffee bar before she returned to report to him in Emergency. He strode across to meet her as she came in through the swing doors.

'Everything OK? How's the ankle?'

'It's bearing up very well, thank you. You seem to have everything under control here.'

'Yes, we had six patients from the crash. The rest had been allocated to another hospital in this area. Josephine was one of the ones who was totally blameless apparently. So we won't have the police coming in to interview her.'

'Thank goodness for that. Josephine needs rest now to enjoy her new baby.' She heard her voice crack with emotion as she spoke and hoped Michel hadn't noticed.

Michel heard the emotional involvement expressed in Chantal's voice and wondered once more what had happened to her before she'd joined the staff in February.

'So you're fit to work again now, are you?'

'Of course.'

'Well, there's a young boy waiting to be seen in cubicle two. His mother is with him.'

'Fine.' Chantal turned away and went to check on her next patient. She found a small boy who'd just arrived after falling on his way to school. He was crying as he clung to his mother's hand.

'Be quiet, Albert. The doctor's here now.'

Chantal looked down at her patient on the treatment table. He was shivering with shock. She spread a cosy lightweight blanket over him. He stopped shivering and looked up at her enquiringly with wide trusting blue eyes, deciding that this lady doctor was OK. Quite pretty, actually. Nice teeth when she smiled at him, which she was doing now.

Chantal glanced down at the notes that had just been given to her.

'Albert, can you tell me what happened when you were walking to school?'

'There was this dog, you see,' he began tentatively.

Chantal smiled. 'I see. Was it a big dog?'

'Oh, it was enormous! But I'm not scared of dogs, am I, Mum?'

'Not a big boy like you, Albert. Now, tell the nice lady doctor how you ran much too quickly when you chased the dog and tripped up on that kerbstone.'

'So where did you hurt yourself when you fell?'

'All down my leg.' He pulled back the side of the blanket to reveal an improvised bandage of old cloths. 'You should have seen the blood, Doctor.'

'I can see the bloodstains peeping through the bandage, Albert. Who put the bandage on?'

'The lady with the dog. She took me into her house and told me I was a naughty boy for chasing him.'

Chantal could see more tears threatening. 'Mind if I have a look?' She was already peeling off the cloths very carefully so that they wouldn't pull on his skin. 'Oh, yes, now I see the problem. Don't worry, Albert, I'll soon have that sorted.'

'What are you going to do to me? You're not going to chop it off, are you? My friend's dad had to go into hospital to have his leg chopped off. He walks with crutches now. I don't mind having crutches but I'd like to keep my leg on if you don't mind. You see, I play football.'

She gave him a reassuring smile. 'I'm simply going to mend the cut that's appeared in the skin.

Can you feel this nice soothing liquid I'm painting all over the cut?'

'What's that for?'

'That's cleaning the wound and—'

'Have I got a wound? Like a soldier?'

'Yes, and you're behaving like a brave little soldier for me. I've just put some painkiller on it so it won't hurt much. Not that you'll need it as you're such a brave boy. How old are you, Albert?'

'Five and a half,' he said proudly.

'You're a big boy for your age.'

Then she fell silent as she focussed on the task in hand.

'There, all done. I've put some stitches in so that—'

'Stitches? How many?'

She solemnly counted them one by one.

'Six.' She was spraying the whole area of affected leg now.

'Six? Wait till I get back to school and show everybody!'

'Doctor, do you think I should keep him at home today?' his mother asked anxiously.

Chantal replied that one day at home would be advisable to give the healing process a good start. She explained how to treat the little boy for the next ten days before his mother took him to see their family doctor who would arrange for the stitches to be taken out.

'Oh, don't they dissolve by themselves?'

'Not this kind of stitches. Because the wound is quite wide and in an area of the leg that will get a lot of movement from an active boy like Albert, it's advisable to put very strong stitches in.'

She pulled back the curtain of her cubicle as she said goodbye to her little patient and his mother. The cubicles were all being used now and further patients were being wheeled in on trolleys.

Better get a move on. Michel didn't like to have too many patients who hadn't been seen by a doctor.

She found herself busy all day with a seemingly endless stream of patients. There was no time to think about herself. She was glad she would be going off duty soon because her ankle was aching now. Actually, it had been aching for the past hour or so but she'd chosen to ignore it. It would be a sign of weakness if she sat down during working hours.

The evening staff were arriving and taking over the patients who were still waiting to be seen. She took the opportunity to go into the office to write her report. Settling herself in front of the computer with her right foot on a chair, she turned sideways and switched on the computer. It was a relief to take the weight off her ankle.

She typed on in her difficult position, listing the wide variety of cases she'd dealt with that day.

Before the crash patients from the motorway had arrived, her first patient had been the child with a frozen pea up his nose. Frozen when it had gone up, according to Dad, but decidedly squelchy and messy when she'd managed to pull it out with her smallest forceps. The blood that came with it was because of the various attempts that had been made to reach it with a variety of household instruments, including a spoon, before the young boy had been brought to Emergency as a last resort.

She'd assured the worried father that the bleeding was only shallow and would stop soon as long as the young patient promised not to pick his delicate little nose.

Following that, there had been the motorbike rider on the coastal road who'd crashed into the back of a car that had stopped suddenly. X-rays had shown a fractured tibia and fibula so she'd called in Orthopaedics to admit him to a ward before they operated on him. The operation had been successful.

'So this is where you're hiding?'

She recognised Michel's voice behind her, lifted her ankle with both hands to support it and turned the desk chair round.

'Don't let me disturb you, Chantal. How does your ankle feel after a whole day on your feet? Tell me honestly. Don't be brave about it.'

'Well, it aches a bit now. It's just because it's tired.'

'OK, that's a warning sign to ease off. Come in after lunch tomorrow and just work the afternoon.'

She raised one eyebrow. 'Are you sure, Michel?

I don't want my colleagues to think I'm getting preferential treatment.'

'And why on earth would they think that?'

'Well, I've had a lot of time off recently and...' She felt flustered as she attempted an explanation. 'You're the boss. If you think it's OK then I'd best take your advice.'

He put on a serious expression. 'I'm absolutely certain. Easy does it.'

'You've been so kind to me.' She was merely stating the obvious while no one was around to hear her praising him. She just felt she'd had preferential treatment and had to be careful.

'I'm just being an attentive doctor to a valuable colleague.' His voice was husky. He cleared his throat, before continuing in a totally neutral voice without a hint of emotion, 'You're a very useful doctor in our department so we don't want to mess up the treatment you've had at this stage.'

She felt another surge of gratitude. 'I was wondering...'

'Yes?'

'I'm truly grateful for the way you've taken care of me since I sprained my ankle and I'm sorry for the way I was so grumpy when you found me lying in the sand.'

'Oh, Chantal, you were suffering from shock. Completely understandable. You were in pain. It was perfectly natural for you to behave like that. Forget it.'

'Well, I've been thinking.'

She paused as she reflected that she really had been thinking too much about this delicate situation. It had started while she'd had to spend a lot of time resting during the early part of her treatment. Now was the time to act before she lost her nerve.

'I'd like to buy you supper one evening as a means of thanking you for all your help in getting me back on my feet'

He was staring at her now, seemingly lost for words. 'Chantal, you don't have to buy me supper.'

'Oh, but I'd like to.'

She'd rehearsed this invitation so often, not knowing how he would take it. She hadn't meant to deliver it in this awkward position, sitting sideways to the desk, holding her convalescent ankle with both hands. She must look so ungainly.

'Of course I know you must be busy in the evenings so if—'

'I'd like to take up your offer, Chantal. Thank you. What did you have in mind?'

He was smiling now, trying to lighten up. She'd caught him completely off guard. It had been the last thing he'd expected from her.

'Well, I thought it would be fun to have supper at that old wooden beach café near the place where you rescued me from that killer stone. I used to be taken there for lunch after a morning on the beach at Club Mickey. It was before my father died, I remember.

'Every August my cousin Julia and her brothers came over from England with their parents for a holiday and that was where we'd all meet up. It was such a treat. Our mothers—they're twins—were always there. Our fathers were both English so the conversation over lunch switched from English to French all the time. It was such a happy time in my life.'

He noted the poignant hint of nostalgia in her

voice before he spoke to reassure her of his interest in this kind invitation.

'I'd enjoy going to the beach café, Chantal. Actually, I've never got around to visiting it. It looks a quaint sort of place.'

She smiled. 'I'm not surprised you haven't tried it yet. It looks very shabby now. The winter winds and rain mean it needs repainting every summer. They haven't got around to that yet this year but it's got its faithful clientele just the same.'

'Will you make the booking or shall I?'

'Oh, we don't need to book. It's first come first served. Just let me know when you're free.'

'How about tomorrow?'

She hid her surprise at his prompt reply. She'd expected him to defer his answer and then possibly forget about it. She wouldn't have had the nerve to repeat her invitation.

'Yes, that would be good. If I'm only working for the afternoon I won't be tired.'

He nodded. 'That was exactly what I was thinking. We'll go straight there when we come off duty. Now, finish your report as soon as you can and go and rest that ankle on your bed with a pillow to elevate it. Be sure to call Housekeeping and order supper to be brought up to your room.'

'Oh, I didn't know that was possible.'

'All things are possible for the medical staff of the Hôpital de la Plage.'

He was reaching across the desk for the internal phone. 'This is Michel Devine. My colleague Dr Winstone will be resting in her room this evening. Could one of your staff take her a supper tray? Yes, about seven o'clock.'

He broke off to speak to Chantal. 'Coq au vin, omelette, or salade Niçoise?'

'Salade Niçoise, please.'

He relayed the message. 'So I'll see you tomorrow afternoon, Chantal. Now, do rest that ankle.'

He turned and moved towards the door to stop himself regretting his decision to have supper with Chantal. Closing the door after he'd passed through it, he leaned against it, breathing heavily.

'You OK, Dr Devine?'

He hadn't noticed a junior nurse coming along the corridor.

'Yes, I'm fine, thank you, Nurse.' He recovered

quickly and smiled down at the young lady who was looking earnestly concerned about him.

He started walking in the other direction. Taking care of Chantal as a colleague posed no problems. But spending a whole evening with her in the romantic setting of the beach as the sun disappeared behind the hills? What was he thinking? It was the sort of situation he'd avoided since Maxine had died. OK he'd play it cool, very cool. No emotional involvement.

Two colleagues having supper together, discussing...well, whatever colleagues are supposed to discuss. Nothing remotely romantic. Books, theatre, cinema. That sort of thing should keep the evening going without too many gaps in the conversation. Ah, she'd lived and worked in Paris, hadn't she? He could leave most of the talking to her.

Chantal could tell it was already morning before she even opened her eyes. She could hear the sound of footsteps hurrying down the corridor. Everybody was going on duty. But she had been ordered to rest.

She opened her eyes and looked at the travel clock on her bedside table. Eight o clock! She hadn't set her alarm for once. No need for that this morning.

The phone rang. It was housekeeping asking if she would like breakfast. Dr Devine had left instructions for them to call. 'Would you like a croissant?'

'Yes, please.'

'And a coffee with milk?'

'Please' She liked dipping her croissant in a large breakfast cup of milky coffee.

She got out of bed and went over to the window, pulling back the curtains. Wall-to-wall sunshine already. Well, it was almost summer. From her window she could see the main gate, the ambulances lined up for duty, one already speeding in from the seafront, making its way to Emergency where everybody would be hard at work by now. Including Michel. She swallowed hard as she thought of her embarrassing attempt to ask him out for supper yesterday evening. She'd been successful but she could tell he had only been polite with her. He would probably be relieved when it was all over. She couldn't think why she'd set it up. Well, actually, she did have an idea but it was too complicated to analyse.

Was she testing herself to see if she really had changed into the ice maiden she tried to portray to the opposite sex? If that was her real reason for this date—if she could even call it that she'd have no problem sticking to the vows she'd made to herself last September. None whatsoever. Her emotions were completely surrounded by ice.

Someone was knocking on her door. She shrugged into her dressing gown and went to open it, taking the breakfast tray from the maid then climbing back into bed.

As she dipped her croissant in the coffee she reflected that her rendezvous with Michel this evening would be harmless as long as she remembered she'd arranged this meal together to thank a kind friend and colleague for all his help. That was the sole object of this evening out together.

'Are you ready to go off duty, Chantal?'

The afternoon had flown by as she'd dealt with

an influx of patients from a crash on the coastal road involving a coach and two cars. She was pulling back the curtains from her cubicle as her final patient was being taken away on a trolley to be admitted to Orthopaedics.

'Have all the patients been seen, Michel?'

'Treated, discharged, admitted and no fatalities. The evening staff have all arrived. I've even dealt with the police investigation and sent them on their way satisfied they've got all the medical details they need for their report. Excellent teamwork by everyone this afternoon, so let's go!'

She wasn't fooled by his bright and breezy attitude. He was as apprehensive as she was.

'Give me ten minutes to clean myself up.'

'Ten minutes? You look fine to me. OK. See you by the front entrance.'

She headed for the staff changing room to change into a pair of jeans and tee shirt, adding the white sweater she'd brought to tie around her neck in case it got chilly later on. Not that they were going to stay long enough for the evening chill to set in. A quick supper, a polite chat and they'd go their separate ways, wouldn't they?

She glanced at her reflection. Mmm, not bad. A dash of lipstick and then she would be ready.

Michel was chatting to Sidonie by the main entrance and Chantal slowed her pace. Mustn't seem too eager to be off.

Sidonie broke off the conversation. 'Hi, Chantal. You look like you're off out. Going anywhere nice?'

'Off to the beach café for supper.'

'Oh, that's where you're going Michel, isn't it? Ah, so you're going together? Keeping up the aftercare of your patient? Very commendable. Well, don't let me keep you. Have fun but beware the killer of stones.'

Sidonie smiled at them as she moved away down the corridor.

Chantal was beginning to wish she'd never dreamed up this supper date. The entire medical staff would have heard about it by tomorrow morning.

'So, shall we go?'

Michel was looking down at her, a wry grin

on his face, probably knowing exactly what she was thinking but hoping he was covering up his apprehension better than she was.

CHAPTER THREE

CHANTAL WAS VERY pleased to see that the Café de la Plage was filling up with lots of happy people. She was glad to have got through a busy afternoon working in Emergency and was now ready for some leisure time. She noticed chattering families, a couple of small babies being rocked off to sleep in their pushchairs, one by a serene-looking, white-haired grandmother and the other by a harassed-looking young mother who was also coping with a lively, demanding toddler while Papa was completely engrossed in a dispute with the elder sister.

It was the sort of warm family atmosphere she remembered from when she had been brought in here as a small child by both her parents, before her father had died. She felt safe here, at home, relaxed—well, almost. There was still a nagging doubt at the back of her mind that she could have made a mistake, asking out the boss on the pretext—no, it hadn't been a pretext! It had been a genuine desire to say thank you to a colleague, now a good friend, who'd been extremely helpful in her time of need.

What other possible reason could she have had? After the treatment she'd suffered at the hands of the duplicitous Jacques she didn't trust any man, not even Michel, who was obviously still in love with his irreplaceable wife.

Michel was holding the back of her chair, politely intent on making sure she was comfortable. She hoped they would both relax a bit more when they settled into their table by the window. Their conversation as they had walked across the sand had seemed strained, contrived almost, as they'd talked about their work and barely glanced at the setting sun, which was low in the sky behind the hills, causing a pink blush over the clouds and strands of gold to weave in and out of the lovely scenery.

She'd had the urge to stop and admire it but hadn't known whether Michel had time for such romantic elements in his busy life. His devotion to duty was legendary at the hospital. He seemed to live for his work and probably hadn't got time for sunsets and sunrises.

She'd remarked on the sunset a couple of times but Michel had seemed to increase his pace and had appeared to be in a hurry to get the dutiful evening over and done with. Well, that's what it seemed like to her and she was beginning to feel the same way herself now they were inside the café.

She'd arranged this outing so it was her responsibility to make sure it wasn't too painful. She put on her dutiful-hostess smile as she looked across the table at Michel.

'Always a good family atmosphere in here, don't you think?'

'Well, I can't really judge because this is my first time here.'

Chantal decided to try again. 'Of course. As I told you, it's a favourite of mine from childhood.'

'Chantal! My husband didn't tell me you were here!' A plump, rosy-cheeked lady was leaning over the table. 'We haven't had the pleasure of serving you in our restaurant this season. Are you still living in Paris?'

'Ah, Florence. Lovely to see you again. Actually, I've left the Paris hospital. I'm a doctor in Emergency at the Hôpital de la Plage now.'

'A doctor? It's not possible that you're all grown up now. Now, what can I get you and your charming companion?'

Michel extended his hand. 'Michel Devine, *Madame*, a colleague of Chantal's at the hospital.'

Chantal could see that Florence was much impressed by her handsome friend and colleague. He could be really charming when he put on that dazzling smile. Florence was handing out menus now and being extremely deferential to the important-looking doctor.

Decisions were made about what they would choose from the menu. Florence put a bottle of red wine on the table. 'On the house,' she informed them, before returning to her kitchen.

'Cheers. Good health,' Michel said, raising his glass towards Chantal.

They could relax now. Michel was beginning to actually look her in the eyes. He seemed to be studying her face now, as if it was the first time he'd ever really seen her. Well, it was the first time they'd been alone together in an off-duty situation and it felt very strange.

She sipped the wine. Mmm, the house wine was always good here and the first bottle was usually a gift to regular clients.

She looked around her. 'The babies seem to be settling at last.'

Michel smiled. 'I love the sound of families enjoying themselves.' He paused, his voice husky. 'Except it reminds me...'

He was looking down at the table now, tracing the pattern woven into the lace. She waited until he looked across at her a few seconds later. There was a sad expression on his face.

'What does it remind you of?' she prompted gently.

'Oh, it's not important. I was simply going to say...'

'Here you two go, a small starter for you.'

Florence was placing a couple of plates in front of them. There was pâté garnished with a tomato salad and gherkins and a basket containing warm, freshly baked bread in the centre of the table.

Chantal made a mental note to ask Michel what he'd been going to say just now about the families enjoying supper together. It had appeared to have had a profound effect on him. But she wasn't going to pursue that line of conversation at the moment. Not when she was feeling relaxed and could see Michel was enjoying himself at last.

He picked up the bottle and poured more wine into her glass. She knew she would have to slow down on the wine at some point. Still, they weren't driving and if she stumbled on the sand, Michel could always carry her. She suppressed a giggle as she reached for more of the delicious bread to accompany the tasty pâté.

'What's so amusing?'

She laughed. 'I was just reminding myself I've got to walk over the sand near where I sprained my ankle so I'd better go easy on the wine.'

He laughed with her. 'No problem. We coped last time, didn't we?'

'There won't be a repeat tonight, I assure you,' she said firmly, biting into a gherkin.

Florence took away their starter plates and placed a steaming tureen of asparagus soup on the table.

By the time the main course was served Chantal's initial hunger was feeling deliciously appeased. They were both eating the roast-chicken dish much more slowly, talking more across the table, and the wine seemed to be disappearing very quickly. This was definitely a fun evening at last. The ice had been well and truly broken.

They had started discussing the theatres in Paris, shows they'd seen, music that pleased or displeased them. All the worthwhile frills of life that got pushed into the background when they filled their days with work, however important it was.

'Yes, I do find I have to make time for leisure pursuits when I'm living away from Paris,' Chantal said. 'I love the countryside and the sea but sometimes I long to go out to the theatre.'

'There's a very good theatre in Le Touquet. I must take you there one evening.'

'I'd like that.' She would, she really would. Going to the theatre was something that good friends and colleagues could enjoy together without it meaning any commitment on either side.

Florence's husband, Giles, who was now waiting on the tables while Florence concentrated on the cooking, paused beside their table to remove the empty bottle and bring back a new one. Michel was now chatting amicably with Giles about wine. It transpired that Giles's brother had a vineyard near Bordeaux so supplies of good wine were easy to come by.

Chantal could feel herself warming more and more towards Michel. She was seeing sides of his character she'd never seen before. Asking him to come out for supper tonight had been a good idea after all. And whatever her motives might have been, she was enjoying herself, delighted that she was getting to know the real man behind the work-obsessed Michel.

The restaurant was now completely full and people were queuing outside. They'd finished their delicious dessert of raspberry tart when Florence asked if they would like to have their coffee served on the veranda.

Michel said that was an excellent idea. It was

one of those splendid early summer evenings that were made to be enjoyed in the fresh air.

Michel chose a secluded table in the corner of the veranda, overlooking the sea. The gentle sound of the waves was so romantic, just the sort of evening for a stroll along the beach, hand in hand with someone close to you. That wouldn't happen with herself and Michel. It was obvious that even though they were enjoying themselves they were both carrying too much baggage from the past.

She took a sip from her coffee cup, her eyes on the man opposite her. His enigmatic expression was giving nothing away. Placing her delicate china cup carefully back on the saucer, she tentatively asked Michel what he'd been going to say when they had first arrived. 'You said this place reminded you of something.'

He tensed. 'Oh, it wasn't important…'

She waited patiently. 'It seemed important to you at the time.'

'Oh, well, it was just a thought about the family atmosphere in the restaurant. I began thinking, as I often do when I'm in a family-orientated place, about what might have been if my wife and I had been able to have children before she died.'

He leaned back in his chair. It had felt as if he was making a confession. Strangely enough it gave him a sense of peace. Chantal was the sort of woman he could trust. She looked as if she would understand what he'd been through, indeed what was an ongoing problem for him, never far from his mind.

Chantal drew in her breath as she looked across the small wicker table, noticing the obvious poignant distress in Michel's expression. A slight breeze from the beach ruffled the edge of the white tablecloth. It was almost as if the ghosts of the past had come to disturb them.

She leaned forward. 'Would you have liked to have had a family?'

He cleared his throat. 'It's my deepest regret that we didn't. It was my wife's cancer that prevented it and then...then she died.'

The silence that ensued was almost palpable. She felt uneasy. Had she caused him more sadness by probing into his past? Maybe if she assured him that she understood something of his pain, that she too had suffered.

'I would have loved to have a baby.' She took another sip of coffee to steady her nerves. Yes, it would help him if she told him what she'd been through and how it had affected her.

She looked out across the sand towards the waves dimly outlined by the lights from the shore. She felt calmness descending on her. Yes, it might help to reassure him that she could understand his distress.

'Last September I was in a long-term relationship with someone. At least, I thought it was permanent. He'd asked me to marry him. He appeared overjoyed when I told him I was pregnant.'

She paused to take a deep breath. 'And then I discovered that he had a wife. I was three months pregnant, looking forward to having our baby. Discovering that Jacques had deceived me triggered a miscarriage.'

Michel reached across the table and took her small hand in his. 'How traumatic for you. The miscarriage that followed his deception…that's impossible to contemplate.'

She nodded, unable to speak for a short while, but the touch of his fingers around hers gave her the strength to continue.

'In the few hours I had between learning the truth and losing the baby I'd already decided that I desperately wanted my baby. I would make every effort to bring up my child in a loving environment. My mother was widowed when I was seven and subsequently she brought me up by herself. She was a wonderful example for me to copy. I planned to give my child the close upbringing that I had with my feisty mother. Even though I would be a single mother I knew I could provide my child with a strong, stable family unit.'

She swallowed hard. 'But that wasn't to be.'

He squeezed her hand. 'Chantal you're young. You've plenty of time to have babies in the future.'

She removed her hand from his grasp and placed it in her lap. It was too upsetting emotionally to have him giving out sympathy when his own suffering was still painful for him.

'Ah, but the problem is I'd have to commit myself and I could never trust my heart to a man again. It would mean opening myself up to potential pain in the future. So I've reconciled myself to the idea that I'm not going to have a family. I've got a good, rewarding career, which totally absorbs me.'

For a few minutes neither of them spoke. They were the only people left outside on the veranda as they looked out at the moonlight shining on the sea. Florence and Giles had retired to their living quarters at the side of the café.

Michel was deep in thought. Such a peaceful scene would hopefully soothe them both. Dared he broach the subject nearest to his heart?

Gently, he broke the silence. 'I know exactly what you mean. I'm utterly devoted to my work at the hospital. For me, taking care of my patients and staff takes the place of emotional commitment now. I determined after Maxine died that I would never allow the love of a woman to enter my life again. You see, I associate the joy of love with the bitter sensation of loss. I don't allow myself to get close to anyone because of that. My only regret is that it means I'll never have children.'

She nodded. 'Like me, you've had to come to terms with the fact that you'll never have a child. The pain never goes away, does it? Tonight when you saw those happy families you got a sharp reminder of what you will always miss. When I'm in hospital, delivering a baby, holding a little miracle in my arms as I did with our patient from the car crash, when Josephine asked if she could call her baby Chantal...'

She forced herself to continue as he leaned forward, seemingly hanging on her every word. 'When I contemplate a barren future sometimes...'

'But there is a way out.' His voice was devoid of emotion, completely calm as he interrupted her.

She stared at him. 'What do you mean?'

He placed both his hands on the table, palms downward. 'We both want a baby but no commitment to each other,' he said slowly. 'We could be parents of convenience. Don't you think?'

She hesitated before nodding. 'Yes,' she said weakly, her voice a mere whisper as her imagination ran riot. What was Michel getting at? Where was this emotive conversation going?

He stood up, pulling his chair round the table so that they were closer together. Was he going to suggest something they could do together to realise their dreams? She could smell the scent of his aftershave, his skin, his body so that she could almost feel the testosterone swirling through his powerful manly frame. She was sensually moved by being so close to him. It wasn't possible to discuss something of this nature without being emotionally involved, was it? Should she stop him before he asked her an impossibly intimate question?

He cleared his throat. 'Maybe there's a solution to our problem. We both want the same thing— a baby. Neither of us wants a relationship. We get on well as good friends with no strings attached. It's not beyond the bounds of possibility that we could...'

She held her breath, her emotions churning as she waited for him to explain.

'We must be totally professional about the situation.'

He paused, as if searching for words.

She sat very still, waiting for him to continue. What on earth did he have in mind?

He reached for the glass of brandy that Giles had placed beside his coffee cup before he'd left them alone earlier.

Chantal had studiously ignored hers at first but now she also raised her glass to her lips.

'How would you feel about investigating the possibility of having donor insemination? We would use my sperm to make you pregnant. There are some excellent clinics we could choose from where the procedure could take place.'

She told herself she was relieved that he'd reverted to his medical voice, making it quite clear there was no emotion to be involved in this situation. So why did part of her wish that he wasn't being quite so professional about his suggestion?

'If you did become pregnant I would help you through the pregnancy, giving you support as I did when you sprained your ankle.'

'Michel, pregnancy and caring for a baby is a lot harder than having a sprained ankle!' she told him sharply. 'It's a lifetime's commitment to another human being. We'd have to draw up an agreement about the parenting of our baby, making sure the child was our priority in a completely unselfish way. There would be so many obstacles if we were intent on getting it right, I'm not sure it would work.'

She could see the hope in his eyes disappearing. 'Even though I must admit it's very tempting.'

Even as she said that she told herself she had to be very careful of this man. She mustn't trust any man in a situation where she might find herself depending on him. She must keep her independence at all costs.

'So, what do you think?'

She squared her shoulders. 'You know, in spite of all the problems I can foresee, I do so want to have a baby!'

'That makes two of us!'

He smiled directly into her eyes, that sexy smile that she knew would be one of the obstacles she'd have to deal with. Could she have the baby she longed for without giving in to her natural feelings towards the father of her child?

'Think about it, Chantal. Take your time, no pressure. We've got to agree between us on the parenting involved and so forth. Then we've got to find a discreet clinic where we can be treated and—'

'So many problems to cope with. It's all a bit overwhelming.' The doubts were creeping in already.

'That's why we'll both take our time.' He stood up and held out his hand to raise her to her feet. 'Let me know if you want to continue with the idea and we'll have another meeting.'

The gentle breeze had turned cold as it blew in from the sea. She shivered.

He pulled off his jacket and put it around her shoulders. 'You're getting cold. We should go. Just don't dismiss my plan completely. It's a pragmatic solution to the problem shared between two good friends. Don't write if off simply because it's not the conventional way of having a baby. Give it some thought.'

As they walked back across the beach he took hold of her hand, telling her to beware of the killer stones that lay beneath the surface of the sand, waiting to pounce onher feet as they had last time they had been here together.

She laughed. That was one of the things she liked about Michel. In spite of the strictly professional image he tried to portray with his staff he was a fun person to spend time with in an off-duty situation. Tonight she'd seen glimpses of the joyous man that he must once have been.

Listening to her laugh, Michel realised he loved the sound of her laughter. He loved lots of things about her. If they did go through with his plan to have a baby together he'd have to be so careful he didn't find himself falling in love with her. Because falling in love was wonderful but the bitter sensation of loss he would feel if or when the love was taken away from him was too awful to contemplate twice in one lifetime.

CHAPTER FOUR

CHANTAL LOOKED AROUND at the patients waiting to be seen in Emergency. The midday sun was streaming through the windows in the waiting room. Summer was well and truly here. Close by on the beach families were enjoying themselves but here in the treatment area the patients were concerned with their pain and anxiety or that of the relative or friend they were accompanying.

She held back the curtain of the cubicle where she'd just treated a patient suffering from sunburn. It could have been worse but she'd advised the mother to keep the child indoors for a few days and then to cover him with hat and loose cotton garments if it was necessary to take him outside.

Applications of non-scented talcum powder would take care of the tiny spots on the chest and underarms which she'd diagnosed as prickly heat. The mother was very young and inexperienced so had hung on every word that Chantal had spoken. She'd also been shown how to rub in the cream she'd been given to soothe the skin where it was particularly painful. The main thing was to avoid direct sunlight and seek shade wherever possible.

Chantal sensed that all eyes were on her now, everybody hoping it was their turn to be seen next. She knew which patient had been waiting for the longest time but her eyes were once again drawn to a young girl seated near the entrance. She must have come in during the time Chantal had been treating the child suffering from sunburn. She looked terribly uncomfortable as she perched on the edge of her seat, pulling a large raincoat around herself. A raincoat, on a day like this?

Chantal walked purposefully across to investigate. 'Is anybody with you, dear?' She kept her tone gentle and encouraging.

The girl pulled the raincoat around her defensively and looked down at the floor to avoid eye contact. How could she explain why she was there when she'd been telling herself she couldn't possibly be pregnant?

For weeks she'd suspected she might be but she'd tried not to think about it. You couldn't get pregnant on the first time, could you? Her fattening tummy and enlarged breasts had convinced her of the awful truth. She'd covered it up for as long as she could but now she knew she needed help. But having got herself to the hospital, she was really scared of what this doctor would say to her.

'Nobody's with me,' she muttered, half to herself.

Chantal made an instant diagnosis that needed to be checked out as soon as possible. This situation couldn't wait. The girl was older than she seemed at first from across the room. Old enough. And a large man's raincoat on a sunny day was a real giveaway.

She took the girl's hand. 'I'd like to help you. Would you like to come along with me?'

She held out her hand. Her patient ignored her hand but began to cry as she made two attempts to stand up. Chantal signalled one of the porters to bring a wheelchair over. They made it into the cubicle before her diagnosis was well and truly confirmed. As the porter lifted the girl onto the treatment couch her waters broke.

Chantal leaned over her patient to remove the sodden raincoat so she could examine her, all the time talking to her soothingly to assure her that she was in good hands. Everyone wanted to help her.

'Would you like to tell me your name?'

'Maria,' was the whispered reply, before the girl's cries became louder. 'No, oh, no, Doctor, Doctor...'

'Don't go,' Chantal told the porter. 'I need you to take us to Obstetrics. Get a trolley, please.'

Seconds later she'd informed Obstetrics she was on her way with a young patient who was in labour.

Maria was clinging to her hand as they made their way through Emergency towards the corridor that led to Obstetrics. She was aware that Michel had spotted her moving out of their department and was striding across to check what was happening. One of the waiting patients had complained to him that he should have been seen next but the lady doctor was taking care of a young girl who'd just arrived.

'I decided this patient needed to jump the queue,' she told him breathlessly, intent on keeping up with the porter and her patient, who was now howling with pain and clinging to Chantal so that she was now bent over the trolley. The porter was holding the door open for her.

She turned her head and paused for a moment to continue her explanation to Michel. 'If you remember when we delivered a baby a few weeks ago in a cubicle it certainly wasn't an ideal situation. Fortunately our baby was OK but...'

'Our baby was more than OK, Chantal, but I take your point. If there's time to get to Obstetrics that will ensure an easier delivery. You certainly seem to have this situation sorted. Keep me informed when you get to Obstetrics.'

As Chantal moved along quickly with her patient she felt disturbed by the way Michel had said 'our baby'. She knew she had to make that life-changing decision soon about whether she and Michel should have their own baby and stop shelving the issue. She brought her whole attention to her patient once more, but at the back of her mind his deep masculine voice was still with her.

'*Our baby.*'

As Michel went back into Emergency to calm the impatient man he couldn't help thinking that even though Chantal seemed to attract obstetrics patients she still hadn't mentioned the conversation they'd had some time ago on the subject. It had taken all his courage to put the idea to her. After all, it wasn't every day that two colleagues went out for supper and ended up discussing the possibility of having a baby together.

He was relieved, as he glanced around Emergency, to see that one of his colleagues had taken the complaining man into a cubicle and the department was relatively quiet again. He could even hear the constant whirring of the air conditioning.

'Dr Devine, could you help me?' one of his nurses called out.

'Of course. I'm on my way.'

He shelved the problem of Chantal's silence on

the subject nearest his heart but not before he'd decided to broach the subject with her as soon as possible. The longer he waited for an answer the harder it would become. Something was nagging him that she'd decided to say no to his unconventional plan, otherwise she would have got back to him in the intervening weeks wouldn't she?

He helped the nurse with her stitching of a wound. She could have done it by herself but seemed to prefer to have him there to supervise the procedure.

The hefty builder lying on the trolley didn't make a sound as the young nurse, her tongue firmly clamped between her teeth, slowly stitched up his wound. The patient looked up at the nurse as she breathed a sigh of relief.

'Didn't feel a thing, Nurse. Tell you what, I bet you were good at embroidery when you were at school last year, weren't you?

'I'm older than you think,' the young nurse said defensively, before glancing up at her boss to see what he'd thought of her prowess.

'Well done!'

She'd only needed a bit of encouragement. His phone was beeping. He went outside the cubicle.

'Michel, do you mind if I stay with Maria in Obstetrics during the delivery? She's only sixteen and there's nobody with her. The cervix is well dilated so I shouldn't be long.'

'Take as long as you like, Chantal. I'll cover for you and send for extra help.'

He was confident that a quick call to the staffing agency would solve the problem. At this time of year newly qualified doctors had registered with the medical agency he found was the most efficient and were anxious to work in his prestigious Emergency department. He dialled the number.

As he was pressing numbers and waiting to speak to a human voice he reflected that one thing he'd noticed about Chantal was that she bonded with all her patients easily and they loved her for it. She took an interest in each and every one of them. She'd make an excellent mother.

He was still waiting for the agency to get back to him, so he called in his next patient at the same moment he decided to deal with the problem of Chantal this evening when they were both off duty. He couldn't do anything about it while she was fully occupied in the delivery of another baby.

Genevieve, the obstetrics sister, was relieved that Chantal was going to remain with their young patient. She'd been brilliant at calming down the young girl. Sixteen years old and she'd made her own way to the hospital while in the first stage of labour. As naïve a maternity patient as Genevieve had ever met. Nobody had explained the birds and bees to that one!

Chantal leaned over her patient as she showed her how to breathe in the gas and air that helped to take away some of the pain when the contractions came. The poor child...she had to stop thinking about her as a child. Maria had told her she was sixteen. Theoretically adult. Well, adult enough to have conceived a child,though she seemed totally bewildered by what was happening to her now.

From the little information Maria had given her she'd gathered that her mother had died in a road accident when she was small and her father had taken care of her by himself since then but he was often away on business.

Papa worked as a salesman and was in Belgium at the moment. He had a mobile phone but he didn't like Maria phoning him when he was working. Anyway, she'd forgotten the number and she didn't have a mobile herself. Too expensive, her father had told her. He always phoned her on the landline to say when he was coming home. Another contraction was beginning and Maria was concentrating on the breathing Chantal had taught her.

The young girl relaxed her grip on Chantal's hand as the contraction passed.

'You're doing really well, Maria. Is there a relative other than your father that I can call?'

Maria shook her head. 'I'm alone in the house when Dad goes away on business. That's why I came here today. I'd only admitted to myself a few days ago that I was pregnant. I thought I'd better get help so— Ooh, that awful pain's coming again, Chantal, help me.'

'Breathe into the mask, Maria.' She checked

with Genevieve, who told her the cervix was almost fully dilated so that their patient could push on the next contraction.

It was a relief when she could tell her patient it was time to bear down. She could push now.

She reached for a dressing sheet and gently mopped Maria's face before the next contraction.

There was a moment of anxiety as she had to tell Maria to stop pushing. Sister was sorting out the cord, which was around the baby's neck.

'Good girl,' Chantal told her patient. 'Yes, one more breath for me, now another. OK, another push and...'

The whole team seemed to exhale a sigh of relief as the baby flopped out into Genevieve's hands. Almost immediately came the wailing cry they all wanted to hear.

As Chantal handed the baby wrapped in a dressing towel into Maria's arms her young patient's eyes were wide with amazement.

'Dr Chantal, I'd put on a bit of weight but I didn't know I was so near to having my baby. I'd tried not to think about it and I daren't tell Papa. Oh, look, it's such a miracle, isn't it? Growing inside me, my baby. I love it. And it's all mine isn't it? Is it a boy or a girl?'

She glanced up at Chantal, who was over-whelmed by Maria's childlike reaction. 'You've got a little girl, Maria. A beautiful little girl.'

'A girl, I've got a girl! A baby girl!'

Chantal became aware that someone else had joined the team in theatre. She could hear a muted male voice in the background somewhere.

He moved to the foot of the bed. 'I was just checking how things are going up here, Chantal. The staffing agency hasn't replaced you yet but I see you've got your hands full at the moment.'

She smiled across at him. 'This really was a miracle.'

'So I see.'

As their eyes met over the scene she knew she had to go through with their mad plan. She'd been hovering and dithering since that fateful evening at the beach café. And also, in this moment of enlightenment she knew that Michel would be a good, caring man to have a baby with. This rush of sentiment was gratifying but worrying if they were to stick to the original plan Michel had outlined.

'She's a lovely baby,' he said, his voice husky with emotion as he watched Chantal taking the baby from the young mother to start the postnatal checks.

He stayed on for a short time, watching her checking the baby's airway and nasal passages. Now she was gently weighing the precious child watched by the young mother who was totally in awe of her baby and the helpful doctor who'd made it all go so well when she'd been in despair. Chantal seemed totally engrossed in her tasks.

He slipped away unnoticed, even more anxious to find out if she'd given some thought to his plan.

An hour later Chantal had settled the new mother and baby in the postnatal ward, promising to return to see her before she went off duty. She spent a few minutes with Veronique, the mature, sympathetic lady in charge of patient home care, explaining that she was worried about Maria, the young girl in Obstetrics, who'd given birth that morning. She outlined as much as she knew about her patient's difficult background while insisting that further details were required as soon as possible.

Veronique took down the details and promised to go and see Maria that afternoon.

'And please try to get in contact with her father,' Chantal said firmly.

'Don't worry, Dr Winstone. I'll treat Maria's case as a priority.'

Feeling a little more reassured that wheels would turn while she got on with her work in Emergency, Chantal hurried along to report to Michel that she was back. She found him in a cubicle reviving a teenager who'd swum too far out to sea. The lifeguards had brought him into hospital, having spent the few minutes in the ambulance working on him. The seemingly lifeless young man was on his side as one of the lifeguards was working in synchronisation with Michel. Between them they'd just achieved the first signs of life.

Chantal waited as she heard a vague groaning

sound from the patient's throat, then more water coming out of his mouth, a flickering of the eye-lashes, a valiant attempt to speak followed by a movement of the chest. She watched as Michel continued to work on his patient. She didn't want to disturb him while he and the lifeguards were engrossed in reviving their patient.

Minutes later Michel pulled himself upright and breathed a sigh of relief. 'Thanks for bring-ing him in, boys.' He smiled at the two young lifeguards. 'We got him just in the nick of time. Another few minutes and it would have been too late.'

He became aware of Chantal standing by the door. 'Good to see you back, Chantal. How are mother and baby?'

Chantal smiled. 'Doing fine in the postnatal ward.'

'That's good! Now, have you had any lunch?'

She shook her head. 'It's too late now. We need to do something about those patients waiting out there. I'd rather keep going till this evening.'

'Me too.' This evening. He mustn't think about the evening yet.

* * *

As she went out of the cubicle a nurse was waiting to ask her for help. She'd brought her young patient back from an X-ray of his arm, followed by the plaster room, and she needed a doctor to outline the treatment required. Was he fit to be discharged or should he be admitted? He'd fallen from his bicycle on the promenade and was still in a lot of pain.

Chantal followed the nurse to the treatment room to check on the X-ray of the scaphoid bone, an important wrist bone, and the subsequent application of a rigid plaster. She was glad that the plaster was a temporary one comprising two halves which could be removed or adjusted as necessary. The patient's fingers were very swollen, she noticed.

She phoned Orthopaedics and asked if they could find a bed for a young patient with a fractured scaphoid. She recommended that he be kept in overnight to be seen as soon as possible by a consultant. The plaster needed to be adjusted by an expert and further treatment was necessary.

Then it was on to the next patient in the seemingly endless queue. There was no doubt about it that balmy summer days increased the number of people waiting to be seen in Emergency.

'The evening staff are arriving.' Michel put his head round her cubicle curtain. 'How long will you be?'

She smiled with relief. 'I'm just clearing this trolley.'

'Leave it. That's an order. I'll delegate it to someone who hasn't been working all day like you. Come now, Chantal. I need to ask you something important. My office in two minutes?'

'OK, you're the boss.'

She wondered what the rush was as she followed him after a couple of minutes. She had a feeling it might be because she'd been avoiding him for a while, feeling desperately unsure of the plan he'd asked her to consider.

'That was five minutes.' He stood up from behind his desk as she went in.

'Yes, it was.' She sank down into the chair near his desk. 'Where's the fire?'

He grinned. 'You can slow down now I've got you here.'

He sat down again and some of the bravado he'd exuded disappeared. All he had to do was say he needed an answer. Yes or no to his master plan? Looking across at Chantal, he realised he'd suddenly run out of steam. She looked as tired as he felt. Maybe it wasn't a good idea to ask her to dinner this evening after all. They'd both been working flat out all day and he expected a lucid answer to his all-important question. Yes or no, not maybe, or give me some more time.

He cleared his throat. It was now or never; take the bull by the horns.

'I've been wondering if you'd had any thoughts on what we discussed at the beach café that evening?'

'Oh, yes, I've given it some thought and... Michel, are you OK?' She was concerned by the agitated way he was now pacing the floor, not looking directly at her and breathing really deeply.

'I'm fine!' he snapped. 'So what conclusion have you come to?

She stood up and walked over to the window where he was now leaning against the wooden shutters fixed back to reveal the evening sun.

'I've given it a great deal of thought.'

'You have? And?'

'I made enquiries at a discreet little clinic I know of in Paris. I spoke over the phone with the director and explained our situation. He assured me they would be able to set the wheels in motion as soon as we come in for an appointment. If, after a consultation and the necessary tests, we wish to proceed, they would be pleased to help us.'

'And would you be happy to go ahead, Chantal?'

She could see the beads of sweat on his brow as he continued speaking. She had to put him out of his misery.

'Yes, I would,' she said, with a confidence that belied the worries still haunting her about the whole project.

He let out a sigh of relief. 'So that's the first hurdle over. You'd taken so long to get back to me I'd given up hope.'

'Michel, this isn't something to be entered into lightly. I've spent many hours agonising over the problems we could face if we go ahead.'

'Me too. That's why I think we need a proper meeting. I've drawn up a list of shared parenting requirements I'd like to discuss with you. Would you care to have supper with me this evening at my house? That way we won't be disturbed by waiters or nearby diners overhearing our unconventional conversation.'

She hesitated. 'Are you sure you feel like making supper this evening?'

Strike while the iron is hot! 'It won't be anything brilliant. An omelette or something simple. We've both skipped lunch so a cardboard box would taste good.'

She laughed and the tense atmosphere began to evaporate.

'Now, this is something I've got to see. A man who can make a meal out of a cardboard box.'

CHAPTER FIVE

THEY CALLED IN at the small store that had been turned into a supermarket since the time when she had come here as a child. This had been in the days when her father had still been alive and they had often came over from nearby Montreuil for a day on the beach. Later, when she and her mother had moved to Paris and had been staying in the area during the long summer vacation she would come in here with other members of her family.

She had particularly enjoyed coming in with cousin Julia, clutching the spending money her mother had given her and deciding whether to blow it all on sweets, a drink or an ice cream. Situated at the end of the promenade, it had been the perfect place for children who had been lucky enough to have some money or an indulgent grown-up with them. In those days, she remembered, it had been a grocery store with a very good bakery attached.

This evening they needed provisions for their supper. Michel had told her he knew there were eggs at home but he was a bit vague about anything else. They definitely needed fresh bread.

'I've never done much shopping,' Michel told her, his expression conveying that he found the whole experience boring.

He was following her, looking a bit lost as they walked down the first aisle. 'As I told you, Chantal, I can whisk up a decent omelette; possibly add something like cheese or ham.'

He reached forward and took packets of both as if anxious to get out of this unfamiliar place as quickly as possible.

Chantal could see that he rarely did any shopping. 'I'll get some salad and bread, Michel. I can see the baguettes over there.'

'I'll get some wine and meet you in the next aisle.'

As she got some freshly baked bread she could see Michel discussing wine over the other side of the shop. He may dislike shopping for food but he seemed to understand his wines. He called her over and she hurried across.

The man serving in the wine area was holding out a glass of wine for her to taste. 'Your husband suggested you taste this one and this one.'

Michel hadn't flinched or corrected the mistake as he watched her putting the glass to her lips, swirling the wine in the glass to let it breathe, as her mother had taught her when she'd been old enough to have a small glass with lunch or supper.

'I prefer this one,' she said, as she made her choice. She had found it difficult to decide. They were both fine wines.

Michel smiled. 'Good choice.' Both men nodded sagely.

As she moved on she heard Michel arranging for a case of wine to be put in his car.

He joined her shortly afterwards, now looking very pleased with himself. A more relaxed Michel was emerging from the work-weary man who could barely disguise his dislike of mundane matters like shopping.

At last they were now into the idea of eating and the trolley began to fill up with impulse buys. They were both feeling hungry so it was soon brimming over. Chantal remembered neither of them had eaten any lunch. Michel was nowhere to be seen now.

She found him at the dessert counter, where he was pointing to a large apple tart and asking the serving lady to wrap it for them. 'I'll take some of that cream and some *crème fraîche* to go with it.'

As they made their way out of the shop, Chantal found they were both in a more relaxed mood. The tension between them as they had entered had been almost palpable. They'd worked all day and had been starving but they'd had to face the dreaded shopping before getting home and cooking. But she'd found it fun to turn what might have been a chore into a pleasant experience.

'We've got far too much food,' she said, as they piled the goodies into the boot of Michel's car.

He smiled. 'As my grandmother used to say, *'Appetite comes when you eat.'*

Chantal laughed. 'Absolutely true! But you'll find yourself eating for days to come with this amount of fresh food, though some of it will freeze, of course.'

He opened the passenger door for her. She climbed in and fastened her seat belt. As they began driving up the hill she looked out at the sun low in the sky at the top of the hill. Below on the sea twilight was dancing on the gentle waves, a golden glow telling them that the day was over and the pleasures of the evening were before them.

Yes, they had a serious subject to discuss but they both wanted the same outcome, a baby to satisfy their craving for parenthood. Parenthood without commitment to each other. She turned sideways to look at Michel. He was looking relaxed, happy even. It could work, this unconventional plan of his. It would work if they were both one hundred per cent committed to the plan.

They were reaching the top of the hill. She could now see a magnificent house standing by itself in a prime position in terms of its view. That couldn't be Michel's house, could it? She held her breath as he turned off the road and swung into the gravel drive.

He turned off the engine and for a few seconds they both remained still, taking in the magnificent view of the sea below them.

'Wow!' she breathed. 'What a view.'

'The view is the reason I bought this place. I'd inherited some money from my grandparents, who brought me up after my parents died. My grandfather was a successful businessman and he had no other relatives to leave his money to. I was an only child. When I got my job at the Hôpital de la Plage I felt I needed a place I could call home, a place where I could put down roots. It was meant to take my mind off the fact that I was on my own now. My consolations were my absorbing work at the hospital and my beautiful house to come home to. Come and look inside.'

A master switch by the door flicked on the lighting system as they went into the spacious hall. There were table lamps, hidden lights in alcoves to light up the pictures on all the walls. Obviously, Michel enjoyed his art collection.

He also enjoyed his photographs. On the hall table there were two photographs of Michel and his wife. One showed them enjoying themselves on a beach, palm trees in the background, his arm around her slender waist. They were both in swimwear, white shorts for him, white bikini for her. The second was their wedding photo taken as they'd stood on the steps of the church. They were a good-looking bride and groom. She could almost feel the love between them.

She experienced a weird sensation of disturbing emotions, which she couldn't understand. She told herself she was happy that Michel had known real love and sad that it had all ended for him. Yes, that was why she felt so upset, why she didn't trust herself to speak as she turned away and focussed her attention on a picture of the view from the house.

She could feel the warmth of the day lingering in the closed-in atmosphere. He went to open a window as she followed him into the spacious kitchen. She glanced around her. It was an absolutely ideal kitchen. The space would be a pure joy to work in for someone who had time to cook for a family or throw large dinner parties but Michel didn't exactly fit into that category.

The kitchen resembled something out of an expensive, glossy magazine but it didn't look lived in. Some of the appliances had obviously never been used.

'What's this for?' She put her hand on an expensive-looking piece of equipment that had been integrated along a wall of electric appliances.

He grinned boyishly. 'I've no idea! I only know how to work the important stuff like the cooker. And occasionally the washing machine when I've forgotten to put out my stuff for the woman who comes in from the agency once a week to keep the place clean.'

He pressed a switch and quiet classical music started.

'Rachmaninov,' she said. 'One of my favourite composers.'

He nodded. 'Me too. You know, the man I bought this house from was in charge of a firm that supplied houses fully furnished to order. His client had defaulted so I bought the house because I liked the view. As long as I've got a cooker, a fridge, music at the flick of a switch and a bed, that's all I'm interested in.'

'It's absolutely wonderful but...'

'Go on, though I know what you're going to say.'

'Do you?' She hoped not. If she was honest she would tell him that it lacked a woman's touch. It lacked any feeling that it was a home.

'You were going to tell me it's like a bachelor pad, weren't you? A place where a man can lay this head at the end of the day.'

She gave him a wry smile. 'You said that, not me.'

'I said it because it's true. It serves its purpose.'

He was uncorking a bottle of wine as he spoke. 'Let's take our drinks on the terrace. That's my favourite place.'

'I can see why.' She settled herself among the cushions on the long wicker sofa as he handed her a glass then sat down at the other end. There were small tables at each end but only one looked as if it had been used. The other still had a label prominently displayed.

'You're quite right, Michel, it's the view that makes this place.'

'And the people in it.' He smiled. 'Thank you for agreeing to have out meeting up here.' He cleared his throat. 'It will be easier to discuss the problems we might encounter with our parenting plan if we haven't got anyone else overhearing us. You say you've already contacted a clinic in Paris?'

She took a sip of wine as she warmed to her subject. 'The director of the clinic is a former colleague of mine. He and his wife became personal friends. They used to give excellent dinner parties. He's an obstetrician/gynaecologist who took early retirement so that he could open his own clinic to help couples who want a baby but need some kind of conception assistance. Most of his work is with fertility problems but he's agreed to check out our plan for donor insemination.'

'Sounds good so far. I've been drawing up a list of parenting responsibilities which we must take very seriously.'

He broke off to move closer to her on the sofa, bringing the bottle with him so he could top up her glass.

At first she felt as if she should be taking notes, but somewhere along the way they were distracted by talking about their backgrounds. She started it by asking Michel how old he'd been when his parents had died.

'I think it's important to know things that our child will need to know,' she explained. 'Conventional, normal couples will already know these things.'

'Oh, absolutely!' He took a deep breath. 'I suppose the rest of the world will regard us as abnormal but if we can ignore the gossip, that will be half the battle. With regard to my background, both my parents were only children.'

He paused and cleared his throat. 'I was also an only child. I was three years old when my parents died. They'd left me with my grandparents when they'd gone off to the Alps for their annual skiing holiday. They were both swept away in an avalanche.'

'What a dreadful thing to happen. And you were only three.'

He nodded. 'I became aware that my parents had been away from home for longer than usual and started to ask questions about when they were coming back. It's difficult for a three-year-old to understand what an accident is. I missed them, but gradually I stopped asking questions and simply accepted that my grandparents had taken their place.'

She could hear that his voice was full of sadness. A sudden image of him as a lonely child flashed into her mind and she felt sorry for him. And now as an adult he still had no family of his own. She was glad she was going to help him. Yes, that was why sometimes she couldn't understand her own emotions when she was with him. It was nothing to do with the fact that he was handsome, charming and charismatic. None of that came into the equation.

She glanced across at him and saw that there was still an air of sadness which had lingered since he told her about losing his parents.

Michel stood up and escaped into the kitchen as if he didn't want to be seen displaying his emotions.

When he returned he was carrying more nibbles. Cheese straws this time.

She saw the dampness on his cheek as he went

past her and once more she felt sorry for the poor little orphan he'd been and was glad that he'd had grandparents to care for him.

'And you?' he enquired, when he was settled once more beside her. 'I remember you said your mother had brought you up by herself.'

'Yes. My father died of cancer. There was a tumour in his oesophagus that was too far advanced to be removed. He was there at my seventh birthday party. I remember wondering why he didn't eat any of the birthday cake my mother had made. A few weeks later he died.'

He put his hand on hers. Neither of them spoke.

'Maybe this is why we're both so committed to becoming parents,' he said gently. 'We both feel we've missed out in some way. To have two parents must be a wonderful experience when you're growing up.'

'We'll have to make sure we give our baby a lot of loving care.' She looked at the man sitting beside her. He would make a wonderful father.

'Come on, let's carry on this conversation in the kitchen,' he said, holding out his hand to help her to her feet.

She felt it was a very special moment as they stood together, looking into each other's eyes. She held her breath as he leaned forward to kiss her on the lips. As quickly as their lips met the kiss ended. Both of them knew this wasn't part of the contract. It was as if they were agreeing to the start of their journey together.

His arm was resting lightly on her waist as he took her into the kitchen

'So, which of these many packages would you like me to unpack?'

They both surveyed the kitchen table. 'I really fancy watching you whip up an omelette,' she said. 'I'll make a salad and that's the main course sorted.'

'And all this?'

'You've got an enormous fridge-freezer over there, which we'll put to good use.' She was already rinsing the salad ingredients, then mixed a French dressing.

'Got any mustard?'

'No idea. If I have, it will be in that cupboard.' She found some and added it to her dressing.

'I'm amazed!' she told him as she watched him cracking eggs into a bowl. 'You look like a real chef.'

He laughed. 'Don't be deceived. This is the only dish I can make. You can serve it up at any point in the day, breakfast, lunch, supper. Now all I've got to do is to whisk it like this then into the pan I prepared earlier and, hey, presto! Oh, I forgot the ham.'

Chantal added it quickly. As she helped him turn out the omelette onto a large serving plate they both stood back to admire their handiwork. Michel might be a wizard in the operating theatre but his pride in a simple omelette was a joy to behold.

He sat at the head of the long kitchen table. She sat beside him. They tore off pieces of bread from the baguette, dunking it in Chantal's vinaigrette, drinking the delicious wine, chattering all the time as if they'd known each other for a long time.

'I'll phone for a taxi to take you back to hospital later, Chantal. This wine was a really good choice. I mustn't drive now. Alternatively, I've got a guest room where you could spend the night. No need for you to decide yet.'

Michel found himself working out exactly how long he'd known this wonderful woman. It had been February when she'd first come into his life so she'd been here about four months now. She'd made such a difference to his working life in Emergency. He found he looked forward to working with her every day. And now she was bringing hope into his life by agreeing to have his baby. Their baby.

If he hadn't decided that he daren't love again it would be very easy to feel emotional about her. But to fall in love was not part of the plan. He couldn't open up his heart to the love of a woman again. Chantal, being very level-headed, had her own reasons not to fall in love. She couldn't trust a man ever again. So they were perfect together, weren't they?

He put down his fork and reached for her small hand. 'You won't change your mind, will you, Chantal?' he asked huskily.

She felt the warmth of his hand around hers and the touch of skin against skin seemed almost erotic. She could feel deep down that being with Michel was affecting her more than it should.

'No, of course I won't change my mind.' She stood up. 'Dessert?' she asked briskly.

He could feel something like an electric current running between them. Deep down inside him was a powerful feeling of wanting to take Chantal in his arms and hold her until the feeling went away. He stood up and put his arms around her, drawing her close. This didn't make sense. She should have pushed him away, told him to stick to the plan. Maybe she was feeling as he was. He bent his head to kiss her.

She parted her lips as every sense in her body ignited with passion and longing. She was feeling overwhelmed by the sensual fluidity of her body as she moulded herself against Michel's hard, virile, muscular frame. She was melting away as he held her tightly in his arms. There was a powerful force gripping her. She knew she should fight it but she had no intention of doing so. She didn't even want to stir in his arms in case the dream ended.

He lifted her into his arms, carrying her towards the door. There was no need for words as he carried her upstairs. They were both intent on giving in to the magic of the moment. There was no need to justify his actions or her compliance. Life was too precious to banish moments like this. There was no yesterday, no tomorrow, simply the present moment.

CHAPTER SIX

WHAT HAD HE DONE? How could he have suspended all rational thinking last night? Michel settled himself back against his pillow. He'd lain for a while with his eyes closed. He could hear the steady breathing beside him. With his eyes now open he dared to look at the sleeping Chantal beside him.

He held his breath in wonder. If he were a real romantic—which he'd tried so hard not to be since he'd lost Maxine—he would say she was a vision of loveliness. Her long dark hair, free from the chignon she swirled it into during working hours, was spread over the pillow. Her lips, slightly parted, were impossibly appealing. He remembered the taste of them from last night. The wickedly sensual effect they'd had on him. How could he have given in to that irresistible desire to make love to Chantal?

He'd done so much damage last night. This was an item that definitely hadn't been on the agenda. They'd agreed to be parents of convenience, not lovers.

He swallowed hard as her lovely long eyelashes fluttered open.

'Hi.'

She gave him a shy but sexy smile before looking around her uncertainly. And then it all came rushing back to her. As wonderful as her memories were of last night, it certainly hadn't been supposed to happen.

She struggled to pull herself into a sitting position but he put out his hand to hold her still, trying not to touch the naked skin beneath the rumpled sheets, that same naked skin he'd explored, tasted, kissed. It had been the most wonderful experience. So unexpected. Now what?

'I'll get some coffee, Chantal.'

He was trying hard to blot out the memory of the magic of their night together. His body had so craved the physical side of a relationship that he'd seemed to have forgotten he shouldn't make love to Chantal. She was out of bounds if they were to have a successful agreement of non-commitment.

He ran a hand through his ruffled hair as he sat on the edge of the bed, his back to Chantal. He daren't turn to look at her. Even now his treacherous body seemed hell bent on leading him into danger again. He had to pull himself together and see if he could bring them back on course. Giving in would change everything in the kind of relationship they'd agreed on.

He grabbed his robe from the floor and stood up purposefully.

She lay very still as she saw him shrugging into his towelling robe. This was the most bizarre situation she'd ever been in. Two people arranging to make a baby together in an unconventional and unromantic way had spent the night together and changed the very nature of the relationship they'd agreed to. Emotional feelings had got the better of them last night and they'd been carried away on a tide of passion and desire for each other. They'd ignored the original plan. So what would happen now?

She looked around the palatial bedroom.

Swathes of ivory silk curtains were still drawn back from the windows in their ornamental tie-backs. They'd slept all night with the windows uncovered and a couple of windows wide open. She remembered at one point how he'd insisted they go out onto the balcony to admire the moon. So he was a romantic after all. He'd kept that hidden before but not last night!

The garden had been so silent and still, fragrant with the scent of the roses. Michel had insisted he could smell the salty sea but she'd said they were too high up. She'd laughed as they'd argued until he'd kissed her so long and hard that they'd had to move back to bed to resume their lovemaking.

Yes, at the time it had felt like love. But love for each other wasn't on the cards. They'd both said that they would love their baby but loving each other was off limits if they were to keep their independence. They'd both agreed not to commit to each other. They must keep their independence if their original plan was to work.

She climbed out of bed and went into the en suite bathroom. There was a spare bathrobe hanging on a hook. Very masculine, much too large.

She was glad it wasn't a feminine type of guest robe. Even as the thought entered her head she told herself that although they hoped to be parents together they shouldn't be jealous of future partnerships either of them might make.

She pulled on the enormous robe and tied the belt twice around her waist as she heard Michel had come back into the bedroom.

She found him on the balcony, placing a tray with croissants and coffee on the small table. She sank down into the large armchair, noticing that he'd replaced the cushions that had been inside the bedroom when they'd both shared the one chair, leaning against each other for warmth, comfort and… She could feel herself blushing at the thought of what had happened next.

'How do you take your coffee, Chantal?'

'Black, no sugar. Oh, you've brought croissants. Breakfast, no less. I'd like milk with my coffee so I can dip my croissant in it.'

He gave her a nervous smile as he passed her cup. 'Strange, having breakfast together.'

'Yes.' It was even stranger, in retrospect, remembering their night together.

They remained silent as they looked out across the garden.

Chantal broke the silence. 'It's even more beautiful in day light out here.'

He couldn't help thinking she looked even more beautiful in the sunshine. That was a wicked thought, a remnant of last night lingering too long. He brought his mind back on track again.

'So, how do we approach the situation now?'

'You mean making a baby together?' She wished she'd phrased that more delicately.

He took a deep breath. 'Well, we both seem well qualified in the baby-making department but...' he paused as if to choose his words carefully '...that wasn't what we intended, was it? We intended to keep our independence and arrange to be parents of convenience. As I see it, we should try to forget last night ever happened and continue with our original plan. What do you think, Chantal?'

'I agree with you absolutely.'

Her treacherous heart was telling her otherwise but she knew she could never trust another man so she banished all her lingering romantic feelings. She'd learned her lesson the hard way with the deceitful Jacques. Last night had been wonderful but it mustn't be repeated if they were to avoid complications.

'Yes, Michel, our original plan for non-commitment to each other will be the most workable solution to becoming parents.'

Michel nodded his assent. He'd enjoyed every moment they'd spent with each other but he'd got his errant feelings under control once more. He mustn't commit himself to Chantal. He'd never stopped loving Maxine and never could. Even if he could banish his memories of her, he'd promised himself never to risk loving a woman again. If he continued to nurture Chantal in a loving way how would he cope if he lost her? Life could be so unpredictable. Grief was a terrible emotion.

'I think we should stick to our original plan,' he said quietly. 'We must try to forget last night. I'm sorry, I shouldn't have…'

She could see he was worried now. 'Michel, it was a one-off experience. Let's stick to our plan as we outlined last night before we…before we both got carried away.'

'Yes, nothing has changed, has it?'

'Nothing has changed,' she repeated quietly as she thought what a false statement that was. False but necessary if they were to envisage shared parenthood and retain their independence from each other.

To make her point, she held out her hand towards him. 'Let's shake on that.'

He stood up and came round the back of her chair to take her hand in his and draw her to her feet. Deliberately she straightened her arm so that they could now shake hands. It was time go back into the sane world where life would go on as usual.

It was business as usual as soon as they got back into hospital. There had been another RTA on the road that fed the traffic into the dual carriageway and patients were being diverted to all hospitals within a reasonable distance. They'd been chosen to take their share of the injured.

By a tremendous effort of mind Chantal managed to put herself into work mode and behave normally when she was working alongside Michel. When he asked her to assist him in the treatment of a difficult leg injury soon after they arrived in Emergency she was totally professional and relieved with the way that he too seemed oblivious to all that had passed between them only hours ago.

'I'd hoped Orthopaedics would take this young man to Theatre but all the theatres are in use at the moment and this operation can't wait.'

Michel looked over the top of his mask at the small emergency team he'd assembled in the larger of the two treatment rooms.

'Scalpel, Chantal.'

He made a long incision down the side of the injured leg. 'As you can see, everybody,' he continued in his teaching voice, 'the tibia, which as you all know is the strongest and most important bone in the lower leg, has been shattered into several small pieces. You will remember I showed you the damaged leg on the X-rays.'

He broke off to speak to his anaesthetist about the condition of their patient. Reassured by his reply, he continued.

'I'm now going to wire the shards of bone together. I always think it's a bit like doing a jigsaw puzzle when I have to deal with a large bone as badly shattered as this one.'

Chantal glanced up at the video screen recording the operation above the table. She could see Michel's hands skilfully fixing the tibia together. He too was taking a look at the screen now as he worked on a difficult section. Their eyes met and she could tell he was smiling beneath his mask. She smiled back, a smile that was meant to reassure him that nothing in their plan had changed. If she continued to make every effort to convince herself it would all work out as they'd planned.

As she was moving between patients later that morning she was surprised at a request from the obstetrics department. Could she spare a few minutes to go and see a returning patient who'd asked to see her? She glanced around the waiting area. Five minutes would be OK, she told the person who'd phoned. There were no urgent cases at the moment.

'It's Maria who wants to see you, Chantal. You

remember the young woman who came in by her-self and was already in labour?'

'Yes, of course. I'm on my way.

Maria was looking radiantly happy when Chan-tal arrived in Outpatients. So different from the bedraggled girl in the enormous raincoat who'd been well into labour without knowing what was happening.

'I just wanted to thank you for helping me when my baby was born, Doctor. I'd like to call her Chantal. I hope you don't mind if I give her your name.'

Chantal smiled. 'Of course I don't mind! I'm delighted.'

She wondered how many more babies she de-livered would be called Chantal. There was a woman with Maria proudly holding the baby who was wearing a pink frilly frock and a tiny hat with a brim that flopped over her forehead.

'I'm baby Chantal's grandmother,' the woman explained.

'A very young grandmother, may I say.'

'Well, my son, the father of this dear little baby, is only eighteen. I was only eighteen when he was born so you can work out how old I am. It was a surprise to me when the hospital contacted me to say Maria had given them my number to call because her father was on business and couldn't be contacted.'

Maria spoke up, looking a little bit flustered. 'Frederick and I had gone out together a few times even though we'd only...well, you know... done it once and I thought you couldn't get pregnant the first time.'

Chantal glanced at the young grandmother. 'Maria isn't the only young girl to believe that old story, is she?'

The grandmother smiled. 'It happens all the time. Anyway, fortunately I can give her all the help she needs. Maria and the baby have moved in with us. Frederick is thrilled to bits at being a father. I've got three more children at home so it's nice to have a baby in the family as well.'

'So you and Maria's father are happy with the arrangement?'

There was a slight pause. 'Let's say he's relieved his daughter is being well looked after, Doctor. He's not really a family man, if you know what I mean. Without his wife he reverted to being a bachelor again and I think Maria was—'

'I was in the way,' Maria said quietly. 'I love being part of Frederick's family.'

'Thank you for coming along to see us, Doctor. Maria told me all about you. She's just been back for a check-up and everything's fine. You did a great job that day.'

'Thank you.'

Chantal felt a warm glow of happiness inside her as she walked back along the corridor to Emergency.

'You're looking pleased with yourself.'

They'd almost bumped into each other as they'd both hurried around the same corner going in opposite directions.

Her warm glow seemed to get warmer now, especially in her face. How stupid of her to start blushing like a teenager again.

'Michel! Where are you heading off to?'

'As your boss I should be asking you where you've been,' he said in a pseudo-stern voice.

'Got a request to go and see an ex-patient who was having a check-up in Obstetrics outpatients.

Do you remember that young girl, Maria, who was in labour when she arrived and I took her to Obstetrics?'

'And ended up spending hours delivering her baby while I was left doing your work and mine.'

He was continuing to tease her with his big-boss manner, while trying to convince himself that nothing had changed between them since yesterday. Yes, he certainly did remember that particular delivery room where he'd been strangely moved as he'd looked at Chantal holding the newborn baby. He remembered thinking what a wonderful mother she would make.

'I didn't spend hours. It was a quick delivery for a first timer. Anyway she's doing well. The baby's eighteen-year-old father is delighted that his mother has accepted Maria and baby Chantal into their large family.'

'They'll all grow up together. One big happy family. Got to go. I'm needed in orthopaedics. They've got a vacant operating theatre at last but no surgeon. Thanks for your assistance in our converted treatment room, Chantal. You did well under the circumstances.'

As he hurried away he knew he would have praised his assistant more if it had been anyone else. But he had to be careful now that he'd shown her how much she meant to him. He mustn't get carried away again, must he? He wasn't at all sure about that. It was going to take an enormous amount of self-control.

She finished writing her end-of-the-day report and switched off her computer. They'd gradually treated all the patients from the RTA and the normal influx of patients. It had been a long day. A long day following a long night. She would have an early night tonight.

'I thought I might find you here.'

Chantal looked up enquiringly as Michel walked in. 'Did you want to see me?'

He perched on the edge of the desk. 'I've been invited to a medical conference in Paris, which starts tomorrow. I had it pencilled in to go over and give a paper there on one of the days, but they've just contacted me to ask if I can be there from tomorrow and stay for the whole of the conference.'

'One of the perks of the job,' she observed dryly. 'How long will you be in Paris?'

'A couple of weeks, possibly longer. Actually, we'll be working hard all the time.'

'Of course you will. And who will be in charge of the department while you're away?'

'The staffing agency is attempting to find a consultant to replace me.'

She stood up. 'I'm sure we'll cope without you.'

'I'm sure you will.'

In a way a break from constantly seeing Michel on a day-to-day basis was what she needed. She would find it hard and would miss him terribly. But at the back of her mind there was a problem that had been niggling her all day. She'd only admitted it to herself when she'd taken a short coffee break in the middle of the afternoon.

They'd made love last night using no protection. She knew the rhythms of her own body as she'd tested the most fertile period in her menstrual cycle before she'd got pregnant with Jacques.

And last night she'd been at her most fertile. If she'd conceived a child naturally, how would that affect their plan? If she'd conceived during their romantic lovemaking then their whole relationship would change, wouldn't it?

'Are you all right, Chantal?'

He was coming round the desk. She forced herself to stand so that she could escape while she was thinking rationally. If he came any closer, if he bent his head near to her as he was doing now…

'I've had a long day, that's all.'

She turned her cheek towards him so that they could say goodbye in the typically French way of a chaste kiss on both sides of the face.

'I've got to go,' she told him breathlessly as the touch of his lips disturbed her more than she'd anticipated.

'Goodnight, Chantal,' he said quietly as he reached the door before she did. He held it open for her. 'Have a good evening.'

'And you, Michel. I hope all goes well at the conference.'

He leaned against the door after she'd gone, taking deep breaths to calm himself. He was glad they'd been sensible just now. Even lightly touching her skin with his lips had disturbed him. Yes, he was going to need more self-control to ensure the original plan was going to work. It was just as well they were going to be separated for a couple of weeks. By the time he got back he would have completely forgotten their night of heavenly madness.

CHAPTER SEVEN

As she lay in her lonely single bed in the medics quarters her thoughts turned to the wonderful night of passion she'd spent with Michel a few days ago. She remembered how they'd had to work together the next day. She'd forced herself to give all her attention and expertise to the patients she had treated. Then in the evening as she had been preparing to go off duty he had told her he had to be in Paris the next day for a conference.

In a way she felt relieved that they would have space between them for a couple of weeks. The brief discussion they'd had when they'd had breakfast together on the morning after their impromptu night of lovemaking had reinforced the idea that they should stick to their original plan. No commitment to each other, parents of convenience. It was easy to say but she was going to find it difficult to implement.

Even now, after just a few days of Michel's absence in Paris, she found herself looking forward to his return. She realised that however she tried to think otherwise, the events of that evening had affected everything they'd planned.

They'd both agreed they wanted to keep their independence, their single status. They would make a baby together, be the most caring parents it was possible to be, given the unconventional circumstances and also the busy professional and domestic lives they would lead. But having thrown caution to the wind and spent the night together, it was difficult for her to forget.

She got out of bed and went over to the window. It was already after midnight but sleep was a long time coming tonight. Dim lights showed in all the wards. She could make out one of the operating theatres, lights blazing as an emergency operation was taking place. An ambulance was pulling up by the entrance to Emergency. One of the night porters and a nurse were already waiting. The hospital never slept, a bit like her at the moment.

She climbed back into bed, leaving the window wide open. There was no air-conditioning in her room. Even a single cotton sheet made her feel too warm. She wondered if Michel was sleeping peacefully in Paris or was he awake, worrying about their relationship? Maybe he was enjoying the bright lights of Paris. There was no reason why he shouldn't. There was no place in her life for jealousy, she told herself firmly. They had no commitment to each other.

She sighed as the sound of an ambulance outside the hospital brought her back to the real world again. The last few days hadn't been easy, especially when she felt as if she was in limbo with the possibility that she might be pregnant already.

They'd only meant to discuss creating a baby by donor insemination. They hadn't meant to go the natural, romantic, intimate way. That usually meant committing to each other far more than they'd meant to do if they were to retain their independence.

She turned over in her bed as she considered the implications. If, in fact, she was pregnant already, that could have a significant effect on their future relationship.

Sleep came eventually but in the morning she had to admit that she was finding these restless nights were depleting her strength. Maybe when her period came she could relax again.

If it comes, said the small nagging voice in her head.

She made sure she was totally professional and efficient during the time Michel was in Paris. The replacement director was good at his job, very helpful and easy to work with. She didn't have time to worry about her personal life as the days passed very quickly. It was only at night she found herself worrying about her relationship with Michel.

She told herself there was nothing she could do about it until he came back from Paris, which would be within the next few days. Michel had phoned to say he and a few of his colleagues were extending their time in Paris for professional reasons. And why not?

The day her period was due came. No period. Not surprising, considering the way she was worrying. She told herself to relax. Two weeks had passed since she'd spent the night with Michel. She would nip out during her lunch-break and pick up a pregnancy kit at the pharmacy.

That evening she shut herself in her small bathroom.

She stared at the thin blue line. Positive. It could be a mistake, but it was unlikely. Modern pregnancy tests were almost one hundred per cent accurate. She had a gut feeling that it was correct. If they'd been planning natural conception on that fateful night, they couldn't have made more effort.

Her initial reaction was that she should phone Michel on his mobile. She reached for hers as she pulled on her slippers then stopped herself from making the call. He would be back from Paris soon. It would be better to tell him face to face. He could be having a night out to celebrate the end of the conference. He wouldn't want her babbling something over the phone about…

Her ring tone was playing. She checked. It was Michel.

She took a deep breath. 'Michel, you must be telepathic. I was just going to call you.'

'Anything in particular?'

It was so good to hear his voice again. 'Just checking when you're coming back. We need to talk.'

'Well, that's why I'm calling. I'm still working tomorrow morning with a couple of colleagues, tying up loose ends, speaking to the press—that sort of thing. I wondered if you could come over on the train so we could visit your clinic? Do you think you could make an appointment?'

'I could try.'

Her mind was jumping around all over the place. It would be reassuring for her to see her friend and former colleague Sebastian, the director of the clinic. He was an obstetrician/gynaecologist who would give them good advice about the dilemma they'd brought upon themselves. She felt so confused. Maybe it was her pregnancy hormones kicking in but she couldn't think straight. Half of her was completely thrilled about her pregnancy while the other half, the sensible half, was worrying about all the implications.

'Will your boss give you a couple of days off?'

'A couple of days?'

'Well, you'll need to stay the night and we can travel back together the next morning. In fact, if you can't get an appointment at the clinic tomorrow afternoon, try for the following morning. OK? I've got to go, Chantal.'

She could hear voices in the background and music as he gave her details of where they should meet. She wasn't jealous of him enjoying an evening in Paris, was she? Jealousy where their relationship was concerned must be ruled out at all costs.

She cut the connection and phoned the clinic in Paris.

Paris was always exciting when she arrived after being away for a while. As she stepped off the train and made her way through the crowds the indescribable hub of sound enveloped her.

The sights and sounds and even the smell of Paris were unique. She still thought of it as coming home. Her little apartment in the sixteenth arrondissement would be empty.

While she'd been on the train she'd phoned her mother, who was taking an extended vacation near Bordeaux, to tell her she was going to Paris for a couple of days and would call in to see her and probably stay the night. Did her mother want her to send on her mail? Not necessary. Apparently the concierge was already sending everything for her.

The good thing about her mother was that she didn't ask probing questions. Never had. She just let her daughter get on with her life. As soon as she'd gone into her teens she'd felt independent—until Jacques had come along. And now there was Michel. Totally different situations to deal with. She shouldn't compare them.

She hurried down the steps of the Metro. The intense warmth and stuffiness of the Metro got worse the lower she went. It was great in winter but overwhelming on a hot summer day like this.

Jumping on the train as the doors were about to close, she felt the welcome rush of air-conditioning. That was better.

She'd always liked jumping on to the Metro and setting off on a journey. Her mother had allowed her to travel by herself from her early teens, having coached her about possible dangers from an early age when they'd travelled together.

It had always been exciting to be travelling by herself. Another step in her independence had been when, soon after she'd qualified as a doctor, her mother had bought the apartment next to her own and given it to Chantal.

It seemed to her that after the years of financial struggle her mother had experienced she loved to take care of her only child. She'd been a teacher all her life but now in her retirement, with a decent pension and a chunk of savings, she could afford to be generous. Chantal felt truly blessed to have such a mother.

As the train drew to a halt at Ranelagh station she was still thinking about what a success her mother had made of her life. Bringing up a child as a single mother had been tough. Chantal was glad her mother could now afford to take long holidays like the one she was enjoying at the moment in Arcachon on the coast near Bordeaux.

She emerged from the stuffy depths of the Metro and turned along the Avenue Mozart. She knew the sixteenth arrondissement from her childhood. Her mother had taught at the Lycée Molière and so they'd based themselves in an apartment nearby.

She had no problem finding the name of the hotel Michel had given her. She gave his name to the concierge, who handed the internal phone to her when he'd established contact.

Michel arrived in the lobby shortly after they'd spoken. She could feel the nervous tension between them as they exchanged chaste kisses on the cheek, like distant friends meeting after a long period of time.

'Have you had lunch?'

'A snack on the train.'

'Do we have an appointment at the clinic?'

She nodded. 'Three o'clock.' She handed him the address. 'It's not far. Would you like to walk and get some fresh air? It's a lovely day out there and I've been cooped up on trains all morning.'

She was beginning to feel quite faint. She took a deep breath.

He put a hand on the back of her waist as they went out into the street. 'Are you OK?'

'I'm fine.'

He took hold of her hand as they walked together. She began to feel stronger. She decided she wouldn't tell him about the pregnancy test while they were walking. They had plenty of time before their appointment. There would be time to find an opportunity before they went in to see Sebastian.

After several streets with high-rise apartments that blocked out the sunshine they came to the edge of the Bois de Boulogne. The sun filtered through the leaves of the majestic trees towering above them as they skirted along the roadside path.

She pointed out the clinic in the distance. The closer they got the more it began to look like a private house.

'That's exactly what it is. Sebastian and his

wife Susanne have lived there all their married life. They brought up four children there and now there's often a sprinkling of grandchildren playing in the garden.'

Michel looked around him as they were ushered into a comfortable waiting room. It didn't seem like a clinic. A welcoming sort of place. He smiled his approval at Chantal.

'I'm glad you chose somewhere far away from our hospital,' he whispered as they sank down into a couple of squashy armchairs.

'Absolutely,' she whispered back. There was another couple across the other side of the room within earshot. She hoped they would go in soon so that she could tell Michel her news. The burden of her secret was beginning to make her nervous. The sooner they could discuss the implications, the better.

The door to the consulting room opened and Sebastian came out, smiling broadly as he extended his hand towards them. 'Chantal, so good to see you.'

As she introduced Michel she saw a second consulting-room door open and the other couple were being ushered in. Of course Sebastian would employ other doctors to work with him nowadays. Too late to break her news to Michel now.

'So fill me in about what you've been up to since we last met.'

She leaned forward in the armchair and looked across at Sebastian. As succinctly as possible she explained that she and Michel were good friends and colleagues who, having lost their partners, regretted the fact that they weren't parents and had decided to explore the possibility of having a baby together through donor insemination.

'So you want to obviate the normal course of having a sexual relationship and a commitment to each other?'

'Exactly!' Michel leaned forward now they'd got that out of the way. 'I will be the sperm donor and Chantal will carry the baby. We do have our reasons.'

Sebastian smiled reassuringly. 'I don't need to know your reasons unless you want to discuss them with me.'

He waited to give them a few moments to consider his words.

Chantal knew this was where she had to intervene. The fact that she was already pregnant was overwhelming her.

'There's something I have to tell you before we go any further, Sebastian. It's a very recent development but extremely relevant.'

She was desperately aware that both men were staring at her now.

Michel's face was a total enigma. As he looked at her fumbling uneasily with her words he suddenly had a blinding flash of intuition. He knew the truth.

He swallowed hard as she managed to speak again.

'I'm already pregnant!'

It was so good to be walking along the leafy footpath again. They'd spoken very little to each other since her announcement. At first Sebastian had been overjoyed at what she told him, saying that solved their problem didn't it?

Both she and Michel had affirmed that they

would have to rethink their relationship. Somewhat bewildered, Sebastian had suggested they go away and come back to see him in when Chantal was about three months pregnant. By that time he could scan Chantal's abdomen and everything would be clearer, relationships, prenatal care and so forth. He'd had only one question to ask regarding the conception. Was Michel the father of this child?

As Chantal sat down on a wooden bench with a view of the Lac Superieur, the larger of the two lakes in the Bois de Boulogne, she could see a man sweating hard as he rowed past. His sweetheart, lover, wife, whatever, was fanning herself with a magazine in the back of the boat. Romance was everywhere in the summer.

'Well, I'm sure we've given Sebastian something to think about today.'

She smiled as she remembered the learned obstetrician's face as he'd tried to conduct a rational discussion with them.

She turned to look at Michel. 'Sebastian is a family man. He couldn't see why we were being so clinical about the process of conception. To him the best way to get pregnant is the natural way. He has to help too many couples who can't conceive naturally. He can't think why we're not totally delighted.'

Michel was staring at her now, thinking that if only they could both get rid of the emotional baggage from their past lives their relationship would be so much easier.

'Let's go back to the hotel,' he said gently, holding out his hand towards her. 'We need to talk.'

CHAPTER EIGHT

THEY WALKED SLOWLY back along the leafy path that gave them shade from the hot sun before turning into the road leading in the direction of the hotel. There was no need for conversation. Both of them were lost in their own thoughts. Michel was holding her hand firmly as if he was afraid she might fall on the rough causeway. It was a new experience for him to have an unborn child in his care that wasn't a patient of his. A baby that he'd created, with the help of this beautiful woman beside him.

It had been an out of this world experience that he was trying hard to forget now. He knew the original plan was the best course of action. He must keep reminding himself that fatherhood was all he wanted.

Chantal was also thinking about the wonder of being pregnant again. She'd known the joy of carrying her first unborn child but that had lasted only three months. She was remembering how she'd had a completely different outlook on life, a feeling of responsibility to another human being. That was coming back to her now. Especially since Sebastian had confirmed her pregnancy. Michel had been over the moon when she'd emerged from the examination room.

He tightened his grip on her hand as they began to cross the road. She turned her head and smiled up at him.

'I know what you're going through,' she said gently as they crossed to the other side.

'Do you? I doubt it.' He gave her a wry smile. 'I've just learned that I'm going to be a father and the responsibility is overwhelming.'

'That's what I mean. I felt exactly the same with my first pregnancy. But that was short-lived and a totally different situation from this. I thought I had a partner who would stand by me. I was wrong. But there are definitely two of us committed to being good parents to our child this time, right?'

He fell silent again as the possibility of losing

Chantal in childbirth taunted him. That was rare in countries where medical care was advanced, but it should never be discounted. He realised his strong feelings for Chantal were intensifying the more he was with her. That was only natural when she was going to be the mother of his baby.

She stood still at the top of one of the side roads. 'I'd like to take a slight detour to show you my apartment.'

'That would be interesting. Is it let to someone else at the moment?

They were already walking down the Rue de l'Assomption. 'No. My mother bought two apartments next to each other when I passed my final medical exams and I became financially independent for the first time in my life.'

'It looks as if it's a pricey sort of area around here.'

'It is, but we were very lucky. My mother had been paying rent for several years on one of the apartments. She scrimped and saved to pay the rent, telling me that it was important she bring up her daughter in a good neighbourhood. She became head of department in the prestigious *lycée* where she was teaching and the salary increase helped enormously. I was also a pupil there so it was a perfect arrangement for a mother bringing up her daughter by herself.'

'Your mother sounds like a remarkable woman.'

'Oh, she is! That's why I knew I could do the same if I had a child by myself.'

His grip on her hand tightened. 'But you won't be by yourself. I'll be there as part of the parenting partnership. Always remember we're in this together, Chantal.'

'Yes, of course we are.'

As she stood in front of the tall, prestigious building where she lived, she felt a moment of panic at the enormity of agreeing to have a baby with someone who would be committed to the baby but not to her. There were so many possible pitfalls along the way.

As she looked up towards her apartment on the fourth floor she had a sudden longing to hide away up there until she knew exactly what it would be like to go through with this unpredictable, unconventional plan. Her apartment could be her bolthole if things got too difficult. She could always return there if ever she felt over-whelmed by future circumstances.

The concierge had come to the door to check on the couple looking up at the apartments. He walked down the steps as soon as he recognised Chantal and they chatted for a short time. She told him her mother was enjoying her holiday. As for herself, she was happy at the hospital she was working in on the coast near Le Touquet. No, she didn't have time to call in because she and her colleague were in a hurry.

Walking off down the street, she knew the concierge had probably found her totally unlike her usual chatty self. But she didn't want to inadvertently divulge any information about her new situation until she'd come to terms with it herself. As the months progressed her secret would be obvious to everyone.

'I've got the apartment right next door to my mother's,' she told Michel, who was no longer holding her hand, sensing her desire to remain discreet in her own neighbourhood.

'You're very lucky to have such an arrangement in a neighbourhood like this.'

They turned the corner and walked more quickly along the Avenue Mozart back to their hotel. He took the keys to two rooms from the concierge at Reception. They went up in the lift.

'You've got the room next door to mine. I was wondering if you'd like to go out this evening for supper.'

She hesitated. 'To be honest, I'm feeling tired.' she said. 'I need a long soak in the bath before I make any plans.'

He smiled down at her. 'Come and have a drink in my room when you feel rested. Take your time. I'll order something from room service if you like.'

She went into her room and headed straight to her bathroom. Good, there was an enormous bath. Large fluffy towels. A nice long soak and she'd be a new woman.

Half an hour later she was in jeans and tee shirt, packed at the last minute in case she found herself in a casual situation during this flying visit. As she knocked on Michel's door she realised she was now feeling so relaxed after her long soak that her feet were still bare. And she was wearing no make-up.

'Goodness, Chantal. I don't think I've ever seen you looking so casual.'

'That's because we're staying in tonight.' As she walked into his room she could smell that indefinable aroma of his aftershave. A decidedly sexy aroma she'd decided the last time he'd worn it. The night their baby had been conceived.

He looked into the small fridge. 'What non-alcoholic drink would you like, Dr Winstone?'

'OK, Dr Devine, I get the message. You don't approve of alcohol for pregnant women, so you're in luck. Neither do I. Not a drop shall pass my lips until I deliver our baby. Is that an orange juice I can spy in there?'

'Yes, and it says it's freshly squeezed, although I doubt it. Anyway, it's the healthiest drink I can find.'

He carried the glass across to a small table by the window, plumping up the cushion in the arm-chair, waiting to check she was comfortably en-sconced before he collected his own drink from the fridge. She felt a frisson of happiness running through her as she watched him.

They were both committed to the child she was carrying. But at this precise moment she found herself hoping Michel would play a big part in her life as well as the baby's. The baby was growing inside her and Michel was growing on her. She told herself that her hormones were affecting the way she thought about the father of her child. These feelings she had for him were only natural. But she mustn't get carried away. She had to stick to the plan they'd agreed on.

For one thing, Michel still loved Maxine. It was obvious to everyone who knew him at the hospital. He'd buried his heart with his wife. He didn't want to move on. If she wanted their relationship to become a real one she couldn't compete with a ghost.

The whole idea was that they should be good parents whilst retaining their independence. She'd had a real relationship with Jacques, who'd gone back to his wife. She knew this arrangement with Michel was ideal. She could have a child and still keep her independence.

She'd got over the spell of nostalgia that had struck her as she'd looked up at her apartment. Yes, it could be her bolthole if it became necessary but for tonight she'd settle for the two of them chilling out in their slippers or, in her case, barefoot.

Michel said it would be a good idea to have an early supper. Better for the baby and also he was planning they should catch an early train so they could be at the hospital by midday. She suggested something light for supper and they settled on chicken and salad. While they were waiting Michel called to reserve their train seats for the morning.

Chantal surveyed the well-presented supper when it arrived. The waiter was at pains to set it all out on a small table, spreading a crisp white cloth and placing a large napkin on her lap. She almost wished she'd made the effort to dress up.

'I feel my old jeans don't match the occasion,' she said when the waiter had disappeared.

'You'd look good in a sack.'

She laughed. 'I didn't have a sack so I pulled on the next best thing.'

* * *

She blinked as she found herself falling asleep in the chair. The waiter had already cleared away and she was feeling decidedly sleepy.

She stirred in her chair. 'Time for me to go back to my room.'

'Do you have to? I mean go back to your room? I've got two beds in my bedroom both with clean sheets on.'

He held out his hands to help her stand up. 'I'm so sleepy I don't mind where I sleep.'

He was standing at the door of his bedroom, holding out his hands invitingly now.

'Come and have a look.'

He moved to take her hands as she stood up.

She looked into the bedroom. 'This room does look more inviting than mine.'

He smiled. 'Which bed would you like?'

'I'll have this one.'

'If you open that drawer they've even provided a nightdress for the lady guest and pyjamas for the man.'

'This hotel has certainly been upgraded since my schoolfriends and I walked past.'

She realised she was waking up now, talking quickly, feeling embarrassed that she'd practically invited herself into his bedroom. As she hurried into the bathroom she remembered how she'd told herself she mustn't sleep with him tonight. She'd drunk only orange juice and bottled water this evening so it had been a conscious decision? She couldn't justify it in any way except her own desire to be near him tonight. Blame it on her hormones again. She didn't want to be alone if she could be near her baby's father. Perfectly natural a mother-to-be should feel that way.

Having justified her desires to herself, she unwrapped the new toothbrush from its packet and scrubbed vigorously. Raising her eyes to the mirror, she saw her intense expression and decided to calm down. She'd made a baby with Michel. There was no need to be shy. She knew she hated sleeping by herself in a hotel. That was the only reason she'd wanted to stay with Michel, wasn't it?

She was in her bed when he came out of the bathroom. He came across and sat on the edge of her bed.

They both started to speak at the same time and then burst out laughing.

'You first,' Michel said.

'I was only going to say that I don't think we should…'

'So was I.'

'What?'

He drew in his breath. 'From a medical point of view I think you need to rest and get a good night's sleep after your exhausting day.'

She smiled. 'Exactly. I just didn't want to sleep alone tonight so…'

'Neither did I. Move over.'

She hesitated. He looked so sexy in his robe, his hair, still wet from the shower, was flopping over his face. She wanted his arms around her, to reassure her that all would be well. But if he put his arms around her…

Too late. She felt him draw her against his naked body.

'Do you have to wear this scratchy, lacy thing?' He was fumbling with the buttons.

She helped him. 'But we mustn't.'

'Absolutely not! But a goodnight kiss won't harm the baby.'

It was the longest, sexiest, most languorous kiss she could ever imagine. She wanted it to go on for ever. She wanted it to develop into something more, despite her earlier vow that they must never complicate things further by making love again.

It was a good thing that Michel had more will-power than she did.

With a large sigh, he dragged himself away. 'Goodnight, Chantal.'

'Don't go,' she whispered. 'Just stay there. Hold me in your arms, nothing more.'

Michel took her in his arms again. He'd always thought of her as being strong, resilient, independent woman. But he sensed that being pregnant again, being in an unconventional situation and all the other problems she was having to deal with, had made her feel vulnerable, unsure of herself.

'I'll always be here when you need me,' he whispered, as she curled herself against him. It was taking all his will-power not to make love to her. He remembered the way she'd clung to him when he'd been inside her on the night they'd made their baby. It was all he could do not to throw caution to the winds and but he had to stay strong.

Someone was tapping on the door. Michel shrugged into the robe he'd dropped on the floor beside the bed when he'd climbed in with Chantal.

He took the tray from the waiter at the door. Placing it on the bedside table he was pleased to see that the waiter had brought coffee and croissants, enough for two people. Chantal could smell coffee, hear someone pouring it. She opened her eyes then pulled herself up against the pillows so that she could accept the cup and saucer he was holding out for her.

He thought once again how young she looked without make-up. And without that tough exterior she tried to portray. That independence she insisted on. But he'd held her in his arms all night and sensed how vulnerable she really was, scared even. At one point she'd seemed to be having a nightmare. He'd cradled her like a baby, shushed her back to sleeping peacefully. She hadn't woken.

He mustn't start falling for her. She was proud of her independence. Wouldn't surrender it to anyone. He must respect that. It was part of her tough personality. The personality that made her so endearing. He mustn't become emotional about her just because she was carrying their baby.

Rather brusquely he asked her if she would like a croissant to dip in her coffee in that disgustingly messy way.

She grinned. 'You remembered! Of course I do. Especially if someone else is going to sort out my bed after I've gone. What time is the train?'

He told her. 'So we'll have to get a move on.'

She swallowed a piece of croissant which had just the right amount of coffee soaked into it. 'Michel, thank you for taking care of me last night. I don't like sleeping alone in a hotel. I felt very safe and I slept like a log.'

'Of course you did,' he told her, wishing she didn't look so beautiful this morning. He'd have to be a robot not to want to take her in his arms again.

He stood up. 'I'll go and use the bathroom.'

'You can have it all to yourself. Throw me a robe and I'll disappear next door.'

The train was about to depart. Michel raced down the platform, having told Chantal to walk slowly.

He was holding out his hand to help her up the step. 'Take your time.'

She was glad they were travelling in first class. So much more comfortable. Michel took out his laptop and became immersed in writing up notes from the conference. Even though she'd slept all night she still felt tired. Good for the baby, she told herself as she closed her eyes.

As they headed for work Michel told her to take her lunch break before reporting for duty. He was carrying her small overnight bag. 'I'll have this taken up to your room. But have lunch first before you go up for a nap.'

'Michel, I slept on the train.'

'Well, have a lie-down, then. I don't want to

see you on duty before two o clock and that's an order.'

As she watched him disappearing into Emergency she found herself wishing he wouldn't use that phrase! At times it amused her. She knew he only said it for a bit of fun but she hated it when he turned back into her ultra-efficient boss. She wanted the real Michel back again. She needed that warm, comforting, sexy man. The man she was trying not to fall in love with.

Because if that happened her life would change for ever and she didn't want that to happen, did she?

CHAPTER NINE

DURING THE WEEKS that followed her obstetric appointment in Paris with Sebastian she found herself looking forward to the next appointment when she would see the scan, the technological proof that she was indeed carrying a baby. She'd seen many scans during her professional life but the excitement of seeing that image on screen would be mind-blowing for her. And also for Michel, who'd insisted he wouldn't miss it for anything. It was in his diary and he'd rescheduled his professional commitments where necessary.

As she waited for her patient to return from X-Ray she couldn't help wishing that Michel would be a bit more relaxed about her prenatal care. She tried to remind herself that when he fussed over her—because that was what it felt like to be told she had to take a break or she must eat lunch—she knew he was worrying about the child she was carrying. His child was all-important to him. She was merely the vessel that was carrying the baby. Well, that's what they'd agreed, wasn't it?

But she realised she'd broken the rules when she'd spent the night at the hotel in Paris. But the care and affection he'd shown her was his way of caring for their unborn child. She had to keep reminding herself it was their child that was important to him and not allow his concern for her welfare to overwhelm her.

Or maybe she should have a word with him. He probably didn't realise how much it was getting on her nerves. Or perhaps she should blame it on her hormones, which made her oversensitive?

The opportunity to speak about it came sooner than she'd anticipated.

A young nurse looked into her cubicle. 'Dr Winstone, we've got a child in the next cubicle with spots all over his back. Would you have a look at him for me?'

The curtain was closed again and she distinctly heard Michel speaking to the nurse in his professional director voice. She waited, not wanting to interfere.

Seconds later he came into the cubicle. 'Chantal. I've told nurse to ask someone else to check the child's spots. Obviously, in your condition you mustn't treat any case that might be infectious.'

'Michel, you've got to stop trying to wrap me in cotton wool!'

She hadn't meant to lose her temper but now he really knew how she felt. 'Our colleagues are beginning to talk about us. They're asking questions about our relationship. Take that heavy man with the hernia you stopped me from treating in case I tried to move him onto his side. I know you took over and treated him yourself but that's not the point!'

'So what is the point you're trying to make?' he asked patiently. He told himself he had to make allowances for her condition. Pregnant women were prone to being over-sensitive. He would listen and try to calm her down. 'It's not good for the baby if you upset yourself like this.'

She took a deep breath. He'd made it quite plain

that everything was for the good of the baby. He wasn't thinking about her as a person. That shouldn't annoy her, given the terms of their agreement, but it did.

She lowered her voice. 'The point I'm trying to make, Michel, is that everybody will soon know we're having a baby together. We can't keep it a secret. Our baby will grow bigger and bigger and then it will arrive, and at that point…'

'Don't patronise me. I understand the situation better than you do.'

A porter was pushing his way through the curtains with her X-rayed patient.

'See me in my office this evening before you go off duty, Dr Winstone,' Michel said in a pseudo-stern tone as he left the cubicle.

The porter was looking perturbed by their exchange. 'On the carpet tonight, are you, Chantal?'

'Possibly,' she said in her most professional voice as she took the X-rays from the nurse who'd accompanied her patient.

The patient raised his head. 'So is my ankle broken, Doctor?'

She placed a cushion under the man's head as

she slotted the X-rays into the scanner on the wall. Pointing to the injured area, she showed him the shattered calcaneum, which had been badly crushed as he'd fallen from a tree in his garden and had taken his full weight on one leg.

She could see it would require expert pinning under general anaesthetic or with an epidural before the foot was put in a cast.

'I'm going to ask one of the orthopaedic consultants to have a look at you. If you don't mind waiting here a bit longer, Guillaume, I'll have you seen as soon as I can.'

Guillaume grinned. 'I'm not going anywhere, doctor. The branches on that tree will have to wait until I get out of here.'

Chantal smiled at him. He was a plucky man, hadn't complained at all even though it had been obvious he'd been in pain when he'd arrived.

'Take my advice and get a professional tree surgeon in.'

'That's what my wife said last week. Wish I'd listened to her.'

'Where's your wife now?'

'Funnily enough, she's on duty here in hospital.

She's a nurse on the children's ward and hates to be disturbed when she's on duty. Thinks it's unprofessional if I phone her mobile, which is usually switched off anyway.'

'Guillaume, you've got to let her know. With your permission I'll contact the ward now and have her come down here.'

'OK, got to face the music some time, I suppose.' He rolled his eyes. 'She'll be so mad at me. I would have been fine if that ladder hadn't twisted.'

Chantal was already speaking to the sister in charge of the children's ward.

'There, your wife is on her way, Guillaume, and I know you'll find her very sympathetic. I've also arranged for a consultant to be with you as soon as he's finished operating.'

Another nurse had just hurried into the cubicle.

'Darling, I don't believe it!'

Guillaume's very concerned but flustered wife had arrived and was bending over her husband. 'Are you OK? Oh, you shouldn't have gone up that old ladder. I told you—'

She broke off in mid-flow and turned to Chantal. 'Is my husband OK, Doctor?'

'He's fractured his calcaneum so I've referred him to one of our orthopaedic consultants who'll be here shortly.'

'Are those his X-rays?'

'Yes.'

'He's going to need surgery, isn't he?'

'I would think so but that's up to the consultant to decide.'

'Of course.'

The distraught wife lavished attention on her husband, who seemed relieved that he wasn't being reprimanded any more. In fact, Chantal could see he was positively enjoying his wife's concern for him.

She waited until the consultant had arrived, assessed the patient and arranged to have him admitted to Orthopaedics for pre-op care.

Sitting at the computer at the end of her working day, she was typing in Guillaume's details, having just made a call to Orthopaedics. The latest news from the ward was that her patient had had the ankle pinned under epidural and was sitting up in bed, enjoying the lavish attentions of his wife.

She heard the door opening and half turned to see who it was.

'Ah, I believe you wanted to see me this evening, Dr Devine.' She swung round from the computer to give him her full attention.

'Chantal, you did realise I was joking this morning when you were treating Guillaume, didn't you?'

'Of course I did. But you had the porter worried. He asked me if I was on the carpet this evening.'

He smiled. 'Have you anything more to report?'

She hesitated. She needed to clear the air, speak about their altercation while he was in a good mood. 'Michel, I've got serious issues with the way you've been treating me since I became pregnant. I don't mind you making fun of me but fussing about my delicate condition is definitely off limits.'

'Not when you're carrying my child,' he said, quietly.

'Our child!'

He sat down on the edge of the desk. 'You really are annoyed with me, aren't you? Look, it's to be expected in the early days of pregnancy. Your hormones—'

'There you go again.' She lowered her voice. 'There's nothing wrong with my hormones.'

She stood up, folding her arms defensively in front of herself.

He strode across the room and drew her gently into his arms. For a few moments she resisted him, standing rigidly, arms like a shield in front of her. But one glance up at his amused expression broke her resolve.

'Maybe I am being a bit over-sensitive,' she conceded quietly.

He bent his head and kissed her, gently, persuasively, ready to agree to any terms she wanted to set if only he could make her happy again.

As he considered the enormity of what she was doing, carrying this baby for him, he found it impossible not to hold her more closely and tenderly against him. He was hoping she wouldn't interpret his tenderness as being too possessive.

He released her from his arms just in case he'd got it wrong again.

'So remind me, what's the date of the scan? I know it's in my diary. Next week, isn't it?'

'Next Wednesday.'

'We'll have to make it a day trip. I've got an important meeting on Thursday. Could you get the scan around two in the afternoon?'

'I've already booked one-thirty.'

'Excellent. And, Chantal...? ' He hesitated.

'Yes?'

'Any time you find me patronising or fussing too much, please tell me at once. Don't bottle it up. Keep the lines of communication open. It's only because I'm concerned about our precious baby.'

She smiled up at him. She had such strong feelings for him now. Stronger than they should be.

The following Wednesday they had a snack on the train so that they could go straight over to see Sebastian. Michel was planning to take her out to dinner somewhere this evening when they got back to St Martin sur Mer. A celebration once

they'd seen the scan. Please let it be a celebration, he thought briefly, before banishing the
awful thought that it could be otherwise. How
on earth did other fathers cope with all the anxiety of pregnancy? As a doctor he should be more
laid-back than he was, able to face the outcome
of all health situations.

As Sebastian waited for them in his consulting
room he couldn't help worrying about his former
medical colleague. He'd known Chantal since
she'd been a medical student and knew about her
trauma last year with Jacques. That fly-by-night
doctor who'd spent most of his medical career
moving around from hospital to hospital on temporary contracts. The scoundrel had led Chantal
to believe all his lies about being single, unat-
tached, in love with her, wanting to marry her.

The entire medical staff who'd worked with
Chantal in Paris had been scandalised when the
story of Jacques's deception had spread around
the grapevine. Everyone had been sympathetic to
her but, being the feisty woman she was, sympathy hadn't been what she'd wanted. She'd given

in her notice and got herself a position in Emergency at the Hôpital de la Plage, back to her family roots so that she could forget the man who'd betrayed her.

He remembered giving her a glowing reference. The Hôpital de la Plage was a prestigious hospital. There were always many applicants when a post became vacant. He'd had no hesitation in recommending her. The hospital board in Paris hadn't wanted her to leave. They'd hoped she would reconsider her position with them as she had been in line for promotion. But Sebastian had explained the whole sordid story of Jacques's deception.

He'd laid it on thick and had taken great delight in the fact that when Jacques's contract had come up for renewal, his well-timed explanation of the odious man's deception had been one of the reasons the board had refused to renew his contract.

'Your patient is here now,' his receptionist told him over the intercom.

'Make them comfortable in the waiting room. I'll call them in shortly.'

He was still checking the notes in front of him

and found himself hoping fervently that Chantal knew what she was doing. He'd had time to make enquiries about her latest boyfriend and had heard nothing but good reports from those in the medical fraternity who'd worked with him. He was a high flyer, excellent at his work, highly intelligent, exceptional at diagnosing difficult cases.

He was a widower who'd been devoted to his wife but unlikely to commit himself to marriage a second time. That worried him a great deal. His wife Susanne, whom he consulted on affairs of the heart, had expressed her concern. She'd advised him to keep an eye on Chantal and make sure she didn't get hurt again.

He went across to open the door, a confident smile in place to reassure Chantal.

'Do come in. How was the journey? You sit here, Chantal, where I can see you. Now, how have you been since I saw you?'

Michel felt very much sidelined. There was an obvious bond of friendship between Chantal and Sebastian. That was good from the point of view that he would take special care of her. He himself had to realise that he'd done very little towards creating this pregnancy and what he'd achieved had been from a purely natural and immensely wonderful experience. So, for once in his life he had to learn to take a back seat.

There was some discussion about blood tests and haemoglobin levels. Sebastian was pleased with her general good health. He touched briefly on Chantal's miscarriage, which had happened the previous September.

Yes, his records showed that she'd had a spontaneous miscarriage thought to have been triggered by the stress of the situation she'd found herself in. Subsequently she'd had a D and C to make sure that the inside of the uterus was healthy again and would be viable for any future pregnancy.

Chantal listened impassively to Sebastian recapping her medical history. She wanted to forget the past and move on to this pregnancy. So precious because she'd never expected it would happen to her again.

Michel was relieved to hear that she'd been well

cared for after the miscarriage but he was also anxious to see the scan of their baby.

A nurse came in from the treatment room to say she was ready to do the scan whenever required.

Michel placed his hand on Chantal's waist as they walked into the treatment room together. She found the touch of his hand reassuring. They were in this together. He was being protective towards her. If anything showed up on the ultrasound that was a problem, she could take it if Michel was with her.

He was helping her up onto the couch now. She gave him a grateful smile for his help and also for being there with her because she suddenly felt scared. She'd had to assume there would be no problems with this pregnancy. But until now there'd been nothing to reassure her.

The nurse was rubbing the gel on her abdomen. At three months pregnant Chantal hadn't detected any roundness or swelling.

She looked up at the screen above the treatment couch. Sebastian was giving a running commentary as they started the scan. Everything was in its rightful place, no abnormalities.

'And here it is, the tiny foetus.'

Sebastian couldn't contain his excitement. He'd never been able to do the first viewing of an unborn baby without feeling it.

Chantal grabbed Michel's hand. 'Look, Michel, our baby. Oh, will somebody take a picture, please?'

'That's all under control,' Sebastian told her. 'We'll give you a picture to take home when— Hang on a minute...'

'What's the matter?' Michel said, anxiously. 'Oh, I see! There's a second foetus, isn't there?'

'Yes, there are two of them,' Sebastian announced solemnly. 'Congratulations, both of you! You're expecting twins.'

Chantal stared at the two shapes that were barely discernible on the screen but they were her twin babies, their twin babies. She gripped Michel's hand more tightly as she turned to look at him. She saw the tears in his eyes beginning to roll down his cheeks as their eyes met. She would never forget this precious moment. For the rest of her life she would remember the moment she'd known for certain that she was going to be a mother.

Michel turned his eyes back to the screen. He needed a private moment to share with those two unborn babies. His love for them was almost too much to bear. And he could feel his admiration and affection for the mother of his children strengthening. As he watched these living babies that they'd made together he felt a strong bond growing between them. A powerful emotion was challenging all his previous ideas.

CHAPTER TEN

HE REACHED FOR her hand across the table. She smiled as his fingers curled around hers. Watching the scan of their babies that afternoon had been a truly moving experience for her and she knew Michel had felt exactly the same. Probably more so, from his emotional reaction. He was a real softie at heart, an absolute pussy cat. She couldn't have believed when she'd first met him in February that he could change so much when she got to know him.

She realised she'd also changed during the last few months. It was pure determination that made her hold out for her independence. Her feelings for Michel were too deep and complicated to analyse. She didn't want to give in to the emotional changes that were taking place in her mind. If she'd wanted a more desirable father for her baby it wouldn't have been possible to find one.

She could hear the little voice that spoke to her constantly in her head as she tried so hard to ignore her strong emotional feelings for Michel. Why was she still so afraid of losing her independence? Michel wasn't like Jacques. Every instinct she had was telling her that he was totally honest. She could depend on him one hundred per cent in any situation. But Michel's whole concern was to become a father. No one could replace Maxine. He was holding her hand now out of gratitude that she'd made fatherhood possible for him.

As Michel continued to hold Chantal's hand he was also thinking about the scan of their babies that afternoon. The strong emotions that had moved him as he'd seen them on screen. He could feel the pain of losing Maxine fading in the face of new life and found that he was becoming more and more caught up in his feelings for Chantal.

'Are you OK, Michel?'

He smiled at her. 'I'm fine. Never better. I think I'm overwhelmed by the scan of our babies this afternoon. I can't stop thinking about it.'

He stopped himself from becoming too effusive. He mustn't get carried away while his emotions were so difficult to understand.

He signalled for the bill. 'We shouldn't stay out too late. It's been a long day for you.'

'And you,' she said, with a wry smile.

'Yes, but I'm not…sorry. Am I being too concerned about you?'

'I'm getting used to it and finding it very charming. Outside of working hours, that is.'

'I think you should take the morning off tomorrow. No, hear me out.' He avoided telling her it was an order, aware that she disliked the word. 'In fact, I'm going to insist and authorise the whole day off for you.'

As they walked outside to the car she didn't demur. She *was* feeling tired. and Michel was quite right. She should take care of herself.

He didn't start the car immediately but simply leaned across and put his arm on the back of her seat. 'I hope you approved of my choice of restaurant tonight?'

'Very smart. Expensive, I should imagine.'

'Nothing too good for the mother of my children.'

'And easier to get to than the beach café.'

He smiled down into her eyes. 'You might be too heavy for me to carry over the sand! Joking aside, you don't look any different. Hard to believe there are two babies in there.'

'It was like a miracle.'

As they sat very still, both engrossed in their own thoughts, Michel could feel the emotional rapport growing between them.

'I've got a proposition to put to you,' he said gently. 'I'd like you to come back home with me tonight so that I can show you the changes I've made since I knew I was going to be a father. I've prepared a bedroom that will be yours to use whenever you want to use it. There's another room beside it that we can use as a nursery. Obviously we'll need to employ a trained nurse to take care of our babies if you choose to go back to work.'

'Michel, I really haven't thought so far ahead.' She paused as she saw the disappointed expression on his face. 'Let's discuss that another time, shall we? But I'd love to go back to your house to see the changes you've made,' she added hastily, so as not to hurt his feelings.

Suddenly she felt that events were going too quickly for her. It had only been a few weeks ago that she'd agreed to have a baby with Michel, even though she'd only known him for a short time and that had been as colleagues.

Now she had two babies on the way, which was wonderful, but the trappings that inevitably went with parenthood had all got to be finalised in the next few months. She would try to take it one step at a time. Michel's endless enthusiasm was great to witness but exhausting when he tried to rush her along with him.

She made allowances for the fact that as the director of Emergency he had to think on his feet, make split-second life-and-death decisions. He was perfect in his professional work.

But domestic life wasn't like that. At least, not in her experience. Were they really going to be compatible during the long years of parenthood ahead of them?

As he started the engine he knew he'd only told her half of what was in his mind. 'Of course, if you prefer to go back to your poky little room in the medics' quarters, spend your off duty confined within those four small walls...'

She gave him a deliberately whimsical smile 'OK, I've got the message. I must say it's very tempting.'

Michel smiled happily. So far so good. As he changed gear to go up the hill he was already planning ahead what he should say. If she approved of the room he'd prepared, would she give him an answer to the question that was uppermost in his mind? He didn't want her to feel she was losing her independence so he must reassure her he would give her space in their new situation together.

'It's a lovely room, Michel.'

'I'm glad you like it.'

He walked across and pushed open a door that led through to a smaller room, which was completely devoid of furniture.

'I had all the furniture taken out because I thought this could be the nursery. And now we know we're going to have twins you can choose their cots and the furniture you would like to go in here. There's a baby furniture shop in St Martin but maybe you'd prefer to go up to Paris to select what's needed? If I'm honest...'

He took a deep breath. 'It would be a great relief if you'd move in here. I would know you and the babies were being well cared for. You'd get away from hospital and have more space and comfort. We could make plans for the future. And when the babies were born you would be used to the house. What do you say?'

Her mind was spinning with the enormity of this new situation. Michel was being very generous and considerate but his main concern was the welfare of his babies. As she'd passed the photos in the hall on her way up here she'd known she mustn't commit herself to any situation that could result in losing her independence to a man who was in love with someone else. She hadn't known that Jacques had a wife. This time she knew where Michel's heart lay and she couldn't compete with a ghost.

'To be honest, Michel, I'm too tired to think

about anything except sleep tonight. So if you don't mind…'

His brow furrowed. 'Of course you must rest now. I had the bed made up in your room because I knew you'd be tired. I'll be right next door if you need anything.'

On impulse she turned to hold out her arms towards him. He'd gone to so much trouble. He was prepared to pander to her every whim.

'Thank you, Michel,' she whispered, her voice barely discernible as she clung to him, unable to cope with the conflicting emotions that were running through her.

He could feel her body quivering as they stood together. It was all he could do not to scoop her up into his arms and carry her to his bed, to make love to her all night as he'd done the night their precious babies were conceived. But wonderful as that would be, it wouldn't solve the problem of their future together.

She pulled herself away from his warm embrace, not allowing herself to respond to the feelings she'd had as he'd held her close.

'Goodnight, Michel.'

He bent his head and gave her a brief kiss before turning away and leaving the room.

It was ages before he could sleep. He put on his bedside light and plumped up his pillows so he could lie back and read if he couldn't sleep. He could check on the report he was writing for tomorrow's board meeting.

He tried to concentrate but he couldn't as his thoughts turned inevitably back to Chantal.

He got out of bed and padded barefoot over to the window that led to the balcony. He pulled his robe around him. It felt decidedly chilly out there in the early hours of the morning. Everything was supposed to seem more difficult before the dawn. That was certainly true of his thoughts about their complicated relationship. He should be the happiest man alive knowing that he was soon to be father of twins. And yet he couldn't help wanting to have Chantal close by him. He enjoyed being with her.

He hoped she was warm enough in the room next door. Of course she was! She would be fast asleep, tucked up in the new bed.

Was he moving things along too fast? Was that

why she seemed so far away from him at times, wrapped up in her own thoughts? Should he have consulted her first before building the little nest for their babies?

Chantal had lain awake after Michel had left her. The idea of having her own room in his house, complete with nursery for their babies, was very tempting. It was what Michel wanted. She thought of the plans they'd drawn up at the beginning of their unconventional scheme. Parenthood had just been a word then. Now it was a reality. It was a lifelong commitment. She'd known that from the beginning but she hadn't thought it through.

She had to admit that if she wanted a lifelong commitment then Michel was the man she would choose. It was the institution of being tied to another person that scared her. But she already had his babies inside her. That was binding enough, wasn't it? Why fight against the warm feelings she had towards the father of her babies? She couldn't ignore these disturbingly strong emotional feelings towards him. If she was honest with herself she would say she was in danger of falling in love with him. Maybe she already had but wouldn't admit it.

She sat up and switched on the light, looking around the room, this beautifully appointed room that Michel had prepared for her. She could be happy here. She could go one further and admit that she would be even happier to be in Michel's bed at this moment. She felt so safe when she was with him. So sure that the physical desires she felt for him were what she wanted.

But Michel was still in love with Maxine and in any case he'd said he would never commit to a loving relationship that might end prematurely and leave him utterly bereft. She must stop fantasising and consider the facts. She should keep her independence. Stick to the original plan and stop becoming carried away with romantic ideas that weren't viable. She was going to be a mother to two babies. That was all she wanted.

She was awakened by the sound of knocking on her door. Michel was carrying a tray. He put it down on the bedside table.

'I've got to leave soon.'

He was being deliberately brusque to counter-act his real feelings at the sight of her beautiful long dark hair spread out across the pillow. What he really wanted was for her to hold out her arms and invite him into her bed. Perhaps if he appeared unavailable it would make her want him.

He hovered by the bedside for a few moments until he admitted his reverse psychology wasn't working on her.

He cleared his throat. 'Make sure you rest today, Chantal. Call me if there's something you need, won't you?'

'Of course.' She smiled up at him. 'Thank you for the coffee and the croissant.'

'Straight out of the freezer into the high-speed oven. Hope it's thawed out enough. See you to-night.'

He made a quick exit in case he changed his mind and made suggestions that he might regret.

She reached for her coffee, wondering why he was in such a rush. She'd barely woken up. She'd hoped he might join her for breakfast at least. Looking across at the window, the silky curtains

held back at the sides by golden tassels, she remembered that she had a whole day to pamper
herself.

First she took a long bath, sprinkling some of
the contents of the bottle of scented bath foam
liberally into the water. When she finally decided
that she should make a move she reached for one
of the large fluffy towels.

As she wrapped it round her she had the disturbing feeling that she was in a luxury hotel. All
well and good for a visit but could she ever call it
home? Was this what she wanted for her babies?

A couple of weeks passed during which time the
crucial question of where she should live when
the babies were born was never too far from her
mind. She found herself working hard, trying to
blot out the doubts that taunted her when she had
time to think.

Michel was as attentive as usual towards her
when they were working together but in a more
professional way. He'd taken the hint that she
didn't want his attentions to overwhelm her. He
reined in his anxious feelings that she was work-

ing too hard. As he noticed her coming out of a cubicle, having dealt with a patient and now prepared to take on another, he couldn't help himself from intervening. Swiftly he strode across the floor.

'Chantal, may I have a word?'

He spoke briefly first to the nurse who was trying to summon Chantal over to her cubicle, telling her he would deal with the problem himself.

'It's lunchtime, Chantal,' he said, quietly.

'I'm not hungry. I'll take a break shortly.'

'You may not be hungry but our babies need you to have regular feeds, don't they?'

He whispered this, knowing it wouldn't be well received.

'And you're looking particularly tired this morning. Try and have some rest when you've had lunch. I'll cover for you if you're late back. I've been thinking it might be a good idea for you to work part time soon. What do you think?'

She drew in her breath. She didn't dare to tell him what she thought at this moment. It wouldn't be good for their precious babies if she allowed herself to let fling the expletives that came to mind.

As she turned and headed for the medics' dining room she suddenly realised that Michel had been quite right. She had been feeling particularly tired this morning and there was a dragging feeling in the lower regions of her abdomen. She made a detour to the women's toilets.

Reaching for the push button to flush the loo, she looked in horror at the tell-tale signs of blood in the lavatory bowl. She put her hand to her mouth to stifle the cry that rose in her throat as she felt blood trickling down between her legs.

'No, no! Not again!'

CHAPTER ELEVEN

SHE LAY VERY still in the small room off the obstetrics prenatal ward. Everything had happened so quickly. One minute she'd felt reasonably OK and the next she'd found she was being loaded onto a trolley and brought up here to Obstetrics.

Michel was sitting beside her, anxious for the obstetrics consultant to arrive.

'Pierre's still in Theatre,' he told her, relaying the message he'd just received.

Genevieve came to ask how she was feeling now that she'd been settled in a bed. She came over and checked the large pad between Chantal's legs.

'Mmm,' was all she said as she changed it.

Michel had left the room to give them some privacy.

'Do you think the bleeding is slowing down, Genevieve?'

'It will take a while before we can assess what's happening, Chantal. Don't get out of bed. Lie as still as you can. Pierre Marchand will be here as soon as he can get away from Theatre.'

Minutes later he arrived, still in his theatre greens.

Chantal stared up at him, anxious to hear his assessment of her condition. Her heart was beating more rapidly than it should as she remained convinced it was happening to her again. This was exactly like the last time, except she'd been totally alone when she'd miscarried last September. This time she had her baby's father anxiously hovering at the back of the room.

She glanced across and gave him a smile of reassurance, even though she didn't feel there was much hope. In the half-hour since the nurse in the ladies room who'd heard her scream had alerted Michel it had become obvious that nobody on the medical staff had been unaware of their unconventional relationship. But the fact that she was pregnant, or possibly that she had been pregnant, added another dimension to their supposedly secret liaison.

She tried to relax as Pierre examined her. He straightened up, his expression enigmatic.

'We'll need a scan, Sister.' He looked down at Chantal. 'I'll have you taken down to the treatment room as soon as possible, Chantal. If things look OK, we'll treat you here with complete bed rest for a few days until things settle down again. If the pregnancy isn't viable…'

Pierre paused, not wanting to upset her any more than she appeared to be. He'd been briefed that his patient had miscarried with her first pregnancy last September.

'It's OK, Pierre,' Chantal said quietly. 'I'm prepared for the worst-case scenario. If the pregnancy isn't viable you would perform a D and C, I presume?'

The obstetrician nodded. 'Yes, but let's stay positive until we find out what's happening, Chantal.'

Michel moved forward and took hold of Chantal's hand. He may be the father of these babies but he felt as if he was getting in the way of the expert Obstetrics team.

She clung to Michel's hand.

'I'm so glad you're here,' she whispered.

He found his spirits lifting. She wanted him; she needed him. He was already thinking of the worst-case scenario. If that happened, would she stay with him so they could try again? His affection for her was growing stronger every day. In fact, he couldn't imagine life without her now.

Michel had a quick word with Pierre before leaving the room. Out in the corridor he switched on his mobile and punched in Sebastian's private number at the Paris clinic.

'I'll come over,' Sebastian said tersely as soon as Michel had given him the stark facts.

Michel tried to convince him that Chantal was in good hands. Pierre Marchand was an excellent obstetrician, but Sebastian insisted that Chantal was his patient and had also been a personal friend of his family for many years. He would be with them towards the end of the afternoon so that he could liaise with Pierre, their Obstetrician. It was important that if Chantal was having a miscarriage she have expert attention to determine the cause of two miscarriages. This would ensure that her next pregnancy had more of a chance of being successful.

'One baby here,' Pierre pointed out as Chantal and Michel gazed at the screen.

'Another one hiding behind it, here,' Michel said, his voice choking with emotion and relief. His babies were still alive, but would they stay so till full term? What was the significance of this bleeding?

'Complete rest is needed, Chantal.'

Pierre spoke with the authority of a consultant who'd had to stress this to patients before. He turned to look at Michel. 'We must ensure that Chantal rests completely. The next few days are crucial. She mustn't get out of bed. All we can do is wait to see if the bleeding stops. Continue with the glucose saline infusion until the condition stabilises. Keep me informed please.'

Michel explained that Chantal's obstetrician was coming over from Paris to liaise with him. Pierre had no quarrel with that.

'Two heads are better than one. Only the best for our important patient.'

* * *

Chantal was delighted when Sebastian walked into her room. She was even more pleased to see that he was accompanied by Susanne. They had all been friends for many years.

Sebastian asked if he could see their obstetrician for a full report as soon as possible.

Michel, who'd been with Chantal all afternoon, put a call through to Pierre, who arrived shortly afterwards. The two obstetricians agreed that complete rest was necessary until Chantal was out of danger. The cause of the loss of blood hadn't been ascertained yet.

'Were you worrying about something, Chantal?' Sebastian asked, gently.

He glanced across at his wife as he waited for his patient's reply. They had their own theory about this unconventional relationship that Chantal was involved in. They'd discussed it at length on the way over from Paris.

Chantal hesitated. 'Nothing in particular,' she said carefully, aware that now she was even more the centre of attention in this small, crowded room. Instinctively she knew what Sebastian and

Susanne were thinking. They'd brought up four children in a conventional, loving marriage. She'd known at her first professional appointment in Paris that Sebastian would be concerned about the unconventional situation between Michel and herself.

'Nothing at all?' Sebastian prompted gently.

She steeled herself and wouldn't be drawn as she told herself this relationship would work. They would make it work.

She shook her head. 'Michel and I have got everything in place ready for our twins. There's even a well-equipped nursery in Michel's house. When I go back to work after out babies are born we're going to employ a trained nurse to take care of them when we're both on duty at the same time.'

Susanne moved forward from the back of the room where she'd been watching quietly.

'Don't go back to work too early, my dear. I spent time at home after the birth of all four of our babies. It's a precious time to bond with them.'

Pierre seemed impatient now. 'With respect,

Madame, childcare isn't under discussion now. Especially when we cannot be sure that these babies will go to full term. We have to be realistic. Chantal has assured us she's not having to worry about anything. Michel will be a devoted father. Sebastian and I both agree that at the moment we have to ensure complete rest for our patient.'

Susanne cleared her throat. 'Have you contacted your mother, Chantal?'

'She's still on holiday on the coast near Bordeaux. I didn't want to worry her.'

'How about your cousin who lives inland from here?'

'I was planning to contact Julia when we knew for certain whether the pregnancy is still viable.'

'The pregnancy will have more of a chance of being viable if we allow our patient to rest now,' Pierre suggested dryly. 'Let's keep in touch, Sebastian, but for the moment I think we should give Chantal the chance to rest.'

In the middle of the night Chantal woke up, initially confused about where she was. She felt somehow different. There was a small light in the corner of the room and a nurse was sitting in an armchair, reading. She stood up and came across the room.

'How are you feeling, Chantal?'

'I think I'm OK.'

'I'll check your pad while you're awake. I last checked two hours ago.' The nurse smiled. 'It's dry, not a sign of blood. Excellent!'

Chantal felt a huge sense of relief. 'I'd love to think my babies are safe now but I know it's early days.'

The nurse nodded. 'Dr Marchand usually puts his patients on at least two weeks complete rest when they've got a threatened miscarriage, especially when they've already suffered one before.'

'Yes, but during my last miscarriage I was in a completely different situation,' she said quietly, almost to herself. 'My obstetrician last September told me that the unpleasant experience I'd been through had triggered my miscarriage.

The nurse was adjusting the speed of the glucose saline infusion 'That does happen,' she agreed quietly. 'Now, please try not to think about it. Try to sleep again. Does my light disturb you?'

'No. It's comforting to know I'm not alone. Last time I was.'

She wouldn't think about the past. Only positive thoughts from now on. She was going to be fine. Her babies would survive.

She closed her eyes, pretending to be asleep so she didn't have to talk any more. It would soon be morning. She'd ring Julia, check on how her cousin's pregnancy was going along. She hadn't seen her for a few weeks.

She found herself wondering how Michel was. She'd had to persuade him that it wasn't necessary for him to miss his sleep. He'd agreed to leave her only when he'd made her promise to contact him if there was any change. He wasn't going home, though. He would be in his usual room in the medics quarters, close at hand if she needed him.

The sun was stealing over the windowsill when she next woke up. She'd made it through the night. The nurse checked her pad for signs of blood. Still dry but she must remain in bed.

It was mid-morning before she rang Julia. Michel had been in to see her and had gone away to organise the staff in the emergency department. He would be back shortly when he was satisfied they could manage without him.

Pierre had been in to see her and had been pleased with the news that the bleeding had stopped. He was going to liaise with Sebastian over the phone and keep him in the picture.

Julia's line was busy. She left a message. Minutes later her cousin rang back and they chatted happily. Chantal relaxed against her pillows. It was always good to talk to her cousin. They immediately struck up the familiar rapport that existed between them and became the two excitable young girls they'd been in the past.

'How are you, Julia? I Haven't seen you for weeks.'

'I'm as big as a house! I'm due at the end of the month. Can't wait to be delivered. Bernard and I don't get out much when he's not lecturing his students or supervising their efforts in the operating theatre. And he's still got patients to see when he's not teaching.

'He's so nervous about me being pregnant. Honestly, you wouldn't think he was a doctor. If this was how he treated his patients they'd all complain. Talk about wrapping me in cotton wool!'

Chantal was giggling already at her cousin's description of Bernard as an anxious father. He always seemed such a confident man when she saw him in hospital but, then, so did Michel.

'Julia, I know exactly what you mean.'

'Oh, you've no idea what I'm talking about, Chantal. You've absolutely no idea…or have you?'

Julia stopped in mid-flow. 'Chantal, is there something you haven't told me? What did you mean just now?'

'I was going to tell you the next time we met up but I've been so busy and…'

'You're not…you're not…?

'I am! Yes, I'm pregnant.'

There was a whoop of excitement at the other

end. Chantal held her mobile at arm's length till the deafening cries died down.

'I'm glad you're pleased, Julia.'

'Pleased? I've over the moon for you. I assume it's Michel's.'

'How did you guess?'

'Oh, come on, it's obvious. You two were made for each other!'

'Well, it's not quite like that. It's a bit unconventional,' she said cautiously. 'You see, we only got together because we both wanted a baby and even then… Oh , I'll explain what happened and what was meant to happen when I see you. Too complicated to tell you over the phone so don't ask. Actually, it's twins.'

'Wonderful, even better! Can't wait to hear the details when we get together. Our twin mothers will be pleased you're keeping up the family tradition. Have you told your mother yet?'

'Hold on a minute, Julia. I haven't dared to tell her. I'm actually in the obstetrics ward under the care of Pierre Marchand. I had some bleeding so I'm confined to bed rest. I've had a scan and the babies are fine but we're not out of the woods yet.'

'Oh, I'm so sorry. You poor thing, cooped up in hospital. Tell you what, why don't I get Bernard to come down and talk to Pierre? They're good friends and Bernard will persuade him you need to be pampered among your own family. You should be up here at the farm with us. How far gone are you?'

'About three and a half months.'

'My, my, you kept that quiet, didn't you? We definitely need to catch up on this complicated and top secret pregnancy, don't we?'

'Julia, are you sure you want me to impose myself on you at this late stage in your pregnancy? You've got enough on your plate with taking care of Philippe and everything else you have to do up at the farm.'

'Chantal, I'm bored out of my tiny mind. Marianne does everything for Philippe, Bernard and, of course, me. She practically spoon-feeds me at mealtimes, standing over me to check I'm eating my greens. "Good for the baby!" That's all I hear.

'She'll be delighted to have a real patient to

fuss over. We've got everything up here in the farmhouse, ancient bedpans, voluminous night-dresses for pregnant ladies, nutritious food from the farm, expert doctors on hand to check anything you'd like checked.'

Julia broke off for a moment to speak to Bernard, who was just arriving in the room.

'Come here a moment, it's Chantal. When you get yourself into hospital this morning we'd like you to speak to Pierre Marchand. Chantal, I'll call you back when I've explained the situation to Bernard. Take care of yourself. See you soon!'

CHAPTER TWELVE

'MICHEL, YOU'VE GOT to believe that Chantal will get the best attention up here at the farm with Julia and me.'

Bernard was doing his best to convince Michel, his colleague and friend at the hospital, that they only had Chantal's best interests at heart.

Chantal lay back against her pillows, trying to stay calm. She was merely the patient and had no say in her treatment apparently. The argument was purely academic now anyway. Bernard had brought her up to the farm to be with Julia. As far as Chantal was concerned, she was here now and here she was going to stay.

She'd assumed that Pierre would have informed Michel but apparently he'd been in Theatre and the message hadn't got through to him. As soon as he'd got Pierre's message Michel had come racing up to the farm to enquire what was going on.

She remembered that when she had been in the obstetrics side ward Michel had suggested it would be safer for her to move in with him. She knew he was naturally feeling protective of her, but was that enough for her to give up her independence? His main concern was obviously for the welfare of his babies. She was merely the vessel that was carrying them.

A couple of hours ago she'd listened to Bernard convincing Pierre that being with Julia and himself at the farm would be the best scenario for their patient. They were all doctors so there would be no shortage of medical attention if Chantal started to bleed again. It would also help her to be with her cousin, away from hospital in the healthy surroundings of the farm amongst the hills.

Julia decided it was her turn to up speak up. 'I entirely agree that it's better Chantal is here with family, rather than spending her time resting—or rather, trying to rest—in the hospital. Michel, you're welcome to come and stay here any time you like. Consider yourself part of the family now that you and Chantal are expecting twins together. And if I'm totally honest, as I'm now nearing the conclusion of my pregnancy I would really like my cousin to be here with me.'

Michel reached for Chantal's hand. 'What do you want, Chantal?'

At last they were all going to listen to her opinion. 'I'm grateful to Bernard that he persuaded Pierre to let me out of hospital to be here with Julia. That's exactly what I want.'

Michel leaned forward and drew her into his arms as Bernard and Julia left them to be alone together.

'So long as this is best for the babies and you, I'm happy,' he said gently.

She found the feeling of his arms holding her was very comforting. It was also stirring up memories of that night when they'd made the babies together.

He looked into her eyes. She loved the sincere expression in his. He was a good man, a sexy, alluring man. She was lucky to be in a partnership with him, even if he was there only because of the babies. Right now she could imagine it was

for real but she had to face the facts of their unorthodox liaison. She listened to his deeply caring voice as he tried to reassure her that all would
be well.

Michel drew her closer in his arms. 'I'll come
to see you every day. Pierre thinks you'll be fine
if you have complete rest for a couple of weeks.
If you'd taken up my suggestion to move into
my house I could have arranged for you to be
nursed at home in your own room. I could have
employed a trained nurse and also taken some
time off to take care of you. I've already made
enquiries at a reputable agency about employing
a trained nurse to help you at home in the prenatal and postnatal stages.'

'You're very kind, Michel, but I like being
with family here. It's more relaxing for me, more
homely. Julia and I grew up together like sisters.'

Whenever Michel spoke about his home, that
magnificent house overlooking the bay of St Martin, she felt worried. Events were moving too fast
for her. She was being carried along on a tidal
wave with little control over events. She was still
overjoyed at the thought that she was carrying

twins but apprehensive about all the trappings of the unusual parenthood that went with it.

'If you're happy to be here at the farm with Bernard and Julia then I'll stop worrying about you.'

She moved in his arms. His lips brushed hers tentatively as if he wasn't sure she would welcome him. She felt a rush of sensual excitement at the touch of his lips but he was already pulling away before she could respond.

She remained still in his arms, moved by the expression of affection on his handsome face. She told herself he loved the babies, not her. The love of his life would always be Maxine.

'Chantal, I've been so worried about you and the babies,' he said huskily.

She remained silent as she tried to make sense of her confused thoughts. 'Michel, it's been traumatic for both of us, believing that we might lose our babies.'

'And I was terrified I might lose you when you first started to bleed. Until the bleeding stopped I couldn't bear to be away from you.'

He broke off, not wanting to upset Chantal with

the thoughts that had plagued him. He'd reviewed all the rare cases he'd witnessed during his career. To lose someone you really cared about was the worst thing that could happen to anyone.

'Michel, we're both in a highly emotional state at the moment. Once I'm fit again we'll review our future plans for the babies, get ourselves back on course with our original plan. Make it work.'

He stood up. 'Of course the plan will work.' He spoke decisively but he realised that his emotions were changing all the time. The babies were at the forefront of his mind but so was their mother, this wonderful woman for whom he felt such strong affection. But he knew he mustn't question their original plan for non-commitment to each other. Chantal valued her independence above everything else.

Chantal also was feeling confused at the strengthening attraction she felt towards him. But these strong feelings she felt for him now would disappear when life became normal again. She was simply feeling fragile and clingy after her threatened miscarriage.

'You must rest now,' he said, in a calm, controlled, almost professional way, the doctor in him regarding what the patient needed most. 'I've got to go back to hospital to see the patient I was operating on when Pierre allowed you to come up here. I'll come and see you tomorrow, if you'd like me to?'

'Of course I want you to come and see me!' She put out her arms as he leaned down towards her. She found herself clinging to him, wishing he would stay, but he was already pulling away, intent on getting back to the hospital where he understood exactly what was going on. Being in this intense, emotional atmosphere was confusing. Would he ever understand what went on inside Chantal's mind?

Would she be with him long enough for him to find out? She was so beautiful, so very attractive. He'd seen the admiring glances that other men gave when they looked at her. There was nothing to stop her having a relationship with another man in the future. He couldn't bear that to happen!

Chantal closed her eyes after he'd gone. She heard his footsteps receding on the stairs then the sound of his car engine starting up. What was this yearning to be close to Michel but then finding it impossible to commit herself to him for ever? For ever was a long time and people changed over the years.

She took deep breaths to calm herself. Yes, she should rest for the sake of their babies. She had to stop worrying about the future.

Michel realised he was driving too fast when he had to brake hard at the hairpin bend halfway down the hill. The lorry coming slowly up the hill veered out of the way at the same time as he did.

He breathed a sigh of relief as he let in the clutch and moved on again, this time more slowly. He hadn't expected that huge lorry to be taking up more than half the road. But that was no excuse for him being totally wrapped up in his own thoughts.

He reached the bottom of the hill and was still plagued by his dilemma in spite of trying desperately to concentrate on his driving. He was on the straight section of road now that led to the hospital. As he relaxed he couldn't help his thoughts turning to Chantal again.

He'd never thought he could love another woman after Maxine had died but his feelings for Chantal were now becoming very strong. He hesitated to call it love, still feeling he was being untrue to Maxine's memory. But was it possible to love two women, one who was here and one who was now a much-loved memory?

He turned into the hospital gates. He must concentrate on work now. Chantal was staying for two weeks with Julia and Bernard and would be well cared for. He must remain as unemotional as he could so that her convalescence would be successful.

Julia came into her room next morning soon after Chantal had woken up. Waiting outside the half-open door, she could see Bernard and Philippe.

'I know it's early for visitors but Philippe so wanted to see you before he went to school and Bernard is waiting to drive him there.'

'Philippe!'

Chantal was very fond of her step-nephew, who came across to give his favourite aunt a kiss.

She remarked on how tall he was now.

'I'm seven,' he told her proudly. 'And I'm going on an expedition today with my class. It's still summer holidays but our class are old enough to go on a geography field trip.'

He chatted on excitedly about the day ahead.

Marianne arrived, carrying a breakfast tray.

'We'll have to go now, Philippe,' Bernard told his son. 'Mustn't miss the coach.'

'I'm afraid it's decaf coffee,' Julia told her cousin as she lowered herself into a large armchair. 'Bernard doesn't approve of real coffee during pregnancy. Once I've delivered this precious baby and breastfed him for a few months I can please myself again.'

'So it's a boy?'

'Yes, I'm carrying a boy. But don't tell Philippe because he'll expect to be able to play with him from day one. I'm leaving the good news as a surprise.'

'They're bossy, aren't they?' Chantal remarked

as she took a sip of the decaf coffee, which was generously laced with hot milk.

Julia shifted herself in the armchair as she tried to get comfortable.

'Do you mean expectant fathers in general or just ours?'

Chantal smiled. 'Probably just ours. I think it's because they're both doctors and know all about what's best for the patient.'

'Or *think* they do,' her cousin put in dryly, handing Julia a warm croissant on a plate. 'Here you go. Try not to make as many crumbs in the bed as you usually do.'

They were both giggling now, as they'd done so many times when they'd been small.

'Chantal, I used to think you deliberately made a mess of your breakfast so that you could get some attention from whichever mother was in charge at the time.'

'You're probably right. When both mothers were chatting the whole time I had to do some-thing to be noticed.'

Julia finished her croissant first and reached for another one. 'I'm glad you've found a good man this time, after what you went through last time. I think you and Michel make an ideal couple.'

Chantal put the remains of her croissant on the plate. 'We're not really a couple, you know, not in the conventional sense.'

'Well, you could have fooled me! So how did you get pregnant, by mail order?'

'Mmm, we had a night of wild passionate love.' Chantal lay back against the pillows as the wonderful memories of that night came flooding back to her. 'It was the most wonderful experience I've ever lived through.'

Julia remained silent for a few moments. 'So, you're in love, aren't you?'

'Julia, I honestly don't know. I was so traumatised after Jacques deceived me I promised myself I would never give myself to another man as long as I lived. Once you commit to someone you open yourself up to being vulnerable and I don't want that.'

'But Michel isn't like Jacques, Chantal. He's a good man, honest, caring and very sexy, impossibly handsome! You couldn't have anyone better in your life. And what's most important, I can tell he adores you.'

'But how do I know that's not simply because I'm carrying his babies? Love, adoration, call it what you like, is an impossible emotion to understand. How do I know that because he's affectionate towards me that it's true love? And even if it is love, how do I know his love will stand the test of time?'

Julia put down her coffee cup and became deadly serious. 'You don't know. Chantal; you've got to trust your instincts and go with the flow. Life changes all the time.

'Last September you set yourself cast-iron rules that would stop you being hurt in the future. But you hadn't met Michel then. You've got to be more flexible. Take life as it comes. Adapt yourself to this new situation you're in. I had to make new decisions about life when Bernard and I were sorting out our differences and I've never been happier.'

Chantal swallowed hard. 'But I'm so confused.'

'So was I, but you've got to make a decision about your relationship soon. If Michel doesn't know how you feel about him he may stick to the idea of a partnership for the sake of the babies. Don't let that happen! Once you totally commit yourself you'll know that was the right course of action. You'll find a way to make it work. Believe me, Chantal, you will.'

The next few days were passing very quickly and Chantal could feel herself getting stronger. Pierre came out to see her a couple of times and phoned every day to check on how she was. As she'd had no further bleeding during the second week, she was allowed out of bed.

Michel came to see her at some point every day, staying for a couple of hours or longer if he had the time. Chantal found herself looking forward to seeing him. She could feel her heart pounding as he bounded up the stairs, moving swiftly across the room to kiss her. But she sensed he was holding something back as they sat side by side in armchairs by the window.

Julia always came in at some point, knocking on the door before she came in. She didn't ask questions after Michel had gone. But Chantal had confided in her that she was glad she had time to herself to think about the future between Michel's visits.

'So, have you had any profound thoughts about your future, Chantal?' Julia asked as they sat together by the window on the day before she was due to leave the farm.

Chantal could feel the warm afternoon sun shining through the wide open French window. She'd been dreading telling her cousin what she'd decided but the decision she'd made after much deliberation seemed the most rational.

'Yes, I've made my decision.' She hesitated. 'I've seen a distinct change in Michel's attitude towards me ever since he saw the scan of the babies. I can't rule out the idea that he's fallen in love with the concept of being a father.'

'Well, of course he has. That's normal. But he also loves you. That's obvious.'

'I'm still very sceptical.' She took a deep breath. 'So I'm not going to renew my contract, which comes up for discussion next week.'

Julia sat still, silently fuming. She knew her

cousin better than anyone. She could be so stubborn when she was convinced she was right. This time she was definitely wrong but how could she persuade her otherwise when she could see her mind was made up?

'I'm going to go back to my apartment in Paris and make preparations for the birth of my babies. Maybe I'll arrange to go back to work part time in my old job at the hospital until the babies are born.'

'Chantal, you may change your mind about being on your own.'

'Mum will be next door and…please, Julia, I'm trying to be rational, not emotional, in not committing my fate to someone else.'

'I don't want to upset you, Chantal,' Julia said in a quiet, resigned tone. 'If that's your decision I'll help you all I can.' She hesitated. 'Did you tell Michel your plans when he was here this morning?'

'No, I thought I would tell him tomorrow. He's planning to collect me in the afternoon and take me up to his house. I thought it would be better if we were by ourselves when I tell him.'

'Oh, it's a good idea that you should be alone when you drop your bombshell.'

'Julia, I'm having his babies. That's what we agreed on at the beginning, nothing more, nothing less. We'll draw up a legal contract together and I'll keep to it.'

Julia didn't trust herself to speak. She eased herself out of the chair and walked back to her room. Her cousin could be so difficult when she wanted to be. She had always been stubborn but never as bad as this before that dreadful Jacques had caused her so much pain. He had a lot to answer for.

CHAPTER THIRTEEN

JULIA HAD LAIN awake for a long time during the night, worrying about what Chantal had told her. She'd known exactly what the poor girl was going through in her confusing dilemma to sort out her emotional feelings for Michel. She'd been in the same situation before she'd married Bernard. She should have given her cousin some sound advice from her own experience, not just walked away, leaving her to struggle by herself.

But Chantal wasn't listening to any of her advice now so her words of advice would have fallen on deaf ears. She could see yesterday that her cousin's mind was made up. It was like that time when they'd gone for an adventure together and hadn't told any of the grown-ups. Chantal had said she knew the path round the cliff edge was safe and it wouldn't take long.

It had been hours before the sea rescue men had

searched the area in their boat and found the two little girls shivering with cold as they'd watched the tide climbing higher up the cliff. They'd had to face the music when their rescuers had taken them home.

Well, Chantal would have to find her own way home this time, wherever that might be, because she'd declared she was definitely returning to Paris, to her own apartment where she would take responsibility for her own future and follow the terms of the legal agreement that she and Michel would draw up. It sounded completely devoid of emotion and intensely hard work. Julia could see it was completely the wrong course of action.

She'd have another try at making Chantal see sense that morning. Glancing at her sleeping husband beside her, she gave a sigh of pure happiness. How could she sell the wonderful idea of marriage and children in a loving marriage to her stubborn cousin? How could she make her realise that anything else would be second best and fraught with problems? Well, that was how she saw it anyway.

Remembering her own doubts and fears before she'd made her lifelong commitment to Bernard she decided she shouldn't be too hard on her cousin. She'd make a start this morning while they were having breakfast together, as they usually did.

As she heard Bernard's mobile buzzing beside the bed she pretended to be asleep, not wanting him to think she'd wasted precious sleeping time on worrying about someone else. She needed all her energy to be devoted to her own welfare and that of the baby, he'd so often told her.

He was speaking in his quiet professional voice now. It sounded urgent. He leaned across. She rubbed her eyes as if coming out of a deep sleep.

'Sorry to wake you, darling, but I've got to go into hospital. Didn't want you to worry where I was. I'll call you later.'

She murmured something vague and turned to face him for his kiss.

As she turned she felt a distinct pain in her lower back. She didn't say anything. Bernard would only start worrying. She was two weeks to her due date now but wouldn't admit to backache until she was sure it was the real thing. It would be much stronger than this, wouldn't it? And there would be other signs before she was convinced. She'd assisted at childbirth on several occasions professionally and had studied numerous textbooks on the subject. But she'd never experienced it herself, had she?

Chantal was sitting by the window in her bedroom, wondering why Julia hadn't arrived this morning. She'd heard Bernard's car leaving earlier as she'd waited for the dawn to break. She'd slept badly because of a real feeling of unhappiness that hung over her. She had to tell Michel the truth today. She had to put on a brave face about it. Make him think she believed this was her only course of action if she was to keep her own integrity.

But if she was truly honest with herself, whenever he was with her she was tempted to take the easy path. Go along with Michel's ideas. Let him make the decisions, as he clearly would like to do. But if she did that she would lose her own identity. She would lay herself wide open to being vulnerable, as she had done with Jacques. She must have been mad to put up with Jacques's whims and fancies! She'd agreed to everything he'd suggested, never queried where he'd been or who he'd been with, welcomed him into her flat with open arms.

Never again, she'd told herself firmly.

It was way past the time that Julia usually arrived. Chantal opened the windows wide to let in the warm sunshine. The sun was high above the top of the hill now. Perhaps Julia was having a lie-in today. Philippe was off on another school trip and had spent the night in a tent and Bernard had left early so who could blame her?

Only two weeks to go now and her cousin was carrying all that extra weight around with her all day. She smiled to herself as she wondered what it would be like towards the end of her own pregnancy with twins.

She would soon know. Time was flying by and she still had so much to organise.

The delicious aroma of hot croissants assailed her nostrils. No need to stay in her room any more. She would spend her last day here checking that she really was getting stronger and was ready to face the outside world and all her problems.

'Come and sit down here, Chantal,' Marianne said, holding back a chair at the long kitchen table. 'I just went in to see Julia but she said she's going to go back to sleep because she had a bad night.'

'Oh, dear! Is she OK?'

'Nothing to worry about, or so she said. I'm going to keep an eye on her all the same. Not long to go now, is it?'

Breakfast over, Chantal had a short stroll in the garden, taking care to walk slowly so as not to tire herself. Yes, she was OK. She increased her speed slightly then paused to smell the scent of the roses, which were beginning to lose their petals. She looked at her watch. There were still a few hours before Michel was due here. She suppressed her feeling of excitement and apprehension. She must stay calm. Stick to her plan.

Staying responsible meant no emotion. Completely rational and calm. Easier said than done.

It was now or never! Michel turned the car up the road that led to the farm. Today was the day he was going to take Chantal home. He couldn't wait to have his babies and their mother under his own roof so he could take care of them. He needed to supervise Chantal's prenatal care and make sure she didn't tire herself as she was prone to do.

He'd accepted that he was very fond of Chantal. At times when he was with her it seemed more than just fondness and affection. He found himself listening more to his emotional self and less to his rational self. Chantal had made it clear they should stick to their original plan. She needed her independence. They had to stick to their original plan.

Today he would be totally businesslike—like when he'd tried to persuade her to move into his house. He would say he wanted to show her the new nursery. As soon as they'd known they were expecting twins he'd asked her how she would like the nursery to be fitted out. She'd told him she'd think about it later and let him know.

She still hadn't got back to him so while she'd been here at the farm he'd called in a professional interior design firm. She would be thrilled when she saw the catalogues and designer plans they'd left for them to look though. Such a wide choice of nursery furniture to choose from! Nothing but the best for their twins and their mother.

Michel arrived halfway through the afternoon. Chantal saw his car coming into the farmyard and went to meet him. As long as she was moving around she felt OK. She'd kept herself busy packing her things ready to move out of the room that had been hers for the last couple of weeks.

He was surprised to see her outside. He smiled and kissed her in the French way of greeting a close friend, a kiss on both cheeks. She remained cool, rational, her mind made up. This was how it was going to be.

'Let's go and sit in the conservatory.' She was leading the way round to the front of the farm-house.

He looked surprised at her suggestion. He'd hoped she would be impatient to be off. 'I hope you're not tiring yourself, Chantal. Wouldn't you like me to help you pack?'

'Marianne helped me this morning. I haven't seen Julia yet today. She was sleeping all morning apparently. Marianne said she'll be down soon to say goodbye.'

As Chantal sank down into one of the squashy armchairs she felt a sudden moment of panic. Michel looked so handsome today in the well-cut grey suit she particularly liked. He looked every inch the successful consultant. He looked like a man who had everything to live for. A good career and in a few months he would be the father of two children. They would be model parents, always putting the needs of their children first.

She took a deep breath. Would that be enough for her? Was she simply running away from having to face her confused emotions every day?

'Michel?'

'Chantal?'

They smiled at each other as they both began to speak at the same time.

'You go first,' he told her.

'No, your turn I think.' She looked directly into his eyes, trying to make sense of that enigmatic expression.

'We need to talk about our immediate plans.'

His serious tone, his nervous expression alarmed her. 'Michel, before you say any more…'

Michel shook his head as she tried to interrupt.

'No, you asked me to speak first. This is really important. I've asked you on several occasions if you will move into my house. It would be safer for the welfare of our babies and much better for your prenatal care and also, if I'm honest, for my peace of mind to have you under my roof. I'm begging you now to reconsider.'

She couldn't speak as she looked at the absolute sincerity in his expression. Tears sprang to her eyes and began to trickle down her cheek at the thought of what she had to do.

Mistaking her reaction, he drew her into his arms.

'Chantal, please say something. Please?'

'Michel I'm going back to my apartment in Paris.'

He looked stunned as she withdrew from his embrace.

'That's what I was going to tell you. I'm carrying your babies and I'm truly committed to the plan we agreed on when we embarked on our parenthood journey together but I've had time to think it through. Too much has happened to me in a short space of time. I can't commit to living under your roof. I need to be totally in charge of my own destiny.'

She dabbed her eyes with a tissue. 'I'm sticking to our original agreement as regards our parenting but that hadn't stipulated moving in with you. I need my own space, my own—'

She broke off as she heard a scream coming from the house. They both stood up as their medical training urged them to go and check out what was happening to Julia.

Marianne was hurrying out through the French windows. 'Julia needs you. You're both doctors so you'll know what to do. She's definitely having strong labour pains now.'

'I'll get Bernard back from the hospital,' Michel said, speaking into his mobile as he hurried into the house. 'Bernard…'

Julia was half sitting, half lying on her bed, doubled up in pain and desperately trying to control her deep breathing. As the contraction passed Chantal got her to lie down so she could examine her.

'The cervix iş well dilated, Julia, but don't start pushing until I tell you.'

Michel had spied a gas and air machine in the corner of the bedroom. Trust Bernard to be prepared at this stage of the pregnancy! He checked the apparatus out before handing Julia the mask.

'There's another contraction coming,' Chantal told her cousin.

'I know, I can feel it! Agh…'

'Breathe into the mask, Julia,' Michel told her as he held it in place.

Minutes later Bernard arrived.

'Darling, hang on in there. You're absolutely brilliant. Yes, keep panting like that. I was driving home when Michel called me. The ambulance will be here as soon as they can get out of the hospital forecourt. There's a traffic jam causing congestion on the seafront.'

Both men had taken off their jackets and rolled up their sleeves and were assessing the dilatation of the cervix. Chantal held tightly to Julia's hand, mopping her brow as the sweat poured from her.

'Don't leave me, Chantal. There's another pain coming.'

'You can push on this one, Julia,' Michel told her. 'OK, that's good, yes, and again.'

'Hold back, Julia,' Michel instructed as he took the baby's head in his hands minutes later.

Bernard was holding his wife now as the baby made his appearance.

'A gentle push now, Julia, and baby will be with us,' Michel told her.

The baby flopped out into his hands and the welcome sound of his first cry could be heard by everybody. So could their sighs of relief at the safe delivery of this much-wanted son.

Chantal looked across at Michel. She had no idea what he was thinking now as he busied himself cutting the cord, checking the baby's airways.

He was behaving as if they were in hospital, as if they were an obstetrics team called in to deliver a patient's baby.

She was glad he was totally calm because she was afraid she was going to pieces. She remembered her cold response to his suggestion that she move in with him. She'd made it quite clear that this would never happen. That must have hurt him enormously. And she also remembered the plans she'd set in motion during the last couple of days. She had to stick to them.

Marianne appeared at the door and was allowed in to see the new baby. 'Oh, he's wonderful. So like Bernard, don't you think, Julia?'

Marianne broke off as she remembered the important message she had to give to Chantal immediately.

'Your car is here, Chantal. The chauffeur says he's taking you to your clinic in Paris. There's a nurse who came with the chauffeur, waiting to help you. Shall I bring her upstairs?'

Chantal swallowed hard. This was what she'd been going to tell Michel just before he'd asked her to move into his house. She'd been in contact with Sebastian and he'd arranged to admit her to his clinic for a check-up before she went to her Paris apartment. He wanted to give her a thorough examination and also make sure that she knew exactly how she was going to prepare for the birth of her twins.

The ambulance had arrived now and staff from the Hôpital de la Plage were now coming up the stairs to take Julia and her baby .

Holding her new baby close to her, Julia was the happiest woman in the world. She only had eyes for her husband and son as medical staff milled around the room, making preparations for their departure.

The nurse from Paris was standing beside Chantal, asking for her suitcase to carry down to the car. The chauffeur had also come upstairs and was waiting in the doorway. Chantal managed to find a way through to Michel.

'Michel, this isn't how I meant it to be. I was going to explain that I need—'

'It's not about what you need now, Chantal,' he told her coldly. 'It's what the twins will require

in the future. Make sure you employ a good law-
yer to legalise our situation while you're in Paris.
That's what you want, isn't it?'

As she sat in the back of the car she knew she
would never forget the expression on Michel's
face. He'd looked like a man who'd been totally
betrayed. Well, in a way he had. She thought of
all the times she'd needed him and he'd been
there for her. She would never forget that hard
expression in his eyes as she'd left him.

The clinic nurse was sitting in front with the
driver, occasionally turning round to check that
her patient was OK.

'Try to get some rest on the journey,' Chantal
had been told.

Rest? Would she ever get rest again from the
guilt she was feeling at turning down Michel's
well-meant and obviously sensible idea that she
should be under his roof with their precious babies. He'd opened up to her and she'd turned him
down flat.

And his parting words still rang in her ears.

He'd told her she should be thinking about what was best for their babies.

After the birth she'd been caught up in the euphoria surrounding Bernard and Julia as their first baby together arrived safely. That was what a conventional partnership was all about. Would this unconventional plan really work?

CHAPTER FOURTEEN

'PHYSICALLY, YOU'RE IN good shape again.'

Sebastian looked up from the notes on his desk, his eyes taking in Chantal's desperately worried expression. She'd been like this, only more so, when she'd arrived yesterday evening. The nurse who'd accompanied her to the clinic last night had said her patient had appeared to sleep for most of the way until the chauffeur had slowed down to allow for the traffic congestion in Paris. At that point Chantal had woken to look out of the window.

Chantal breathed a sigh of relief at Sebastian's words. 'In that case, I could go back to my apartment, couldn't I, Sebastian?'

'Chantal, you're free to come and go as you please. You and your mother live quite near, so I expect to see you frequently before the babies are born. Is your mother back from holiday yet?'

'Yes, I'll phone her shortly to say I'm coming back today. She knows I'll be back some time this week but I wanted to be sure I checked with you first that all was well.'

'Well, as I said before, you're physically fine again.' He hesitated. 'I'm not sure about your emotional state. Are you sure you can cope with this unorthodox situation you and Michel have created for yourselves?'

Trust Sebastian to hit the nail on the head! He knew her too well.

'I'm not at all sure,' she admitted tentatively. 'But I'm going to give it a good try.'

'Yes, but is it what's best for the babies? You and Michel seem like an ideal couple when you're together. Nobody would know that there wasn't a loving bond between you.'

'Please, Sebastian! It's not as simple as you think. We've both got emotional baggage from the past that prevents us from committing to each other.'

'Chantal, I honestly think you should go and see your mother now. Brigitte's the one who should be advising you, not me. Family is always best in discussions of this nature. I'll give you just one piece of advice, if I may. If there's any chance at all of you having a conventional loving partnership where you commit to each other for life, you must take it.'

Walking down the Rue de l'Assomption towards her apartment block, she could feel butterflies in her tummy. The thought of explaining to her mother everything that had happened to her while she'd been on holiday was making her feel very apprehensive.

Sebastian had reminded her when she'd been leaving the clinic that her mother was a strong, dependable lady. She would take it all in her stride, as she always has done.

She'd nodded in agreement before saying, 'That was why I knew it was possible to give the babies a happy future. I saw how my mother coped by herself.'

'Your mother always gave the impression it was easy,' he'd replied. 'But that was because she didn't want to worry you.'

She stopped walking now to reach for the bleeping mobile in her bag.

'Maman!'

'Chantal, I've just got your message about coming home. That's wonderful. Where are you now?'

'Practically home. I stayed with a friend last night.'

'You should have told me you were here in Paris. I would have…'

Her mother was still talking as Chantal entered the apartment building. The concierge came to meet her, taking control of her trolley case while giving her an effusive welcome. He came with her in the lift, taking her right to her own door before leaving.

Her mother was standing in her own open doorway. They hugged each other.

'It's so good to see you again, Maman. How was the holiday?'

'Come in, come in and let's catch up.'

She followed her mother into her kitchen and sat down at the table.

They drank coffee together, her mother still recounting how wonderful her holiday had been. Chantal was more than happy to simply hear about the sun, the sea, the wonderful restaurants.

'I've eaten far too much during my holiday. I've put on two kilos so I'm going to be careful of my diet until I'm back to normal or none of my clothes will fit me. I had to buy this new blouse. Do you think it—?'

Her mother stopped in mid-flow as she looked across the table.

'You look well,' she said carefully. 'You seem to have put on a bit of weight yourself since I last saw you.'

She waited for her daughter to say something.

Chantal took a deep breath. 'I'm pregnant, Maman.'

'Congratulations, *chérie*! Well, you have been busy while I was away. Are you in a relation-ship, then?'

'It's rather unconventional, actually.'

'Don't worry. I'm totally unshockable. How un-conventional is it.?'

'Well, the father of my babies is…'

'So it's a multiple birth?'

'Just twins, Maman.'

'Fine.' Brigitte reached for the coffee pot and refilled their cups while waiting for her daughter to continue with her unexpected news. She told herself to stay calm. All would be revealed sooner or later and while she was delighted at the thought of being a grandmother she wasn't so sure about the 'unconventional' side of things. But whatever it was, Chantal would have her full support.

'Do you know the sex of your babies?' Brigitte took a sip of her coffee.

'No. My obstetrician asked if I wanted to know but I told him I thought I should allow the babies' father to accompany me to the obstetrician's when their sex is revealed. You see, Maman, I have to be very careful to involve him at important stages of my prenatal and postnatal treatment. We haven't drawn up a legal document yet...'

'So you're going to draw up a legal document?' Whatever next!

Chantal paused, cleared her throat, looked

down at her hands and still it was difficult to actually find the right words.

'You see, Michel and I are colleagues—well, actually he's Director of Emergency, which, as you know, is the department I'm working in, so technically he's my boss. We became friends and went out for a meal together. We sort of found ourselves discussing how we'd always wanted to be parents but that it wasn't possible now.'

Brigitte nodded. She was beginning to guess what was coming.

'It turned out that Michel's wife had died and, well, you know what happened with Jacques. So we agreed to try for a baby together. The idea of a committed relationship didn't come into it. We agreed we would go to a clinic for artificial insemination where Michel would provide the sperm and I would carry the baby but...'

She paused for breath.

'Can you slow down a bit, dear? I think I'm with you so far. Just give me a moment to digest this bit. Don't worry, I've read about AID. So you actually went ahead with this, did you?'

Chantal knew she mustn't show weakness at

this point. She must stay firm, she told herself as she searched her handbag for a tissue and blew her nose.

'Well, in the intervening weeks, as we slowly got to know one another better, the dynamic between us changed slightly. Michel decided we should have a meeting at his house to discuss the unconventional partnership we were going to enter into.'

'And...?'

At this point Brigitte had a good idea what might have happened. The way that her daughter was speaking about this doctor called Michel indicated that she had the highest regard for him. Human nature being what it was...

'Well, when we went to his house that evening we were just good friends, discussing an unconventional situation that could work out for both of us.' She paused.

Brigitte couldn't wait to hear what happened. 'So, you both got together that night did you?'

'Mum! How did you know?'

'Chantal, I wasn't born yesterday. It was bound

to happen. Two friends wanting a baby. Much better to do it the natural way.'

'But we didn't mean it to happen. We just sort of got carried away and then…well, in the course of one night together…'

She had to stop again. She found herself blushing as the memories of their lovemaking flooded back.

Brigitte smiled. 'I gather you and Michel enjoyed yourselves on the night your babies were conceived?'

'Yes, we did. But we were both intent on keeping to the plan we'd initially made that we should have an uncommitted relationship. Good parents but keeping our own independence.'

'Just a moment, Chantal. You didn't think you could honestly do that, did you? Not after you'd made love?'

'Yes, we did think the plan would still work. And at first it did. But as soon as my pregnancy was confirmed I found myself in the middle of a maelstrom of emotional changes that I found difficult to deal with. Then a few weeks ago I had some bleeding, which seemed to signify that I was miscarrying. Thank heavens my babies are still safe!'

'Exactly! Thank goodness the babies are still safe. That's the main thing. I have to say you hit the nail on the head when you said you've been in the middle of a maelstrom of emotional changes. You've had to deal with hormonal changes and from a personal point of view you've had to come to terms with the reaction of your babies' father. How did Michel react when it seemed as if you might lose the babies?'

'He was desperately worried. He'd become very concerned about the babies' welfare as soon as he saw them on screen at the first scan. It was almost as if he'd fallen in love with them. And he transferred that concern to me because I was carrying them. He became possessive, always suggesting I should take care when I was working, stop for a proper break at lunchtime...'

'Well, of course he did. And quite right too. I like the sound of this young man.'

'Well, yes, he did care about us a lot, the babies and me. Then he asked me several times to move in with him so he could take care of us.

He has this magnificent house on the top of the hill overlooking the bay of St Martin. You know where I mean, Maman? Right at the top before the road goes down the other side.'

'Yes, yes, I know where you mean. I was driving over there last year on my way to Montreuil. I think it was built a couple of years ago. It's a beautiful house and what a view! So when are you moving in?'

'Well, I said I'd think about it. He asked me again yesterday.'

'Yesterday? And you…?'

'It was just before Julia gave birth and we became involved in delivering her baby. She's had a little boy, Maman.'

'But that's wonderful! She must be over the moon. I must phone my sister to congratulate her on becoming a grandmother.'

Brigitte couldn't help wishing Chantal was settled like her niece with a good man by her side. This man Michel could well be the one for her even though she didn't seem to have realised it yet.

'Now, to get back to your unconventional situation, Chantal. After Michel had asked you about moving in and you'd helped to deliver Julia's baby, what was your answer?'

'I said no again and this time I made it clear it was final. I need to keep my independence. After Jacques deceived me and caused me to miscarry I vowed I would never trust another man.'

'I know you said that then, my love, but circumstances change. I was away on holiday when it all happened and you coped all by yourself. Didn't tell me a thing till weeks afterwards. You try to be too independent. Always have done. Just like your father.'

Brigitte was watching her daughter carefully as she spoke again.

'Chantal, tell me exactly why you can't marry the father of your babies?'

Chantal glared at her mother. 'Because he hasn't asked me, for a start, and if he did? Well, he just won't. He's still in love with his dead wife. I can't compete with a ghost, can I?'

'Ah, so you have thought about it, then?'

'Well, of course I've thought about it but that's as far as it got.'

'If he did ask you to marry him rather than just move in with him would you?'

'Mum, I need to be independent. As I told you, Jacques's deceit triggered my miscarriage. Not only did I lose my baby but I lost the ability to love. As I lay on my bathroom floor in the throes of my miscarriage I remember feeling a change come over me. It felt liberating at the time as I vowed never to commit myself to another man. I knew that would ensure I would never be vulnerable again.'

'But Michel sounds totally different from Jacques. Surely you can see that?'

Chantal could feel tears threatening to roll down her cheeks and remove the hard exterior of herself that she had just tried to portray.

'Yes, I can see that,' she said quietly. 'And that's the problem. The more I fight the feelings I have for Michel, the more I want him, not just because he's the father of my babies but because...because I think...well, I'm sure now that...I love him.'

She choked on her words, desperately reaching again for a tissue.

Brigitte took a box of tissues from a nearby shelf and handed it to her before sitting down again and waiting silently. She felt she'd said enough to bring Chantal to her senses. She mustn't be seen as a nagging mother. She longed to cradle her daughter in her arms as she used to do when Chantal had cried as a child. But she was a big girl now and had to make her own decisions.

She knew she'd needed to break down that icy exterior her daughter had built around herself since she'd been so badly hurt last year by that scoundrel. It had taken a good, thoughtful man like Michel to thaw her out. And it had taken her own tried and tested method of getting through to her daughter's inner self. Chantal had trusted her with the secret she hadn't even admitted to herself.

Her eyes were dry now. 'Mum, I know you think that marriage and a loving, lifelong commitment to a partner are best for a family but you managed alone brilliantly.'

'Chantal, I had no choice! I *had* to make a success of my parenting when your father died. I hadn't *chosen* to be by myself, bringing up a child on my own. Many a night I cried myself to sleep, wishing my wonderful husband was still with me. But I had to keep strong for both of us.'

Chantal reached across the table and squeezed her mother's hand. 'I never knew,' she breathed. 'You always appeared to have everything under control.'

Brigitte wiped a tissue over her own eyes now. 'My advice is go back and find out if Michel would still like you to move in with him. If he does, tell him you will. When you're both under one roof and have babies to care for, love will blossom. I'm sure of it. And when he asks you to marry him...'

'If he asks me to marry him.'

'OK, if he asks you to marry him be sure to say yes. Love and marriage go together. I should know. Those few years I had with your father before he died were the most wonderful, the most...'

They were both reaching for the tissue box now.

'Mum, don't you think it's too late for me to go back to Michel and tell him I've changed my mind about moving in?'

'It's never too late to change your mind. Especially if you're a woman. We're well known for it.

But you'll have to grovel.' She gave her daughter a conspiratorial grin.

'Grovel? What do you mean?'

'Eat humble pie, tell him you got it all wrong. Men like to be told that they were right all along. But the important thing is that you tell him. If you do manage to convince him you've changed your mind about moving in with him then you can rest assured that it's quite safe for you to let nature take its course. If you keep an open mind about the situation once you're under his roof, he'll come round to thinking about marriage. He'll find he can't resist making love to you when you're living together and—'

'You really think so?'

'He's a man, isn't he? You're an attractive young woman who's carrying his babies. Your pregnancy is well established now and making love will help to ease the tension between you. Make the first move if you have to. Believe me, he'll love you for it.'

Chantal looked out of the car window at the view of the sea sparkling in the glowing twilight. Before she'd left her mother's apartment she'd phoned Sebastian to tell him she'd changed her mind and was going back to see Michel. He'd insisted on sending his chauffeur to drive her, saying it would be much better she didn't tire herself on the journey.

It had only been as Sebastian's chauffeur had driven off the motorway that led to St Martin sur Mer that she'd phoned Michel to find out where he was. Her mobile had rung for a long time before he'd answered. He had probably been deciding whether to take her call or not.

When he'd finally answered he had been brisk and to the point. He was at home. 'Why do you want to see me?'

'I just need to see you.'

'Well, OK. But make it soon because I have to go out tonight.' He cut the connection.

Predictable reaction, Chantal thought nervously as the car climbed higher up the hill. How long did she need to convince him she'd changed her mind for ever?

The chauffeur lifted her case out of the boot and waited by the door. Butterflies were once again fluttering around in her tummy. The chauffeur had already opened the car door but she remained in her seat watching, watching and planning what to say.

The front door of the house opened.

Slowly, she got out of the car.

Michel, towel in hand, was in his dressing gown, his dark hair wet and rumpled from the shower. He pushed it back from his forehead and took the case from the chauffeur, who returned to the car and started the engine. He'd already told Chantal that Sebastian had asked him to return to Paris that evening.

As the car drove away she felt very apprehensive. Michel's cold manner was scary. She'd never seen him like this before.

She followed him into the house. He dumped her case by the door and went through to the veranda. He stood by the rail of the veranda, looking out at the view, his arms folded, his back towards her.

'I thought you would still be in Paris. If you've got the name of your law firm I'll give them a call in the morning but right now I have to—'

'We need to talk,' she said quietly as she sat down on the nearby sofa. 'I stayed at the clinic last night. Sebastian gave me a full examination today. I had a scan this morning.'

He swung round and moved to her side, looking down at her with an enigmatic expression.

'How are the babies?'

'They're fine. Sebastian asked if I wanted to know the sex but I said I would like you to be with me when we found out—if you do want to find out. It would be the right thing to do and... Oh, Michel, I've changed my mind about moving in here. If you still want me here under your roof I'd love to make this my home while I'm waiting for the babies.'

She'd hoped to control her tears this time to give him a rational explanation in words but possibly her tears would convey her feelings.

'I was wrong, I was so wrong,' she managed to say. 'Can you ever forgive me for being so difficult when you were so kind?'

He sank down beside her and drew her into his arms. 'There's nothing to forgive, he whispered. 'You're carrying my babies, that's enough.'

'No, you deserve more from me, Michel. More commitment to your needs as well as mine.'

His arms tightened around her. 'Chantal, I thought I could never love again but I was wrong. I've been trying to ignore my feelings for you. Trying hard not to fall in love with you. Yes, I'll always love Maxine but my heart is big enough to love both of you. If only you loved me back I would be the happiest man on earth.'

'But I do love you, Michel! I was also trying hard to ignore my feelings for you and pretend I wasn't—'

His lips on hers prevented her from saying anything further.

'Words aren't enough to pledge our love,' he murmured as he scooped her up into his arms and carried her upstairs.'

There was moonlight streaming through the open windows when she awoke. The first thought that occurred to her was that she was home at last, her real home with Michel. She'd never felt happier.

As if sensing that she was looking at him, he opened his eyes.

'You're still here. I thought I might have dreamt it all. If we've conceived two more babies it's going to be a bit crowded in there.'

He placed his hand over her tummy. 'No, I'm confident there's only two in there. I can hear them asking when they can go to sleep again.'

She gave a sigh of happiness. 'It's taken too long for me to admit I was in love with you. The main reason I fought against my true feelings for you is that when I miscarried my first baby last September I vowed I would never trust myself to a man again. Jacques's deception hurt me so much.'

He drew her into his arms. 'Tell me about it,' he said gently. 'I want to know everything about what happened to you.'

She took a deep breath as the awful memories came flooding back. 'Jacques's wife turned up at my flat. I had no idea he was married. I was carrying his baby. I wanted that baby so much. I wanted to be a mother...well, anyway, there was a lot of shouting between them. Apparently that wasn't the first time he'd betrayed her. Finally the shouting stopped and they left together.'

She snuggled close to Michel. He was stroking her hair. She felt safe in his arms.

'Please go on, darling. I need to know if I'm to understand what changed you.'

'I began to feel ill. I thought it was simply the horrible experience I'd just been through. I told myself I was strong enough to forget his deception and move on. I would give my unborn baby all the love I was capable of. My mother had brought me up by herself after my father died so I could do the same.'

She broke off to compose herself again. 'I didn't realise it had triggered a miscarriage. When I found myself on the bathroom floor, doubled up in pain, I felt a change coming over me. I became hard. I vowed that no man would ever cause me such pain and anguish again.'

He kissed her gently on the cheek. 'My poor darling. I can see now why you were wary of commitment. You thought all men were the same, didn't you?'

'Until I met you,' she whispered, looking up into his eyes where she could see her own love mirrored there.

She moved in his arms as she felt desire mounting between them. His lips were on hers. She welcomed the gentle feel of his kiss, the sensual, exciting touch of his hands exploring her body. They blended together, making love once more until they climaxed together, both of them knowing that their love for each other would last for ever. Nothing could break the bond between them.

Chantal came round from her sensual snooze in Michel's arms. She looked up at him and saw he was wide awake, his eyes dreamy and loving as he returned her gaze.

'Michel, you forgot you were going out, didn't you? Will someone be waiting for you?'

'Ah, yes, my mythical date. Pure fantasy. Nothing wrong with that when you're still hurting from the fact that the mother of your babies has refused to move in with you. But I'll forgive you now I understand the reasons behind your desire to remain totally independent of any man after your horrible experience with Jacques.'

'And I'm relieved you've realised it's possible

to love Maxine at the same time as you're loving me.'

'Only you could have made me realise that,' he murmured.

She smiled up at him. 'And only you could have made me fall in love again.'

His lips brushed hers. 'If I were to say four little words to you, would you give me an answer?'

'That depends on what the little words are. Please don't keep me in suspense.'

'Tradition requires me to get out of bed and go down on one knee.'

She remained silent. She would remember these precious moments for the rest of her life, she knew.

He was looking up at her from the side of the bed, gazing at her with such love that she thought her heart would burst.

'Will you marry me?'

He held out his hands towards her. As she clasped them she felt a shiver going down her spine. She'd been utterly transformed since they'd both confessed their love for each other.

'Yes, oh, yes, of course I will. Michel, I love you so much I...'

He was holding her in his arms again, covering her face with kisses as they vowed they would love each other for the rest of their lives.

He knew that he would never forget how beautiful his bride-to-be looked when she agreed to marry him.

EPILOGUE

As CHANTAL AND Michel changed their twins' nappies in the nursery they could hear the sound of their guests arriving downstairs and in the garden. They'd chosen to wait until the babies were four months old before having an official party to publicly celebrate their wedding and the birth of their babies.

They'd had a wonderfully quiet, low key wedding in October at the church in Montreuil for close family and friends but today was a big event where they were going to show off their babies.

Chantal looked up at Michel and smiled. 'What a difference a year makes!'

He laughed. 'Any regrets?'

'You must be joking. Last June I was still agonising about the past and the effect it had had on me. Today I'm the happiest woman alive. Mother of two, wife of the most wonderful—'

'Oh, spare my blushes, Chantal! When you've finished with that nappy bin on your side of the cots, could you pass it this way? Eugh! What a stink!'

Chantal laughed. 'You can be so romantic, Michel.'

He dropped the bin on the floor and drew her into his arms. 'If it's romance you want, darling, you've come to the right man. I was just wondering if we've time to…'

A loud wailing sound came from both cots.

'Michel, they're both hungry, remember.'

He kissed her on the cheek and released her. 'OK. Later. You take Rose, I'll deal with Christophe.'

They settled themselves in the comfortable feeding chairs by the French doors that led onto the balcony, from where they could see their guests arriving. The perfume from the roses wafted up from the garden.

Chantal looked down at her little daughter who was sucking noisily on her bottle. The little blue eyes gazed trustingly back at her. Had she ever imagined a year ago that she would be as blessed as she was now? And to be a mother with a boy and a girl. This was where she truly belonged. They were a real family.

Someone was tapping on the door.

Michel looked up from baby Christophe. *'Entrez!'*

Angeline, who helped them with the babies and some of the housekeeping, came in.

'Chantal, would you like me to take over the feeding for you? The caterers are setting out the lunch buffet in the marquee and I've got time to help you now.'

'Good. You can take Christophe.' Michel stood up, cradling his son, and handed him over to Angeline. 'I'll go and change.'

Chantal smiled at Angeline as she settled herself in the seat that Michel had just vacated. Angeline had proved to be a brilliant addition to the household. She'd had nursery training but was also happy to help around the house and turn her hand to anything that needed to be done. A distant relative of Marianne, Julia's housekeeper, she was exactly what they needed.

Chantal hadn't wanted to keep on the obstetric nurse they'd employed for the first month of the twins' lives. She'd wanted to be a hands-on mum, taking care of her own babies. And she found that she was in no hurry to return to her medical career. Being a full-time mother was all she'd ever dreamed of. Especially when Michel was happy to help her whenever he wasn't on duty at the hospital.

She could hear the hum of conversation downstairs. Rose took her little rosebud lips from the bottle and looked up at her mother as if to say she didn't want any more. The bottle was almost empty.

She lifted her daughter over her shoulder, rubbing her back gently until she heard and felt the reassuring burp that told her Rose had been winded.

'I'll put Rose in the playpen for a few minutes, Angeline. Christophe can join her when he's finished feeding.'

It had only taken her a few minutes to change into the cool white linen skirt and jacket she'd chosen for the occasion. With her hand on the banister as she hurried downstairs, she paused for a moment to look at the friends, relatives and medical colleagues chatting to each other in the large entrance hall.

'Chantal!' Pierre Marchand, the obstetric consultant who'd been such a help during her pregnancy, called out. 'You look wonderful! Nobody would think you were the mother of two babies.'

She smiled as she continued down the stairs.

'Who's looking after the shop today?' she asked her medical colleagues as she was warmly welcomed into the group. 'So many of you are here today! Thank you all for coming. I hope we don't get an emergency.'

A chorus of agreement rang out as she passed through the hall, saying a few words to everybody before going out into the garden.

The marquee on the lawn was also crowded with friends, relatives and a large number of medical colleagues. Chantal again found herself hoping there wouldn't be a major disaster that would send them all scurrying back to the hospital. She noticed many of her colleagues were drinking fruit juice or fizzy water just in case.

The caterers had set out an excellent buffet at the far end of the marquee and guests were wandering outside in the garden, enjoying the summer morning.

Michel came across from the group he was entertaining when he saw his wife. 'You look wonderful,' he whispered. 'Everybody's asking to see the babies. Shall we go and bring them out here before it gets too hot?'

She nodded in agreement as he took her hand and led her back up the stairs. In the nursery their babies were kicking their legs in the playpen. Chantal had laid out their clothes on the bed. That was supposed to be her own bed but she preferred to sleep in the next room with Michel, leaving the adjoining room door open. Consequently, 'her' bed acted as a dressing space for the twins' clothes.

'Shall I help you, Chantal?' Angeline was already lifting baby Rose from the playpen.

Michel lifted out Christophe but handed him to Chantal. 'I'm no good with buttons and zips.'

He watched as his babies were decked out in the beautiful garments Chantal had chosen for their public appearance today. The babies were wearing little white two-piece outfits, a dress for Rose and trousers for Christophe.

Chantal took the baby hairbrush and passed it gently over their soft blond hair. Gently she gathered Rose into her arms and Michel picked up Christophe. Together they went down the stairs. The people in the hall gave a collective sigh as they appeared. 'Oh, look at the babies! Aren't they gorgeous? What a beautiful picture they make as a family.'

They made their way slowly through the admiring crowd, out into the garden where there were more 'oohs' and 'ahs' of appreciation.

Sebastian and Susanna gave their approval at the brilliant progress of the babies.

'Thank you so much for all your help during the pregnancy,' Chantal whispered to Sebastian.

'It was an absolute pleasure to see the outcome, Chantal. Thank goodness it's all been such a success. May you have a long and happy family life together. I know you've got a ready-made family with your boy and girl but are there any plans to enlarge it in the future? You're both completely natural parents.'

'Oh, yes, we've got plans,' Michel told Sebastian.

'Glad to hear it,' Susanna said.

'Chantal!' Julia, followed by Bernard and the boys, came hurrying across the lawn. The two cousins were soon catching up on everything that had happened in the last few days since they'd last seen each other. Philippe was carrying his baby half-brother Thibault and showing him his baby cousins.

'They're our second cousins,' he was saying in a serious voice, as if his eight-month-old brother knew what he was talking about. 'You see, our mother is Chantal's first cousin so…' He glanced up at his father. 'Do you think Thibault understands what I'm saying, Papa?'

Bernard nodded gravely. 'Of course. Like you, he's very bright for his age.'

Chantal moved on to the seat under the trees where she'd spotted her mother deep in conversation with her twin. It was obvious that Brigitte and Berenice were trying to catch up with their news as she and Julia had just done.

Both sisters turned at the sound of Chantal's voice and they both insisted on holding the babies. Brigitte took Rose into her arms. Michel followed shortly with Christophe and handed him over to his great-aunt Berenice.

The sisters were besotted with the babies. 'You can leave them with us,' Brigitte said. 'Go off and talk to your guests. We'll take care of them. Don't hurry back.'

'Come and have a look at the roses with me,' Michel said as he took Chantal's hand.

She knew exactly where he was taking her. They'd been here many times before. There was a secret garden, which was difficult to find unless you knew it was there. They went through the ivy-clad archway and were finally alone.

'I just had to have you all to myself for a few minutes.' He drew her into his arms. 'You look absolutely radiant.'

As she responded to his kiss she reflected that they were going to be together for the rest of their lives but she would always remember this special moment. They were a real family now but there was still romance in their lives, always would be.

'This is where they are!'

A whole crowd of colleagues from the hospital staff had joined them, followed by the wine waiters, who were topping up their glasses.

'Here's to the happy couple! May all your troubles be little ones.'

She recognised the English voice of her eldest cousin, who was a consultant in a London hospital. He was Julia's elder brother.

'Congratulations on the birth of your twins!' Everyone was joining in the toast, raising their glasses.

'I was so happy when I saw the twins on the screen after your threatened miscarriage,' said Pierre Marchand, the obstetrics consultant at the Hôpital de la Plage who, in liaison with Sebastian in Paris, had seen Chantal through her pregnancy. He also raised his glass. 'I'm so glad we didn't lose them. Chantal, you were a brilliant patient at that difficult time. You did everything I

told you to and look at you now, positively blooming with good health!'

'To the twins?' Genevieve from Obstetrics
lifted her glass for another top-up. That definitely calls for another toast. You're not on call,
Pierre, are you? Well, thank goodness for that!'

'Speech!'

Michel rose to the occasion, welcoming everyone, paying compliments to his beautiful wife,
his wonderful babies, saying thank you to everyone who'd helped during the pregnancy. Everyone cheered as he swiftly brought the impromptu
speech to its conclusion.

Sensing the demand for further speeches would
arrive as the champagne flowed, he put his arm
round Chantal and guided her away from their
no-longer-secret garden. Grandmother Brigitte
and Great-Aunt Berenice had waved them away
when they'd returned to claim their babies, telling them they needed more time with the little
darlings.

Their guests were milling round the buffet now.
The band had arrived and was in place on the
lawn, playing music for dancing. Michel took her

in his arms and guided her round the lawn in a slow foxtrot. Everybody cheered as they finished. Chantal knew she would remember this day for the rest of her life.

'Have the guests all gone now?' Michel asked when Angeline came to help them settle the babies.

Angeline nodded. 'The last taxi of guests has just driven off and my taxi is on its way up the hill. Thank you for ordering it for me, Michel.'

'Thank you for all your help. The babies are both asleep, as you can see,' he whispered. 'That sounds like your taxi in the drive now. Good-night, Angeline.'

They were alone at last. Michel took Chantal's hand as they tiptoed away from the sleeping babies in their cots. As they went through into their bedroom he unzipped the strapless blouse beneath her jacket.

'I've been wanting to do that all day.'

'I've been waiting for the time when you could safely do that all day! Oh, that's better.' She kicked off her kitten-heeled shoes and curled up in an armchair beside the bed.

'Let me help you into bed, darling.' Gently he lifted her onto their enormous bed.

'Comfy enough?' He snuggled up to her, struggling to throw the rest of his clothes away onto the thick carpet.

She turned towards him.

He put out a hand and gently stroked her face. 'How are you feeling?'

'Fit and healthy. Not a bit tired. Fabulous day, don't you think? I was so apprehensive this morning about all the arrangements we'd made.'

'So was I. It went off very well, didn't it? Good planning, Chantal.'

'I was going to say the same to you, Michel. We make a good team.'

'No planning needed tonight.'

She sighed. 'All night alone together.'

'Apart from our babies.'

'They're snuggled up together side by side just like we are.'

'Well, not exactly…' She snuggled against him as he drew her into his arms. Life couldn't get much better than this.

* * * * *

Mills & Boon® *Large Print*
Medical

November

200 HARLEY STREET: THE PROUD ITALIAN	Alison Roberts
200 HARLEY STREET: AMERICAN SURGEON IN LONDON	Lynne Marshall
A MOTHER'S SECRET	Scarlet Wilson
RETURN OF DR MAGUIRE	Judy Campbell
SAVING HIS LITTLE MIRACLE	Jennifer Taylor
HEATHERDALE'S SHY NURSE	Abigail Gordon

December

200 HARLEY STREET: THE SOLDIER PRINCE	Kate Hardy
200 HARLEY STREET: THE ENIGMATIC SURGEON	Annie Claydon
A FATHER FOR HER BABY	Sue MacKay
THE MIDWIFE'S SON	Sue MacKay
BACK IN HER HUSBAND'S ARMS	Susanne Hampton
WEDDING AT SUNDAY CREEK	Leah Martyn

January

200 HARLEY STREET: THE SHAMELESS MAVERICK	Louisa George
200 HARLEY STREET: THE TORTURED HERO	Amy Andrews
A HOME FOR THE HOT-SHOT DOC	Dianne Drake
A DOCTOR'S CONFESSION	Dianne Drake
THE ACCIDENTAL DADDY	Meredith Webber
PREGNANT WITH THE SOLDIER'S SON	Amy Ruttan